THE RED KNIGHT

BY K.T. DAVIES

PUBLISHED BY
ANACHRON PRESS

All Rights Reserved

Other Anachron Press Titles

Day of Demons: A Dark Fantasy Collection
Anthology

Vex: A Modern Viking Saga
Short Story by Colin F. Barnes

Dark Metaphor
Short Story by Colin F. Barnes

City of Hell Chronicles: Volume 1
Anthology

City of Hell Chronicles: Trifecta
Anthology (3 tales)

Find these and more at:

www.anachronpress.com/books

Acknowledgements

My thanks to first readers, Ewan Davies, Cam Field, Jane McCard and John Giles, and to editors JJ and Russell Smith and Jane McCard. Thanks also to my publisher, Colin F. Barnes.

For Ewan, Raven and Gabriel.

Prologue

Shame drove Kurn through the rain and mist and up the scree trail at an angry lope. His comrades had the Bear at bay, but he was here, hunting nothing more fearsome than a pregnant sow.

Rain-slicked stones skittered beneath his feet spotted here and there with blood. He was close. A woman's scream echoed from the dark caves gouged into the ragged line of hills that squatted beneath the cloud-shrouded mountains. It was the great scream, the earth shaker—the scream of birth. He froze; steam rose from his near naked body, indigo war paint ran down his limbs. *Fool.* It was only the cold that made him shiver, only the chill breeze sweeping off the snow wrapped mountains, not spirits. There was nothing here that could stop him gutting the bitch and casting her get onto the rocks for the buzzards to devour. The Dura Sat had commanded that the invaders die, and so they would. All of them.

"You'll catch your death up here, son. It's a bad place to be running around half naked," said the old woman.

Kurn was angry that he'd flinched. He hadn't seen her because she was small, and as grey and hunched as the tumble of rocks she was standing beside. She must have been hiding, and had crept out when he was looking up at the caves. She hadn't just appeared out of thin air. The mist was playing tricks with his eyes.

"Move, peasant, or die with the invaders!" The hard words bolstered his courage, and hid his embarrassment.

Her hooded eyes flashed a cold, hard grey. She did not withdraw or feebly brandish her crooked staff to keep him at bay as he would have expected. Instead she strode towards him. Much to his surprise, it was Kurn—Slayer of Wolves, who gave ground. He slipped a few feet down the slope, pushed back by nothing more than the force of her presence.

She pointed a finger at him. "You're very rude, I—"

Another scream, full of deep desperate grief, rang from the caves. Kurn smiled. The old woman looked worried. "The Dura Sat, Clan Lord of all Tamalan, has marked the Bear's mate for death. Step aside, old woman."

She gave a short, hard laugh. "Oh, please. I thought appearing out of nowhere would be enough to convince any fool that this hunt is over. I suppose there's no accounting for feckless youth is there? Very well, *boy*, I'll lay it out plain because I don't have time for games. I've got some bread in the oven and it's going to burn if I leave it much longer."

He should just end the hag and finish his task, but it was bad luck to kill a lunatic. He raised his spear. The old woman chuckled. Wisps of grey hair haloed her face, caught by the same chill wind that carried the sound of anguished sobbing from the caves.

"Just go, and—"

"Hush, foolish child. I'd put aside a goat for this, but who am I to make such choices?" She narrowed her eyes, and stared at him as though calculating his worth. "Fuck 'em'. I'm going to give you a chance boy—a chance to run an' thwart the will of the gods. What say you to that, little lamb?" She looked up at the mountains and shook her staff, carved bone charms jangled against the wood. "Aye, you heard me. Now you—" She jabbed the staff at Kurn, "fuck off home to your mother."

To the Void with bad luck. Kurn cast his spear at the old witch.

She gave a long rattling sigh. The spear quivered…in the ground beside her.

He couldn't have missed. She was small, but not *that* small, and no more than ten feet away. He couldn't have…

The woman froze his thoughts with a glance. Her cold grey eyes were suddenly huge and feral.

"So be it," she said.

A warrior born, his body had wit enough to defend itself while his brain came to terms with what was happening. He drew his sword as the old woman sprang at him and even made an attempt to block when she turned into a snow leopard mid-leap. It was only when the shapeshifter anchored her claws in his chest, and rode him to the ground that he realised his battle-honed skills and lightning reflexes were not going to be enough to save him. Powerful hind legs shredded his stomach and thighs and sprayed his guts across the hillside. He spumed a gout of blood over the creature's death grey pelt as it sank its teeth into his throat and crushed his windpipe.

The last thing Kurn saw was the shadow of the mountains. The last thing he heard was a baby screaming its first lungful of breath into the cold, morning air.

Chapter One

The horse pawed the parched ground in frustration. Jamie knew how she felt; the heat was crushing and there was still no sign of Countess Duvessi.

"Don't worry, old girl, we'll be going home soon and then you'll be able to eat yourself stupid on sweet, Antian grass."

The horse nickered softly and gave him a friendly nudge. As he stepped back, pain lanced through his swollen ankle. A curse sprang to his lips, but he clenched his teeth and swallowed it. He couldn't voice a complaint, not while the Company were out there somewhere fighting for their lives. For the hundredth time that day he scanned the horizon, searching for any sign of the 1st. It had been a risk going after Trevisa's cavalry, but if the intelligence was good it was the best chance they'd had to cripple the troublesome general.

He peered at the Suvian lines and wondered which one was General Trevisa. The Fox, as he was called, was a cunning old bastard, and had led them a merry chase across Suvia for weeks now. Twins willing, that game would end today. If only he knew how the 1st had fared. Worry knotted his guts; he was the Captain's squire and should be with them, but instead of fighting with his comrades, he was stuck on a hill, waiting for a gaggle of overindulged courtiers to come and watch the battle. *Asha's paps.* Breaking his ankle was, without doubt, the most stupid thing he'd done since that drunken night in Weyhithe, and all for the sake of a rabbit supper. His friends had called him 'Bunny Bait' for two weeks now, and showed little inclination to stop, despite it not being even slightly amusing. The teasing and the punishment far outweighed his crime in every way. If only he'd kept his mouth shut about being able to speak bloody Suvian. He wasn't a liaison; he was a warrior, so why had the Captain agreed to send him to Countess Duvessi? The Prince's lover was a grand pain in the arse. Always hanging around camp, making a nuisance of herself. Just thinking about her and her idiot friends set his teeth on edge.

"This is so unfair, and such a bloody waste of *my* time. All to keep a prince's whore happy..." Jamie's gaze wandered across the acres of lavender that lay between the hill and the General's army. Counting the units arrayed in battle formation before a squat, white farmhouse, he estimated Trevisa's force numbered between six and seven hundred.

He squinted against the sun's glare. The brilliance of the lavender and the painfully bright azure sky made his eyes water, but the view across the plains was breathtaking. *If Duvessi can be bothered to drag her fat arse out of bed she'll have a vulture's view of the slaughter from up here.* It didn't matter a damn if she turned up. What mattered was that there was only one unit of reserve cavalry with Trevisa, and he wouldn't dare engage without the support of the rest. Of course, if his cavalry turned up, it would mean that the 1st had lost; a thought he refused to contemplate. To distract himself, Jamie directed his attention to the forces lined up opposite the Suvians.

Two solid ranks of mounted knights projected an aura of steel-clad menace across the battlefield; they were the 2nd Company of the Antian Royal Guards, second only to *his* company. Being possessed of more wealth than friends, Prince Ranulfi had also employed the services of the mercenary Free Companies, which was how Trenham's Irregulars came to be fighting alongside the Antians. In marked contrast to the iron discipline of the Antian destriers, the Irregular's nags pranced skittishly before the Suvian battle lines. Jamie smiled.

After four hours of standing around in the spirit-sapping heat, Jamie was about to give up and go look for the 1st when a weary train of servants staggered over the crest of the hill.

Jamie was politely bustled aside as some of the servants erected a large, gold-striped pavilion. He watched in amazement as others unpacked a sumptuous feast and the elegant tableware on which to serve it, while down on the fields below the hill, warriors were preparing for battle. The more robust of Duvessi's servants had the dubious honour of unloading the Countess from her lathered palfrey, much to the poor beast's obvious relief.

Jamie seethed quietly as the rest of the spoilt courtiers dismounted, and took a leisurely stroll about the hilltop. Naturally, they were complaining that the wine hadn't been properly chilled, and that the sun was too hot for the time of year. Jamie wanted to bash their heads together. *The sun was always too hot in this damn country.* Not one of the whining coxcombs seemed to notice or care that the battle was but a drawn sword from starting.

The Countess eventually deigned to notice him. She beamed a smile so wide that her eyes vanished into the folds of her fat, little face. Jamie took a deep breath and forged a smile of his own, mindful that he was representing his Captain and the 1st. She giggled, and thrust out a ring laden hand for him to kiss. Dutifully, he raised her doughy fingers to his lips.

"*Dearest*, Jamie," she cooed, "'tis delightful to see you again. Did you miss me? How is your poor foot?"

He hoped the treaties King Daris had made with Ranulfi were worth the gross indignities his knights, *and* squires, were being forced to endure for the sake of the kingdom.

"My foot's much better, thank you, Countess, and to be in the abundance of your gracious company is, as ever, beyond my humble ability to express."

She giggled, and looked at him expectantly. He groaned inwardly and offered her his arm. She seized it with the enthusiasm of a hungry buzzard, and marched him off to the pavillion.

While tucking into the lavish feast, Duvessi regaled Jamie with the account of the harrowing, two mile journey that she and her companions had endured to get there. Despite her constant assurances that her appetite had quite abandoned her, she devoured a platter of sweet meats, two entire capons, and a bottle of Suvian Ruby as she recounted her harrowing tale. Eventually, Jamie managed to coax the weary travellers from the table by assuring them that the honey-glazed lamb wouldn't spoil in the heat. It didn't matter a damn; they'd soon lose their appetites when the killing started.

Under Jamie's direction the servants erected a silk canopy on the edge of the hill, and set a dozen gilt chairs beneath it.

The Countess flounced onto a chair, and sighed. "Can you smell that, Jamie dear? Suvian lavender is the finest in the world, its scent is incomparable. 'Tis heartbreaking to see it trampled, and yet, it releases the most magnificent perfume when crushed. Perverse is it not? the pleasure one can derive from destruction."

Jamie's attention was focused on the battlefield and he only remembered his manners when she gave a tactful cough. "Forgive me, Countess. Indeed, 'tis a mortal tragedy."

Her full, red lips puckered into a sullen pout. "You seem terribly distracted today, Jamie dear. Is it the heat? Redheads suffer dreadfully under our sun, and *you're* forced to wear all that heavy armour, you poor darling. I shall speak to Captain Stenna about it. You look like a lobster, boiling in the pot. Have a drink dear, you'll feel better for it, I know I do." She giggled and held out her glass for a refill.

She was right about one thing; he couldn't maintain his usual mask of attentiveness or feign interest in her trivial conversation. His heart and thoughts were with his comrades.

"So who's in charge of our lot?" One of the noble sycophants demanded. He was tall, and wearing an outfit so festooned with ribbons that he reminded Jamie of a maypole.

"Captains Stenna and Vorbek have field command," he replied.

Maypole scowled. "I thought Calvigneri was in charge? This won't do at all. I'm sure you understand, Lord Turlowe."

Jamie stiffened. "As I've already mentioned, several times, *my father* is Lord Turlowe. Unless he and my two older brothers all suddenly drop dead, Twins forbid, it would be somewhat presumptuous, not to mention rude for me to assume the title."

Maypole sniffed. "What rank are ye then?"

"I'm currently a squire in the First Company of the Royal Guards. I hope one day to be a knight, but as yet I have not attained that singular honour."

"You Antians are a strange breed. I cannot imagine a noble Suvian of even the lowest rank submitting to such humiliation. You fraternise with peasants and…" Maypole flourished his kerchief towards the battlefield. "What are they doing, *Squire* Turlowe?"

"The Fox's left flank is turning to face Trenham's archers." Jamie tried not to sound like he was talking to an idiot, even though that was clearly the case.

"I'm not a dolt, sir. I can see they're moving, but to what purpose? Those mercenary dogs are far too cowardly to engage. Look at them; charging about like their arses are on fire, it's pathetic. Ranulfi should have them all flogged."

The Countess and her guests immediately set about debating the finer points of military tactics, of which they knew vastly more than any mere general, judging by the sureness of their pronouncements.

Flustered and irate, the Countess dragged Jamie into the argument. "Jamie my sweet, please explain why Trevisa has turned to face the mercenaries. Does he feel threatened by them? Can a few little arrows really scare those brave soldiers?"

"They can do a great deal of damage, Countess. Have you noticed that they've been creeping ever closer to Trevisa's flank?"

She nodded uncertainly. Jamie grinned. "My Lady knows full well, I'll wager, what happens when some varlet is left to get behind. Unchecked, the mercenaries would wreak all shades of havoc upon Trevisa's rear."

The Countess giggled, and gave his arm a playful squeeze. "Really, Squire Jamie, how bold you are."

"And wrong. Look—the cowards are running. Typical mercenary scum." Maypole gave a smug grin.

He was right; the Irregulars turned tail and began to flee the field in disarray. The Fox's left flank howled in triumph, and set off in pursuit; hounds that had the scent of blood. Jamie saw the Suvian officers frantically signalling for them to hold the line, but few heeded the command. The bait was taken.

To their credit, Trevisa's archers saw the danger, and let fly a blizzard of arrows when the 2nd began to rumble towards them. The sky darkened with shafts, but either through nerves, or lack of judgement, they loosed far too early. At the extreme limit of their range, most of the arrows fell short, or bounced harmlessly off the heavily armoured knights and horses. Meanwhile, the Irregulars raced erratically about the field, scattering rolling waves of dust in their wake.

Jamie held his breath as the 2nd charged the Suvian line, gaining speed with every thunderous step. Even over the distance he could hear Althus Vorbek, Captain of the 2nd, roar an order. Sunlight flashed from a hundred gleaming lance points as his knights levelled their weapons.

Trevisa's centre set their pikes and braced to receive the charge. Jamie fought the urge to cheer when the 2nd's herald gave a sharp blast on his horn, and the knights changed formation. About 200 yards from the centre, they doubled their line into two ranks, wheeled away from the wall of pikes, and charged at the disorderly left flank. Trevisa's reserve cavalry reacted quickly, but they were out on the far right flank. They would have to ride wide of their own lines before they could countercharge the 2nd—wasting time that the left flank didn't have.

Several of the Countess's companions were unable to watch the slaughter and fled to the pavilion. Those who stayed gasped as the Antians tore into the left.

"This is horrible," the Countess breathed.

"This is war," said Jamie.

"They may have mauled the flank, but it was a mistake to charge; your comrades will be surrounded," Maypole slurred. "They've made a fatal error, Squire Turlowe."

"Tell me, sirrah, do you know the cognomen of the Second Company?" said Jamie.

Maypole held out his glass and waved it impatiently until a servant refilled it. "I cannot say that I do."

"It's called, the Anvil."

"Is that because it gets beat upon often?" The nobleman laughed.

Down on the field, the centre of Trevisa's line turned to engage the Antian cavalry.

"Ha! D'you see?" said the Suvian almost gleefully. "Wait until the Fox's cavalry charge them in the side. See how they like the taste of Suvian steel."

That was enough. Jamie rounded on the drunkard. "Damn it, man, whose side are you on?"

Maypole fixed him with a bloodshot glare. "The side of Suvian honour, sir! Not low, *foreign* tactics."

Blood sang in Jamie's ears, his hand strayed to his sword hilt. *Easy, Jamie; he's not worth it.* Heeding his own council, Jamie took a breath. He was a Royal Guard and wouldn't dishonour himself or the Company by spilling the blood of an imbecile.

He fixed the drunkard with a stare as hard as coffin nails. "You're not worth the rust on my blade, and you know nothing of honour."

Maypole had a sudden attack of sobriety. His bleary eyes focused on the sword and the blood drained from his ruddy cheeks. Mumbling empty curses, he staggered back to the pavilion. The rest of the group sat locked in silence; frozen by the horror unfolding before them. A hot breeze rolled over the hill, bringing with it the sweet smell of lavender infused with the stench of blood.

Anxiety chewed Jamie's guts as he tried to follow the battle through the shifting veil of dust. Now that they had destroyed the flank, the 2nd closed with Trevisa's centre. The Suvians were well armed, and supported by archers, but they were no match for the Anvil and were being steadily beaten back towards the farmhouse that shone like a pearl amid the carnage. Jamie thought their cause was lost, but the embattled Suvians weren't finished yet. They raised a ragged cheer when their Cavalry were finally in position to charge the 2nd.

"I think perhaps your comrades were rash, Squire Turlowe," another of the guests suggested. "The Anvil is about to be struck a resounding blow by the flower of Suvian knighthood."

Jamie didn't miss the note of smugness in her voice. *Blood will out.* It didn't matter that Trevisa was their sworn enemy, he was Suvian, and the Royal Guards were foreigners who meant nothing to them. *The puling sots don't mind that we bleed for their cause.* Their hypocrisy didn't surprise Jamie; it disgusted him. He turned his attention to what was happening on the field.

Even without their garish battle standard, there was no danger of confusing the Suvian knights with the Anvil. Their horses were decked in flowing silk caparisons of every conceivable colour. The knights all wore mirror-bright mail and flamboyant helms crowned with gilded crests and rampant heraldic beasts.

The Anvil were head to toe in unadorned steel plate over which they wore quartered surcoats in their company colours of black and green emblazoned with King Daris's Griffin. When the Suvians were close, Vorbek bellowed a command, and half of the 2nd reined their destriers about to face them.

"Your horses are nimble...for such heavy set beasts," another of the courtiers remarked.

"The Guards destriers are the finest horses in the world," said Jamie.

"Our horses are bigger."

"They are indeed rangy beasts, but as I'm sure you know: size isn't everything. It takes years to train a destrier. They are, quite literally, worth their weight in gold." *Just like their riders.*

The Suvians rode well, but they lacked discipline. Jamie could see that they were coming in too fast, and their line was ragged. This would not end well for them.

He loathed the long hours Captain Stenna made them drill, but the reason why was about to be made painfully clear. The Suvians hit the Anvil piecemeal, and instead of smashing through, they broke against them.

Suvian horses careened into each other and crashed to the ground in horrific tangles of broken limbs. Riders were catapulted from their saddles and crushed beneath the trampling hooves of their terrified mounts. When the dust settled it was plain for all to see that the Anvil had lived up to its name.

The slaughter had captivated the Suvian nobles' attention, but Jamie caught a glimpse of something else, moving at speed to the right of the hill. He squinted through the dust towards the wide swathe of trees that hemmed the fields on that side. When he realised what he was looking at, it took all the self-control he possessed not to whoop with joy.

The Countess fluttered her fan. "Tell me, Jamie dear, does the First Company of the Royal Guards have a…*eke namerinaria*…a cognomen?"

Jamie grinned broadly. It seemed he wasn't the only one who'd noticed the late arrivals. "Indeed, Countess. The First are also called, *the Hammer*."

The Captain of the Hammer never felt the heat of battle. When she fought, she was always cold.

As the 1st cantered around the edge of the wood and onto the battlefield, Captain Stenna calculated the distance to the enemy. She checked her horse, flexed her plate sheathed hand, and drew her sword. The Company manoeuvred into formation, gathering pace with every stride. Alyda raised her sword aloft and roared the order to charge.

The Suvians didn't see their approach thanks to the dust storm that the Irregulars had raised. Although the haze provided excellent cover, it was like riding through a blizzard of burning ash. Choked and half blind, the Hammer's destriers braved the stinging hail without hesitation, and in moments they were on the unsuspecting Suvians.

Alyda roared a warcry as the 1st smashed into the rear of Trevisa's cavalry. The air was ripped from her lungs by the bone-jarring impact. The high cantle of her saddle groaned, but she kept her seat and drove her horse,—a huge, ill-tempered black called Lyco—into the flank of an orange caparisoned mount and its rider. The Suvian horse crashed to the ground screaming. Lyco trampled the fallen beast with uncommon fury and crushed its skull into the dirt with his massive hooves. An arm reached up from beneath the dead horse and clawed the air. Alyda brought her sword down in a slicing arc. The arm fell away.

All sound merged in the roaring tumult of battle. It was a terrible song, composed of screams and the clash of steel. The Hammer played the tune well. Alyda glanced to her right. Her second, Kieran Lorhine, was hacking a path through the Suvians with controlled savagery. On her left, Nev Vysten, one of the Company heralds, was smashing in the side of a knight's head. *Just as it should be,* thought Alyda, as the Hammer and the Anvil schooled the Suvians in the brutal art of war.

Alyda wheeled her mount. A Suvi in a swan-crested helm plunged from the melee and charged her. She smiled and drew back her sword. When Swan Helm was a stride away, Alyda nudged Lyco sideways and swung her blade at the knight's head. The speed of his charge doubled the power of the blow. His visor creased beneath her blade, his head snapped back, but he didn't fall. Cursing, she snatched his horse's reins and dragged its head round before hitting him again. Her sword rang against his helm. He swayed, but somehow the bastard managed to stay in the saddle. Infuriated by his stubbornness, Alyda dropped the reins, grabbed a wing of the gilt swan on his helm, and yanked the flailing knight towards her. He thrust out blindly, but only succeeded in slicing his horse across the withers. The animal screamed. Alyda wrapped her arm around the knight's neck and smashed him in the head with the pommel of her sword until blood ran through the breathes of his crumpled helm. When she let him go he slid from the saddle like a boned fish.

Before she had chance to catch her breath, an axe winged out of the chaos and ripped her sword from her hand, narrowly missing taking her fingers off. Alyda felt a flutter of panic. She ignored it, and looked for her attacker. *There.* The Axe thrower was wearing a garish yellow sur-coat, patterned with black chevrons. She flicked Alyda a curt salute and drew her side sword before spurring her horse at Alyda. She looked like a wasp; coming in sword raised, ready to deliver a fatal sting. Alyda didn't panic; this wasn't the first time she'd lost her sword during a bat-tle. As the Wasp Knight roared towards her, Alyda reached down and grabbed her right spur.

Trease had taught her the words of command the day she'd been awarded the Fey prize. It had taken her sev-eral attempts to master the subtle inflections of the alien tongue, but she now spoke them fluidly in her mind and as she did, the spur changed.

A shiver ran down her spine as the metal flowed over her mailed fist like honey and encased her gauntlet in shimmering silver. The Wasp Knight hammered a blow towards Alyda's head. She raised her hand, and a long slender blade extended from the living metal.

Their weapons met with a resounding *clang*. Fey silver locked against mortal-forged steel. The shock of the impact numbed her fingers and spiralled up Alyda's arm. She would have dropped her sword, but the hilt of the eldritch weapon had melded around her gauntlet as though blade and hand were one. Alyda's attacker recoiled as though *she'd* been stung. Sensing its rider's surprise, the Wasp's horse leapt away from Lyco. The Suvi took one last look at Alyda, and spurred her mount into the roiling mass.

Alyda might well have done the same if someone she was fighting suddenly produced a Fey sword. But then, she wouldn't have missed with the axe in the first place.

She touched the Fey blade to her heel and willed it to be a spur once again. When that was done, she quickly dismounted and scooped up her sword. The moment her arse was back in the saddle something bright flashed towards her face. She raised her arm instinctively, and blocked a spear that was aiming for her visor. The leaf-shaped blade screamed across her vambrace, adding another scar to the metal before it snagged in the mail voider that protected her armpit. Her assailant gave a hollow roar, and tried to drive the spear into her chest. As she fought to stay in the saddle, Alyda could feel the riveted links of mail splitting under the pressure. She grabbed the spear shaft, and guiding Lyco with her legs, turned him to face the Suvian. The spear broke through the mail, and sliced through her arming jack. The blade slid against her side. She sucked in a sharp breath as pain scorched a burning trail across her ribcage. Swearing, she dug her heels into Lyco's flanks and he kicked out at her attacker's mount. The horse shied, the spear withdrew, cutting her again.

Rage lent her strength, and she yanked the spear towards her, dragging the Suvian half out of the saddle. Before he realised what she was doing, Alyda hacked at his outstretched arm and struck him on the elbow. There was a loud crack. The knight howled and dropped the spear. Alyda jabbed him in the throat with the butt of his own weapon. She was about to sheath her sword in his neck when the call to disengage sounded across the battlefield. Discipline won out over anger. She pulled the blow and waited to see if he would withdraw or stand.

Cradling his injured arm, the Suvian bowed. Alyda felt a stab of disappointment, but raised her sword in salute and let him go. As he wearily coaxed his mount back to his lines, she made a note to remember the snarling boar on his helm and shield, just in case their paths should ever cross again.

General Trevisa and his honour guard picked their way across the bloody field to where Alyda, Vorbek and Trenham were waiting. Like most stallions, Lyco was not a docile beast, but today had been tough even for him. He stood quietly, veins bulging, lathered in sweat, as exhausted as his rider. Alyda loved her horse, but wished she didn't have to fight two battles in one day to make the angry bastard behave.

Trenham pulled off his mail coif and emptied a canteen over his head. The water ran gold through his copper curls. Alyda's mouth watered. She ached to shed her steel skin, and drown herself in a barrel of ale, but this wasn't over until Trevisa surrendered. Seeing Trenham and the Irregulars take their ease was an exquisite torture. Her side ached, her throat was raw, and sweat was pouring down her back. Much longer out here beneath the harsh Suvian sun and she was sure she'd cook in her own juices like a clay-baked hedgehog. Vorbek offered her a wineskin. She shook her head. *Soon.* Behind her, the Company battle standard fluttered in the languid breeze. When she moved, her side burned, but the pain was useful, it kept her sharp and angry; ready to fight again if the Fox decided to retire sword in hand. After all the trouble he'd caused her, she almost wished he would.

The Hammer formed up beside the Anvil; Trenham's mercenaries lounged under the trees. She did a quick head count and was relieved to find that the Hammer had taken relatively few losses. She was damn proud of her knights; they were battle worn and weary, their scarlet surcoats rent and stained, but when she caught the eye of any one of them, she was met with a look of cool determination. *Hard as iron, cold as stone.* That was the Company motto, the creed they lived and died by. *Just as it should be.*

"Ay up, Shorty," Vorbek rumbled. "He's here."

General Trevisa reined in his mount about thirty feet away from them. He was flanked by two weary officers, one of whom carried Trevisa's magnificent standard. Alyda had chased the old bastard halfway across Suvia in the past month, but this was the first time she'd seen him at close quarters. He was older than she'd imagined, but sat poker straight in the saddle, a knife bright gleam in his eye. After a brief discussion with his officers, Trevisa sent his herald over.

"Who will speak on behalf of this force?" the herald asked. He looked expectantly at Vorbek.

"I will." Alyda nudged Lyco forward. "I'm Captain Alyda Stenna, of the First Company of the Antian Royal Guards."

The herald gave her a disdainful look which, purely by coincidence, was when Lyco decided he didn't like the herald's horse and lunged at it, teeth bared. Alyda pulled him up, and tried not to smile as the Suvian's horse shied. Trevisa shook his head and urged his horse forward while his herald fought to control his jittery mount. The Fox looked exhausted, as though the weight of the world rested on his thin shoulders. The old man's face was etched with deep lines, his grey brows were knitted in a deep, permanent frown. He bowed stiffly to Alyda. She raised her sword, but didn't bow.

"My la...*Captain.* I would with your permission, withdraw from the field, undertaking upon my honour not to bear arms against your noble companies for the remainder of this conflict."

No surprise they're always fighting if they treat war like a fucking game. She fixed him with a steady gaze. "General, there are only two ways you may leave the field today: dead or surrendered."

Trevisa spluttered, and slapped the pommel of his saddle. "Madame! Do you doubt my word, my honour?"

Vorbek and Trenham sniggered behind her, she ignored them. "I know nothing of either, General, but I do know that you're beaten, and must either lay down your arms, or lay on. The choice is yours...for now."

Patience had never been one of Alyda's virtues, and it was particularly lacking after a day like today. Her orders from Ranulfi had been simple; stop Trevisa. She would have preferred not to send the Company in again, but she was more than willing to do so if he wouldn't yield, and gods help him if he forced her to it.

"This is not how civilised people behave! This is not how we conduct war!" Trevisa snarled.

Alyda smiled. "It is now."

"I warn you, Captain Stenna, your vile practices have not gone unnoticed. You have few friends in Suvia, and would be wise not to make an enemy of me."

Either he was talking out of his arse or he knew something she didn't. "I confess, you have me foxed, sir."

Trevisa seemed to momentarily forget that he needed to open his mouth in order to speak. When he remembered, the words, "Heathen magic!" exploded forth. "Do not try to deny that you are a *witch*," he hissed. At the mention of the word 'witch' his herald touched a blue bead that was dangling from a chain on his wrist. Alyda recognised the Suvi charm to ward off evil. If people weren't still dying all around them it would be funny.

"If I was a witch d'you think we'd be having this conversation? Don't you think I would have turned you into a frog by now and then fucked off home?"

"Have a care woman! *You are known*. The Brotherhood of the Redemption is seeking you."

"They found me, this morning. It did not go well for them."

Trevisa gasped. "What have you done? They are a holy order, blessed by the Eklesiasti himself."

"Then rejoice, for they have gone to their gods."

"Your wickedness is breathtaking! Be advised; although you have the advantage now, Captain Stenna, the tide can turn and…" The colour drained from Trevisa's face.

"My son?" he asked, his voice trembling.

"Fought well and died bravely," she lied. She could have crushed him with the truth, but unlike his son, the Beast of Levray, she wasn't cruel. She wouldn't tell Trevisa that his first-born had died a slow, painful death in a pool of his own shit and guts. It had not been a good death, but one that he richly deserved.

"So, that's where you were this morning. Defiling a holy order, and murdering my son." Trevisa trembled with the effort of trying to master his emotions. "If you were a man I'd call you out for what you have done, Captain Stenna."

He was starting to annoy her now. "Man or woman, your challenge would be refused. There's no honour to be gained fighting an old man."

"How dare you!" he hissed.

She swept her arm in a wide arc taking in the scope of the carnage. "Because it is *your* dead who litter the field, General, not mine!"

Stung, Trevisa scanned the battlefield as though seeing it for the first time. His eyes blurred with tears. Blood drenched the lavender, staining the purple crimson. The flower of Suvian knighthood lay broken in graceless death. The cries of the wounded and the dying accompanied the eager screams of the vultures gathering for the feast. Without saying a word, Trevisa unsheathed his sword and tossed it on the ground. He then snatched his standard from the herald and handed it to Vorbek. Alyda patted Lyco's neck. Now it was over.

"It is done, and the Fox has tasted defeat for the first time; goddess be praised," said the Countess.

Jamie had watched her quaff about a pint of wine, but rather than being in her cups she seemed more alert than he'd ever seen her.

"I had no idea you'd find the battle so interesting, Countess."

A tiny stitch of a smile tugged the corner of her mouth. "No, of course you didn't, Jamie dear. You weren't supposed to."

Until that moment he hadn't noticed what a penetrating gaze she had, or how uncomfortable it felt to be the focus of it. On the battlefield, Trevisa's soldiers were throwing down their arms.

"It isn't entirely work," she said, "not this time. This time my reasons are personal."

She patted the seat next to her. Jamie accepted the invitation, grateful to rest his swollen ankle, although he didn't have the faintest idea what she was talking about.

"Many years ago, when I was an innocent girl—" She laughed. "I assure you there *was* such a time—I had a lover. He was a poor knight, the third son of a third son, but a finer, more gallant heart you could not hope to find." She turned the stem of her glass, and stared into the crimson depth with such intensity, Jamie thought the crystal might shatter. "You remind me of him. Not your fiery locks—his hair was as black as my heart, and he didn't have freckles." She chuckled. "No, 'tis more...*how* you are, both an innocent, and a warrior. 'Tis a rare combination, my dear and trust me, I've seen them all."

As bewildered as a newborn, Jamie forced a polite smile. All he wanted was to return to camp and find his comrades, but he was stuck here until her noble drunkenness decided to release him.

"Trevisa took a liberty with me all those years ago. That's why they called him the Fox; he was always stealing into the chicken coop." She breathed a gentle sigh. "When my lover, *my angel*, challenged him, Trevisa had him killed. Back then I was without influence, and nobody else cared a whit about the murder of a vagabond knight. Ah, but it broke my heart, and set me on an...*interesting* path."

She handed her glass to her body servant, and dabbed a kohl-stained tear from her cheek. Jamie noticed that the servant's knuckles were crisscrossed with dozens of pale scars, and that he had a very workmanlike hunting knife hanging from his belt that was quite at odds with the satin breeches and ill-fitting wig.

The Countess smoothed faint creases from her gown. Her hands were small, plump…scarred. "I have waited almost thirty years for this day. Patience, dear Jamie, can remain a faithful virtue when all others are lost to you." She took his hand in hers. "Thank you for *your* patience and for reminding me of the only person I have ever loved. I'm pleased you were here to share the moment when I finally saw him avenged. That you are so like him, and that your comrades were my weapons only sweetens the cup. Now, Jamie dear, I have two little gifts for you."

"There really isn't any need, I—"

"No, I insist, and not even kings can resist me when I am adamant. You must take them. I had a…" She smiled. "Suffice to say, I no longer need them, but you might." She unfastened a fine, gold locket and chain from around her neck and dropped it in his palm. She then unfastened another, this time of silver with a carved piece of horn hanging from it.

"The locket is just a keepsake, a little something to remind you of me. The other is more useful. I fear you have some dark roads to walk, Jamie dear. It won't save a life, but it will keep it for a time. Goddess forbid, *you* should ever need it." She wrapped his hand around the gifts. "Do as you will with the locket, but look after the horn. 'Tis old magic—*good* magic."

"Magic is outlawed in Suvia. Aren't you afraid of the Redemption?"

She giggled. "Surely you've learnt that there is only one law in Suvia, if not the entire world?"

Jamie smiled. "Don't get caught?"

"Precisely. Now go, I release you. I can see you're itching to be away. Please pass on my congratulations to Captain Stenna." The Countess kissed his cheek before drifting over to the pavilion. Her servant gave him a knowing smile and followed her.

Jamie wasn't sure, but he got the distinct impression that he'd been a pawn in a game he hadn't realised he'd been playing.

To take his mind off his embarrassment he opened the locket. Pressed behind glass was a curl of hair that had faded to the colour of dried blood. Painted on the other half of the locket was the portrait of a young woman. She had an unremarkable face, except for her eyes. Even though the years had blurred and cracked the paint they still stood out. Bright as pins, and as sharp as needles; the young girl crossed the decades and fixed him with a penetrating gaze.

The Antian camp that had earlier been mired in sullen anxiety erupted in cheers of joy and relief when the Hammer and the Anvil returned in triumph. It took Alyda half an hour to make her way through the jubilant crowd and back to her command tent, by which time her side was a constant, throbbing ache that pulsed pain with every breath. She lifted the tent flap to find that Vorbek had beaten her back. The Northerner was already sprawled in a chair, mug of ale in hand, a broad grin plastered across his bloodied face. Alyda tugged off a gauntlet, but she'd need help with the rest of her armour. She was about to shout for Polyn, when Jamie hobbled in, sweating like a cob stallion.

"Sorry I'm late, Captain—the road was choked with Suvi prisoners on their way to Lemarasch Keep," he said and set about unbuckling her armour.

Alyda took off her helm and sweat drenched arming cap. Long, black braids uncoiled down her back, sodden and heavy. Vorbek also wore his hair in the triple braids, as was the tradition in the Guards. Not only were they an easy way of identifying the various ranks, but they also provided excellent padding under a coif—something Alyda was most grateful for given how much her ears were ringing. Vorbek's squire, Keris, was struggling to remove the knight's dented breastplate. The task wasn't made any easier by Vorbek reaching over her for a jug of ale that was on the table.

He snagged the pitcher and poured Alyda a drink. They charged their mugs, splashing froth over the maps spread across the table. The two squires rushed to save them. Alyda couldn't care less, the long anticipated battle, and probably the war was over, and they'd won. She gulped the ale. It was sweet and cool, and gone all too quickly. She held out her tankard and Vorbek obliged her with a refill.

"I was feeling a mite lonely for a while there, Stenna," he said.

Alyda raised an eyebrow. "You'd better not be complaining. Some of us have fought *two* battles today."

They laughed—victory more intoxicating than any ale. Alyda looked at Trevisa's magnificent standard propped in the corner of the tent. It would also be going back to Antia; the question was, *with whom?*

The Captain of the Hammer snatched a coin off the table, and gestured to the captured colours. "Heads or tails?"

Vorbek scratched his matted beard before answering. "Tails."

Alyda flipped the coin, sparking a golden trail through the air. It hit the table, pirouetted, and finally came to rest with the stern face of King Daris uppermost.

Alyda flashed Vorbek a grin. "Don't feel bad, old friend—I just can't lose today."

Vorbek laughed. "Aye, so it seems. Enjoy it, Shorty. There are too few days in a lifetime when everything falls just right."

The tent flapped open. Trenham breezed in wielding a wine bottle instead of a bow. Alyda probed her side, cautiously exploring the extent of her injury. The mercenary flopped onto a chair and dragged the cork from the bottle with his teeth, before spitting it away.

"You should get your surgeon to take a look at that, or perhaps use some o'that *heathen magic* to heal yourself." said Trenham, grinning.

Alyda gave him a dead-eyed look. "You're about as funny as pox. As for this, I can wait. Gedthis has a tongue sharper than any blade. Let me at least—"

Vorbek coughed, and indicated with a frown that someone was behind her. Even before she turned around she knew who it was.

Gedthis stepped into view and glared daggers at her. "I'll get to work, shall I?"

Vorbek and Trenham declined the surgeon's invitation to leave while he worked. They decided to stay and offer ale, wine, and advice. Alyda accepted the wine, but the medical advice and alcohol were pointedly refused by the surgeon.

Gedthis cut open Alyda's bloody shirt and poked at the gash where the spear had sawed along her ribs. "I had hoped you wouldn't end up being skewered this time, Captain. Don't you do all that practicing to prevent this sort of thing from happening?"

"I'm obviously not very good yet, Gedthis," said Alyda through gritted teeth.

"Luckily for you, I am."

"So, Squire Turlowe, did you enjoy being in the company of the Black Countess?" Trenham enquired.

Jamie frowned at the mercenary. "Do you mean Countess Duvessi?"

"Aye. Not that I'd call her the Black Countess to her face—I'm too fond of breathing." He winked at Alyda. "I heard she was quite taken with you, Jamie lad. Must be those flaming locks, eh? All women of taste find us red-heads irresistible—isn't that right, Captain Stenna?"

Though it hurt, Alyda had to laugh. The Irregulars had been attached to the Guards since they'd arrived in Suvia three months ago. During that time she'd got to know Trenham and his company. Despite his terrible sense of humour, he'd proven himself to be an excellent com-mander of competent fighters. He also knew her father, which was enough for Alyda to stay on friendly terms with him, even if she didn't trust the mercenary as far as she could spit.

"I must thank the Countess," she said. "Short of telling us what colour breeches the Beast would be wearing, she was right about everything else. She's a damn good intel-ligencer."

Trenham nodded in agreement. "Aye, she's done well for us and her prince. Although, she's made an enemy of the Brotherhood and they have long memories." He leaned across the table and lowered his voice. "Tell me, d'you know what happened to Prince Jerim's troops? I heard they didn't even disembark."

Alyda and Vorbek exchanged a look of caution. Despite his affability, Trenham was still a mercenary, and they were always sniffing around for information that might lead to the next contract. Alas, it wasn't a secret that Prince Jerim and his brother, King Daris were at odds, but she wasn't going to be drawn on the subject by Trenham.

"The Governor of Cathlan fell ill and returned home on the orders of the King." She wasn't one for lying and didn't think she'd convinced Trenham of anything other than her loyalty.

"Ah, I see." The mercenary smiled. "Well, as pleasant as this has been, I'd best be going. It's a long way back to Careth. We must do this again sometime; it's been both enjoyable, and profitable." He patted his coin pouch, tipped the knights a salute, and left.

Alyda took another swig of wine, but it was doing little to numb the pain Gedthis seemed intent on inflicting. "Asha's Paps, Gedthis! It hurts more now than when it fucking happened."

"I doubt that very much, Captain." He got up and wiped his hands on his apron. "I need to get something from my tent. Try not to do anything, or go anywhere while I'm gone."

"That cowardly *fa'cachta*," Alyda swore in Tamalak when she was sure Gedthis was out of earshot.

"I take it you mean Jerim and not the sawbones?" Vorbek asked.

"Aye, Gedthis isn't averse to bloodshed."

"I think we may be sent to chastise a certain younger brother when we get home."

"Probably. Although you never know—Jerim might really be ill."

They were still laughing when Gedthis returned with a cloth covered bowl.

"That's very kind of you Gedthis, but I'm really not hungry at the moment," said Alyda.

"I'm glad you're in high spirits, Captain. There are other wounded who aren't feeling quite so light-hearted."

"I'm not surprised if he's been ministering to 'em." Althus side-mouthed.

The surgeon narrowed his eyes and whipped the cloth off the bowl. Alyda was relieved to see that it contained nothing more sinister than hot water and herbs. Gedthis fished a threaded needle from the water. It looked unnecessarily long.

"Lean over to the side please, Captain," said Gedthis as he expertly twisted a knot in the steaming, linen thread.

Alyda did as he asked, and hoped she looked more at ease than she felt. Althus gave her a reassuring nod; he knew the drill.

"Squire Turlowe!" Gedthis snapped. "For gods' sakes, hold the damn lamp still. I'm good, but not even I can work in the dark. This might sting a little, Captain." He wrinkled his nose and uncorked a small bottle of something that smelled like wine vinegar.

"So when do you think you'll be ready to leave for Toresta?" Alyda asked Vorbek.

She knew he answered because she could see his lips moving, but she didn't hear a word he was saying. As Althus started to speak, Gedthis poured the liquid over her side. Pain dug fiery talons into her flesh and stole the breath from her lungs. She didn't cry out, like all knights in the Guards she took the pain, dragged it into her gut and held it there until it died.

A welcome breeze wafted into the tent, cooling the sweat that was running down her face. Alyda looked to the entrance and saw a shock of white blonde hair; it was Della, one of the company heralds. Alyda beckoned her in.

The herald limped in and peered at Alyda's side. "That looks nasty. I thought you said it was a scratch, Gedthis?"

Alyda glared at the surgeon. *Now* she wanted to call him a *fa'cachta*.

"It is a scratch," he snapped as he deftly stitched the stinging flesh together. "Don't be so dramatic."

Della smiled apologetically at Alyda. "I'm sorry, Captain, but there's some Suvies outside. Shall I tell them to come back when he's finished or…?"

Alyda shook her head and blessed Gedthis with a barbed stare. "No, bring them in. It's only a scratch."

Vorbek stood up and wiped his mouth with the back of his hand and straightened his braids. The herald showed two Suvians into the tent; dressed in their finery they looked as out of place as snowdrops in a desert. Alyda knew Count Lemarasch; he was an aide to Prince Ranulfi. He always seemed a decent sort and, unlike most of the prince's staff, possessed of more than half a brain. She had no idea who the other one was, but judged that if he'd ever been a warrior it had been a long time ago. The stranger had a full, almost perfectly round belly, and was wearing possibly the most elaborate uniform she'd ever seen. If martial prowess was measured in gold braid he must surely be a god of war.

Round Belly swept past Lemarasch, "My dear Antian friends, I—"

He began boldly enough, but on seeing the surgeon's red work, he choked. His eye widened, his mouth closed, then opened, then closed again, making him look like a freshly landed fish.

Alyda wasn't in the mood to deal with idiots, and gave Lemarasch a questioning look. He shrugged apologetically and stepped past the gasping Round Belly.

"Captain Stenna, Captain Vorbek, allow me to congratulate you on the Prince's behalf. It was a fine victory, but this is clearly not the appropriate time to discuss business with you, Captain Stenna. Please, forgive our interruption." In a whisper intended only for Alyda he added: "I'm really *very* sorry about this." Then in a louder voice: "Captain Vorbek, perhaps you could assist us?"

"What can I do for you, Count Lemarasch?" Althus asked.

The old nobleman frowned. "It's the standard you took—that of General Trevisa. General Calvigneri..." he indicated Round Belly, who inclined his head very slightly to the captains, "…would like to know how much you would be willing to take for it."

"Ah, well. I'm afraid you'll have to come back later and speak to Captain Stenna after all, for 'tis the First that has claim to those colours."

Gedthis dropped the needle in the bowl and rinsed his hands turning the water pink. "Another excellent job, even if I say so myself. Please keep it clean, Captain. I'll be back later to check on it."

Alyda grunted and sat back. The stitches pulled, and her side felt raw, which did nothing to improve her rapidly deteriorating mood.

Round Belly produced a silver vinaigrette from his sleeve and took a sniff before clearing his throat. "Captain Stenna, how much do you want for the standard? I'll pay handsomely for it, *in gold*. 'Tis just a pity I was delayed, or I would have taken it from the field of honour myself." He tried to thrust out his chest, but merely succeeding in presenting his belly like a proud mother-to-be.

Take it himself? Alyda looked at Althus. The Captain of the Anvil shrugged. Round Belly was dressed in a theatrical fantasy of a military uniform. The man reeked of perfume and self importance. His white gloved hand rested on the jewelled hilt of a sword that looked more suited to peeling apples than spilling blood. She'd wager a month's pay that he'd never even seen a battlefield, let alone fought on one.

"I'm sorry, *General*, but the standard is going back to Antia with the First." She was too tired to go into detail about what she thought of his offer, or in which orifice he could shove it.

Calvigneri's sickly smile vanished. "Captain, I must insist that you sell me the standard. I'm sure you understand it cannot be taken from Suvian soil. Honour is at stake, I must return with it to our Prince's headquarters, I absolutely must!"

Alyda was on her feet before she knew it. She took a step towards Calvigneri. Startled, he hopped back.

"General Calvigneri, that…" she stabbed a finger at Trevisa's colours, "is a *battle standard*, taken in combat and paid for with blood. It will hang in a place of honour at Trelanlith Arth so that in years to come, when this day has been forgotten and we have long since turned to dust, the knights who come after will see it and remember those who fell in its taking."

Calvigneri's gaze flicked nervously from Alyda to the standard and back again. He gulped. "S…so you won't sell it?"

"No."

After an uncomfortably long silence, Lemarasch rescued Calvigneri. "My Lord, I believe it's time to inspect the troops."

"Yes! Yes, of course," Calvigneri spluttered. "Why didn't you remind me earlier, Lemarasch? Captain Stenna, Captain Vorbek, I cannot say that it has been a pleasure." The General almost tripped over his sword in his haste to leave. When he'd gone, a wide grin spread across Lemarasch's angular face.

"Thank you, Captain—I'll dine out for months on this tale." He bowed and left.

Althus chuckled. "You're a born diplomat, Ali."

She sat back down and put her feet on the table. "Aye. 'Tis a gift."

Chapter Two

Lord Hyram prayed a silent prayer to no god in particular that the day would pass quickly and uneventfully. He loathed parades, disliked public holidays, and despised wearing heavy robes and chains of office on hot July days. Acid burned his gullet while he waited for Daris to finish reading his report. He looked out of the window to pass the time, but the impressive view of the capital afforded him little pleasure. Far below, beyond the garland decked walls of Weyhithe Arth, the winding streets were thronged with what looked to be the entire population of the city and every town and village for miles around. The air hummed with excitement, as the great unwashed waited to greet the knights of the 1st and the 2nd on their triumphant return from Suvia. Hyram wanted to vomit. He traced the path the parade would take from the city gates to the Arth, *if* everything went to plan. His stomach lurched when he considered what would happen if it didn't.

"I cannot fault Stenna and Vorbek," said Daris, when he'd finished reading the report. "They were exemplary, were they not?" He tossed the report on the table. Dressed in his ceremonial armour he looked every inch the warrior king. Hyram noted with unreasonable annoyance that he was wearing his hair in three braids in honour of his precious Guards.

"Yes, my Lord, your knights' prosecuted war with brutal precision. It will be a desperate day before *King* Ranulfi contemplates the shores of Antia with hungry eyes."

"Good, let's hope he's learnt the lesson his cousin did not." Daris rocked on his heels. "So… How badly did my brother disgrace me?"

Hyram knew he'd have to tread carefully with this subject. "From what I've gathered, not a great deal—at least, not with the Suvians. According to reports they're struggling to come to terms with the aftermath of their first real war for over twenty years. I don't think they noticed the slight."

"So who did?"

Hyram closed the window. "The Free Companies are certainly aware that the Prince did not disembark a single soldier. The Cathlan nobles have also been bragging about how their Governor slighted you, but then they would; they're his subjects."

"And he is mine, damn him to the Void!"

"I'm sorry, my Lord. I don't know what to suggest."

"Why don't you suggest what you've hinted at before; that I have my brother quietly done away with?"

Hyram sighed inwardly. His mistake had been in mentioning that accidents sometimes happened to troublesome younger brothers who threatened the stability of a kingdom. It had only been the slightest suggestion, but enough for Daris to almost soul bind him into swearing never to consider harming Jerim—to the point where Hyram dreaded what would happen if the imbecile had a genuine accident. If only he'd done away with the poisonous little fuck without attempting to gain approval from Daris, then they wouldn't have to deal with his constant scheming.

Daris paced angrily. "Why does he seek to infuriate me so? Have I ever denied him anything?"

"You've always treated your brother well, better than he has perhaps deserved. He has always been…difficult, my Lord. I don't think it's in his nature to be amicable, or to recognise where his best interests lie." This was Hyram's most diplomatic way of saying Jerim was a power-obsessed madman. The Councillor didn't hedge out of fear, but out of love. He didn't want to add to Daris's problems. Unlike Jerim, Daris was a prince amongst men irrespective of rank, and happily for the people of Antia, had been born first. Hyram knew it hurt him deeply that the love he bore his brother had only ever been repaid with scorn. They'd fought since childhood, then, as now, Hyram had stood between his cousins, protecting one from the schemes of the other.

"Enough of Jerim. Today is not a day I want to think about him. Truth be told, I'm glad he's *too ill* to attend the celebrations—he'd only darken the day with his malice and I would have my Guards welcomed home with joy in every heart in Weyhithe."

Hyram smiled, but his stomach was churning. Not all hearts were full of joy, of that he was certain. His was gripped by fear and anxiety. His gaze was drawn back to the window. Down in the Great Ward, the 4th Company of the Royal Guards were preparing to ride from the Arth. Hyram was rarely roused to anything more than casual cynicism by martial displays. They were so damned pompous—little more than excuses for overindulgence, and buffing the egos of boorish thugs. Today however, he was keenly interested in the parade. Somewhere among the teeming crowds, his best agents were on the trail of the King's enemies. While the knights basked in the adulation of the masses, his people were hunting killers in the shadows of Weyhithe. He didn't know who he was looking for, but the threat, the merest whisper of the word *assassin* was too serious to ignore.

Daris clapped him on the shoulder. "Come, cousin, there's no need for such a serious mien. Put Jerim from your thoughts and enjoy the day."

"Forgive me, my Lord. 'Tis only the heat that vexes me." Hyram smiled in a bid to convince Daris of the lie.

Garian wasn't tall, or particularly strong or, alas, a deadly swordsman. He was however, quick, intelligent, and very good at his job. But if the axe had been thrown with a little more accuracy, and a little less haste, he would now be nothing more than a twitching corpse sprawled in the doorway. Spurred on by the sharp reminder of mortality that had splintered the woodwork inches from his head, Garian charged into the room. The axe man looked surprised that he'd missed and hesitated before reaching for a sword that was hanging on the back of a chair. Garian didn't waste a breath, and vaulted the table between them. He kicked the chair away, pinned the axe man against the wall, and held a knife to his throat to keep him there.

"Don't move," said Garian.

The man nodded slowly, then headbutted him. Because he didn't have room to throw his head back the blow lacked strength; even so, he hit Garian hard enough to momentarily stun him. The axe man made a grab for the sword. Blinking away tears, Garian kneed him in the balls, reversed his grip on the dagger and thrust it, two-fisted, into the man's shoulder. He felt the tip skid off bone before cutting through the muscle. A solid shiver leapt up his arm when the blade finally hit the wall. The man let out a shrill scream.

"Let's try again, dog shit, and if you so much as breathe in a way I don't like, I'll kill you. Do you understand?" Only the slightest tremor in his voice betrayed Garian's fury. The axe man nodded. "Good. So, *Gilhas*—who and where?"

Gilhas's eyes widened at the mention of his name. Garian hoped he could bluff him into thinking he knew more than he did. All he knew for certain was that he was running out of time.

Gilhas clamped his lips together in a hard line. Garian twisted the blade. The bloody key unlocked his mouth and Gilhas let out another high-pitched scream.

"So help me man, I will flense the fucking meat from your bones if you don't tell me what you know."

Gilhas's resolve began to crumble; tears pearled and ran down his bloodless cheeks.

"Are your new friends worth dying for?" Garian pressed.

"She…she had me buy poison… that's all, I swear on the Twins! That's all I did."

"Tell me everything," Garian demanded, praying that there was more to tell.

"A ca…captain, one of them comin' back fr…from Suvia, that's who she's after, but I don't know which one."

Garian twisted the knife again, eliciting another agonized scream from Gilhas.

"For Asha's sake! I swear it, I swear…" he blubbered.

"What does she look like? What's her name?"

"No name, short, 'bout your height, black hair— Hadami looking. A red cloak, g…grey cap."

Garian pulled his dagger from Gilhas' shoulder. The injured man yelped and slid down the wall leaving a scarlet smear on the panelling.

"You, innkeeper! Get your arse in here now." Garian ordered the woman who was loitering in the hallway.

"Watch him until the City Guards arrive. If he's gone when they get here, you'll take his place in the King's dungeon, understand?" He sheathed his knife, and wiped his bloody nose on his sleeve.

She prised the axe out of the door frame. "Aye, sir, as you say, sir. Don't worry I'll cut the fucker in 'arf if he tries to move."

Garian didn't give a damn. Gilhas was a taken piece. Now he had to decide his next move, and do it quickly. There was no way he'd be able to battle his way back to the Arth in time to tell his master what he'd found out, the streets were rammed, and even if he did make it, the word of a petty criminal like Gilhas wasn't enough to cancel the parade. Out of time and choices, he headed over to the East Gate where the knights would enter.

On the way over he collared a Sergeant of the City Guards and told her to detain every woman who fit the description Gilhas had given him. The indignation of the gypsies was a small price to pay compared to the riots that would follow if one of the King's knights was murdered. He had no idea which one was the target, but at least they'd both be in the same place at the same time.

The Hammer and the Anvil reached Weyhithe in time to see the sun pierce the dark horizon before beginning its ascent into the clear, blue sky. Alyda smiled. It was going to be a perfect day.

By mid morning, her knights were dressed in their finest harness, and waiting in a tent that had been set aside for their use until it was time to enter the city. Outwardly, Alyda maintained an air of cool detachment as befitted a Captain of the Royal Guards. Inside, she was as excited as a child on the eve of Midwinter.

Althus beckoned her over, the green and black plumes in his helm brushed the canvas roof with every movement. He was being besieged by an army of young ladies and gentlemen who'd brought flower garlands for the knights.

"Mornin', Captain Stenna, you've scrubbed up well." Althus grinned and politely ducked so that more garlands could be added to the half dozen that were already draped around his neck. "Don't go fainting in the heat now, Shorty—I know what a delicate flower you are."

She gave him the lizard eye. "If I do pass out, promise you won't try to revive me with a kiss."

"Ach, I'm hurt!"

"Call me a flower again and you will be."

Satisfied that it was immaculate, Jamie folded the Captain's red velvet cloak over his arm. There was just one more item he needed.

He lifted the Silver Spur from the Captain's trunk as though it was made of the most delicate crystal rather than... whatever it was made from. The spur was the highest honour the King could bestow on a knight. Jamie remembered the day Daris had presented it to the Captain like it was yesterday. Today would be another great day to remember.

The squires and pages had been given a tent of their own and were frantically busy, polishing armour, cleaning cloaks, paying minute attention to every buckle and stitch to ensure the knights they served would look their best for the parade. Everyone was excited. They all talked at once, voices growing louder, and louder, as they fought to be heard. The young warriors boasted extravagantly of how they would dazzle the noble young ladies and gentlemen at the feast with tales of their daring exploits in Suvia, but not Jamie. The only person he could think about was the Captain, and making sure everything was perfect for her.

"So Turlowe, d'you think Captain Stenna will bed Corvinius tonight? Or has her affection turned to Vorbek?"

Hedden was the newly appointed squire of Rann Lacgarde and had only been with the Company for a couple of weeks. He'd come as replacement for the Standard Bearer's previous squire who'd been killed in Suvia. Unlike his predecessor, Hedden was obnoxious and abrasive, and for some unknown reason had decided to tease Jamie whenever he got the chance. It was expressly forbidden for squires and knights to fight each other, but Jamie was finding it increasingly difficult holding to the rule when it came to Hedden.

Hedden sneered; he was a couple of years younger than Jamie, but a good deal taller. "Well, copper top, what d'you think?" He either hadn't noticed, or didn't care that a space had cleared around them. "Who do you think the Captain will have between her thighs tonight? Or maybe she'll do both? I've heard Hadami women are given to taking more than one lover at a time."

Jamie laughed; he wasn't intimidated by Hedden. He'd always been a likely looking target for bullies; he wasn't tall and, as Countess Duvessi had noted, was cursed with a boyish face, but in his case, looks were deceiving. Jamie was a veteran who'd fought in the line, and looked his enemies in the eye when he'd killed them. Hedden was an untried recruit, full of piss and wind.

"I neither know nor care who, if anyone, the Captain will take to her bed tonight," he said, "but I do know that I wouldn't take you to mine if you were the last warm body in Antia. Now don't start crying because I've spurned you, it's embarrassing."

Hedden flushed as scarlet as the Company colours and barged from the tent, hounded by the mocking laughter of the other squires. Jamie winked at Keris who was watching him with an expression somewhere between curiosity and admiration. He liked her; she understood what it was to be a captain's squire, and she made him laugh. He gathered up the cloak and was about to leave when she came over.

"I thought you were going to belt him," she said.

"So did I, and then I remembered he's an idiot and not worth being kicked out of the Guards over."

She laughed. "Aye, true enough, although, if he'd said anymore about my Captain, I'd have punched him myself." Her eyes lit up. "Is that the Silver Spur? Can I have a look?"

"I...alright, but I have to take these to the Captain. Come, walk with me, and be careful with it."

They passed the horse lines; like their riders the knights' mounts had also been groomed within an inch of their lives and kitted out in their finest harness. The Captains' mounts both had great plumes attached to their crinets, Lyco's in flaming red and Vorbek's horse in black and green. Jamie pretended not to notice Lyco dragging two grooms over to a bale of hay, while they dangled from his reins like ornaments.

Keris held the spur up to the light. "I've seen Trease's spur from a distance, but I've never touched one."

"Ah, well, there are only two knights alive who've won them. I was her squire when she received the honour." Jamie beamed, unable to resist showing off just a little.

Keris gave him a lopsided grin. "Yes, Jamie, I know, I was there too. They say they're a pair. What d'you think?"

Jamie shrugged. "I don't know, but I suppose it would explain why only two knights have them. They're Fey made, I can tell you that for certain. Look at the engraving, no human smith could produce something so detailed."

Keris nodded appreciatively. "It's beautiful, but I wouldn't know Fey work if it bit me. I'm the daughter of a farmer, not a lord. We don't have too many Fey treasures tucked away in the family vaults, unlike some." She elbowed him playfully in the ribs.

Outside the officers' tent they saw Lieutenant Lorhine and Lieutenant Tiran. The two officers were locked in a heated debate.

"I think you'd better use the other entrance," said Keris when the senior knights began shoving each other.

Aye, I think you're right."

Keris smiled and handed him the Silver Spur. "It's really stunning."

"Aye, well, I spent about two hours cleaning it last night."

"Your Captain's lucky to have you."

Jamie slapped her on the back. "Thanks Ker, it's nice of you to say so. No one else understands what it's like being a Captain's squire."

"I think we're very alike, you and I." She picked a speck of lint off the Captain's cloak and smiled in an odd, shy sort of way.

"Aye, we could be family, like brother and sister—you know what I mean," said Jamie.

Her smile vanished. "Brother and… I'll see you later Jamie, you don't want to keep Captain Stenna waiting."

"I thought you'd got lost," said Captain Stenna.

"Sorry, Captain, I had to help the grooms with Lyco." He knew she wasn't really annoyed. Despite the raised eyebrow and folded arms, the half-smile and bright gleam in her eyes betrayed her good humour.

She threw on her cloak. Jamie looped the gold braided ties through the rings set near the shoulders of her breast-plate, careful not to leave finger marks on the shining metal. Her parade armour was exquisitely decorated, but could turn a blade as well as her battle harness should the need arise. Unlike her battle armour, this set was mirror bright, and every surface was etched with roses and curling vines. It was a fine testament to the skill of its maker.

Jamie dreamed of one day owning a suit of armour made by Master Bainley. When he was finished draping her cloak, he handed her the Silver Spur. A shiver ran down his spine as he watched her hold it against her right boot heel. There were no buckles or straps; the metal simply flowed around her boot, seamlessly locking itself in place around her ankle. The Captain saw that he was watching and winked.

Outside, someone shouted; "The Black Lancers have left the palace!"

Vorbek clapped the Captain on the shoulder. "Lock up your sons and daughters, Weyhithe! The Hammer and the Anvil are coming to town. Knights! To your horses!"

Cassian checked the girth on his saddle and cinched it up another notch. On his signal, the Standard Bearer unfurled the company colours. The sable field rippled in the gentle breeze that swept through the walled canyons of the Arth, animating the silver griffin emblazoned across it. He cast a critical eye over his company as they prepared to leave. Their coal black horses were immaculate, their blackened armour pristine. The 4th was ready to ride.

Cassian was looking forward to seeing Alyda and Althus again, but he didn't enjoy banquets. He'd stopped being embarrassed by how he looked years ago, but still found social gatherings awkward. Hefting the Guard's ceremonial mace, he admired the bronze griffin that topped the ironwood shaft. Every minute scale had been polished to perfection. He raised it aloft and ordered the Lancers to move out.

By the time they reached the East Gate, Cassian's ears were ringing. The noise and colour, the tidal roll of bodies pressed against each other was as disorientating as the battlefield, the only difference was that nobody was trying to kill him. He raised the mace, the 4th came to a halt behind him, and the crowd fell silent. Moments passed; Cassian and the citizens of Weyhithe held their breath until the gates split and a blade of sunlight sliced through the shadows crowding the street. The hundreds of spectators gave a thunderous cheer, so loud it shook the glass in the windows. The gates were thrown open to reveal the Hammer and the Anvil waiting outside.

Lyco stamped and snorted imperiously when the Lancers' herald sounded her horn. The blast cut through the noise of the crowd and sent a shiver down Alyda's spine. From behind her, the call was answered.

Cassian rode forward and halted between the gates. When the roar died down he gave the formal greeting. "King Daris the Seventh, bids me welcome you in love, honour, and fealty. Do you enter here in faith, at the bidding of the King?"

Alyda's mouth was dry; she had to swallow before giving the reply she'd been rehearsing in her head all morning. "The First Company of the Royal Guards humbly accepts the graciousness of King Daris and enters his city in love, honour, fealty, and faith."

It was a rare day when a destrier of the Guards was startled, but something, probably the sudden cheer, caught Lyco by surprise and he reared. Alyda's heart missed a beat. For a moment, while her horse beat the air with his hooves, she was sure she was going to be dumped unceremoniously on her arse. She hung on and when he came back down, she set spurs to his flanks and drove him through the city gate.

Garian was no horseman, but making the ugly brute rear was reckless, even for one of the Royal Guards. He was watching proceedings from a balcony that overlooked the road. Threats, promises, and coin had convinced the owners to be elsewhere while he availed himself of the best vantage he could find to search the crowd for the assassin. All he had to go on was a vague description and a well developed nose for trouble.

He scanned the crowd while the Captain of the Black Lancers and the Captain of the Hammer bellowed non-sense at each other. When the Captain of the Anvil had given his response they would ride together to the Arth at the head of their companies. Three Captains, one of whom was going to die if he didn't save them. *No pressure there, then.* He would have to correct the description of Stenna. Tamalak women were generally brawnier than Antians, but she was only half Tamalak. She was tall, but had inherited the more slender build of her Hadami mother. She obviously knew she was fair, even though her expression was perfectly composed, Garian saw the flush in her cheeks and the twinkle in her eyes. She was clearly enjoying the adoration of the crowds. This was in marked contrast to the Captain of the 4th. The man was as pale as a corpse, and looked about as happy. Garian could well believe the rumours that the knight had Fey blood; there was something not quite human about that long, angular face. In any company it would have been impossible to mistake Althus Vorbek. The Captain of the Anvil was a giant, half bear, half troll—typical Tamalak.

Garian ignored the knot of desperation tightening in his gut and searched the crowd again. Thus far, he hadn't spotted anyone who even came close to matching the description Gilhas had given him, and the knights were about to set off for the Arth. He'd have to stay with them, but if he went down into the streets he'd be trapped in the crush. There was nothing for it; if he couldn't go down he'd just have to go up.

He'd learnt as a boy that the architecture of Weyhithe lent itself very well to the needs of those who wished to travel quickly and, more importantly, *unobserved* around the city. The sewers were a grim alternative, but of no use today. Jutting balconies and pitched rooftops that overhung the narrow side streets at regular, easily traversed intervals, most definitely were. The tightly packed buildings were horribly dangerous when fires broke out, but extremely useful at times like this.

For the early part of the route Garian was able to keep pace with the knights, but his progress stalled roughly mid-way to the Arth when he came up against a damaged roof, its blackened roof beams exposed to the sky. Cursing, he searched for an alternative way forward while keeping an eye out for the assassin. About eight feet below him was a narrow balcony. He could use it to climb across to its neighbour on the next building along, and then back up onto the rooftops. Having picked his path, he jumped down, smiled politely at the startled spectators on the balcony, and made to climb over the side. He was halfway across when he glanced down and caught sight of something that froze him in his tracks. Standing at the point where the road curved round a bend, was a Hadami woman wearing a grey cap. He watched, heart pounding, as she took something from the basket she was carrying. Frustratingly, he couldn't make out what it was before it disappeared under her red cloak.

He looked around for the fastest way down, and spotted a drainpipe about four feet away. It was old, rust pitted, and covered in flaking paint. It could be a *very* quick way down if it was as rotten as it looked. As soon as he committed all of his weight to it, a metal bracket snapped off and spun into the crowd. He froze and thought light thoughts. The pipe groaned ominously, but didn't peel away from the wall. He wasn't going to hang around long enough for it to change its mind and slid down, bracing his feet against the wall to slow his descent. About eight feet from the ground he dropped, slightly behind and to the right of the Hadami.

Her face was turned away from him as she watched the knights' approach. He tried to push through the crowd to get a better look at her, but was blocked by the soldiers who were keeping the road clear. All he could make out was her profile; her face was framed by thick, black hair, typically Hadami, and her skin was tanned. She smiled at some fellow as he squeezed by her, but the moment he passed, the smile vanished. Garian slipped his knife from its sheath and held it blade-up by his side. As he continued to watch the woman, doubt crept in and he began to question his instincts. She looked so ordinary, cheering and craning to catch a glimpse of the knights. But wasn't he ordinary? Was she like him? Was she a killer, or an innocent?

When the knights drew closer he got his answer. She glanced around to see if she was being watched. For a second their eyes met. That was all it took, for both of them. She flicked another glance towards the knights who were almost level with her, and then back to Garian. She shouldered her cloak aside, revealing the business end of a small handbow.

Hesitation kills. Garian never forgot anything his master taught him, especially not that piece of wisdom; it had saved his life on more than one occasion. The assassin could either stick to her intended target, or go for him. While she was deciding, he rushed her, and stabbed her in the heart. There was a brief flash of anger in her dark eyes. He pulled her close, and kissed her; just a pair of lovers, locked in a passionate embrace. She struggled, tried to cry out. He drove the knife deeper. She breathed her last breath into his mouth; it tasted of blood.

The knights rode on; waving to the crowds, completely unaware that death had been stalking them. Garian supported the assassin's dead weight against him, and danced her down a side street, her hot blood soaking into his shirt. Even out of view of the main road he continued the pretence of courtship until he turned down another, darker alleyway. After making sure it was deserted, he pulled the knife from her chest and let the body fall.

Other than the small bow, which he decided he'd keep for himself, she was carrying papers that identified her as a Hadami of the Vodoni clan. Whatever she was, she wasn't Hadami—she didn't have a single tattoo. Her pouch contained a few small coins and a glass vial of dark brown liquid. He carefully removed the waxed stopper and wafted his hand across the mouth of the vial. It smelled acrid, with a slight hint of rotten fruit. He didn't recognise it, but guessed it was poison, either that or the worst perfume ever created. He put the stopper back in and dropped it in his pouch. He'd test it later; right now he had to get rid of the body.

After uttering a few choice oaths, he managed to drag the grate off a nearby sewer. He tipped the body into the darkness, there was a muffled splash and she was gone, carried away with the rest of the city's waste. Garian was confident that his dark blue shirt would hide the blood stains well enough to pass a casual inspection. He should go straight to Hyram and make his report. Should—but wouldn't. He'd tell the City Guard they could call off the hunt, then he was going to find a quiet inn somewhere. Killing left a foul taste in his mouth. A few mugs of ale would help wash it away, or at least numb him enough that he didn't care.

Alyda's heart quickened when she saw the spires of Wey-hithe Arth spearing into the sky above the city's rooftops. Lyco sensed her excitement, and trotted proudly through the gates of the barbican.

The Arth had been built on a massive outcrop of stone that loomed above the city. A fortress of one kind or another had stood in the same place since the Tamalak Clan Lords had ruled Antia, over a thousand years ago. It had been destroyed and rebuilt many times over the centuries, always rising from the ashes bigger, and more impressive than its previous incarnation. Queen Thea had softened its hard edges over the years by planting gardens and importing fine sculptures, but for all the embellishments it remained a fortress, there to guard the city and busy river port.

The Arth protected the city, but it fell to the 5th Company of the Royal Guards to protect the Royal residences. Resplendent in russet and silver, the knights of the 5th patrolled the Arth walls.

The whole of the court and hundreds of guests were waiting in the bailey. King Daris, Queen Thea and their sons, Princes Talin and Olin were seated on a raised dais in the middle of the ward. It was the greatest honour to be received by the King and his family, but it was the presence of Matlin Trease, the Commander of the Royal Guards that caused Alyda to sit a little straighter in the saddle. The Knight Commander was standing in front of the dais. Physically unremarkable, he was a slight man who could pass unnoticed in any crowd, but Trease's reputation was legendary, and the man's presence more daunting than the Arth itself.

As she rode before him, Alyda was conscious of every movement, every shift in weight and posture, aware that nothing would escape his critical gaze. By some miracle Lyco was behaving impeccably. His neck arched gracefully, his hooves picked at the cobbles with uncustomary precision. It had been a gamble riding the foul-tempered destrier into the city, but he'd earned his place amongst the warriors who'd fought in Suvia. Perhaps on some level he understood the honour and had decided to be reasonable, or perhaps the long gallop she'd taken him on this morning had made him more tractable. Whatever the reason, Alyda was grateful for his rare good mood.

High above the bailey, Hyram closed the window against the thunder of three hundred knights dismounting and the raucous cheering of the crowds. He much preferred it up here with the gulls, far from his official chambers and the mundane matters of state. This was where the real work was done. It was from here that he waged a subtle war against those enemies who threatened the stability of the kingdom. He'd been careful to ensure that those few who wandered the dusty reaches of the tower never noticed the door to his chamber. At no small cost, he'd acquired a little Fey made cat that he'd placed outside on the door lintel. Its particular magic caused the eye to slide over the door without really noticing it. It was petty magic, and wouldn't deter a determined search, but it was enough to distract a casual glance. Of course, the downside to privacy was that no one had ever been in to clean. A heavy mantle of dust had settled over the room. The carved oak panelling was thick with cobwebs, and his old four-poster bed was sinking into stately decay. His desk groaned under the weight of books and papers, piled in precarious stacks, some of which were so high he imagined they might very well crush him to death should they ever fall.

He was dangerously close to running out of space for his vast, and still growing, collection of books and scrolls. He guessed that he had—at most—enough floor space to grant him another year's grace, but then he'd have to move into a bigger room or, gods forbid, get rid of some of his beloved books. The fire crackled and spat in the grate, he dabbed sweat from his brow and opened the window he'd just closed.

The noise of shouting peasants was a lesser evil than frying in his own fat. It was an unfortunate superstition that he'd developed, but he couldn't bring himself to let the fire die. He knew it was irrational, but he was sure that the moment the flames died would be the exact time he'd need to destroy something quickly. That fear, that madness of his own creation, kept the fire burning, and the sweat running down his face. At times like these he considered that for a supposedly intelligent man, he could be exceptionally stupid.

After hours of anxious pacing and pointless staring out of the window there was a familiar knock at the door. It creaked open, Garian peered inside. Hyram's sense of relief that the boy was alive was almost immediately usurped by annoyance that he'd kept him waiting. It may have been an unavoidable delay, but no one had ever accused Hyram of being reasonable.

"Don't stand there gawking, get in here!" said Hyram.

After giving his report, the boy handed over the papers he'd taken from the assassin. When he'd devoured their meagre content, Hyram tossed them on the table and sighed.

"Was there anything else that might indicate who wanted to spoil the party?" He didn't try to hide his disappointment; he was a starving man that had been fed just enough to enrage his hunger. These crumbs of information were not enough.

"If there'd been anything else, I'd have brought it, my Lord."

"Watch your tone boy, I'm in no mood for your insolence." Hyram propped his chin on his hands and glared at the papers, trying to imagine the hand that had forged them, and the reason behind the deed. "We were lucky this time." He tapped the papers. "But why the bloody knights? Why not Daris, or Thea, or the princes? Why such a crude attempt?"

Garian poured himself a glass of wine. "You sound disappointed."

Hyram recognised the tone, the awkward body language. The boy was unhappy about something. It was probably the killing. It didn't sit well with some people, not even after they'd done it a few times; the revulsion never left them. Garian seemed to be such a person, which was a pity—for him. He'd have to learn to wall off his feelings or it would destroy him, Hyram had seen it happen. He hoped it would be the former; he'd spent a lot of time training the boy.

"There are far too many missing pieces, we must rectify that. And where in the Void have you been by the way? You look a mess, and you smell worse."

"Oh you know; killing an assassin, saving lives, the usual."

"After that—you stink of cheap ale and pipe smoke."

"I had *one* ale. I didn't think you'd mind; I haven't slept for two days."

"Do not try to take advantage of my generous and kindly nature, Master Tain. You may rest all you want after the feast tonight."

"Why, I'm not…"he sighed, "I'm going to the feast, aren't I?"

Hyram smiled, took a scroll from his robes and tossed it to his apprentice.

Garian eyed the parchment suspiciously. "What is it?"

"Your promotion, *Captain* Tain. You'll have to imagine the fanfare and all that foolishness. Your salary will be increased accordingly."

A flicker of genuine pleasure lit his apprentice's face, but it was fleeting. The mask of bored indifference was back in place almost instantly. He'd taught the lad to hide his feelings, but sometimes he thought he might have done his work too well.

Garian tucked the scroll into his shirt. "And I quite fancied a parade. Oh, well…"

"Alas, there's no parade, but I do have a uniform for you to wear tonight. It's in the chest over there."

His apprentice approached the chest with a healthy measure of caution. Hyram stifled a chuckle as the boy flipped the lid and cautiously poked at the contents which were a saffron doublet and pair of lime green hose.

"It's what the servants will be wearing. I think they're your size; they looked small enough."

"I really don't know what to say my Lord," Garian intoned.

The King gave a rousing speech. When he finished, hundreds of doves were released, and rose petals fell like red rain, carpeting the Arth in scarlet. It was a magnificent end to the parade. Trease officially dismissed the Guards, and without further delay preparations began for the feast.

After making sure the Company horses were stabled and fed, Alyda slipped away to her room. She could have gone to one of the many receptions being held in their honour, but chose instead to steal some time alone before the feast.

Once she'd bathed and changed, she let her feet wander where they would while she ordered her thoughts on the day's events. She would be seeing her parents tonight, for the first time in many months—too many if she was honest. Guilt threatened to take the shine off the day, but she wouldn't let it. If any people on earth understood why she did what she did, why she hardly saw them from one year to the next, it was her parents. They had joined in her the free spirit of the Hadami and the hearth-bound heart of the Tamalak. *And what a restless, striving creature they've made me.*

After what felt like hours of wandering through the amber shaded labyrinth, she found herself in a windowed corridor. The leaded panes had captured the dying rays of the sun and spun a web of light and shadow across the marble floor. On the windowed side, an arched doorway led to a lush courtyard garden. Alyda allowed herself to be drawn by the subtle scent of flowers that wafted into the corridor.

The garden was a tranquil refuge in the heart of the busy castle. The walls dripped with twining honeysuckles and hundred petal roses bowed on slender stems. In the centre, a marble fountain burbled quietly. Alyda went and sat beside it and trailed her calloused fingers in the cold water. Lulled by the song of the fountain, she closed her eyes and let her thoughts drift amid the perfume.

Bear always got the good stuff, Talin mused groggily when he woke from the Pel-induced slumber. He'd never dreamed of nymphs before; they were delightful, and outrageously rude. He grinned, the warmth still lingering in his groin from the almost embarrassingly real dream. That was damn good Pel: strong—despite having been mixed with chocolate to take the edge off the bitterness.

He stretched out on the bench beneath the ancient wisteria knotted into the garden wall. It was one of his favourite hiding places, one he used quite often when he needed to escape the tedious demands of his so-called 'duties'. He'd already swapped his fine robes and princely circlet in favour of a plain grey shirt, black breeches, and an old pair of boots. When Bear got back from wherever in the Void she'd gone to get wine, they would sneak into the city, and join in with the celebrations by way of visiting their favourite brothel. The drugs and wine were splendid; now all he needed was a tumble with one or two of Madame Medelle's best before he had to come back and sit through yet another dull state feast. Why he had to be there while his father entertained a bunch of charmless knights was beyond him.

He immediately forgot all thoughts of escape when the dark haired woman wandered into the garden. Dressed like a Tamalak, he particularly liked the way the scarlet tunic was split to her waist, revealing the fitted hose and doeskin boots. She had long, black hair, held back from her lovely, if rather serious face, by a simple silver band. She looked familiar, but he couldn't place where he knew her from. He stifled a yawn. The Pel was still fogging his brain; it wasn't like him to forget an attractive acquaintance. Whoever she was, she hadn't seen him lying in the shadows and he wasn't in any hurry to reveal his presence. It was terribly rude to spy on her, but she looked so content, he didn't want to announce himself and spoil the moment for either of them.

He watched her until the sun dipped behind the walls and the layered shadows of the Arth were banished, one by one, as torches were lit, and the windows poured gold into the darkened garden. She opened her eyes, stretched and got up to leave. Talin was trapped by indecision. If he showed himself, he'd be in the awkward position of having to explain why he hadn't made himself known earlier. He could stay hidden, and she would leave none the wiser, but then he wouldn't find out who she was and that suddenly struck him as something he very much wanted to know. Damn it, he was the heir to the throne. He didn't have to explain anything. Before she reached the door he stepped from the shadows, and cleared his throat.

"Good evening, my lady," he said, and flashed what he knew to be a charming smile.

She looked more angry than surprised. He girded himself for a tongue lashing which would last just until she recognised who he was, and then the fawning and giggling would begin. Her hard expression softened. She looked him up and down and relaxed her stance. He waited for the apology and coy smiles that invariably followed chance meetings with his noble self.

Close up, she was even fairer than he'd thought. Perhaps he wouldn't have to go into the city for a fumble after all. Being the heir to the throne had always proved to be a powerful aphrodisiac. Perhaps he could charm her out of that, very nicely fitted tunic, despite the Tamalak reputation for being a little on the cold side. He stopped his thoughts travelling too far down that road when he noticed she hadn't bowed, or curtsied or even stammered an apology. He smiled again. She looked as though she expected *him* to speak. He felt a rare thrill; *she doesn't know who I am*. That put bells on the hawk, and made the game much more interesting.

"Forgive me, my lady, I didn't mean to startle you," he bowed.

She arched an eyebrow. "Then perhaps you shouldn't lurk in the shadows, sir."

"True enough. Although in my defence, I didn't speak up because I didn't want to disturb you. You looked so peaceful."

The corner of her mouth twitched into a tiny smile. He wasn't sure he liked this game after all.

"Well, I'm glad I didn't scare you." He added.

Her smile widened. "Rest easy, sir, you didn't scare me."

Was she laughing at him? That wasn't the response he was used to.

Silence descended as he fumbled for something to say that wouldn't betray who he was, or make him sound like a lack-wit. *Prince* Talin could talk about anything, he had a thousand conversations stored for when he met an awe-struck subject, but he didn't want to play the Prince card yet, it smacked of failure. The game was still on, although it had to be said, the cards were not falling in his favour at the moment. Despite that, he found he rather liked the equality; the honesty of the encounter. The awkward silence was refreshing compared to the gushing, false pleasantry his title engendered in almost everyone he met.

"Are you here for the feast?" He cringed the moment the words left his mouth. It suddenly occurred to him that without a crown to prompt a favourable reaction, he might actually be rather dull. It was a sobering thought. She must have sensed his embarrassment, and rather than mock his failed attempt at making polite conversation, she smiled and played along.

"Aye, I am. How about you?" she said.

Before he could answer, Bear staggered into the garden. Talin sighed. Late or early, Iris was never where you wanted her, when you wanted her.

"Tal, is that you," she asked in a loud whisper. "Tal?"

She was already drunk, and set on becoming more so— if the half dozen bottles of wine cradled in her arms were anything to go by.

"Here, let me help you." Talin rushed over and whispered in his friend's ear; "She doesn't know who I am, keep it that way."

Bear winked, dumped the bottles on him and went over to the woman. Talin held his breath, unsure what his friend would say or do.

"Good evening, lovely lady. Allow me to introduce myself," she sketched a deep and somewhat unsteady bow. "My name is Iris Berwick, but my friends, *of whom there are many*, call me Bear, and you are…?"

It wasn't often that Alyda was mistaken for a noblewoman and as amusing as flirting with the gentleman was, she really should introduce herself. Of course, she knew from past experience that as soon as she did, his attitude would change. He'd either run a mile, challenger her to an arm wrestling contest, or want to talk about the war in Suvia, which was a pity in this case. He was good looking—tall, sandy haired, a bit soft round the middle, but nothing that a little exercise wouldn't sort out and she knew precisely the kind of exercise she'd like to put him to. The thought made her smile, but she put it from her mind; he and the woman were probably lovers. And in truth, they made a handsome pair. She was big, voluptuous, with sparkling eyes and a head of wild, ebony curls.

"Good to meet you, Bear. My name's Ali. I didn't mean to intrude…"

"What? Oh. You mean me and him? Asha's paps! He's like my brother—the one I wouldn't fuck." She laughed so hard she almost fell in the fountain. "Oh my, no. I mean, I don't mind a bit of strange from time to time, but I couldn't possibly with *him*. He's my oldest, dearest friend, and I think we're related—isn't that right, Talin?"

Talin grunted and folded his arms. "I really couldn't say. You've done that thing where you're nice, *and* a bitch all in the same breath, it confuses me."

"As you can see, Lady Ali, he's not the most erudite fellow, but that isn't his fault. Gods love him." She gave Talin a hearty, drunken hug. "I'll not hear the poor idiot blamed. Y'see, he was dropped on his head when he was a babe and it's left him a little slow."

"Pleased to meet you, Talin."

"Pleased to meet you too, Ali."

"Oh I see," said Bear. "Its all coy smiles and lingering eye contact, is it? Fine then." She scooped up a bottle of wine, had second thoughts, and picked up two more. "I'm going. I can see where I'm not wanted. I'll send Medelle your apologies, Talin." She tossed a tangle of curls over her shoulder and staggered from the garden, clutching her spoils.

"Where's your woman, Corvinius?" Princess Matia snarled from behind a smile. "I thought the lanky cunt would be here by now, swaggering around like she owns the place."

Rufus chuckled. For all that her venom burned, being drunk dulled the sting of Matia's scorpion tongue.

"She's a Knight Captain of the Royal Guards. It's our duty—nay, our god given right, to swagger, Highness."

Matia smiled sweetly. "*Our?* Oh, forgive me Rufus, I'm so accustomed to you whoring yourself like an oversexed game cock, that I sometimes forget you're a Knight Captain, albeit a rusty one."

Matia was such a vicious little poppet. He fancied that one day, probably in the not too distant future, instead of kissing her slender neck, he'd be forced to break it and do both him and Jerim a favour.

"That reminds me—with 'Lyda being here, I won't be able to attend to you tonight." He winked. "She needs her turn with the game cock."

The Princess threw back her head and laughed, but her dark eyes were hard, and promised vengeance for the slight. He enjoyed provoking her; he liked the way her small breasts swelled in their silk cage as she fought to control her temper. Corvinius called a servant over who was carrying a jug of wine. The boy re-filled his goblet, slopping wine over his hand in the process.

"Oaf!" Corvinius hissed, and backhanded him across the face.

The boy mumbled an apology, and backed into the crowd.

"I don't think your half-breed whore will mind a stained cuff," said Matia, clearly amused.

"None of my whores concern themselves with what I wear, unless... you're not trying to tell me something, are you, Princess?"

"You're drunk, so I'll let that go, but have a care Corvinius, you're not indispensible."

He raised his glass and took a long drink, savouring the rich, full-bodied taste, and the look of impotent rage on her face. "Oh, but I am, Highness."

He was convinced he'd done a marvellous job of keeping Lady Ali amused. She'd laughed at his stories, and teased him about the truth of some of his more outrageous claims. He had enjoyed himself immensely, despite being shocked by quite how much of his life was defined by being a prince. It had proved most enlightening, if a little depressing and yet, despite his best efforts, she still insisted on leaving.

"I really have to go," she said, just when he thought he'd convinced her to stay.

Other than his parents and Bear, nobody denied him anything, ever. He was at a loss and a little angry, and yet, strangely pleased with how the evening had gone.

"I hope you're leaving because you have to and not because you want to?" he asked, wary of what an honest answer might be, but also excited by the prospect of being liked for who, rather than what, he was.

"Yes, it's because I have to. It's been a long time since I've seen my parents."

"If only I could say the same. I hope we'll meet again, Ali."

"I'd like that." She smiled, but stayed an inch beyond the point at which they might be close enough to kiss and forget the world for an hour or so. "Farewell, Talin." She said, and left his mother's garden.

He was sure, no, *he hoped*, he heard a hint of regret in her voice.

Alyda slipped into the hall through a side entrance. She was relieved that there was still a long queue of guests waiting to be announced. She hadn't been looking forward to explaining to Trease why she was late for a feast being held to honour her and her Company.

The first person she spotted was Corvinius. He was talking to Princess Matia, Prince Jerim's Guthani wife. She was there in her husband's stead because he was 'too ill' to travel according to the official story. Alyda didn't go over. In part it was because she was appalled by the Prince's shameful behaviour in Suvia and wasn't sure she'd be able to feign politeness if his name was mentioned, but that wasn't the only reason she didn't rush to greet her lover.

She'd expected to be pleased to see him after all the months away, but now, watching him drunkenly flirt with Matia, she realised that she didn't feel much at all.

It was no secret that Corvinius had the morals of a tomcat; that had never been an issue between them. He was charming and handsome and asked nothing of her that she wasn't prepared to give.

The relationship had worked for both of them, but over the last year he'd changed. His sharp wit had turned vicious, he'd become jealous, and increasingly bitter about the bad reputation of the 5th. He reserved his most savage criticism for Commander Trease, who he blamed for denying him a field command. It suddenly struck her that she no longer cared for Corvinius, hadn't for a very long time, if truth were told. It only remained to tell him so. And when she'd done that, she would find Talin and carry on where they'd left off in the garden.

"The Lady Nusrama Falrin Na' Stenna, and Sir Konstantin Stenna!" The Court Herald declaimed.

Alyda brushed down her tunic before going over to greet her parents. It had been almost a year since she'd seen them, but her mother never changed. Her hair was as black as a raven's wing, and even though she was wearing a voluminous Shemisana gown, she was youthfully lean and moved with grace. Alyda kissed her on both cheeks. Age hadn't been as kind to her father. His back was bent from years of hunching over plans and drawings, but the old warrior turned engineer was still head and shoulders above most people in the room. His wavy hair was thinning and more silver than gold these days, but his bright green eyes were as lively as she remembered.

He swept her up in a bear hug. "It's so good to see you, Ali!"

She winced, the tightness in her side reminding her of Suvia. Her mother narrowed her eyes.

"What have you done?" she demanded.

"Nothing, it's just a graze," Alyda answered lightly when her father put her down. "How are the horses?"

Her mother raised an eyebrow, but didn't press. "They're good—I'll be going to the summer pastures from here to get the measure of the yearlings. Are you looking after Lyco? He looked thin the last time I saw him. Antians don't know how to take care of Shemisana horses, and when can I take him for stud? I've some mares that I want him to cover while he's still able."

Alyda smiled. "I've missed you too, Mother. You can have Lyco next year. Don't worry, he'll still have enough fire in his belly for your mares, but I need him now; it wouldn't do for a captain of cavalry to be without a horse."

Alyda saw her mother tense, but before the usual argument over horses could start, her father broke in.

"—Karl sends his love, but we're busy at the moment with a big order, which is why he and Greta couldn't come I'm afraid." He smiled apologetically.

"Ah, my poor, overworked brother. Don't worry, he's already sent me a letter telling me how hard you're working him."

Her father smiled sheepishly and hugged her again. "I'm blessed to have such talented children. I'm so proud of you both."

"*We're* proud of you both," her mother added. "Now, what did you do to your side?"

At last, Garian had heard something interesting. A big order of siege engines meant trouble for someone. He made a mental note to find out who the old mercenary was working for. Other than that solitary scrap the night had been a complete waste of his time. He was exhausted and bored of listening to inane small talk. What made it even more of a chore was being forced to wait on the King's guests whilst wearing hose that were so tight, they threatened to ruin his chances of ever siring a child.
But all of those indignities paled in comparison to being struck by the Captain of the 5th. Garian was murderously furious, and would repay the bastard with interest for striking him. For now, he'd have to swallow his ire. He'd keep his eye on the arrogant knight, not least because he was rather obviously flirting with the wife of the King's brother. She didn't seem to mind the attention, quite the

contrary. That she was there, and her husband wasn't would also be of interest to Lord Hyram.

The knight and the Princess probably thought they were being discrete. They hardly made eye contact, and kept a respectable distance from each other, but occasionally, when they must have thought they were unobserved, their eyes would meet or their hands would touch and they would whisper to each other.

To Garian, who was trained to read people, it was obvious that they were not the slight acquaintances they pretended to be. No surprise there. Corvinius was renowned far more for jousting between the sheets than at the tilt rail. He'd make sure to keep an eye on them; see if he could turn up any dirt that he could use against Corvinius. One way or the other, he'd pay him back.

As he was watching, a page delivered a message to the knight. Corvinius dismissed the girl, and took his leave of Princess Matia. Garian followed him at a discreet distance, filling proffered glasses as he went, while thinking how easy it would be to stick a knife in the knight's back. Corvinius sidled over to Captain Stenna and snaked his arm around her waist. It made Garian smile to see her shrug him off.

"There you are, 'Lyda my love." Corvinius slipped his arm around her. "His Majesty has requested that you join him on the terrace."

Alyda uncoiled his arm from her waist. His presumption irritated her, and he was drunk. She also caught the faint whiff of Pel on his breath.

"If you'll excuse me…" She bowed to her parents.

"Aye, well, duty calls and all that," said her father.

"Don't be long," said her mother, "King or not, we're your parents, and I think that gives us more of a claim on your time."

Despite her annoyance at Corvinius, she had to laugh. "I'll be back soon, Mother, I promise."

As they walked through the hall, Corvinius again tried to slip his arm around her waist. It wasn't a sign of affection she liked, or one that they'd ever shared. She knocked his arm aside and rounded on him.

"I don't know what's got into you, Rufus, but don't do that again."

Corvinius chuckled. "You're not embarrassed that I showed affection in front of your parents are you? I'm sure they'll be delighted that you've gained the interest of a *real* gentleman."

"You excel at being wrong about so many things, Rufus."

"I was trying to be friendly. You should be pleased that I lavish time and attention on you. Play your hand well, and I might even be persuaded to sire a child on you one day; give your family a leg up in the ranks. Twins know, they need it. Why, even the bastard of a Corvinius would be a step up from a horse breeding gypsy and a barbarian Tamalak."

His words stung, but it would be a cold day in the Void before she'd let him see that he'd got to her. She smiled. "You might belong to one of the oldest houses in Antia, but your family tree has few branches, and your bastards are ten-a-penny, so if you don't mind, I'll decline your generous offer. Goodbye, Rufus."

When Alyda was allowed through the cordon of guards and onto the terrace, she saw King Daris talking to Commander Trease and Lord Costaine. She was glad he was busy; it gave her time to calm down, and let her anger at Corvinius dissipate. When they finished, Trease beckoned her over.

"Good to see you again, Alyda. Your parents are well I trust?" the King asked.

Alyda saluted. "They're well, Majesty, thank you."

"Good, good. Please give them my regards. Now, I've been talking to Matlin about a new recruit that I'd like you to meet." Daris smiled broadly. "I need you to take him back to Trelanlith and knock him into shape. Come, I'll introduce you now, while he's still sober."

Daris led her over to where Queen Thea was talking to a veiled Khusani ambassador, General Tyrus, and some other people who had their backs to her. Alyda got the sinking feeling that the 'new recruit' was the King's eldest son, the renowned rake, Prince Talin.

"It's about time that he finished off his martial training, somewhere away from the…" the King coughed, "…distractions of Weyhithe. After talking it over with Matlin, I thought, where better to send my son than to the Hammer? 'Tis only fitting that the future king serves with the best. I'll warn you now though, he isn't used to hard work, or discipline, or even getting up in the morning. Talin! Come here and meet Captain Stenna." Daris called out to one of the people talking to Queen.

Alyda registered that the King was still talking, but when the heir to the throne turned round, she stopped listening. The person who she'd spent the evening with, wasn't simply Talin, he was *Prince* Talin; the heir to the throne of Antia. Swords, arrows, and lances she could handle, crushing embarrassment was a much more awkward foe to get to grips with. She felt such a fool. How could anyone fail to recognise the heir to the bloody throne?

The Queen ushered her son over. "Please make sure he doesn't break his neck, Captain Stenna, Talin can be quite reckless."

His eyes widened. "It's an…er, an honour to meet you. Yes. *You*. Captain Stenna. Ali, Alyda Stenna. Who is…that is to say, who you are."

The King muttered something under his breath.

Queen Thea frowned. "Tal, are you drunk already?"

Alyda wondered if now was a good time to ask if he wanted to join the 2nd.

Unlike his father, Talin had no desire to be a warrior. He liked to hunt and, upon occasion, play martial games, but he'd spent the time he should have been training with the 5th, whoring and drinking with Bear. As for the Captain of the Hammer, he'd only ever seen her from a distance, head to toe in steel, just another of his father's implacable knights. If he'd known who was underneath all that tin, he might have taken more interest in his martial studies. He recalled hearing Trease say that she was 'highly competent'. That was gushing praise coming from old Granite Face. If only he'd said she was beautiful and excellent company. Bear was going to laugh her arse off when he told her what had happened. He hoped the Captain would understand that he hadn't intended any mischief by hiding his identity. He hoped the contrite smile he gave her would convey how sorry he was; it always worked on his mother.

He was therefore disappointed to see that her face remained perfectly composed; untouched by emotion, as unreadable as stone.

Chapter Three

The 1st had been back at Trelanlith for a week. As the days passed, the Company slowly re-adjusted to peacetime duties. It wasn't easy; the transition from battlefield to barracks took time. On this particular day, Alyda was struggling. Sunlight was pouring through her office window, drenching the room in syrupy, will-sapping warmth. She fought valiantly to muster some enthusiasm for going over the accounts with the Paymaster, but it was a losing battle. The air in her office was as thick as honey and when her vision wasn't swimming, her gaze constantly drifted from the books to the window. Outside, knights were drilling on the parade ground, something she found infinitely more interesting than the ledgers spread before her. Malby cleared his throat. She looked round. The Paymaster was looking at her expectantly.

"Sorry, Mal, what did you say?"

Malby's thin lips tightened. "I said, it would leave a balance of two hundred and seventy crowns, and eighty shillings rounded up. This doesn't include the second quarter, when we were in Suvia. I've kept those accounts separate. Would you like to see them now or after we've been through these?"

"Alas, it'll have to be later—tomorrow in fact. I have to take one of the new knights out on the Chase now."

Malby pulled a face, but didn't voice his displeasure. Like everyone else in the garrison, he knew who the new knight was. "Of course, Captain, but the sooner I have the final figures approved, the sooner I can send in the accounts. You know—"

"—Saddles aren't made for free, and every rivet and link must be paid for. Yes, I know Mal, I know. We'll finish this first thing in the morning."

She knew that the Paymaster would prefer it if they didn't do all that riding and fighting. It made the accounts untidy. Later that evening he'd no doubt air his grievances with his equally ill-used comrade, Surgeon Gedthis. They'd retire to the infirmary, as they did most nights, and put the world to rights over a glass of port or three—which, Alyda noted, had been accounted for as '*medicinal supplies*'.

When Malby left, she took her sword from where it was hanging on the wall beneath the shrine to Sestrian and Ashania, the patron gods of Antia. Unlike the weapon, the shrine was thick with dust. She'd had the blade re-honed since Suvia, but she drew it out of habit and checked its edge. It gleamed, as clean and bright as the day she'd made Lieutenant, the day her parent's had given it to her. It was a fine weapon, and had served her well since the Border Wars. Etched into the blade was an inscription that she didn't need to read to remember: *I serve the one, who serves the one, and neither shall be parted from the Other*. Alyda rubbed her thumb over the incised words before sheathing the blade and going to meet the Prince.

Lacgarde was leaning on the stable door, watching Talin from beneath the heavy slab of his brow as the Prince tacked up his horse. When he was done, the Company Standard Bearer grunted his approval. In the short time he'd been with the 1st, Talin had learnt that the knights had a specific way of doing just about everything, from saddling a horse, to buckling on a sword belt. There was the ordinary, inferior way, and then there was the Company way. The knights were ridiculously fastidious, but he couldn't help but be impressed by their devotion to the Company they served. They ate, breathed, and slept *the Company*.

Even though they'd only recently returned from campaign, the knights' appetite for hard work and rigorous training was voracious. The contrast between the 5th and the Hammer couldn't have been greater. He now understood why the 5th were regarded as the worst of the best, and how the Hammer had earned their fearsome reputation. Their loyalty and dedication bordered on the fanatical.

Lacgarde pointed to a speck of dust on one of the gleaming stirrups. "I'd wipe that off, if I was you, Highness. The Company comes back dirty—it never leaves that way."

Talin brushed it off, doubtful that anyone else would have even noticed it. "How long have you been with the Company, Rann?"

"Over ten years this summer, Highness. I made Standard Bearer less than two years ago." The big man beamed proudly, displaying the many gaps in his smile. "I came to the First from the army, chosen from a half dozen squires out of the Eighteenth, my mother's regiment. It was a proud day for my family."

Talin nodded thoughtfully. "So you've known the Captain for some time?"

"Aye. She was nineteen when she joined the Hammer, but she won her spurs a couple o' years earlier, fighting with her father's Free Company."

"She is young though, to be a Captain in the Guards."

Talin wasn't trying to be contentious; he was genuinely fascinated by Alyda who, at only 25, commanded not only the Company, but also the loyalty and respect of veterans like Lacgarde. The Standard Bearer stiffened.

"The Captain's earned her commission and her command *many* times over with finer deeds than most who've climbed as high in the ranks. You should know that, if you don't mind me sayin', Highness."

Talin shook his head; not even he was thoughtless enough to forget that she'd saved his father's life. "Forgive me, I'm not being clear. I'm not questioning her ability, or her right to command. I meant, what is she like as a person?"

Lacgarde looked less than convinced by his assurances. It was going to take longer than a week for him to win the trust of such a close knit band of warriors.

The knight leaned heavily on the stable door and scratched one of the jagged scars that creased his jaw. "She's quicker to smile than she is to frown, but Twins help you if you cross her. She's cocky, but in a way that lifts you up, an' makes you feel you can do anything, not the way that makes you want to punch someone in the mouth, if you know what I mean, Highness?"

"Aye, I think I do, remind me to introduce you to my friend Bear…or perhaps not, now that I think about it."

Lacgarde patted the grey's neck. "It goes without saying she's a fine horsewoman, nigh-on born in the saddle. You know her mother's a Shemisana headwoman? That's their version of royalty, so it is." The Standard Bearer grinned crookedly. "She has a calm head and a cold heart in a fight. I'd not like to go against her."

Talin couldn't imagine Lacgarde being wary of anyone. The man looked like a rough-hewn statue of a human, only on a much larger scale.

"Don't mistake me—she's not the strongest knight in the Hammer. That's me, despite what that pup Lorhine would have ye believe. Neither is she the weakest by a similar margin. She is one of the quickest and can see an opening and attack it faster than anyone I know. She never hesitates." Lacgarde leaned in close. "And that's a thing you'd do well to learn, Highness: see, think, and strike, all in a breath. If you can master that you'll not go far wrong."

"Thank you Rann, I'll try to remember." Talin was about to lead his horse out of the stable when he noticed Lacgarde was scowling. "What is it?"

"Begging your pardon, Highness, but where's your sword?"

"In my quarters—why?"

The knight frowned. "You should have been told. All knights must go about armed, even within the Arth. It's been so since the attack on your father, when Captain Aysgarthe was killed."

"I didn't know. I'll go get it now."

"You don't have time. 'Captain said she'd be here on the hour and she's never late. If you aren't here when she arrives she'll have yer balls for earrings." He unbuckled his sword and handed it to Talin. "Here, take mine. I've got a spare, but if you could get it back to me as soon as you can, I'd be grateful."

Talin accepted the weapon with a nod of thanks.

There was no question that the Great Hall was magnificent. The fine oak panels were draped with the Company's many battle honours. Ancient weapons were fanned above the fireplace, forming a steel crest around the huge sea drake skull that hung above the mantle. The hall was a sight to quicken any warrior's blood, but for Alyda the spirit of the Company resided in the stables.

Every block of stalls was immaculate, kept clean by the army of grooms who snapped to attention when she passed. The moment he heard her footfall, Lyco thrust his big, ugly head out of his box and snorted a greeting.

New grooms soon learnt to keep a respectful distance from the warhorse's stall. The first nasty bite was usually enough to teach them caution. Alyda had heard that sending the youngsters to his stall had become an unofficial welcoming rite. She'd let it continue, so long as nobody got hurt. The Company had many traditions and they all helped to strengthened bonds, which were vital to a fighting company. When the tide turned against you in battle, sometimes the only thing that got you through was faith in your comrades.

She brushed the shock of mane from the destrier's eyes. He snorted, but for all his show of annoyance, he lowered his head so that she could stroke the side of his face and neck. Her fingers found an old scar and traced its path down his neck to his shoulder, she leaned against him, felt his warmth, the pulse of his blood. She could have spent all day there, but duty called.

"I've got to go now, old friend, but I'll take you out tomorrow—today I need Nua's speed."

When she reached the corner of the block where the Prince's horse was stabled, she heard the familiar voice of her Standard Bearer. She wasn't given to eavesdropping, but she deemed it a forgivable sin when she heard her name mentioned.

When she'd listened to what Rann had to say, she had to agree that he was almost right, if a little over-dramatic. She'd certainly bollock the Prince if he was late, or if she found him unarmed, but she'd let him keep his balls, for a first offence, at least.

The bell tolled the hour. She waited until the last chime was dying before rounding the corner. After all, she was never late. When he saw her, Lacgarde snapped to attention and saluted. She pretended not to notice that he was standing behind the stable door to hide that he was unarmed. She also pretended not to notice the distinctive meat cleaver of a sword that Prince Talin was wearing.

A groom brought Nua over. Alyda swung into the saddle, aware that the Prince was watching her every move. When he mounted up, she noted that he did it Company style. Alyda let him ride out of the yard ahead of her. When he was a good way off, she turned to her Standard Bearer who was still loitering behind the stable door.

"Tell Kieran I need to speak to him about the repairs to the tilt yard when I get back. Oh, and it would be a coin pouch. I don't wear earrings."

Lacgarde's eyes widened. He saluted so hard his knuckles cracked on his chest. "Aye, Captain. Tilt yard, coin pouch. Got it."

"Another fine horse, Captain Stenna," said Talin as they rode away from the Arth.

"Aye, she's an excellent riding horse, but she's too timid to make a good warhorse."

"Unlike that black demon of yours. I saw him earlier trying to savage one of the grooms. What's he called again?"

Alyda laughed. "He's called Lyco. Nua gave birth to his foal last year. I hope it'll grow to be a mix of their best traits and not a really big, evil-tempered bastard. I don't think even I'd want to tackle that."

"What does your mother think? I hear she's the expert."

"Dear gods, she doesn't know that Lyco's spent some of his precious Shemisana seed covering an Antian mare."

"Indeed? Does she judge Antian horses to be inferior to Shemisana bred animals?"

"Little better than donkeys in her opinion."

Talin chuckled. "Donkeys?"

"I'm afraid so."

"They look cosy, don't you think?" Nevenna whispered to Della. The Heralds were in the hayloft, watching the Captain and the Prince ride out.

Della shrugged and rolled back in the hay. "I wouldn't say so. She looks bored, if you ask me."

"You sure that isn't wishful thinking?" Nevenna teased. "I thought you'd got over your infatuation."

Della tipped straw from her boot and fixed her lover with a frosty stare. "Don't try to provoke me. I just admire the Captain for what she's achieved. I spent an entire year pursuing *you* before you even noticed I was alive."

"Oh, I noticed you alright. Always giving me the cow eyes and showing off. I just had to be sure you were serious, and not chasing me for a wager—or a joke." She winked.

Della sat back on her haunches. "Why do you say such hurtful things?"

"Because you're ten years my junior and as beautiful as sin. You could have your pick of the Company, but you chose me, and I'll never know why. I've got piles older than you are."

"Piles? Urgh. You're such a charmer." Della leaned forward and planted an angry, passionate kiss on Nevenna's lips.

Breathless when they parted, Nevenna's voice trembled. "Whatever your reasons, I'm glad of them. Wager or not, you mean everything to me."

Della picked a twist of straw from Nevenna's unruly hair. "I remember the first time I heard you sing. It was up on the borders, when we camped in those ruins. The snow was falling so thick, and heavy; I thought it would drown us. You stole my heart that night and have kept it ever since."

"And I'm never going to give it back. Now come on, we really must get some practice in."

Della grinned and pulled off her shirt. "Oh, I intend to."

The rugged landscape of the Chase was the perfect place for the Hammer to hone their riding skills and train their mounts. To the east, the ragged shadow of Trelanlith forest blurred past as Alyda raced along one of the many narrow tracks that hatched the heather studded moorland. The nearby forest had been home to the first Arth, which had been in its prime many hundreds of years ago—when the Fey walked amongst humans and traded magic with the Clan Lords. Its crumbling ruins now lay in the forest's jealous embrace, abandoned and almost forgotten.

After a good long gallop, Alyda reached a ford across the river Tennen. She pulled up to let Nua have a well-earned drink and to wait for the Prince to catch up. She'd deliberately chosen some of the more challenging trails to test his skills, those where gravel ran like water and did not forgive a misplaced hoof, or a poorly balanced rider. He'd done better than she'd expected and had kept up for most of the way, but she'd lost sight of him about a mile back. Minutes passed and there was still no sign of him. Worrying images of the Prince lying in a ditch with his neck broken, flashed into her mind. She decided to go look for him when much to her relief, he cantered around a bend in the trail.

He pulled up beside her. "I took a wrong turn."

"These paths aren't the easiest—you've done well, Highness. Shemisana tradition holds that the Horse Lord favours those with a pure heart and that his creatures will always keep those people safe. I think it's meant to encourage children to keep their behinds in the saddle."

"You don't believe it?"

Alyda laughed. "Gods, no. Even the best riders fall from time to time. But my Mother believes it, which is why she finally let me join the cavalry."

"Wasn't your father a Free Company Commander?"

"Aye, but she doesn't like soldiering, probably because of what he used to do. The cavalry is *almost* acceptable—horses are sacred to her gods."

"But not your gods?"

What could she say? That she believed in what she could touch and see, but that she'd take the word of her betters that there was something more to life than was apparent. In truth, she didn't care one way or the other. "I'm pleased you can ride, Highness. It'll make my job a damn sight easier."

Talin dismounted and led his grey over to the water. "You didn't answer my question."

Either he was religious, which, given his reputation, she doubted, or he was just extremely nosey. Alyda toed a stone into the river. She rarely discussed her family, religion even less, but he was a prince and she was duty bound to answer him.

"There are Antians, Tamalaks, Cathlans and even a couple of heathen Hadami in the First, all because of your Father. He's done a great deal to bring the kingdom together, but there are still some subjects that are better left alone, religion being one of them." She wasn't much of a diplomat; she lacked the patience for it, but she hoped she wasn't too blunt. Offending the future king wasn't a wise career move. "I respect the gods of my family as I respect the gods of my knights, although I've never had a particularly strong devotion."

"You're quite right; a person's beliefs are their own affair. You must forgive me, Captain, being nosey is a habit born from idling one's time away at court." The Prince smiled. "Where does the trail lead?" he said, looking across the ford at the rimpled path that cut through the forest.

Alyda silently cursed her lack of foresight. She hadn't realised how close she'd brought them to the ruins. "It leads to the old Trelanlith Arth, Highness."

"That's where they tried to kill my father."

"Aye, it is."

"I'd like to see it, if you wouldn't mind showing me?"

She never wanted to see the demon-haunted hole again, but she could hardly refuse. As much as it was framed as a request rather than a command, it wasn't done to say no to a prince.

"Certainly, Highness."

They mounted up, and rode into the oppressive gloom of the forest. The loamy soil muffled the sound of the horse's hooves. Even the birds seemed to sing more quietly the deeper they went. Conversation dwindled to silence. Alyda wondered if, like her, Talin could feel the weight of centuries pressing down on him as they rode between the ancient oaks. After a short time, they began to see broken remains of carved stones, jutting through the dense undergrowth. Alyda hadn't been to the ruins since the day of the attack. She wasn't reassured that it looked exactly how she remembered it.

They came to a fork in the trail that was marked by a broken column. The weathered spike of dark stone was etched with faded markings, the meaning of which as forgotten as those who had made them. Alyda took the left fork. The trail was overgrown, and had just enough clearance for them to pass if they lay along their horses' necks. Thankfully it was short and soon opened up into a large clearing.

A carpet of moss was slowly spreading over the remains of a white, marble floor, of what must have once been a grand hall. The clearing was ringed by a double row of broken columns that reached to the sky like supplicant fingers. Alyda hated it. Bad memories were locked into every stone and bough. She shuddered when she looked at the spot where *it* had died. Nothing had grown there, not the smallest weed had encroached on the blasted ground. After two years, the wound remained.

Shoving her unease aside, Alyda dismounted and tethered her horse loosely to a branch. The Prince did the same. Both horses stood rigidly alert, ears erect, nostrils flaring, questing for scents or any sign of danger.

"It was a spring morning," she said. The loudness of her voice sounded out of place. Like dancing on a grave, she felt it was somehow wrong to break the silence. She continued, more subdued. "His Majesty had arrived at Trelanlith the day before. He was touring the Guards' garrisons. I was honoured to be asked by Captain Aysgarthe to escort the royal party on their ride out…"

Alyda was delighted and surprised when the old man told her she'd be riding as escort for the royal party. She kept her excitement in check, remembering her father's advice to her when she'd been accepted into the 1st, '*Be dedicated, confident, and at all times composed.*'

The day of the attack came as easily and clearly to mind as though it had happened yesterday. She'd buckled on her spurs in the Great Hall, while trying to ignore the pounding in her skull and the almost overwhelming urge to throw up. Unfortunately her parents had failed to advise her against the dangers of drinking contests—not that she didn't know them from previous bouts, but somehow that lesson never stayed learnt.

Participating last night had unfortunately been unavoidable. She couldn't possibly let an outsider beat the Guards, not even if the herald who'd issued the challenge was a member of the King's retinue. Alyda had won, and saved the Company honour, but the price of victory was a brutal hangover. She shivered; it was unseasonably cold. Hopefully the cold air would clear the fog from her brain. *Never again* she swore and threw her uneaten breakfast to the deer hound that was snuffling around the tables hunting for scraps.

When the royal party were ready to leave, Alyda led the horses onto the parade ground. The King was accompanied by his bodyguards, a man and a woman who didn't introduce themselves, Commander Trease and Captain Aysgarthe. The King barely marked her presence, but she didn't escape inspection from the Commander of the Royal Guards. Until that day she'd thought Aysgarthe's inspections were exacting, but quickly realised he was decidedly lax compared to Trease. She couldn't have looked as rough as she felt because he didn't say anything when he finished. He just gave a curt nod, which she took to be a good sign.

The memory was so vivid, she shivered.

The Prince smiled. "...I said this isn't what I expected. It's so...peaceful," he was obviously repeating himself.

"I...er... No, indeed. It hasn't changed at all," she said.

She was distracted by old ghosts clamouring for her attention—drawing her back to the past. She paced across the clearing, half expecting to see blood splattered on the broken stones.

"The Commander laid a map out on here." She ran her hand across a fallen column that lay at the edge of the clearing. It felt smooth. A profound cold reached through her gauntlets, despite the dappled sunlight patterning the ragged edge of the clearing.

Trease and the King were bent over the map, lost in conversation. She was still mounted as was Aysgarthe. The gruff captain was sharing a joke with one of the King's bodyguards…

Alyda paused, took a breath. Talking about what happened never got any easier. It was so far beyond anything she'd ever experienced, before or after; it was more like reliving a nightmare than an actual event. Though she knew she hid it well, she felt sick and embarrassed.

"One minute the world was as it should be. The next…"she groped for the right words. "The air seemed to…thicken. I couldn't breathe. It felt like I was drowning, choking in the open air. I think I must have started to pass out, and then a powerful blast of wind blew up out of nowhere and Nua threw me." She didn't think it necessary to describe how Captain Aysgarthe's horse had reared and thrown him against a tree. How his skull shattered against the trunk, leaving a bright smear of blood and brains on the pale bark.

"The next thing I remember is opening my eyes and seeing the Commander and your father lying over there by the column. I didn't know if they were dead or alive. The two bodyguards were the only ones on their feet. They went to your father. Captain Aysgarthe was dead…"

Alyda climbed unsteadily to her feet, narrowly avoiding being trampled by her terrified horse as she bolted down the trail with the other mounts. The bodyguards were shouting at her, but she couldn't hear what they were saying above the ringing in her ears. It took the raw agony of one of them screaming to shock her from her dazed stupor.

"It was a Shadewalker—that's what your father's scholars called it when we described it to them…"

Alyda got her first look at the Shadewalker when it knocked the male bodyguard across the clearing. The nightmare creature was a sickly grey-white and heavily muscled. It stood on all fours, and was almost five feet tall at the shoulder. Its gaping maw bristled with far too many teeth. The bodyguard was still down when the beast sprang at him again. He reached for his sword but it was on him in an instant and tore out his throat with one huge, savage bite.

"He went down fighting." She didn't describe how the beast shook its head from side to side with the bodyguard hanging from its jaws like a rag. The memory was so vivid; she could almost taste the iron tang of the guard's blood that had sprayed across the clearing.

"The other guard charged the beast. I went to see if I could help your father. The Commander was beginning to come round, but the King wasn't moving. If he hadn't groaned I would have thought—" She didn't need to say more.

Talin nodded, his jaw was set in a stony grimace.

"Commander Trease got up and drew his sword, he ordered me to get your father away from there. I started dragging him towards the trail. You know about the Commander's sword?"

"All I know is that it's supposed to be Fey-made. You must forgive me, Captain Stenna; I wasn't the most attentive student of history. My brother is the scholar."

"No, I understand, Highness. I spent more time in the stables than the classroom. All I can say is that the blade was the only weapon we had that could hurt the cursed creature. When it turned on the second bodyguard, the Commander laid into it...."

The Shadewalker's tail was thick, and plated with scales, the tip was drawn out into a wicked barb. Trease was on his feet, but still looked dazed. He blocked a vicious tail swipe, but didn't see it lunge at him with a raking forepaw...

"It slashed the Commander—shredded his mail like it was paper..."

Alyda saw Trease clutch the bloody gashes in his chest, saw him fall. Before the beast could finish him, the bodyguard put herself between it and the wounded Commander. The Shadewalker *laughed*. The guard let her blade speak for her, and sliced the beast across the throat. The strike would have slain any mortal creature, but she didn't so much as scratch a scale. It lazily swatted at her with a forepaw. She avoided it easily, but the attack had only been a feint. While the guard was distracted, the creature's tail scythed in low to the ground and flicked up at the last minute like a viper.

"I shouted a warning. I'm not sure if she heard me or if at the last second, she saw the tail strike. Either way, she got her sword up in time to block the barb, but the force of the blow threw her against that column. Her leg twisted under her; I heard it break..."

With Trease and the bodyguards either dead or unconscious; the beast now turned its attention to Alyda and transfixed her with its baleful gaze. In all the fights she'd ever been in she'd never experienced real terror. When she locked eyes with the demon, when those sulphurous eyes glared at her, burning with depthless malice, she understood the true meaning of evil.

The King slipped from her nerveless fingers. She was frozen with fear. It felt like it was daring her, *willing* her, to run. No one would know. She could sprint down the track and leave the King and the others to their fate. It was a simple choice; run and live or stay and die.

She weighed her life against her honour and for all that she wished it was otherwise, the scales refused to tip in the coward's favour. A monstrous laugh bubbled from the beast's throat when she stepped over the King's prone form and set her guard. It advanced slowly, apparently in no hurry to finish her. Alyda tried to draw a deep breath, but her throat was tight, her chest filled with the thunder of her pounding heart. She had to control her fear. The beast opened its dripping maw and smiled. *Hard as iron and as cold as stone. You're a Royal Guard, the best of the best.* She told herself. *Cold as...as... Stop shaking!* The beast took a step towards her. She was paralysed with fear. *I'm going to die...*

"Stenna!"

She snapped her head round and saw Trease. He was up on his knees, his face was ashen, and blood was pouring from his chest. With a mighty effort, he threw his sword to Alyda. She dropped her own weapon and caught the Commander's mid-flight, and thankfully, hilt first. Furious, the beast roared and leapt at her. She sidestepped as much as she dared without leaving the King exposed. The beast twisted and tried to rake her with all four sets of claws. Alyda pivoted on her heel, and lashed out with her sword letting the momentum of the spin throw the blade out in a wide, horizontal arc. The shock jarred her arm as the blade ripped open the Shadewalker's stomach. A single claw caught her, cut through her armour and peeled the skin from her shoulder, its tail whipped across the back of her leg, just above the knee.

She went down. White hot pain burned her senses; the world tilted, and shrank to a dim tunnel. She was falling. Desperate not to die face down, she thrust the Commander's blade into the ground, fracturing the brittle crust of marble. The earth shuddered, her vision blurred. *Hard as iron... Damn it! Do not pass out!*

The Shadewalker crashed to the ground about eight feet away and let out a high-pitched squeal. Black blood and steaming innards spilled from the gaping wound in its stomach, the beast shuddered then lay still. The only noise in the glade was the sound of her laboured breathing, she sagged against the sword.

The beast twitched.

Her breath caught in her throat. She looked up. Its eyes snapped open; locked on hers. Horrified, she watched it drag its legs beneath it and stand up. Its guts trailed in the dirt. It gathered its hindquarters and prepared to leap. The ground seemed to tremble; all she could do was hold onto the sword and wait for death. The beast leapt…

Talin broke the spell. "How did you kill it?"

"A lucky blow, Highness." The answer was close enough to a lie to make her feel uncomfortable, but the truth was far more difficult to explain.

She didn't remember killing it.

Her last memory was of seeing it leap. Her next recollection was of there being a great weight on her, pinning her to the ground…

She opened her eyes. The beast was lying across her, its skull almost cleaved in two. Its head was inches from her face; its rank breath was hot against her cheek, its great yellow eyes still burned with fevered hatred. There was another presence staring out at her from behind those dying eyes, one that was filled with the malevolence of the Void.

The Shadewalker drew a last, shuddering breath and was still. Before she had chance to thank the gods, a reedy tendril of smoke rose off the body, swiftly followed by another, and another. The damn thing was starting to burn. Even though it was dead, the bastard was intent on killing her. She tried to squirm from beneath the carcass, but her left arm and leg were pinned. She would have cut her way out but she'd lost the sword. She craned her neck and saw the Commander's blade lying tantalisingly close. Faint hope turned to despair as even at full stretch, it was just beyond her reach. The Shadewalker's body began to swell; there was a loud hissing followed by a soft *whump*. Stinking, burning fat bubbled over the curve of its flank. It dripped on her, sizzled against her armour. Flames began to light along its back, hungrily devouring scales that had been impervious to steel. Alyda yelled her frustration and pummelled the carcass.

It moved—but she hadn't moved it.

Terrified, she again strained to reach the Commander's sword. Desperation lent her a fingertip of extra stretch, and she was able to touch the blade, but it wasn't enough. The beast lurched; its ruined head lolled drunkenly against her. A forepaw hung in the air above her, claws poised. *How can it? The damn thing's on fire—ho…?* An armoured hand grabbed the dangling paw and yanked it back out of sight. The pale face of Commander Trease appeared above the beast, followed by that of the bodyguard who reached through the flames and grabbed hold of the Shadewalkers back leg. The bodyguard coughed, but her armour protected her from the heat.

"When I say, '*push*,' give it everything you've got." Trease shouted to Alyda. "Now! Push!"

Coughing, and half blinded by smoke, Alyda pushed the burning corpse for all she was worth. For a terrifying moment it didn't move, then, very slowly, *too slowly*, it rolled back, freeing her. She scrambled clear of the conflagration, her armour hot to touch and blackened by the oily smoke…

"I think it was more than a lucky blow, Captain," said Talin.

She opened her mouth to protest, but Talin raised his hand. "Please—hear me out. I know you'll never accept the praise you deserve, but you must let me thank you for saving my father's life, and for bringing me here."

It would seem churlish to argue, but in her heart she couldn't accept his gratitude because she wasn't sure she'd earned it. Two years had passed, two years of waking up drenched in sweat, and of seeing those feral, yellow eyes in the darkness of her dreams, but never a hint about how, or if, she'd killed the damned thing.

It was late by the time she'd finished telling her tale. Long shadows were stalking across the glade; night's gloom crowded the treeline. It was time to leave.

They mounted in silence; Alyda let the Prince ride ahead. Before she left the glade to the shadows and the ghosts, she raised her fist to her heart, and saluted the dead.

Chapter Four

On the day that the citizens of Weyhithe came out to bid farewell to the Hammer, Garian slipped quietly out of the city, his departure marked by no one. It would have taken a decent rider about two and a half days to reach the border between Antia and Cathlan; it took Garian three. A city boy by birth and choice, he wasn't fond of horses and the brutes knew it.

As he rode deeper into Cathlan, he had to admit it was a wildly beautiful land. Snow crested mountains cradled glassy tarns in jagged crowns. Below them, the valleys were robed in purple heather, and clouds of fat, white sheep drifted across the verdant hillsides. For centuries, mines had been delved into the mountains by those who hunted the gold and iron buried deep within, but for the most part the hand of man had passed lightly over Cathlan.

Garian's route crisscrossed the province. He stopped briefly in a handful of villages, towns and hamlets, quietly gathering reports and leaving new orders as he went. Like Garian, the King's agents were very ordinary people, drawn more from the ranks of the humble than the privileged. Shepherds, bakers, innkeepers, and their ilk could be counted in the ranks of unobtrusive soldiers who fought in the Shadow War, a conflict that had never officially started. There were no rules of engagement, quarter was never asked, or given, and from what he'd seen so far in his nineteen years, it would probably never end.

On his way back to Antia, Garian mulled over the information he'd collected. Individually the disparate reports didn't amount to much that would be of interest to anyone…at first glance. However, now that he'd brought them together they formed a picture of events unfolding in Cathlan.

There had been a bread shortage in Carngarthe that had tripled the price of a loaf in just one week. He'd found out that the shortage had been caused by Prince Jerim's factors buying up the bulk of the grain coming into the capital of the province. In Trenatha and Shordain the blacksmiths and armourers had been paying top price for ore in order to keep up with demand from the Free Companies that were, as they said often and loudly, "just passing through". Only they'd been there for weeks, and showed no sign of leaving. Most worryingly, there had been enough Guthani trade delegations coming and going in the last month that by his calculations, the whole of Cathlan could have been supplied with enough hides, horn and silver to meet demand for the next twenty years.

These were just a few of the many little scraps of infor-mation he'd gathered on his travels and pieced together. When they were viewed as a whole cloth it looked very much like Prince Jerim's battle standard. Hyram might see things differently, but he doubted it. If the apprentice had eyes to see it, the master surely would.

The King and his brother were separated by two years and vastly different characters. Daris was passionate, whereas his brother was temperamental; the King was quick to anger and quick to forgive. Jerim never forgot a slight. Garian served Daris because he did only what was necessary to protect the kingdom. Jerim lived to control the lives of his subjects.

Hyram had told him that it was Jerim's constant scheming that had prompted Daris to make him Governor of Cathlan and marry him off to a Guthani princess. According to Hyram, it was because he spent his every waking moment fermenting petty plots and breeding ill will in the court.

Garian remembered his master's volcanic rage when, only six months after Jerim had gone, reports began to filter back that the new Governor had been heard to say that Cathlan should be a kingdom in its own right—with him as its ruler. Garian was rarely surprised by the baseness of humans, but he was still staggered that a few greedy men and women thought the misery and destruction of war was a price worth paying to put a crown on their heads.

He reached a crossroads. He could either ride straight to Weyhithe and deliver his report, or go and investigate a piece of information he'd picked up on his travels. He wanted to go home, his aching behind wanted him to go home, but he found himself turning towards the coast road anyway. Hyram had trained him too well.

It didn't take Garian long to find the cliff path the journeyman had told him about. He dismounted and led his horse into the deepest part of a weather-beaten copse, startling a flock of seagulls into the sky. He cursed and hoped no one had seen their panicked flight as he tethered his mount out of sight of the path.

Forcing his way through the tangled gorse that grew in abundance on the seaward side of the path, he crawled on his belly to the crumbling cliff edge. Sure enough, the distinctive black sail of a Guthani ship loomed into view as he inched forward, exactly where the journeyman had said it would be. A passing conversation with a fellow traveller had yielded gold, and all for the price of sharing a fire on a cold evening. *You can't make luck like that,* Garian thought. The scent of trouble caught in his nostrils and fired his hunter's senses.

It wasn't a Wolf Raider. Their vessels were bigger and like their namesakes, the fearsome pirates hunted in packs. This was a lone, sleek hulled ship, built for speed, not for hauling over other vessels. He was glad that it wasn't a Raider; he didn't like the thought of being attacked by one of the sea drakes that always accompanied their ships.

The cove was guarded by jagged fangs of rock and from what Garian could see there was no obvious benefit to be gained anchoring so close to danger, other than to avoid being seen. Garian counted half a dozen men and women on the narrow strip of beach. They were standing near a row boat that was rocking in the foaming surf. Four of them were wearing brightly coloured woollen leggings favoured by the Guthani and bronze scale mail hauberks that came to their knees. They had axes hanging from their belts and painted shields slung across their backs. You didn't need to be a spy to work out that they weren't merchants. Three of the group held crossbows at the ready, and were scanning the cliff top. He smiled. They were no doubt looking for people like him. He tugged his scarf up over his face, to hide what his hood did not.

One of the group—a tall bristle-bearded fellow, beckoned for two men dressed in brown robes to follow him up the beach. He handed something to the thinner of the two, but it was impossible to make out what it was over the distance. The thin man tucked whatever it was into his robes. After a brief conversation, Bristle Beard returned to the others. The robed men set off along a narrow path that snaked up the cliff in long, lazy switchbacks.

Bristle Beard and his warriors climbed aboard the boat and rowed out to the ship. Garian studied the route the robed men had taken, marking the spot where the path came out at the top. He shuffled back from the edge and pelted along the cliff path to get ahead of them.

The path ran parallel to the cliff, in a roughly north south direction. He might have been a poor horseman, but he was an excellent sprinter, and easily beat them to the head of the track. Two horses were tethered nearby. He guessed they belonged to the men and wondered if he had time to search the saddlebags before they arrived. Tempting though it was, he had more pressing tasks to attend to.

When he was satisfied that he'd prepared as well as he could, Garian hid behind a wind-twisted tree, south of the path. It wasn't the best hiding place, but it gave him a clear view of the path and the horses. The constant roar of the sea and gusting wind stole their words, but as the men drew nearer, he could hear that their accents were Guthani. The first up the path was the one who had been given the package, closely followed by his companion.

Now that they were closer, he saw they were wearing the robes of priests of Sestrian. Garian didn't think much of their disguises. They were wearing shirts and breeches beneath the robes, unlike real priests of Sestrian who didn't allow themselves such comforts even in the depths of winter. They were also wearing sturdy boots. Most of the priests Garian had ever met were bookish fellows, used to shuffling through cloisters and had little need for hobnailed boots. But what shouted imposter louder than all their other mistakes were the sword-shaped bundles strapped across their saddle bows. Priests of Sestrian never carried weapons. *Bloody amateurs,* he thought as he watched them mount up and turn north, most likely headed to Carngarthe.

He slid a bolt into the track of the crossbow and stepped out from behind the tree. Before they had chance to break into a gallop he drew a steady breath and took aim at the one with the package. He exhaled and squeezed the trigger. The bolt buried itself between the man's shoulder blades. He cried out, and fell from his horse, reins still gripped in his hand. The other Guthani immediately kicked his mount in the ribs and took off along the track, riding low across the horse's neck.

Garian dropped the heavy crossbow, scooped up the small handbow he'd taken from the assassin, and sprinted after him. The path curved out of sight around a rocky outcrop about thirty feet away. Beyond the rocks was a stand of birch trees, split by the track. As he approached the bend, he heard the horse scream. He rounded the corner in time to see it staggering to its feet.

The stunned rider was on his knees. He looked up; Garian levelled his handbow. The man narrowed his eyes and threw something at Garian before diving off the path. It felt like he'd been kicked. Garian glanced down; a knife was sticking in his thigh. He gritted his teeth and took aim, tracking slightly ahead of the man. He pulled the trigger. The man gave a strangled cry and crumpled, the shaft of the bolt jutting from his ruined eye. Garian took a step toward him and stumbled, a sharp pain gripped his leg.

"Bollocks."

Hooking the bow onto his belt, he wiped his hands and took a firm grip on the hilt with both hands. There was a hot, stab of pain and a rush of blood as he pulled it from his leg. Cursing the names of as many gods as he could think of, he bound the wound with his scarf.

Other than being covered in his blood, the knife looked clean. He sniffed the blade, but couldn't detect any unusual smells that might indicate the presence of poison. If it had been treated with anything he'd find out soon enough. Angry that he'd been hit, he kicked dirt over the blood on the path and limped over to the body.

He found a handful of gold coins in a pouch, and a sheath for a throwing knife hanging down the dead man's back. When he finished searching the body, Garian rolled it into the undergrowth. The man's horse had bolted, which was a pain in the arse—he would have liked to have searched the saddlebags. The rope he'd used to trip the horse had snapped when the animal ran into it. Rather than untying both ends as he should, he tossed them into the grass either side of the track. He was annoyed, in pain, and bleeding, and the scarf was doing little to stem the blood flow.

Garian limped back along the path to the other Guthani, cursing with every painful step. *Why was nothing ever easy?* At least the horse was still there, its reins clutched tightly in the dead man's hand. Garian felt neither sympathy nor regret as he looked into the dead, dusty eyes of the Guthlander. He briefly considered that he spent a lot of time searching the corpses of people he'd killed. It didn't bother him; at least that's what he told himself.

The man had some coin, a dagger, and a leather wallet tucked into his jerkin. Inside the wallet was a piece of parchment with some kind of list written on it, but he wasn't sure. He couldn't read it. This vexed him more than the wound in his leg. He had a talent for languages, which had brought him to the attention of Hyram when he'd visited the orphanage all those years ago. *Such a kind patron, the master of spies.* At least he'd picked Garian and the others for their brains, and not their youthful good looks, unlike some of the other 'patrons'. He dragged his mind from the grim past and back to the slightly less grim present. The script looked familiar, perhaps some archaic form of Guthani, but he just wasn't sure.

Annoyed, he tucked the wallet into his shirt and kicked the body into the grass before searching the saddlebags. He was again frustrated to find they only contained some food and a change of clothes. He just hoped the note was important enough to warrant two dead bodies and a knife wound.

It was dusk by the time he'd finished tidying up the most obvious signs of a fight. After some consideration he decided to leave the Guthlander's horse. Its shoes were probably marked, and he wasn't dressed like a man who owned two horses. The last thing he needed was to be pulled by some overzealous provincial militia, curious as to why a cove like him had two horses and a stab wound. He didn't want to end up being hanged as a horse thief. Although, the way his luck was running it wouldn't surprise him. As for the Guthani, he had to assume they'd been headed to Prince Jerim in Carngarthe. He didn't rule out the possibility there were other plotters, but given what he had found out already, that seemed unlikely.

That night, Garian camped off the path in a small copse. He didn't light a fire, but sat huddled in his blanket, cursing quietly at the pain that shot through his leg every time he moved. He'd brought a small supply of bandages with him, but by the time he'd set camp, they were already soaked through. He wrung them out and reapplied them before trying to get some sleep.

After a restless night, he woke up damp and cold, sometime before dawn. Mist had pooled around the feet of the trees and the world was washed in shades of grey. The sombre morning matched his mood. He got up and tested his leg—it was stiff and sore but the bleeding had stopped. He had a good idea where he was and figured he could be over the border by evening, if he cut east onto the main road south.

By nightfall he was back in Antia, and by his estimation, two days from Weyhithe. He wanted to press on, but his leg had started to bleed again after a long day in the saddle. There was an inn nearby where he'd stayed before.

It had clean rooms and hot food—two things he was badly in need of.

As he got closer, he saw a Hadami caravan had pulled over by the turning to the inn. Crescent moons and wildflowers were carved into the doorframes and painted on the sides of the wagons marking them as Vodoni.

Hyram wasn't as scathing about this clan as he was other Hadami. He considered them to be excellent herbalists who often traded him herbs that they gathered on their travels. He saw one of the wagons was having a broken wheel levered off its axle. While it was being repaired, the rest of the Hadami had taken the opportunity to set up cooking fires and let their horses graze.

The smell of food and hot chai made Garian's empty stomach growl. He nodded politely as he passed a Hadami man who was standing by the roadside, smoking a pipe. The man returned the gesture and approached him.

Garian was eager to reach the inn and rest his leg, but he couldn't ride on without appearing rude and there were too many Vodoni around to start causing offence. The pipe smoker was middle-aged and typically well dressed. He was wearing a scarf wrapped around his head in neat folds, and a pair of exquisite gold earrings. Garian noted the curling tendrils of his family tattoo peeking out of the collar of his grey, silk shirt. His outfit was completed by a pair of grey linen trousers tucked into calfskin boots, and a rapier hanging from a finely tooled baldric. The hilt of the weapon was an elegant construction of woven steel and brass, displayed either as a warning or for show. Garian wasn't sure if he was talking to a master swordsman or a braggart; neither was appealing.

"Good evening, friend. You wouldn't be with the blacksmith, would you?" The Vodoni asked.

"Good evening, sir. No, I'm afraid not. I'm heading to the inn." Garian pointed down the side road.

"Ah, t'was a hopeful enquiry—I'm growing impatient waiting for the man and rather wished you were he. My apologies, sir."

Garian decided to take the beautiful sword as a warning and not merely for show. Few braggarts had the grace or confidence to be polite to strangers.

"As you're headed that way, I wonder if you would do me a small favour?" the swordsman asked. "If you see a Hadami lass at the inn, would you be kind enough to ask her to hurry back? I sent her to fetch some ale, though it would seem from the time she's been gone that she's waiting for it to be brewed."

"I'll most certainly pass on your message if I see her, sir."

It didn't hurt to keep on the right side of strangers, especially those who according to Hyram could brew some of the most lethal poisons in Antia.

The inn was a welcome sight, huddled against a pine clad hillside beneath a sky streaked with ragged slashes of red and gold. Two dun-coloured dray horses were tethered outside. A huge cart stacked with hay was drawn up beside them. The freshly cut grass scented the air with the sugary sweetness of wildflowers. A round of raucous laughter escaped through the gap under the door. Garian felt the tension of the last few days begin to ebb away.

When he opened the door he was hit by a wash of hot air and beery smokiness. The room was crowded; all he could see was a wall of broad backed farmhands, judging by the smocks they were wearing. They were watching something, but he couldn't make out what it was, probably a cock fight. He wasn't interested; all he wanted was a bed, some food, and a few pints of ale. He began to edge around the rowdy group to get to the bar when a meaty arm thrust out and blocked his way.

"Weems closed, s'get lost," slurred the owner of the arm.

Garian cast a glance beneath the fleshy arch and saw a girl huddled on the floor. She saw him. Her big, blue eyes were shining with unshed tears. Garian sighed. He looked up at the beer bloated face of the Ox in his way, then back to the girl. Without saying a word, he turned and left the inn.

"Fire! There's a fire outside, 'tis the cart!" one of the thugs finally noticed and raised the alarm.

Ignoring the girl, the farmhands bundled outside to rescue the burning cart and catch the spooked horses. Garian had been watching them through a hole in the kitchen door, willing the dolts to notice the flames before they got round to raping the girl. As it was, he'd had to watch them give her a beating which had tightened a cold knot of hatred in his gut. When they were all outside, he sneaked in to the bar. Cowering in the corner behind the counter was a man in an apron and a heavily pregnant woman, they were probably the innkeepers. Whoever they were, they looked scared witless. He put his finger to his lips; they nodded and kept quiet.

"Can you sit a horse?" he whispered to the woman. She nodded vigorously.

"Mine's out back," said Garian, "take it and ride to the Hadami caravan on the main road, tell them what's happening. They may have seen the smoke already, so don't rush and risk your unborn, alright?" Keeping his eye on the door, he steered them out through the kitchen.

When they'd gone, Garian went to help the girl. She'd pulled herself up and was leaning against the bar. Her face was bruised and her clothes torn, but her huge, blue eyes were defiant.

"Quickly, girl, get over here." Garian beckoned her over.

She eyed him suspiciously and stayed where she was. He could see through the window that the glow was diminishing.

"For fuck's sake, hurry up!" he hissed. A moment later, the Ox burst into the bar, smoke curling from his charred smock.

He glared murderously at Garian. "You little bastard!" he bellowed and charged.

The Ox was slow and lunged clumsily over the bar. Garian swayed back, easily avoiding the ponderous attack even with an injured leg. Before the Ox had chance to throw another punch, the girl snatched a jug off the bar, and belted him over the head with it. The stout, earthenware vessel bounced off his skull. The Ox swayed, momentarily stunned by the blow, giving Garian time to slip a bolt into the handbow. When he recovered what few wits he possessed, the farmhand lashed out, and viciously backhanded the girl across the face, lifting her off her feet. She landed amid a billow of petticoats and lay still.

Garian rarely *wanted* to hurt people, even though he did it often enough, but seeing the girl hit like that made him particularly keen to take down the Ox. He rested the bow across his forearm and squeezed the trigger. The bolt struck the Ox in the cheek. Garian cursed—he'd aimed for the bastard's eye. The Ox bellowed his fury, and ripped the shaft from his face. Meanwhile, the others were stumbling back inside.

There was no point trying to reload. At most, he'd get one more off before they mobbed him. *All I wanted was a bed for the night.* The door to the kitchen was just behind him. All sense told him to run. He'd done what he could for the girl and had a duty to get his report back to Hyram. It was sheer folly to try and hold them off until help arrived, particularly in his condition. He wasn't a hero; he was a spy—a killer.

"Why isn't anything ever fucking easy?" he muttered and drew his knife.

None of the farmhands were keen to be the first to tackle him when he drew the long-bladed hunting knife. They backed off and threw mugs, chairs, and anything else that wasn't nailed down. Even on one leg, he was far nimbler than his assailants were accurate. He could have kept them at bay all day, but then one of them had the wit to drag the semi-conscious girl to her feet and hold a bailing hook to her throat.

"Drop the knife, you little cunt," the drunk snarled.

Garian considered his options; it didn't take long. As soon as he dropped the blade, the cowards were on him. He was dragged over the bar by his hair and beaten to the floor. He could hear the girl cursing and shouting, but all he could see through the web of his laced fingers were feet and fists, raining blows from all directions. He curled into a ball, tried to weather the brutal onslaught like he used to do when he was six, when his father got bored of beating his mother. They kicked him, stamped on him, punched him… After what felt like hours, he was picked up, hoisted above shoulder height, and thrown through the window. He hit the ground and rolled onto his back. When he opened his eyes, he saw glass shards falling all around him. Someone was crying…was it his mother? No, she was already dead. Was he dead…?

"Weems gonna kick ya to death, ya runty little bastard," one of them sneered.

Ah. Not quite yet then. Unlike their boots, the threat lacked impact, why, dying like this was almost funny. After all the fights he'd survived against iron-hearted warriors and cold-eyed killers, he was going to be kicked to death by a gang of drunken farm hands. At least Jerim wouldn't get his message. It would probably be used to wipe one of their big, hairy arses the next time nature called. If he'd had the strength he would have laughed.

A kick in the ribs flipped him onto his stomach. As his conscious mind ceased to function, primitive instinct took over and he tried to crawl away from the source of pain, harsh laughter ringing in his ears. Suddenly, the laughter stopped. Something was in his way, stopping him crawling. He looked up. Through the blur, he saw a pair of calfskin boots. The last thing he heard before he passed out was a dog growling.

The smell of bacon crept into Garian's dreams and dragged him by the nose to hungry wakefulness. He opened his eyes to see a painted wooden ceiling. A thick downy quilt obscured the rest of his surroundings. Warm and sleepy, he wanted nothing more than to burrow into it and sleep for another week or two. Alas, duty wouldn't allow him to indulge the fantasy. He propped himself up on his elbow and took a look around.

Everything ached and his head was pounding. Considering the beating he'd taken, he felt in remarkably good shape, and very hungry. He was in a wagon; the boxed-in bed was against the wall opposite the split door, the top half of which was ajar. The door creaked gently back and forth, allowing the smell of cooking and a wavering slice of sunlight to slip inside.

He was slightly perturbed to discover that he was naked except for bandages wrapped around his sore ribs and thigh. But there was something else his sleep fuddled mind was struggling to recall. *The wallet.* Panicked, he was about to leap out of bed when he saw it lying on a chest next to the bed with his other belongings. He grabbed it and checked that the parchment was still inside, which it was. Relieved, he lay back and closed his eyes, but he couldn't sleep. The mouth-watering smell of food was too good to ignore. He wrapped the quilt around him, and limped to the door.

He opened the door; it was morning, his breath tumbled out in delicate, frosty curls. The sun was climbing over the horizon, but hadn't yet chased the chill from the air. He wondered how long he'd been out. The Hadami wagons had been moved closer to the inn, the window of which had been boarded up. The burnt cart was gone, leaving only a blackened patch of earth to mark where it had been. There was no sign of the drunks. The swordsman he'd met earlier was sitting by a fire in front of the wagon, expertly flipping bacon in a large frying pan. It sizzled noisily next to a cluster of juicy tomatoes and a heap of glistening mushrooms. Garian's stomach rumbled.

The Hadami called over his shoulder. "Come and join me, young sir. I'm about to break fast."

"I'm not really dressed for it."

The Hadami turned round. "Ah. I see what you mean. Your clothes were a mess. My beloved took them to wash after she cleaned you up. Wait there, I'll go find out where they are."

The Hadami went over to another caravan and tapped on the door. Garian was pleased to see it was opened by the girl from the inn. She looked well, save for a few bruises. After speaking with the swordsman, she disappeared inside and returned a few moments later with a bundle of clothes. Instead of giving them to the swordsman, she brought them over herself. It was only when she reached the steps of the wagon that he remembered he was naked save for a quilt and quickly made sure that it was covering his modesty. A bruise darkened her cheek and her lip was swollen, but her eyes were just as beautiful as he remembered; no, they were more beautiful.

"Good morning, lady," he mumbled.

A knowing smile spread across her face. "So it would seem."

Garian blushed, which wasn't like him, but the way she looked at him was disarming, like she knew what he was thinking, although right at that moment it probably wasn't hard to guess.

"Here, take these." She thrust the bundle into his arms. "My mother tried to wash your clothes, but they were ruined." She draped the garments over the door then skipped down the stairs and joined the swordsman by the fire.

The clothes were a good fit—whoever had chosen them had gauged his size better than Hyram. He would never have chosen grey linen trousers or the pale blue shirt, but he couldn't deny they were comfortable. He had to admit defeat when it came to the headscarf. There was obviously a knack to winding the slippery fabric around a head, but he couldn't fathom it. He'd learn how to do it at some point, and then maybe add Vodoni to his repertoire of disguises.

When he'd finished dressing, he scrutinised his reflection in the polished copper pots hanging on the dresser. He decided he felt better than he looked. He had to get back to Hyram with the parchment, but he couldn't stop thinking about the girl. The way she'd smiled at him. Why had she smiled at *him* like that? It didn't make sense. He was thin and short. His hair was too brown, and too wild, and his eyes were too dark and staring. Most of the time he hid his true face, he was a good actor, he had to be; his life often depended on his ability to dissemble.

Right then, with no need for subterfuge, he saw himself for what he really was: a cold-hearted gutter-snipe, a killer. The only difference between him and the average piece of street scum was that he wasn't out to cut a purse, or mug a drunk. He was above average scum, the kind who put a crossbow bolt in a man's back for a piece of paper. That he killed in the name of the King didn't make it any better. He was worthless, just like his father used to say. *A girl like her could never be interested in a killer like you.*

"Fuck off." He growled at his reflection and settled a less fierce mask over his sharp features.

As weak as a new born calf and just as graceful, he climbed down the steps of the caravan.

"Come, sit. You must be hungry; the healing my wife gave you takes a lot out of a body. You'll be going *Thinne* if you're not careful," said the Hadami.

He and the girl touched the crescent moon pendants they were wearing. Garian had heard the term before. *Thinne* didn't mean a lack of weight; it signified a lack of essence, a death of spirit. If a person lost too much of their essence they would became evil spirits. Hadami legends were full of cautionary tales of the Thinne, hunting the living. Garian knew that all manner of fell creatures still haunted the dark and lonely places of the earth and stalked the unwary, but the only monsters he'd ever encountered, and there had been a few, had all been human.

The Hadami handed him a plate piled with food. Garian was ravenous, but refrained from devouring it like a hungry dog.

"How long have I been here?" he asked between mouthfuls.

"Two nights. You drifted all of yesterday, my Mati— *mother* that is, thought you might not wake up. She stayed with you until she was sure you weren't going to leave us."

"I'm grateful. What happened to those bastards who attacked us?"

The girl looked at the swordsman.

He wiped his knife on the grass. "They were dealt with."

"I don't remember much after being thrown through the window," said Garian.

The Hadami gave a half smile. "I can see by your face you will not rest until you have a full account."

"I would appreciate that, sir."

"Well, now let me see… We saw the smoke and met the Innkeepers on the road. They told us what was happening. Maire and I reached the inn first, just in time, I think. It looked like those savages were intending to kill you."

Garian nodded. "Aye, I believe so. Did you have a hound with you? I seem to recall hearing a dog growling."

The Hadami smiled apologetically. "We have started in the middle, this is wrong." He wiped his hand on his trousers before offering it to Garian. "Allow me to introduce myself. I am Korstoi Kristi, Hetman of this Charaval. This is my daughter." He gestured to the girl.

As much as he wanted to introduce himself as *Captain* Garian Tain, he refrained. "Garian Tain, cartographer," he said and shook the Hetman's hand.

The Hetman's daughter leaned over and offered her hand. He tried not to seem too eager to take it, or smile too warmly when she touched him.

"I'm pleased to meet you, Garian Tain. I'm Sulithabai Kristi, daughter of Korstoi Kristi and B'ha'Maire Na Strolzogyr."

The Hetman clapped him on the back. "It was most remiss of us not to introduce ourselves. Don't mistake me—we're not Shemisana, we are Vodoni! A Shemisana would have killed themselves for committing such a terrible breach of etiquette." The Hetman laughed heartily. "Now where was I? Ah, yes. The Innkeeper told us what was happening, and my beloved and I made for the inn as quickly as we could, followed by the rest of the Charaval. The pigs who attacked you were too drunk and stupid to back down. May the gods forgive me, but a part of me is glad that they didn't." Korstoi sheathed his knife. "We gave them the chance to surrender because unlike them, we are civilised people. It was more than they deserved. After three of them had gone to their gods the rest lost their appetite for violence."

Prompted by the Hetman's account, Garian's memories came flooding back. He suddenly remembered the screaming and the sound of bone's snapping, of flesh being torn apart, and when the screaming stopped, hot breath against his cheek, and a pair of inhuman, blue eyes staring down at him.

"She's a shifter!" Garian spluttered.

Korstoi Kristi raised an eyebrow. "Did I not say I was the Hetman of this Charaval? Ah, but you do not know our ways. As Hetman it was my pleasure, and my duty, to marry a Moon Maiden. The Silver Weavers and the Vodoni have ever been joined thus. Don't they teach you stone dwellers anything these days?"

"Alas, our education is somewhat lacking when it comes to Moon Maidens and Silver Weavers," Garian confessed without shame.

"It's been a long time since I was called a maiden." The woman swept from behind him. She looked younger than the Hetman, although her hair was grey. It was her eyes that marked her out as something other than an ordinary, middle-aged woman; they were disconcertingly blue, more akin to those of a wolf than a human. Now he remembered her. She was the one who had been looking after him. He stood up and bowed.

"Ack, sit down, child, finish your food, you need to get your strength back. You've been through a lot."

"You're most kind. I believe I have you to thank for tending to me. My leg feels much better."

"And so it should—now it hasn't got poison running through it. It's a good thing our paths crossed or you'd have most likely bled to death before the next day was out, and then my darling Suli…Let's just say, the gods are good."

Garian didn't give a fuck about the gods. His professional pride was wounded, he was certain the knife had been clean. "Are you sure there was poison?"

She laughed sharply, revealing canines that were slightly too long. "Oh yes. It was Red Widow Bark. The bush grows in southern Guthland where it's warm and damp. It's good for those with thick blood and weak hearts, but only as a last resort, as it kills as often as it cures. It has no smell that *you* could discern and it keeps its strength for many days, even when applied to a blade. Like the one you got stuck by, I imagine." She folded her arms and fixed him with a challenging stare.

"You're right, Da. He is brave." Sulithabai winked at Garian. "There aren't many who'd dare question Mati on the subject of herbs."

The Hetman threw up his hands in mock surrender. "Now Maire, my love, go easy on the boy. We haven't finished our breakfast yet, and you know how slow-witted men are when their bellies are empty."

"Don't try to wheedle me, Korstoi Kristi. Now, you'll have to excuse me. Clothes don't wash themselves."

Maire kissed her husband, far more passionately than Garian thought proper for a middle-aged couple.

"Take care of yourself, young man. I'd hate for all my hard work to be wasted." Maire grinned at him and strode off between the wagons.

"I've never even heard of Red Widow Bark," said Garian.

"Don't be hard on yourself, 'tis a rare herb," offered Korstoi. "I doubt that even in Guthland there are many who know what it's used for, and even fewer who know how to prepare it. My wife is exceptional, you know."

Garian nodded. "Indeed. I must ask her about the anti-
dote before I leave." He turned to Sulithabai. "Are you…
like your mother? I mean, you didn't change back at the
inn…"

She flashed him a dazzling smile. "No. I'm not a shifter
as you put it. I'm just an ordinary girl."

"I don't think you're the least bit ordinary," said Garian
before he could stop himself.

"I suppose I should get on too," said the Hetman. "I'll
see you later, Suli…Suli? Never mind." The Hetman got up
and left.

The next morning, Garian woke in the Hadami wagon,
only this time he wasn't alone. Suli was with him. They'd
spent the whole of the previous day and most of the night
talking. When they knew all there was to know about each
other and had drunk their fill of mead, they'd made love.
He'd tried to stop himself; he didn't want to offend his
hosts, but he couldn't help it. He wanted her more than
he'd ever wanted anyone, and apparently, hard as it was
for him to believe, she wanted him. Whatever the truth he
hadn't needed much persuading.

Now, lying next to her, he could hardly believe his good
fortune and tried not to think about what would happen if
her parents weren't as understanding as she'd assured him
they were. Worse still was the thought that he might wake
up any minute and find it was only a dream. He buried
his face in her thick, golden hair. It smelled of rosemary,
wood smoke, and her.

"What are you doing?" She mumbled sleepily.

"Smelling your hair."

"You're a strange human; you know that don't you?"
She nestled her behind into his groin. He was instantly
aroused.

It was past noon when they finally got up. The pain in his leg had faded to a dull ache. On any other day he would have been happy about such a swift recovery, but not today.

Garian and Suli broke their fast in silence. They hadn't spoken about him leaving, but they both knew he had to go. Suli had told him that the Vodoni would also be moving on now that they'd given their statements to the local magistrate. Garian hoped the thugs would hang, but what concerned him most was when he would see Suli again. They had shared so much in the last few days; it felt like he'd known her all his life. The thought of being without her, even for a short time, was almost unbearable.

Korstoi returned his gear to him without comment. The Hetman must have realised that the items he had with him were a little out of the ordinary for a cartographer. His circumspection would be rewarded after Garian had left. He and Suli had agreed that she could tell her parents why a cartographer carried two crossbows and a finely balanced hunting knife.

Garian had broken his sworn oath and told her everything about himself. Like making love with her, it felt right, more; it felt good to be able to talk to someone about what he did. Other than his mother, nobody else had ever shown any real interest in him as a person. He couldn't repay her kindness by being anything other than honest with her.

Hyram would be incandescent with rage if he ever found out, but Garian didn't care. She already meant more to him than anyone he'd ever known, including his patron. He'd be damned if he would found their relationship on lies. He wasn't convinced the Vodoni would regard 'spy' as an acceptable occupation for a son in law, but he knew without a doubt, that he'd give it up in a heartbeat if that was the only way to be with her. He would do anything for Suli, she was as vital to him as breathing.

She kissed his neck. "You're thinking again, Captain."

"Are you sure you're staying in the area? What if you go elsewhere? How will I find you?" he asked.

She laughed and kissed him again. "Don't worry. I've told you, we'll be around here for most of the summer. We always are, and if father suddenly decides to go elsewhere, I'll send word or you can come find us—that's what you're good at isn't it?"

"Very funny, my lady. I just don't want to lose you. I mean, a girl as handy as you are with a jug is quite a prize."

She laughed and leaped into his arms, taking them both to the ground.

Later, when Garian finished saddling his horse, Suli's father gave him some food for the journey, a pipe and some Pel for the road.

"Do not take my daughter's affection lightly," said the Hetman as he tightened the girth on Garian's horse. "I am far less gentle than my wife if you cross me."

Garian wasn't offended; the warning was only what he'd expect from a protective parent. If he could, he'd rip his heart from his chest and show the Hadami how full it was with love for his daughter. Instead he'd have to settle for using words to express how he felt.

"I'd gladly die for your daughter, sir, but mostly I want to live for her, now that I know what life is for."

The Hetman laughed. Garian realised he sounded like a fool, but he meant every word of it.

"I think you missed your calling…*master cartographer,*" said Maire who came over to bid him farewell. "You should have been a talespinner with such a honeyed tongue." She took something from her pocket and pressed it into Garian's hand. It was a crescent moon pendant, identical to those worn by the Vodoni. "Farewell, master Tain. May the gods guard you." The shapeshifter and her husband left Suli and Garian alone to say their goodbyes.

"You remember where to meet me in two weeks' time? If you don't come, I'll take it that you have changed your mind," said Suli.

"I'll be there. Just don't go getting yourself into any more fights."

After kissing her for the twentieth time, Garian mounted up and turned for the Weyhithe road. When he looked back he saw that she was waving. That was the picture he wanted to remember, the image that would keep him company on the lonely journey home. Being without her for two weeks would be agony, but despite that, he was overjoyed. For the first time in his life, someone was watching him ride away.

Korstoi and Maire came up behind Suli as the boy rode into the distance. The Hetman was tired to the bone; hopefully the stress of the last few days would be worth all the trouble they'd gone to. As if sensing his thoughts, Maire turned to their daughter.

"Are you sure he's ours?" she asked in a rare moment of uncertainty.

Suli smiled. "He isn't *ours*, Mati dear, he's mine, and I'm his."

"That wasn't part of the plan. Maire smiled. Oh well, the gods work in their own way, I suppose."

Korstoi laughed and put his arms round his daughter and his lover. Storm clouds might be gathering, but where there was love, there was hope. He kept the thought to himself; to voice it would have invited savage teasing from both women. What could he say? Like the city boy, he was a hopeless romantic.

Chapter Five

Two days after leaving Suli, Garian sighted the walls of Weyhithe. Pennants were flying from the highest towers of the Arth and gulls glided in lazy spirals above the smoke-plumes of a thousand chimneys. When he neared the gates, he caught a whiff of stale city air. No one could call it pleasant, but it was the smell of home.

He found his way to Lord Hyram's room some time before dawn. He wasn't surprised to find his master sitting at his desk, surrounded by the nubs of a dozen dead candles. The dark circles under Hyram's heavy lidded eyes told the apprentice that his master had not been sleeping well. Garian briefly entertained the possibility that it might be from worrying about him, but after the old man spent the next hour soundly berating him for not sending word, for helping the girl, for getting injured and just about everything else he could think of, he discarded that fantasy.

After a few minutes' pause to build up a fresh store of anger, Hyram continued with his tirade. "We do not send a second dog into the badger's den if the first one doesn't return! You're out there on your own, so be more bloody careful. I have spent too much time and effort training you for you to go risking your neck helping strangers when you're about the King's business." the old man seethed.

Garian wasn't stupid enough to say anything in his defence. He waited quietly for the storm of Hyram's temper to blow itself out.

The spymaster snatched up the paper Garian had taken from the Guthani. "And this damn thing is all we have to show for it—a bloody inventory! Without names or dates, it's as much use as a eunuch in a brothel." He gave a heavy sigh and rubbed his eyes. "Ships, warriors, grain and equipment, and a lot of it, but nothing that can link it to Jerim, save this mark here." He stabbed the paper with his finger. "This is most certainly the sigil of Ulyan Redbear. I've only seen it on one other document, but I'm certain it's his mark."

Frustration etched in every crease of his sweating brow, Hyram poured a glass of wine and threw it back in an angry gulp. "Stopping it reaching Jerim might delay the little bastard's plans, but not for long, I'll wager. We must find out what he intends, or more accurately, when and where he plans to attack. Urgh! I could strangle him with his own guts and not lose an hour's sleep."

Garian had heard of Ulyan Redbear—he was a powerful Guthland thane and Princess Matia's cousin. It was a reasonable leap to think that one ambitious princeling would help another if it was of mutual benefit. Guthland was a violent, lawless country where if you could take power and hold onto it, it was legitimately yours. When he was twelve, Hyram had taken him there with a trade delegation. He prayed to the Twins that he'd never have to go there again—he didn't want to visit anywhere twice in a lifetime where rotten fish was regarded as a delicacy.

"Well, Captain, have ye anything to add?" Hyram dared him to speak.

Garian saw the trap. "No, my Lord."

"Damn right, you don't. Red Widow Bark! You'd have been as bled as a slaughtered pig hours before you got here if those Vodoni hadn't found you. Idiot boy. Have ye learnt nothing?"

It was touching to see how much Hyram cared, but Garian didn't think it prudent to say so, or mention that he'd fallen in love. That revelation would most certainly push the old man over the edge. The King's Councillor had been married off young to a woman he hardly knew, as was the way with nobility, who matched for blood rather than love. They had two children. His daughter, Merin, was the Captain of the 3rd Company of the Royal Guards. The other, a son, had died at birth with his mother. Hyram never spoke of them. From what Garian had seen over the years, Hyram had devoted his life since then to serving Daris.

His master threw himself into his chair and stared so intensely at the note on the table, Garian half expected it to burst into flames.

"I must speak with the King about this. I want you examined by what passes for a proper physician. Go and see that quacksalver Lorstadt—tell him I sent you, and get some rest, d'you hear me?" Hyram growled.

"Yes, sir." Garian made a hasty exit before his master thought of anything else for him to do. Lorstadt was the King's physician, but if Hyram said go see him, he would do as he was bid, this time. If Hyram knew he'd spent a day making love instead of rushing back to Weyhithe with the inventory he would've skinned him alive.

Queen Thea was sitting by a window in the royal apartments, embroidering a tapestry. Stitch by stitch, red roses grew on the white silk. Hyram paced the room.

"Come, sit by me," said Thea without looking up from her work. "You're wearing a hole in a very expensive carpet."

The Councillor obeyed his Queen. Thea's slender fingers twisted a knot into the thread. Her shears flashed as she neatly snipped the end. Female aesthetic qualities were mostly wasted on him, but even he knew that Thea was a rare beauty. He'd known her for a long time, they had aged together—he far worse than her. Fine lines creased the corners of her eyes and mouth, but her fair hair was still lustrous and her dark brown eyes as disarming as they had always been. If, *Twins forbid*, he ever had to take a wife again he would do well to find one half as fair as Thea.

"Is it bad?" she asked at last.

"I think so, my Queen."

"I cannot help but think that if Daris and I hadn't married, and he had wed a Guthani Princess as was intended, none of this would be happening."

"Not at all," Hyram lied smoothly. "Jerim would have found a reason to attack Daris even if he'd married Ashania herself. It's his nature to cause mischief. You can't blame yourself, Thea."

"Perhaps, and I know I shouldn't listen to court gossip, but when I hear them whispering about wasted alliances…"

"Ignore them. They're jealous and bored."

"Oh, I know, and I do ignore them for the most part. But every now and then I wonder how different, how much easier it would be for everyone—including you—if Daris had blood ties with Guthland."

"Guthani kings do not value such things; all that matters is having the strength to hold the throne. Alliances last only as long as they are useful and not a moment longer. They are foolish and greedy people, which is why they still live in huts made of dung."

"Aye, there have been two kings and one queen on the Dragon Throne since Daris and I were married."

Hyram cared little for the company of women, but Thea's smile never failed to brighten his mood. She had come a long way, this daughter of a minor noble house. Fate and chance had conspired to throw her and Daris together, during the turbulent days of Daris's father's reign. Hyram had fond memories of when she first arrived in Weyhithe. She'd blown in like a breath of fresh air, but was completely unprepared for the vicious intriguing of the courtiers. For their part, they thought her little more than a brood mare from the country, a bumpkin. It came as a great surprise to those who tried to use her, how quickly she learnt to play their game. With a little help from him, she made her tormentors regret their presumption. He sighed. Wonderful times, so very long ago. *Were we ever that young?*

The door to the King's private chamber burst open. Daris swept in, and tossed Hyram's report on the table.

"I cannot call the Council to censure him now." Daris raised his hand, forcing Hyram to swallow his objections and wait impatiently for the King to finish.

"It isn't because I don't want to, cousin. Twins know, I'd love to deal with him immediately, but if I move now it will provoke him to act—and if your intelligence is correct, Jerim is more prepared for war than I am. You must find out who supports my brother. I have to know who I can rely on in Cathlan and here in Antia, and find out if he's approached the Tamalak nobles."

"What about the boys? What about Talin?" Thea asked, unable to mask her concern.

"Talin can stay where he is, at least until the Council meet. There's no safer place he could be than with the Hammer. Olin is here with us, but set one of your hounds to watch over him, Hyram."

Hyram bowed. "Of course, there is the tournament at Trelanlith soon. I don't wish to be alarmist, but every mercenary and vagabond knight in the kingdom will be there, and accidents happen during tourneys."

A look of fear flitted across Thea's face, but it was too late to take his words back, even if he'd wanted to, which he didn't. It was a known fact that along with boar hunting, tournaments provided the perfect opportunity to eliminate heirs to thrones.

"You must send for him immediately, Daris," Thea insisted.

Daris frowned at his Councillor. Hyram made sure to look suitably abashed even though he wasn't, and Daris knew it. So long as he made a show of contrition the King wouldn't have to throw him in the dungeons.

"I'm sorry, love, but I can't. If I brought Talin home for no good reason it would be a sure sign to our enemies that something was amiss. Don't worry, I'll send word that he cannot take part in the tourney."

"But they could send assassins; murder him in his bed. Tell him, Hyram!"

Daris knelt beside her, his expression softened, all trace of kingly authority vanished. "They could do that here." He took her hands in his and kissed them.

She kissed him, and brushed a strand of hair from his face. "No they couldn't, I wouldn't let them."

Hyram examined his finger nails. He never knew where to look when they got all mawkish.

"Talin is a grown man, Thea, not a child—despite how he acts. I promise you, he'll be perfectly safe at Trelanlith."

She looked unconvinced. Hyram sympathised but now that he thought about it, there was another good reason to keep Talin away from Weyhithe. Daris and Thea only had two children. If assassins were sent, it was better they were not in the same place at the same time. *An heir must sur-*

vive. He knew it was cold, but someone had to be practical for the sake of the kingdom.

"I need to gather my forces—*quietly.*" Daris laughed. "Forced to sneak in my own kingdom, damn my brother! I'll send word to our lords in the south; I think it's time they organised some training exercises. Mark me, Hyram; I undertake these preparations in the hope that Jerim will see sense before his schemes ruin us all. I must give him the chance to stand down before I plunge the kingdom into civil war. I will not close the door on that, I cannot, not until he raises his banner against me—do you hear me, Hyram?"

"Yes, Majesty." Hyram bowed. His conscience was clear; whatever he did it would be for the good of Daris, and the kingdom, and what the King didn't know wouldn't hurt either of them.

Alyda pushed back on her chair until it rocked gently on two legs. The wood creaked in protest, but the stout oak could take the abuse. She picked up the Silver Spur and idly flicked the wheel while she waited.

She never grew tired of looking at the Spur, even the tiny rowels were decorated with intricate vines and flowers. After her sword, it was the most precious thing she owned. The words of command began to form in her mind. She felt the metal start to flow beneath her fingers. It was as though she was holding a living creature, one that wanted to change; to leap to life in her hands, but now wasn't the time to play. Reluctantly, she put the words from her mind. The Spur was still, nothing but cold, dead metal.

Nevenna was waiting with her. She was looking out of the window, watching her fellow knights practicing manoeuvres.

"When do you think we'll go?" she asked Alyda, her gaze tracking the wheeling horses.

"No idea. Trease just sent orders to get the recruits trained up quickly and to, *maintain standards*. That's his way of saying, be ready for battle.

"Will it affect the tournament?

Alyda flicked the rowels of the Spur. "I shouldn't think so. I don't think we'll be going far if we get the order to move out. No need to prepare for a long sea voyage, if you see what I mean.

Nev grinned. "Aye, Captain. I'm pleased about the tourney. I fancy Del's going to do well in the melee this year."

"You're biased, but speaking of the tourney; how angry was our newest recruit when you told him?" Alyda asked.

"Teeth-spitting furious." The Herald grinned. "I was particularly impressed by the stream of invective he came out with; very imaginative."

"Well, he has been studying under the master. I hear he and Kieran have become firm friends."

"Aye, unfortunately Kieran isn't developing the manners of a prince—more that the Prince is becoming as rough as a cavalryman. What do you think his Highness will do?"

A little later than expected, Alyda heard the sound of heavy footsteps echoing in the hallway. "I think we're about to find out." Alyda swung her feet off the desk and pretended to read some papers just before Prince Talin burst in. She glanced up. He'd obviously come straight from the practice yard and as Nevenna said, looked completely furious.

"Captain Stenna!" the Prince demanded, "I have an issue that I must raise with you immediately."

"Are you a knight in training or a Prince currently?" Alyda asked.

He frowned, halted in his tracks clearly confused by her comment. "What?"

"Well, Highness, a knight wouldn't burst into their Captain's quarters in such a dishevelled state unless they had been ordered. Neither would they rudely demand the attention of their commanding officer." The Prince looked utterly bewildered. If she wasn't so mindful of her duty she would have laughed her arse off. "If you're a prince, then of course, you can do as you please. You can barge in, shout—dance on my desk if you so desire. Only, if it please you, decide which you are before we continue as it's very confusing for a simple soldier to fathom."

"How dare you!" Talin spluttered.

"Ah, you are the Prince then." Alyda stood up and saluted. "Forgive my lack of manners, Highness; I mistook you for a knight."

The Prince stabbed an accusing finger at Alyda. "You…I…urgh." Cursing incoherently, he stormed from the office.

Nevenna laughed. "That showed him, or you're getting posted to the borders."

Alyda grinned. "You mean *we're* getting posted to the borders Lieutenant—I couldn't possibly leave the Company behind."

Nevenna stopped laughing.

When Nevenna had gone, Alyda set about her paperwork in earnest. The Prince would either come back or leave Trelanlith in a sulk. Either way, she might as well get on with some work while she waited to find out which it would be. She told herself she wouldn't mind if he left— she hadn't wanted him there in the first place. The trouble was she couldn't entirely convince herself that was true.

There was a knock at the door. Prince Talin entered. He'd bathed, his hair was neatly braided in a single plait, and he'd put on a pristine scarlet surcoat. He saluted and waited for her to address him.

"Yes, Highness?" she said at last.

"Captain Stenna; I would like to apologise for my conduct."

"Apology accepted. Was there anything else?"

"Yes, as a matter of fact there is. Lieutenant Vysten informed me that I cannot take part in the tourney next week. I'd like to know why."

"Because I ordered it."

"Yes, I got that part. I'd like to know *why* you ordered it."

"Under normal circumstances, I'd say it was none of your business, but then not every knight is the heir to the throne. You've been forbidden because it's too dangerous. Lieutenant Lorhine says you have skill with lance and sword, but the practice yards are very different to an open tourney. Nobody here wants to kill or maim you. The same cannot be said for some of the knights who'll be attending. Don't mistake me; most are honourable warriors, but they're coming here to win fame and glory. Unseating a Prince would be a bragging right, and we cannot risk the life of the future King. I'm sure you understand." From the sour expression on his face it was evident that he didn't.

"This is ridiculous, I've fought before—completely naked on one occasion. I assure you; there is no adversary more furious than a cuckolded lover." He grinned. "I'm sure I can look after myself fully armed and armoured. Please, Captain. I don't want to write to my father and ask his permission, but I will. This is the only time in my life that I've ever wanted to participate in a bloody tourney; you have no right, or reason to deny me."

Alyda took the letter bearing the King's seal from the drawer and slid it across the table. His face darkened as he read it. She hadn't wanted to pass responsibility to the King; her shoulders were broad, but it was clear that he wasn't going to accept her word and leave it there. She understood entirely, and would have been just as determined in his position.

"It seems I owe you another apology, Captain Stenna. I thought the order was yours. I should have known my parents wouldn't let me slip the leash entirely." The Prince tossed the letter onto the table.

"Tell me, Captain, why was I only informed this morning? The date of the letter is over three weeks ago."

"Telling you now means you're only going to be miserable for one week, instead of four."

He smiled. "You care if I'm miserable?"

Damn. He'd seen something she didn't even want to admit to herself.

"I care about the morale of all my knights," she said, quickly brushing the comment aside. She looked down at the papers to hide the flush she felt rising in her cheeks. The door burst open. It was Jamie, he'd been running.

"Captain," he spluttered. "Lieutenant Lorhine and Lieutenant Tiran are fighting."

The Great Hall was in uproar, tables and benches had been overturned and a knot of knights and squires were gathered in the centre of the room, enthusiastically shouting encouragement and curses. When they saw Alyda and the Prince, the noise died down and the crowd flowed apart to reveal Lorhine and Tiran. Lorhine had Tiran in a headlock and was punching him in the face. As he drew back his fist to hit him again, he glanced up, and froze.

"Let him go," said Alyda, her voice barely louder than a whisper. Lorhine immediately released Tiran. The knight dropped to his knees, gasping for breath.

"Both of you; my office, one hour. If you so much as look at each other before then, I'll kick you out of the Arth myself." Without waiting for either to reply she stalked from the hall, icy silence trailing in her wake.

"Would you rather be hung or dishonourably discharged?" Polyn asked Jamie.

He glared at the page. Normally he'd throw something at her, and follow it up with a lecture about not asking stupid questions, but he wasn't going to berate her in front of Hedden and his cronies.

"Hanged, without a doubt," he muttered and continued to change out of his muck and into something more presentable for the hearing.

"Hmm, I don't know," the page mused. "I saw someone being hung once. It took forever. He went purple and pissed himself...it was horrible. I think I'd take the discharge."

Jamie snorted. "You might as well be dead with a dishonourable discharge."

Pol folded her arms defiantly. "I still don't want to hang."

"Do you want to shut up? Your constant prattle is giving me a headache," said Hedden. His friends sniggered.

Jamie knew he should ignore him, but Hedden was like a splinter under his fingernail; inconsequential, but really annoying. "Only the Commander or the King can dishonourably discharge a knight, and only the King or a juried court can order a hanging. This isn't anywhere near that serious." Jamie tugged on his best boots and stamped his feet until they were snugly wedged into the stiff leather.

"I should be allowed to go with you. I'm your junior, and the Captain's page." Polyn flopped back on her bunk. Her freckled face screwed up.

Before Jamie could answer, Rudi Lauwen looked up from the sock he was darning.

He jabbing the needle in Pol's direction. "I'm Lieutenant Vysten's squire. If anyone else should be allowed in, it's me."

"Or me," Hedden chipped in.

"Why in the Void would you be allowed in, Hedden? Lacgarde won't be there." Jamie realised he shouldn't have taken the bait a second after he had.

"Because I'm wonderful, *Turd*lowe. Why else?" Hedden basked in his friends' laughter.

Jamie was seething, but forced a tight smile. "Y'know, Hedden we really are lucky to have you in the First. Did your village have to wait long after you left?"

Hedden narrowed his eyes suspiciously. "Wait for what?"

"Another idiot." Jamie threw his muddy clothes at Polyn and left before Hedden talked himself into a beating.

Talin crept into the Captain's office and commandeered a seat by the door where he would be out of the way. The last thing he wanted after this morning was to draw attention to himself. The room was hot and crowded with knights waiting for the hearing to begin. Talin knew it was terribly selfish, but he was privately grateful to the brawling officers. The fight had completely overshadowed his embarrassing little outburst.

Alyda was sitting at her desk, huddled in quiet conversation with Lieutenant Vysten. Her unsheathed sword lay before her, a cold, gleaming symbol of the military court's authority. When her squire came in, Talin pulled him down onto the bench beside him.

"Just the man I wanted to see."

"Me, Highness? I'm honoured."

"Aye, I thought if anyone knows what's going on it will be you, Master Turlowe."

"You flatter me, Highness."

The squire neither looked nor sounded in the slightest bit flattered, but he'd damn well stay and answer Talin's questions whether he liked it or not.

"Captain Stenna looks to be in a grim mood. Is a scrap all that serious?"

"Serious enough; particularly as it's between officers. The Captain says discipline is our foundation."

"That sounds like Trease. She reminds me of him—especially when she does that thing where she shouts without raising her voice."

Jamie gave Talin a disdainful look. "She's a Captain of the Royal Guards; she commands respect."

Like his older brothers, young Turlowe had inherited the irritating ability to sound smugly superior to everyone they spoke to, including a future king. It reminded Talin of his youth spent with the other noble children of the court. He and Bear would mercilessly tease the older, and equally as annoying, Turlowe brothers when they forgot their places. It was so easy to get a rise out of them; every single member of the family had a temper as hot as Naran pepper.

"Although, *unlike* Trease, she's lovely, even when she's angry. Don't you agree, Jamie?" Talin may have been teasing, but he meant it and was glad of the chance to voice his feelings, even though they were disguised as a jest.

"I really wouldn't know, Highness," Jamie mumbled.

There it was: the old, Turlowe Flush. The lad went from pasty to beetroot in seconds. Ah, but teasing a Turlowe was like fishing in a barrel, and not half as much fun without Bear there to share the joke. Captain Stenna and Lieutenant Vysten finished their conversation and the hearing was brought to order.

"So who do you think came off worst?" Talin asked Jamie.

Jamie shrugged. "Hard to say, Highness."

It was obvious to a blind man that Lorhine had beaten the damnation out of Tiran. The Tamalak knight hadn't escaped entirely unscathed; he had a few cuts and bruises, but Tiran was a mess. Talin wondered if his nose had been straight before the fight, because it certainly wasn't now. The disgraced knights saluted the Captain. She returned it, but the look on her face was as cold as the Ice Halls of Tamalan.

She tipped a nod to the Paymaster. He dipped his quill and prepared to write.

"Lieutenant Tiran, why were you and Lieutenant Lorhine brawling?" she asked.

Tiran cast a withering sideways glance at Lorhine. "Captain, Lieutenant Lorhine has insulted me many times before today. This assault was the culmination of months of persecution."

Lorhine drew a breath. Talin hoped the big knight wasn't about to talk himself into even more trouble, but Alyda shot him a warning look and he held his tongue.

"If you feel you've been persecuted, why haven't you seen fit to tell your commanding officer about it?" She jabbed a thumb at herself. "That's *me*, in case you've forgotten."

Tiran gulped. "I felt it was my duty as an officer to deal with the situation myself...without involving you, Captain."

"That's not your decision to make and you know it. Any dispute between officers under my command is my concern, and should be brought to my attention. Now, why do you feel you have been persecuted, Lieutenant Tiran?"

Talin whispered to Jamie. "Did you know about this?"

"Me? No, Highness. I'm the Captain's squire; sensitive conversations tend to stop when I enter a room. I heard rumours, but nothing specific, and I don't poke my nose into the senior knights' business. It's not how we do things."

"No. Apparently you beat the shit out of each other, which is seldom the best way to resolve a dispute, if you ask me."

"I wouldn't dream of asking you anything."

Before Talin could rebuke him, the squire added;

"It would be rude to question a prince."

Tiran cleared his throat. "Lieutenant Lorhine has consistently thwarted my attempts to encourage the proper and respectful worship of Sestrian within the Company. He has threatened me in the past, and today he attacked me in front of half the Company."

Alyda turned to Lorhine. He looked like he was going to explode. "Let's hear it, Lorhine."

"Captain, this…this, *zealot*," he spat the word like it was poison, "has been causing trouble from the moment he was promoted. I've had to put up with his bullshit for a year now. Before he got made up he was infuriating, since then he's behaved like a bloody tyrant."

Lieutenant Vysten scribbled a note and passed it to Alyda. She read it before continuing to question Lorhine. "I'll ask you the same thing I asked Tiran: why didn't you come to me? Or don't you trust my judgement either?"

"I trust your judgement implicitly, Captain. I thought I'd give him a chance to see his foolishness for what it was and put an end to it himself. I thought it was the best way to deal with the situation for the good of all. I see now that I was wrong."

"How astute. A shame your insight's come a bit late in the day. Now, what happened?"

"He's been trying to force his lance to worship Sestrian—*only* Sestrian. He punishes those who don't follow his devotions and favours those who do. It goes against everything we stand for—"

Tiran opened his mouth in a wide 'O' of outrage and rounded on Lorhine. "All Antians should be proud and grateful to kneel before the blessed Hawk of Dawn, He who is the Lord of all!" Tiran thundered. "You wouldn't understand, Captain, but it is the solemn duty of all pure Antians to—"

Alyda raised her hand and cut him off. "Pray tell, Lieutenant Tiran; what wouldn't I understand? And what in the Void is a 'pure' Antian?"

"Well, Captain…you're half Tamalak and half Hadami, I don't expect you to understand the strength of feeling we pure-blood Antian's have for Father Sestrian. Although, I'm sure you agree; a strong faith is vital if we are to have a strong kingdom."

Alyda gave Tiran a look that Talin hoped she'd never bestow on him. "Lieutenant Tiran, after what you've said and done, I can't imagine I'd agree with you that shit is brown without checking first."

"Be assured, Highness, Tiran is in a minority," Jamie whispered.

"Are you sure, Jamie? You're the Captain's squire, remember? Who'd tell *you* if he wasn't?" he immediately regretted his words. He was angry at Tiran, not Turlowe. Bear was right; he could be such an ass at times.

Jamie looked like he wanted to punch him. "With all due respect, Highness; I'd know."

Before Talin could offer one of his rare apologies, Alyda slammed her fist against the table. The unexpected display of temper stilled the room.

"What you have failed to realise is that I promoted you in spite of your 'strong faith', not because of it." Although she was clearly furious she still didn't raise her voice. "I had hoped your unbending devotion would soften when you gained more responsibility. Instead, you've used your promotion to pursue your stringent beliefs even more aggressively." She sounded disappointed. "This shows a woeful lack of judgement, and a lack of respect for the Company and our values. You talk of strength, but what you've done undermines, not only the morale of the Company, but the respect due to King Daris, who you have sworn an oath to serve. What gods a person chooses to worship is a matter for their own conscience; that is the King's law."

"It is the business of all devotees of the Hawk to ensure his faith flourishes," Tiran declared, as though he hadn't heard a word she'd said. "Sestrian is the first amongst gods and none shall deny Him! Not even a king."

"This fool is close to treason," Talin hissed.

"I'd like to think he doesn't realise what he's saying, but in truth, I don't think he cares," said Jamie.

Talin nodded. "He sounds brim full of conviction, and utterly bereft of doubt. That's never a good thing."

Alyda shook her head and turned her attention back to Lorhine. "What caused the fight, Lorhine?"

"A disagreement between fellow officers, Captain Stenna."

Talin noticed her right hand ball into a fist, but this time she didn't slam it into the table. "I'll ask you once more, Lieutenant. If you still feel unable to tell me, I will have no option but to discharge you from the Company."

Lorhine winced, but the threat proved enough of an incentive to loosen his tongue. "I told him never to beat the squires in his lance again. A lad ended up in the infirmary this morning." He paused; perhaps in the hope that he'd said enough. The look on the Captain's face said it wasn't. He took a deep breath. "I told him if he did it again I'd have no choice but to inform you."

"Go on, Lieutenant," Alyda insisted.

Lorhine swallowed hard. "He said, 'Go and run to the half breed and…'" He shrugged. The room held its breath.

"And what? Gods, this is like pulling teeth. What else did he say, Lieutenant?"

"Nothing, Captain…That's when I hit him."

Alyda raised an eyebrow and looked at Tiran. "Lieutenant Tiran; have you been beating my squires?"

"They...they need disciplining from time to time," he murmured, unable to meet her gaze.

Lorhine rounded on him. The big knight was shaking with rage. Talin thought he might hit Tiran, but he didn't. As much as Tiran deserved a punch for what he'd said, it was good to see Lorhine finally exhibiting some of the vaunted, 'Guards discipline' he'd heard so much about.

"You do it because you enjoy it, you miserable—"

"Not another word, Lorhine, or you'll be spending the night in the guard house," Alyda assured the furious knight. "As for you, Tiran, you know that a good officer upholds discipline by example, not by beatings."

Tiran stared resolutely at his feet.

"Do you deny beating the squires in your charge?"

He shook his head. "I...I do not. As I said, they need disciplining. Roland wasn't in the infirmary for longer than an hour or so. It was just a—"

"Enough. It's quite clear that you do not respect the Guards, or the laws we live by. And yet, you fought bravely on campaign."

That got his attention. He looked up.

"With that in mind, I'm going to give you the opportunity to resign your commission with honour. If you don't, I'll be forced to ask Commander Trease to convene a full disciplinary hearing in Weyhithe." Alyda paused a moment to let the weight of her words sink in. "If that happens, and you're found guilty of the charges that I will bring against you, I promise, your discharge will not be honourable."

Tiran looked like she'd run him through. "But you can't...my family have served in the Guards for generations!"

"And you have shamed their service." She looked and sounded completely unmoved by the knight's plight, but Talin noticed her fist rested white-knuckled against the scarred tabletop. "You have until sunset to make your decision. The offer is more generous than you deserve." She tapped the note Nevenna had passed to her. "The boy you put in the infirmary is ten years old. You are dismissed, Lieutenant Tiran."

Stunned, Tiran staggered from the room. Lorhine stared straight ahead, bracing himself for his turn. Talin felt sorry for him, but doubted if even the words of a prince could sway the Captain's decision.

"Lieutenant Lorhine, no matter what the provocation it is unacceptable to strike a fellow knight, let alone another officer. What kind of example does this set for the younger members of the Company?"

"With all due respect, Captain Stenna, it shows 'em that bigots and bullies will not be tolerated in the Hammer."

Her eyes flashed. *If looks could kill,* thought Talin.

"If you ever command your own company, which I seriously doubt given your current attitude, you'll be able to make those decisions. But while you serve under me, you will do as you are told. You're not a fucking Clan Lord; you're a Royal Guard, a knight. We follow the rule of law and order, not *'whoever hits the hardest wins'*. Can you get that through your thick Tamalak skull? You can either serve this Company and abide by its rules, or take your sorry arse back to Tamalan. Now, what's it to be?"

"I wish to serve, Captain!" he confirmed without hesitation.

"Then you shall wear a single braid, Lorhine. Until you learn to command yourself, you will not command others... and you will not take part in the tourney. You are dismissed, and this hearing is closed."

When everyone except Jamie had gone, Alyda sat back and put her feet on the desk. Her spurs scratched a few more grooves into the ink stained leather.

She was already regretting giving Tiran the chance to request a disciplinary court; he was stupid enough to think he might win and put them all to more trouble than he was worth.

"Damn laws," she muttered.

Jamie handed her a glass of wine. "Pardon, Captain?"

"I was just thinking that if this goes to a full trial, Trease will discharge both of them."

"But that wouldn't be fair; Lorhine was provoked."

Alyda snorted. "The Commander wouldn't give a damn about that. He'll go by the letter of the rules and I'll lose a good officer as well as a bad one.

"He was defending you."

"Aye." Alyda laughed. "He'll think twice before he does that again, I'll wager."

That night, the Great Hall buzzed with conversation about the fight and the hearing. Talin was surprised that there was some sympathy for Tiran, until he remembered that the knights thought losing your commission was a worse punishment than death. He thought they were well rid of treasonous cur, but kept his own council. Prince or not, it wasn't his place to comment on Company business. He spied the man he'd come to find, sitting on his own by one of the huge fires that blazed at either end of the hall. He went over.

"Mind if I join you?" Talin asked Lorhine.

"No, Highness, but I warn you—I'm miserable company this eve."

"I've got a bottle of Dragon's Blood."

Lorhine kicked a chair towards him. "I feel less miserable already."

They cracked the bottle and set about putting the world to rights. Hours passed; the hall emptied, the roaring fire burnt down to glowing embers and the Prince's bottle of

Dragon's Blood became one amongst many. All deference to rank and status vanished along with the drink.

"My Larissa is the most intelligent, beautiful, funny person in the whole kingdom; no—the world," Lorhine slurred.

Talin shook his head. "Because you are a man of good taste, I'll allow she may be the second. *The* smartest, most beautiful, just about perfect, woman in the world isn't called Larissa. Trust me; I know what I'm talking about."

Lorhine snorted. "So who is this paragon, you think rivals my Larissa?"

Talin was far too drunk to guard his tongue and smiled as he pictured her face. "Her hair is as black as a moonless night and her eyes are as bright as emeralds. She's a brilliant commander of fearsome warriors and she has a smile that could melt the Ice Halls of Tamalan. You know of whom I speak."

Lorhine laughed and slapped Talin on the back, almost knocking him off the chair. "Ashania's sweet paps! 'Tis a good thing you're a prince, or I'd say you aimed too high."

"If only my title impressed her. If anything, it goes against me. She doesn't see me as a person. To her I'm nothing more than a duty—an inconvenience." He threw up his hands in frustration. "You know her Kieran; how do I get close?"

The knight shrugged. "Buggered if I know—she busted me down to a single braid, remember?"

He sighed. "I'm a desperate man."

"Alright, Sest's sake—you look glummer than death. Now listen up: there's a reason you don't see a ring of betrothal on her finger. She's the Captain of the Hammer—heart and spirit. She eats, breathes, and sleeps the Company. True; she used to screw Corvinius, but he was just a fumble, someone to scratch that itch we all get. Don't get me wrong, Highness I wish you luck, but if you manage to '*get close*' as you put it, you'll be a better man than most because there's plenty have tried and got nowhere."

"I wish I'd never asked."

Kieran grunted. "So do I! I don't like thinking about the Captain like that. It makes me feel strange, and not in a good way."

As the night wore on, they fell into an easy silence. Sometime during the small hours of the morning, Lorhine stumbled off to bed; leaving Talin alone with only his thoughts and a pair of deer hounds for company. The coals of the fire turned from rubies to bones as he wondered how he could prove to the Captain of the Hammer that he was a better man than most.

The tournament was mere days away and it was too bloody hot to sleep. Talin got up and snagged a jug of water off the table. An anaemic breeze stirred the curtains but did nothing to lift the oppressive heat that smothered the room. He swept the curtain aside, and climbed out of the window onto the gently sloping roof. It was an improvement, but not by much. He needed sleep; another hard day of honest work lay ahead of him.

The routine duties of the 1st had been suspended as final preparations for the tournament got underway. He'd been forced to sit through dozens of tourneys over the years; but he'd always preferred taverns to arenas and the cock-pit over the tilt yard. Very soon he'd have to watch a bunch of puffed up egotists show off their martial prowess before the adoring masses, and for the first time in his life, he was jealous of them.

He wanted to be admired by the crowds, not as a prince, but as a knight and a warrior. What irked him most was that he knew *why* he wanted it—who he was desperate to impress. *That bloody woman.*

He lay back and stretched his aching limbs against the cool slates. Rather than spend the week before the tourney getting drunk and sulking, he and the newly demoted Lorhine had volunteered for the work gangs preparing the Arth for the games.

It had seemed like a good idea at the time, before he knew just how much work was going to be involved. They'd spent most of their time helping to build a grand viewing stand and raising a huge earth mound in front of it. Kieran told him that the mound was there to protect spectators from runaway horses, and to give the squires and seconds somewhere safe to stand, ready to re-arm their knights or hold tokens taken from other competitors. The work had been backbreaking but the results of their labour were rather impressive if he said so himself. He could watch the melee with the other honoured guests while sitting on a seat he'd made.

But it was small consolation for not being able to participate. He drained the jug; the water was warm and did nothing to wash away the bitter taste in his mouth. Of all the events, the melee was the one that had most appealed to him, one that he could have done well in. It still burned that he'd been forbidden to take part.

Working with Lorhine had kept him busy and he'd had someone with whom he could share his misery, but the work itself was killing him. Lorhine had a limitless store of stamina and made no allowances for Talin's woeful lack, no matter how much he'd begged or threatened. He'd fallen into his bed exhausted every night for the past five days. If only it wasn't so bloody hot tonight.

He yawned and closed his eyes. He saw Alyda. He sat up. Why was he even pretending? *She* was the real reason he couldn't rest. Every time he closed his eyes he saw her. Saw her, but couldn't have her. This had never happened to him before. Damn the woman, he was the heir to the throne. The bloody heat just added to his woes. He climbed back inside and threw himself on the bed, resigned to another sleepless night.

On the day before the tourney, everyone was hard at work preparing the Arth for the biggest event Trelanlith would see all year. Talin was hot. Sweat stung his eyes as he beat some roof beams into submission with, he had to admit, more enthusiasm than skill. At mid-day, a break was called and he and Lorhine sat in the shade of the stand to eat their bread and salt beef, and sup a mug or two of warm, weak ale.

"Tonight, the gates of the Arth will be thrown open to every shade of fighter who fancies themselves a knight," said Lorhine between mouthfuls of food. "The boastful, the honourable, the deadly, and the foolish. They'll all come, looking to test their mettle against the First...and I have to sit and watch 'em. Oh, sweet Asha! I wish I'd hit the bastard harder for all the pain he's caused me."

"He's gone—forget him. Think about next year; Weyhithe Tournament is but a handful of months away. I'll come and cheer you on."

"It's not the same. I wanted to win *our* tournament. No offence, Highness."

Talin grinned. "None taken—*Squire* Lorhine."

As much as he wanted to prove himself to Alyda and the Company, now that his anger had cooled he had to acknowledge that his father was right. Breaking his neck in the lists wouldn't prove anything other than his mortality; of course he'd never admit that. He'd learnt a great deal during his time with the 1st, not least that he was not, nor ever could be, one of them. He was Prince Talin. One day he'd be King Talin. *King.* Gods help them all. That thought alone was enough to keep him sober and straight for the rest of his life.

"Will Captain Stenna be competing in the tournament?" he asked.

Lorhine wiped his mouth with the back of his hand, and gave him a knowing grin. "Why don't you ask her? She's over there, digging the privies." The knight nodded towards the main gate. Sure enough, she was over by the curtain wall, digging one of the long privy trenches.

Three braids hung down her back, but instead of armour or a scarlet surcoat, she was wearing an old pair of breeches, battered boots and a patched leather vest. Her bare arms were bronzed and, as was common among both Tamalak and Hadami, heavily tattooed.

A page struggling to drag a cart laden with food over to Alyda's gang gave Talin an idea. He slapped Lorhine on the back, and called the girl over. After a brief negotiation involving two silver pennies, she let him have the cart.

Alyda buried the blade of her shovel in the dirt. After a well-earned break, they would set the boards and pitch the tents over the top and that would be another job done.

She dropped back into the trench to retrieve a pick and wondered how many drunks would be hauled out of the filth this year. Last year, nine people had taken a dip, three in one go when one of the boards had broken. That piece of bad luck had cost her half a royal. This year she'd wagered a crown there would be five; being pushed didn't count. She stuck the pick in the bank and began to climb out. Someone, a dark silhouette against the sun, offered her a hand up. When she was out of the hole, she was pleasantly surprised to see that it was Prince Talin.

"You get around, Highness; I thought you were working on the stand. What brings you over here?"

"The girl was having trouble with the cart, so I gave her a hand. Do you mind if I join you? I haven't eaten yet."

"Not at all."

"Will you be competing in the tourney, Captain?" he asked and helped himself to his second lunch. Alyda got some food and they sat down next to the privy trench with the rest of the crew.

"No, it wouldn't look good for the host to get dumped on her arse." She grinned. "I'll be on hand to attend you and the other honoured guests."

"Excellent—shaking hands and making small talk are my particular areas of expertise."

"I imagine they're very useful skills for a prince," she said.

"They are indeed, along with outstanding bravery, great wit, and a charming personality."

She laughed. "Don't forget modesty."

"I've decided to eschew modesty. I don't think it will get me what I want. What do you think, Captain? What will help me win the prize: boldness or modesty?"

Her smile vanished. She got up. "If you'll excuse me, Highness, there's something I need to attend to back at the Arth." Without waiting for him to answer, she inclined her head and strode off across the parade ground.

Talin cursed under his breath as he watched her go. For a moment it had been like that evening in the garden, and then she was gone. Once again, he'd been thwarted by the hard as iron, Captain of the Hammer and the wall of steel she habitually dropped between them. He knew she liked him, he could feel it, see it in her eyes when she looked at him. He threw the remains of his bread into the trench. Like his hopes, it was destined to be buried under a tonne of shit. Until he'd met Alyda Stenna he'd revelled in the power and privilege of being a prince. Now, he felt cursed by his title

Chapter Six

Kasper Thorgulsen inhaled the smoke coiling up from the dish of burning herbs. His battle-scarred chest expanded as he drew the heady fumes deep into his lungs. Rivulets of sweat ran down his naked body; his eyes began to water, his vision swam.

The Raven Daughter beat out a rhythm on the goatskin drum. Her hand was a blur as she flicked and twisted the slender bone across the taut goatskin. Swaying in time to the hypnotic rhythm, her bare breasts were a pleasing distraction. Reluctantly, he tore his gaze away from his wife's naked body. Taking the black handled dagger in his right hand, he held his left arm over the gleaming copper bowl and drew the blade across his forearm. The sharp kiss of steel woke his drugged senses; blood dripped into the bowl. Bethanglyn ceased her playing and leapt to her feet, eager to inspect the augury. Thorgulsen stepped aside while she read the signs.

"What does it say?" he demanded.

"There will be conflict," she said, turning the bowl in her hands as she peered at the contents.

Thorgulsen laughed. "I didn't need to slash my arm to tell me that, Beth."

"True enough, it is your wyrd; crow friend, fattener of dogs, widow-maker—"

"I know who I am, woman. Tell me something I don't know."

She put the bowl down and wrapped herself in her cat skin cloak. First she makes him slash his arm, and then she denies him the pleasure of looking at her body, which was the only good thing about the damned ritual in the first place. He wondered why she didn't just kick him in the balls and have done with it.

"Sometimes it's best not to know too much, my love." She pitched her tone just right to leave him unsure if she was mocking him, or showing genuine concern. Knowing Beth, it would be the former.

"And sometimes I have to break people's bones to make them tell me what I want to know. Now I pray you, wife: tell me what your damn spirits showed you."

"Is there an 'or else' after that, my husband?" She took the knife from his hand and slowly licked the blood off the blade.

"Just tell me, witch." He ignored the sudden desire to fuck, and pulled on his trews.

"It wasn't clear. This place is too close to the Ward and it's a surly bastard. The spirits are afraid. They fed poorly and said little. But be assured, your hair will be more silver than gold before you join them. That's all I can tell you."

He snorted. "Why doesn't that surprise me?"

Bethanglyn trailed her arm across his back. Her sharp nails drew heat to his skin and sent a pleasant shudder down his spine."Would you like me to cast the runes?"

"Does it involve me cutting myself?"

"No, the runes do not demand blood."

"Then why didn't you cast them in the first place?"

She looked up at him, her eyes bright, and a sly smile on her lips. "'Tis always better to bleed for what you want."

"Remember you said that…"

Later, when the fog caused by Bethanglyn's herbs had cleared, Thorgulsen marched through the temporary encampment, over to where Telvier's Free Company standard fluttered in the breeze.

His senses might have cleared, but his annoyance at his wife still lingered. A true daughter of the Trickster, if she wasn't careful she'd go too far with him one day and not live long enough to regret it.

Thorgulsen's hirths had finished pitching their camp. A dozen prow-fronted tents circled around an iron fire pit. Painted shields hung from carved ridge beams, proclaiming that the Blue Boar, Leaping Salmon, and Black Aurochs were present. The warrior elite sat around the fire, preparing their war gear for the Ant's games. They nodded their acknowledgements to their Thane as he passed. Hirths did not bow to anyone—not to their leader, not to kings or queens, not even to the gods.

Thorgulsen had scouted the place as soon as they'd arrived. He wasn't impressed. The main body of the castle was three-sided, built around a large square, hemmed in on its forth side by the gates and curtain wall. The Arth was plainly built and as squat as a toad. It might be the home of the famous *Hammer of Antia*, but it was an ugly cowpat of a keep. His hirths wouldn't use it as a dog kennel, let alone a place where they could hang their shields. More importantly, it looked impossible to defend against a serious attack, which was good, given why they'd come to Antia.

He was pleased to find that the Steelskins were as complacent as Jerim said they would be. It would make this little task that much easier to accomplish. He didn't like the country, the food, or the people. The sooner he was home, the happier he'd be. A sharp pain stabbed his right knee. It was an old wound gained in a reckless youth—a reminder of wilder days. He scratched the thick scar where the Narwhal had speared him. Its magical horn might have been worth five times its weight in gold, but the cost of taking it had long outlasted the coin.

Thorgulsen's recollection of his youthful foolishness made him smile, even as he cursed the pain that had brought it to mind. He had more fire in his belly back then, and not a whit of caution. *Void bound* they'd called him; he'd dared all, risked everything to earn enough gold to raise a warband and pay the enormous dowry Beth's family had demanded.

For all her strange ways, she was worth every scar and pain he'd gained gathering the mountain of gold they had asked for her hand. In return, the Raven Daughter had taught him many things, the most important of which had been patience. It had taken him a long time and a lot of killing to become a Thane and Warleader, but he had done so where many others had failed and been swept aside.

He was now closer to the Dragon Throne than he could have dreamed possible in his youth. The youngest of seven, he'd left home with only an axe and the skill to wield it. Now he was a wealthy and powerful Thane—only a sword's length behind his cousin Ulyan on the path to the throne. If this campaign went as planned, he would be in the perfect position to take the throne from Redbear when he became too fat and lazy to defend it. He smiled. To the Void with spirits, he didn't need auguries to tell him that this was going to be a good year; he could feel it in his bones.

The long black wig had been frighteningly expensive, each strand of hair knotted individually. Luca Telvier sat at his dressing table, carefully burning curls into the lustrous black hair with a hot iron. Like the silver backed mirror that captured his powder pale reflection, it was the finest money could buy. He smiled at himself in the glass. Nothing could curb his vanity, not age or excess—not even the touch of lover's rot that had marred his once good looks.

The hair hissed in the iron, heat fixing another ringlet into the flowing locks. Satisfied with his endeavours, he put the iron back in the fire and carefully pulled the wig over his shaven pate. Studying his reflection in the mirror, he teased and twisted errant curls until he was satisfied that everything was perfect.

"Such a waste." It had been a while since he had spoken Antian. He needed to let his tongue get used to the feel of the dreary language—not the worst thing he'd ever had in his mouth, but distasteful all the same.

"Luca my boy, there's not a body within a thousand miles who can appreciate your artistry." Antians, like their language, were a dull and uninspiring people, but his current employers were even worse. "Uncultured dung eater," he muttered as he plucked a rogue hair from his nostril. "Not a shred of style or an ounce of manners. Good thing their coin is plentiful."

"Talking to yourself, Telvier? said Thorgulsen, who had entered unannounced. "They say it's a sign of madness," The mercenary spun round. Out of habit his hand flitted to the knife up his sleeve. When he saw his employer filling the entrance to the tent, he fluffed the lace at his cuff, and painted a broad smile on his face. Without waiting to be offered, Thorgulsen came in and helped himself to a glass of wine. The pig downed it in one.

"You wanted to see me." Thorgulsen grunted in barely understandable Antian, despite the hours of patient tutoring Telvier had given him when they were in Cathlan.

"Yes, Thane, I wanted to know if you had decided to attend the feast this eve. It will afford us a prime opportunity to get the measure of the Royal Guards. You might want to savour the wine—it is rather delightful, if one takes the time to taste it." The mercenary smiled tightly.

"It tastes like goat's piss. As to meeting the Antians, I'd rather stay here and pleasure myself. I didn't come to Antia to play—I came to make the crows fat."

"Of course, but it will appear strange if someone as important as you came to take part in the tourney, but didn't go to the feast. It would be perceived as a slight, and we do not want to put our hosts on their guard." He wanted to add, 'you great flaming dolt' but kept that to himself. "It will also give you the opportunity to see your patron's nephew."

The Thane shrugged. "I'll meet Prince Talin soon enough, this mock fighting and feasting is a waste of time. Raven Matia should make that skragling Jerim put his metal up now, or by the time he's finished fucking about, we'll all be as soft bellied as the Ants cowering in their steel skins."

Thorgulsen poured more wine and threw it back as quickly as the first glass. Telvier had killed men for less, and as big as the Guthlander was, a knife in the throat would bleed him out just like any other bloated pig. Alas, now wasn't the time to indulge in such a luscious fantasy. He'd save that one for later. Right now, he had to convince the great fool to go to the feast. Lack of attendance would be noticed.

Thorgulsen waved the glass at him; the crystal looked out of place in his big, ugly paw. "D'you have any ale?"

"Alas, I only have the thirty-gold-crowns-a-bottle Suvian Ruby you're knocking back. Very remiss of me not to have ale, I don't know what I was thinking."

It amused Thorgulsen to see the muscle at the corner of Telvier's eye twitch every time he took a swig of the expensive and rather pleasant wine. Thorgulsen knew full well that it was the good stuff, but it didn't hurt to let the mercenary underestimate his intelligence.

"I'm bored. Let's go kill the princeling; it'll save us a job later." Thorgulsen sucked wine from his braided moustaches and chuckled. Telvier scampered over to the tent flap and peered out nervously.

"I pray you, Thane, please guard your words. There are many strangers wandering through the camps and a tent wall isn't proof against eavesdroppers. Prince Jerim is sensibly biding his time to make sure victory will be certain when we make our move. Didn't your own kinsman suggest you come here to get the measure of the Antians and have a *legitimate* reason to be in Antia?"

The Suvian didn't miss much, he'd give him that. "To the Void with Redbear, Guthani go where they please. Nor do I need to get the measure of any man, woman or beast so long as their blood is red, and I'll wager my weight in gold the Steelskins bleed as red as anyone."

Telvier plucked a lace-trimmed kerchief from his sleeve and coughed.

"Oh, I understand your frustration, my Lord. I too cannot wait until we're wading, knee-deep through the entrails of our enemies, but if Jerim's plan works, the booty will be plentiful and the fighting *easy*. Do not mistake me; I like a good, bloody fight, but I much prefer it when the odds are stacked in my favour. Jerim's plan is sound and will work, so long as our allies play their part."

Thorgulsen thought Jerim's plan was a sack of shit. It didn't say much for Telvier's skill as a strategist if he couldn't see that.

"This subterfuge is pointless, it will end the way these things always end; in blood, shit, and death. We have the advantage of numbers and surprise; we should get on with it before the Ants get wind of our plans."

"Fun though that would be, a bloody civil war, will not achieve the result Prince Jerim is after. He doesn't want to rule people who hate him, it makes them terribly intractable. If he can force his brother to abdicate in his favour with a minimum of bloodshed, so much the better for Prince Jerim and Princess Matia. When the royal couple are happily ensconced in Weyhithe and Redbear strips Cathlan to fund his attempt to take the Dragon Throne, you'll be carried along with him I should think. This way everyone benefits." Telvier grinned.

"You're a bright fellow. You want to watch that."

The Suvian dabbed at his neatly trimmed moustache. "Oh, I do, my Lord, and don't worry about my loyalty or circumspection; you've paid handsomely for both."

Thorgulsen smiled. They both knew that if a better offer came along, Telvier would rip up their contract and stab him with the quill they'd signed it with. It was the only thing he liked about the Suvian; his honest dishonesty—refreshing in a world full of insincere sincerity.

"Asha's paps!" exclaimed Bear.

Talin had been dozing and almost leapt from the tub when his friend burst into the bathhouse.

"I was going to wait for you outside, but life's too short. Surely even a prince has only the same amount of skin to scrub as an ordinary man? Or are you doing more than bathing in there?" She grinned and slammed the door behind her. "Sest's teeth, I could feel myself aging waiting for you to finish sudding yourself. No need to reach for a towel—the water's murky enough to hide the crown jewels, not that I haven't seen your gems before. D'you remember that night near Pridmore when we had to run for our lives?"

Talin groaned. "How could I possibly forget when you never miss an opportunity to remind me?"

"I'll never forget your lily white arse glowing in the moonlight as we ran through the woods."

"Hello, Iris. Yes, nice to see you too. Yes I'm very well thank you, and yourself? No, please don't stand on ceremony, come in, and make yourself at home."

Bear flopped onto a bench, black curls tumbling around her face. She was laughing, but she looked tired, dark circles ringed her eyes. "Do forgive my shocking manners. I'm weak with hunger, having ridden for days to get here, *at your bidding."*

"Hunger? The day you ever go hungry, Iris Berwick, is the day I sprout wings and fly. You want to be careful; you're getting awfully broad in the beam. Think of your poor horses."

She laughed. "I don't want to worry you, Highness, but I think there's a dead maggot in the bath. Oh, no, wait a minute, it's your cock."

"Where are the guards when I need them?" Talin demanded, looking around the empty bathhouse.

Bear unfastened her puce coloured cloak, and tossed it on the bench. "They died of old age waiting for you to finish polishing your sceptre."

He raised an eyebrow. "Speaking of royalty, you didn't exactly rush when I summoned you. I'm sure that's treason."

"Aye, well, I would have come sooner, but Mama and Papa wanted me to spend some time managing my estates. All rather dull really, but they're far more likely to behead me for being disobedient than you are, which is why I'm late. But enough of my hardships, I'm here now and it is time to make merry! I met a lovely brother and sister on the road. They're simply dying to meet you in about… an hour from now. So if you wouldn't mind hurrying up, Highness. If we're quick we can enjoy a bite to eat, a bit of a fumble, and still be fashionably on time for the feast, although, gods know where my trunks have got to." She tossed him a towel.

He'd sent for Bear because she was his best friend, and he could always rely on her support and, upon occasion, her advice. Only, now she was here he wasn't so sure it was a good idea. She'd never had a serious relationship in her life and going on current form, probably never would. She could either lend a sympathetic ear or laugh in his face. He got out of the tub and started to dry himself.

"As much as I appreciate you setting me up, I'm not interested."

"What's this? Prince Talin passing up the chance for a bit of fun with a lusty country lass? Are you ill? I assure you, she and her brother are very easy on the eye. Here—have a bit of this, it'll loosen you up." Bear pulled a small silver box from her doublet and tossed it to Talin.

He caught it and flicked open the lid. The familiar smell of Pel tickled his nostrils. Inside were four gold-dusted pellets of the drug. It smelled rich and earthy, and woke old lusts in him. There had been a time when he would have taken two pellets and no one would have been able to guess he'd taken any at all. Now just the smell of the stuff was making him feel light-headed. That's why Bear looked tired—too much Pel. He snapped the lid closed and threw the box back.

"Not for me, thanks. I'm limiting my vices to alcohol and chasing unobtainable women."

Bear shook her head, took out a golden ball of Pel and popped it in her mouth. "As you wish, although I don't approve of either. I take it you're mooning over Captain Stenna?"

"You do too much of that." He hadn't wanted to say it, but she'd pricked him. His affection for Alyda wasn't trivial. Bear's smile faltered.

"Now, now, Mother, you know a little bit of Pel keeps me calm, or would you prefer it if I lost my temper? That always goes well, doesn't it?"

"You could just do with taking less—you look worn out."

She snorted. "I can handle it, I have a strong constitution. Anyway, enough of me; tell me about your unobtainable woman."

He let her change the subject. Perhaps she was right, perhaps Pel didn't affect her like it did other people, or perhaps it was an argument that would have to wait for another time.

"She likes me, I can tell, but she won't let me get near. I'm at a loss."

"She's a Royal Guard; perhaps she isn't impressed by the title? Maybe you should go for a lower rank, if you've got a taste for warrior women all of a sudden."

"You can be such a dolt, Bear. It's not the type—it's her. I can't close my eyes without seeing her. It's driving me to madness. She's always in my thoughts, I—"

"Alright, alright, Asha's paps, I get it. You're love-sick."

"In the worst way," he said and finished dressing.

"I can see why; she has a fair countenance, long, shapely legs, a curvaceous behind, and nice dugs. I might try for her myself. Perhaps that's it—rather than a princeling—she might want a lusty warrior like herself. Now don't look so glum. If I do bag her, I promise I'll let you watch." She grinned mischievously.

Talin wasn't amused, it was probably the Pel, but damn it, that was no excuse to trample over his feelings. "Have a care, Lady Berwick."

"Sweet Asha's orbs, I'm being *'Lady Berwick-ed'*. What have I done wrong?" She asked. Her face a picture of innocence.

"I'm serious. If you can't be helpful, you can go."

She threw up her hands. "Alright, alright, I won't move on the Captain. You saw her first, and in truth, she scares me. Besides, there are plenty of other pretty things here and all at the mercy of my god-given charm. It would be unfair to take from my oldest and dearest friend, who, had it not been for a lucky accident of birth, would have probably died a virgin."

Talin threw his towel at her. She ducked and it hit the wall with a wet *splat*. "If I didn't know better, I'd swear you were the heir to the throne and I merely the hanger-on."

"Yes, I know what you mean," she muttered, as she examined her cloak. "I'll tell you what I'll do; I'll speak with her friends, find out as much as there is to know about her. What she likes to eat, what her favourite colour is, all that stuff. Let's see if we can't come up with a way to get you into her breeches." She raised her hand as Talin was about to tell her not to bother. "No, don't thank me, Highness. You can make me official wine taster to the King when you're on the throne, or give me a huge castle and fill it with gorgeous servants. By the way, do you have a spare room in your quarters? We can't possibly share; your snoring is really quite awful."

She picked up the towel and used it to rub at a stain on her cloak. While she was busy Talin filled a bucket from the tub of cooling water.

"Here Bear, let me help you with that," he said, and tipped the bucket over her.

The polished oak tables stretched the length of the Great Hall. They were not laden with dainty or exotic dishes; the food was simple, wholesome fare, well prepared and plentiful. It was a banquet to feed warriors and lacked neither quality nor quantity. If nothing else, Thorgulsen couldn't fault the Steelskins' hospitality.

He was sitting with Telvier and their Lieutenants. Bethanglyn was dancing with a lad whose face had turned as red as his hair. The boy didn't seem to know what to do as Beth swayed against him. She occasionally threw a glance over her shoulder, just to make sure he was watching. The Thane sipped his ale, and feigned disinterest in his wife's antics, but they were duly noted. *Let her play her little games.* One day he would plant his seed in her belly and that would kill her powers. Then she would have to cover her auburn locks and stay at home like a good wife. There'd be no more air fucking with Antian milksops then.

He stopped watching his wife and turned his attention to the knights of the Hammer. They were easy to pick out of the crowd, not only because of their scarlet surcoats and long braids, but they were also the biggest warriors in the hall. Even the women were a good head taller than most of the men present. Picked for what they looked like rather than skill, like prize cattle. He smiled to himself. *Let them graze, the wolves are watching.*

Telvier leaned across to him, gold teeth shining amid the black. "Alas, Prince Talin will not be taking part in the tourney."

Thorgulsen wasn't surprised. "These Ants are as soft as horse shit. If a Guthani princeling didn't take the chance to prove his worth it would bring shame on his entire house."

The Suvian quirked an eyebrow. "Perhaps, Thane, but not three months ago, these particular knights taught my countrymen a hard lesson in fighting that they will not soon forget. There are many Suvian families in mourning because of these 'soft' knights. Even the Brotherhood of the Redemption has declared them demonically possessed, which is high praise in some circles. Don't make the same mistake as my fellow Suvians, Thane. Do not underestimate them."

"They may have plucked a few peacocks, but they'll find Guthani hirths more than a match."

The mercenary stiffened. Thorgulsen took a swig of ale, content for now to watch the cattle.

Jamie wasn't sure how he'd ended up dancing with her. One minute he was making his way through the crowd, the next he was been dragged off by the Guthani. As pleasurable as it was having her lithe body pressed against him, he was relieved when the musicians took a break and he was able to disengage himself.

As he made his escape, a weighty arm fell across his shoulders. Startled, he looked round expecting to see an angry cuckold. It wasn't, it was the Prince's lover; Lady Iris Berwick. She clamped her arm around his shoulders and steered him over to an empty table where she pushed him into a chair against the wall and sat down beside him, trapping him behind her huge skirts.

"Here you go," she said and pushed a flagon of ale towards him. "You look like you've worked up quite a thirst."

"Er, thank you." He took a long drink, confused by the sudden interest he was receiving from the most unexpected quarters. Confused, but not complaining. Lady Berwick wasn't as pretty as the Guthani, she was perhaps a little square in the jaw and broad in the back for his tastes, but her breasts were magnificent. After a moment he realised he was staring at them and forced himself to look up at her face. Her eyes were light brown, almost golden, not that he could see much of them; her pupils were huge. When she breathed he caught a strong whiff of Pel.

She coughed. "I said: I know your brothers."

"Er...yes. Me too."

"While our parents argued about taxes and the state of the kingdom we court brats were sent for lessons together—etiquette, fencing, history and gods help us, dancing. I'm not sure who had the least fun, our parents or us. How are your brothers doing? I haven't seen them in years?"

"They're well, but I don't see them much either. Thom is in Suvia—with the ambassador in Toresta."

She smiled. "Ah, that sounds like him. How's your Captain? You must see more of her than you do your family."

The ale was beginning to take its toll and he let his gaze drift down to her breasts.

"She's well—and yes, I suppose I do."

"Is she still seeing that handsome bastard, Rufus Corvinius?" Lady Berwick beckoned to a page who was weaving through the crowd with a jug of ale.

Jamie had to catch himself before the ale made an honest man of him. He was a squire and had to show respect for all senior knights, even a piece of dog shit like Corvinius.

"I don't believe …I mean, I don't know, my Lady."

Lady Berwick smiled and took the jug from the page. Despite his weak protestations, she re-filled Jamie's mug.

"They are nice aren't they?" She flicked her gaze down to her chest. Jamie almost choked on his drink.

She laughed. "Don't be embarrassed, if I didn't want people to look at them I'd cover them up."

He was about to mumble an apology when someone put their hand on his shoulder.

"I see now why you ran away, sir knight."

He immediately recognised the voice and the musky perfume. They both sent a thrill of excitement running down his neck, straight to his groin. Lady Berwick's lips parted in a languid smile.

"I cannot imagine what possessed him to leave such a delightful companion. Please, join us. I'm Iris by the way, but my friends call me Bear."

The Guthlander slid onto Jamie's knee as light as a whisper, quite the opposite of the solid presence of Lady Berwick. He was either in a really good situation with two attractive women flirting with him, or a really bad situation for the same reason. He took another drink and decided not to think about it.

"Bear? How appropriate. My name is Bethanglyn."

Lady Berwick looked surprised, but then she laughed. "It's awfully hot in here, don't you think? I wonder—would you like to go for a walk? Perhaps, Squire Turlowe could be our guide, show us a thing or two?"

"I'd like that very much," the Guthani purred. She slipped her arm around Jamie's shoulder. "What say you, sir knight?"

If this was a dream Jamie did not want to wake up. He got up and sketched a slightly unsteady bow. "I'd be delighted."

A tented city surrounded the Arth, and the hall was thronged with happy guests. Despite the revelry, Alyda could taste the steel in the air. It was going to be a hard tournament.

Nevenna passed her a mug of ale. "Good thing we enlarged those stands.

"Aye, success in Suvia has brought a few more challengers—all keen to make their names.

"Let 'em try. Have you seen how many Guthlanders there are? There's even a Thane."

"I've seen him." Alyda had marked the Thane the moment he'd walked in. He was as tall as her, but twice as wide, and as cold-eyed as they came. He was sitting next to someone who, by his dress, had to be Suvian. She could just make out his rat-thin face and bright, little eyes peering from beneath an extravagant wig.

"They're an odd couple aren't they," said Nevenna as they surreptitiously eyed the outsiders.

Alyda shrugged. "That's what happens at tournaments, Nev. People come together who'd never meet otherwise." Logical as that sounded; there was something odd about their association.

"Aye. Warriors come together; share food and drink, swap tales and then try to smash each other's brains in." Nev laughed.

"Captain Stenna, there you are." The crowd parted and the Prince stepped forward. He inclined his head to Alyda and Nevenna.

What was I thinking? The realisation that she had been a fool struck her the moment she laid eyes on him. She'd allowed herself to think of him as just another knight, an ordinary man, but he wasn't, and right then the illusion was shattered.

It had been easy to forget he was the heir to the throne when he was out on the practice fields, covered in mud. Tonight he was wearing a fine fillet of gold and his doublet and hose were blood red velvet, embroidered with gold and studded with rubies. He was also wearing the company surcoat, but a single scale does not a dragon make. It wasn't only his attire that marked him out, it was his whole bearing. This was the real Talin, *Prince* Talin, and far beyond the reach of a mere knight.

"Good evening, Highness," she said. Every word felt like lead in her mouth. "Would you care to watch tonight's entertainment?"

"It would be my pleasure, Captain Stenna. Other than Bear's disappearing act, what is the entertainment?"

"We have an earth mage, Highness."

When they were seated, Alyda gave a nod to the robed and hooded mage who was standing in the middle of the hall, waiting for her signal. He raised his hand. The huge candelabras flickered and dimmed to nothing. At the same time, the roaring fires died back to barely glowing embers. An excited murmur rippled through the hall as pages cleared a space around the mysterious figure. Time passed, a few nervous coughs echoed in the darkness.

Alyda thought she saw a light, smaller than a candle flame, appear next to the mage. Fascinated, she watched the light slowly float around him. Before long, dozens, then hundreds, and then what seemed like thousands of tiny, pin pricks of light were swirling around the mage and bathing the hall in a radiant glow.

Alyda had always imagined mages to be imposing individuals who exuded power, and then she'd met Kilner. He was short, and fat; quite a homely fellow, but his skills were undeniably impressive.

The crowd gasped as the lights swirled around him. He flicked his wrist, and a twisted hazel wand appeared in his hand and he began to weave intricate patterns in the air.

The lights were now shining so brightly that people were forced to shield their eyes or look away. The flickering motes flew apart and formed into a half dozen, roughly head-sized spheres that floated above the awed crowd for a few seconds before silently exploding into millions of tiny, gem-like points of light. The mage waved the wand and the lights flew together and formed into giant, shimmering butterflies, glittering dragonflies and exotic birds that flew up to the rafters, before diving down and scattering the thrilled audience.

For the next half hour the magician dazzled them with a myriad of conjured animals, flowers, and mythical beasts, all created out of light and fire. Then, as suddenly as they appeared, they vanished, surprising everyone.

The room was once again plunged into darkness. For a moment there was silence, then the fires roared back to life and the candles sprouted flames. The hall erupted into rapturous applause, only there was no one there to receive it. Like all good magicians, Kilner had vanished.

Alyda was ready for her bed hours before the watch bell rang midnight. When it chimed the twelfth hour, she sighed and poured herself another glass of water. The diehards would carouse into the small hours, particularly those who weren't fighting on the morrow. She on the other hand, had a long day ahead and had completely run out of small talk and the stamina to be talked at. Unfortunately, she couldn't escape. Protocol forbade her to leave before the Prince, and he and his friends showed no signs of retiring.

At least when he was pretending to be a knight she could go to bed when she pleased. As soon as she had the uncharitable thought she regretted it. He'd worked hard to fit in with the Company, walking a narrow path between being a prince and an ordinary knight. He'd done so well that she'd almost forgotten he was the heir to the throne. Tonight, when she saw him with a gold circlet on his brow, surrounded by adoring subjects, she remembered, and now she longed to be elsewhere, away from the laughter and the crowds, and most of all from him.

"The Captain looks bored, wouldn't you say?" Talin asked Nevenna.

Alyda was with one of the local dignitaries. She was nodding in all the right places, but was obviously bored rigid. He empathised.

"Oh no, Highness. That's the Captain's thoughtful face; she's having a wonderful time entertaining your Highness and our other guests." The Lieutenant smiled.

He wasn't convinced. Talin recognised from personal experience the practiced face of diplomatic politeness. He also noticed that Alyda kept stealing furtive glances towards the door.

"Oh, please don't mistake me, Nev. Captain Stenna has been a most polite and attentive host, but I know just what a chore it can be, being pleasant to dozens of strangers who are all desperate to talk to you. It's a particular torture if they also happened to be dull." He laughed; the knight smiled awkwardly, unsure how to respond.

His humour had soured as the evening had worn on and what he'd meant to be a joke had come out sounding sharper than he'd intended. Before the feast he'd resolved to confess how he felt to Alyda. But the moment she'd laid eyes on him, her smile had vanished and she'd spent the rest of the night avoiding him, or being so coldly polite he could have yelled. He caught her eye and beckoned her over, she complied with little enthusiasm.

She saluted stiffly. *This is maddening.* He could smell her perfume, delicate and sweet—the distinct fragrance of Suvian lavender.

"Captain, I must thank you," he gave a nod to Nevenna, "and your Company, for a most splendid evening."

Alyda inclined her head. "I'm pleased you've enjoyed yourself, Highness."

He wanted to take her away somewhere they could be alone, where he could speak honestly and openly, without a bloody audience. Looking at the press of people still waiting to meet him and bore him with their petty anecdotes, he knew that would be impossible. So be it. If he couldn't play the part of suitor, he'd be the chivalrous knight and give Alyda the opportunity to escape.

Talin feigned a yawn. "As enjoyable as tonight has been, I fear I must retire."

Her face brightened. "So soon, Highness?"

That hurt, but he stayed in character. "I'm afraid so, but I've had a wonderful evening."

She bowed respectfully. "Goodnight, Highness."

He saluted Company style. "Goodnight..." He almost said 'Ali' but caught himself. "Captain Stenna."

When the Prince and his entourage had gone, Alyda waited a polite length of time before excusing herself.

Hours later she lay in bed, watching the inky darkness lighten to gloomy grey. Muttering curses, she got up. Damn the man for invading her thoughts and stealing unbidden into her dreams. And damn her stupid self for enjoying it.

Chapter Seven

A cold wind whistled through the shutters but it was warm in the hay, lying between the two naked women…

Morning. Tourney. Jamie sat bolt upright, his heart hammering out of his chest. With a sickening jolt he remembered how one thing had led to another. What had seemed like a fine idea last night could have him thrown in the guardhouse today. He jumped up and began to search through the pile of discarding stockings, petticoats and gowns for *his* clothes. He shouldn't have drunk the wine they'd found, he shouldn't have brought them here. Sweet Asha! He should have thought with the big head, and not the small, but it was too late now. He heard a giggle and looked round to see both women were awake and grinning at him.

"Good morning, Jamie," Bear yawned.

Jamie hid his modesty behind his shirt and backed towards the ladder.

She laughed, "Don't you think it's a bit late to come over all shy?"

"I, er… I have to go. I—" He tripped over the ladder, but managed to grab hold of it as he fell and slow his descent. He landed on his arse with a bump. Cursing, he scooped up his clothes just as the barn door was thrown open.

The Guthlanders didn't wait to be invited; they strode in and began searching the stalls. Jamie struggled into his hose, and made to leave. A grey beard with a face like a badly patched quilt stepped in his way.

"Can I help you?" Jamie asked his heart sinking into the pit of his stomach.

"Depends on who you've been fucking up there." The Guthlander thrust his chin in the direction of the loft where a light drizzle of hay was falling from between the boards. "Best hope it's not who we're looking for, *runt*," Greybeard drawled, "or your little pig pizzle will be coming off, yes?" His two companions moved up either side of him, blocking the way out.

Jamie reached for his sword, and then remembered it was still up in the loft. He cast a glance around the barn. There were a couple of pitchforks leaning against one of the stalls, but he doubted he'd be able to reach them before the Guthlanders were on him.

"It's none of your damn business what I've been doing or with whom," he said with more confidence than he felt, "now get out of my way."

Greybeard gave a throaty chuckle, and took a step towards him. Jamie stood his ground, weight on the balls of his feet. The hay rustled. He turned, praying that he wouldn't see Bethanglyn. It was Bear; she was clutching his sword against her bare chest.

"I can assure you, he's no runt." She grinned and tossed the sword to Jamie.

The Guthlanders laughed. Greybeard said something in their guttural tongue and slapped him on the back before leaving. Jamie was stunned and set for a fight that hadn't happened. Bear let out a filthy laugh.

"What's so funny?" he asked.

"Apparently they think you must be stronger than you look." A slender arm wrapped around Bear's shoulder. "If only they knew the whole of it, eh?" She grinned and rolled back into the hay.

"Dear gods. I pray they never do," Jamie muttered before charging off to find the Captain.

"Where have you been?" Alyda couldn't wait to hear his explanation.

Jamie looked as tired as she felt. She shook her head at Polyn who was helping her on with her cloak. Polyn did the same; obviously enjoying seeing her senior squirm. Alyda looked him over. He was armed and armoured, ready for the junior's competition but his surcoat was rumpled, his belt twisted, and he had straw in his hair. She should throw the book at him, and by the look on his face that's what he expected.

"I overslept, Captain, too much wine. May I report to the parade ground? The squires' melee is about to start."

Alyda was caught somewhere between amused and annoyed. "You've got a brass neck, Squire Turlowe."

"Yes, Captain. Sorry, Captain."

"Don't worry, Jamie; it's nothing we can't cure. You may not head over to the parade ground—you may head over to the stables and help muck out for the rest of the day."

He snapped to attention and saluted, but she could see he was devastated. *As he should be.*

"If you're late tomorrow, you'll be cleaning out the privies on your own—with a spoon."

"Yes, Captain…shall I report here tomorrow, Captain, or to the stables?"

"Neither. Go straight to the parade ground and sign in for the melee. You're too old to compete with the juniors, and I can think of no better punishment than letting you get a good beating at the hands of the senior knights. Dismissed, Squire Turlowe."

When Bethanglyn walked in, Thorgulsen composed a bored expression. He didn't want to look like he'd been waiting for her. Yawning, she poured herself a mug of ale. He resisted the urge to jump up and knock her across the tent.

She threw herself onto a couch, a lazy smile on her lips. "Aren't you going to ask where I've been?"

He shook his head. "I know where you've been, cunt. You reek of sex."

Her smile broadened. "What if I told you the spirits had commanded me to do it? To learn about our enemy, flesh to flesh, blood to blood?"

"I'd say you were a lying whore." A cold breeze suddenly blew through the tent, knocking over candles and scattering papers. He reached for the knife in his belt. Beth smirked. As suddenly as it had come, the wind died.

"Don't let jealousy make you stupid, Kasper. Powerful forces are at work here."

Thorgulsen spat, it was only a breeze, but it didn't hurt to find out what the mad bitch had been up to. "And what do your spirits say we should do about these *powerful forces?*"

"They say if you want to die in your bed, surrounded by your grandchildren, you should kill the Red Knight tomorrow. Don't worry, I'll point him out. Pay heed, Kasper. I may be a mad bitch, but the spirits never lie."

On the second day of the tournament, the sky was quilted with layers of fat grey clouds, but the threat of rain hadn't deterred the crowds. If anything, there were more people there than there had been yesterday. It still irked Talin that he wasn't going to compete in the grand melee, but he could cheer Bear on, if she managed to get ready in time. His friend was crashing about her tent searching for something while her pages ducked around her, trying to fasten her armour.

"Damn, but this armour has shrunk since I wore it last," she grumbled. "I need some new harness; the varlet who made this was second rate in skill, but a grand-master when it came to charging for his work."

"Don't blame the armourer, blame over-indulgence."

Bear snorted. "That's rich, coming from you."

Talin laughed while the pages valiantly tried to make both halves of her cuirass meet. After much pulling and tugging, Bear shooed them away and took a deep breath before gesturing impatiently for them to try again. This time when they pulled the back and breast plates together, the two halves met with ease.

"There, a perfect fit—if I don't breath. So how much gold have you bet on me to win, and do I get a cut?" She asked, testing her range of movement with a few twists and lunges.

"Alas, dear friend, I haven't made any wagers." He raised his hands to silence her protest. "I must remain impartial. I assure you if I was able to bet, you would certainly be my choice…for second."

Bear planted her fists on her hips and glared at him. "You are joking?"

Talin wasn't sure if she was being seriously angry or playfully angry. Either might result in something being thrown at him, and he got ready to duck. "It has been a while since you competed. I think that Guthani Thane might get the better of you, unless you cheat."

Bear snorted. "The one with the stupidly large axe and stunningly beautiful wife? You know what they say about those who wield oversized weapons."

"They're really strong?"

"They have small genitalia. Although, there must be something about him to have a wife like Beth. Now she's a woman worth risking my neck for, even if she is a heathen witch—or possibly because of it."

"I suppose she's fair enough, if you like that kind of thing."

"You only *suppose* she's fair? Why, her beauty would make the Fey jealous. Oh, I forgot." Bear gestured for the pages to leave and sat down beside him. "How is wooing Lady Ali progressing? Spare no details, I'm like a priestess. You can, nay, *must* tell me everything."

Whenever Talin thought about Alyda, his stomach sank. "There's nothing to tell." He got up and paced the tent. "Captain Stenna isn't the kind of woman to be wooed, not even by a prince."

Bear shook her head. She did a passable impersonation of someone who cared, but he could see in her eyes there was no real sympathy or understanding. He wasn't angry, he wasn't even surprised; she'd always been the same, although the Pel made it worse. The damn stuff blunted the feelings of even occasional users, and Bear lived on it.

She got up and flexed her shoulders. For all her complaining the fine blued armour fit her perfectly. "I'm sorry to hear that, but I've seen the way she looks at you, I've *smelled* her excitement when you're near. No-one can hide that, believe me." She gave him a wicked grin. "I think there's conflict between the Lady's desire and the Captain's duty; one that a determined suitor might force if he'd a mind to."

Talin shrugged. "Perhaps, or perhaps I have to accept that this woman is beyond me. Anyway, enough—I'm tired of being miserable. I must go and be bored by our guests."

"Ah, yes. I saw the Khusani caravans arrive earlier. Those veils quite provoke my imagination. Did they bring any more toys with them this trip? I'll never forget that bird: chirruping and tweeting and flapping its little brass wings. Such a marvellous construction, so cunningly wrought. It must be magic—nothing made of metal could sing as sweetly as a real bird."

"I'm sure they will have brought more toys to beguile the court, but the bird wasn't magical. Mother had it examined by mages; it's just a clever toy."

Bear gave him a sidelong look. "I've heard they only cover themselves from head to toe when they're in foreign parts, but back in Khusan—Nara in particular—they walk around naked. Do you think there's any truth in it?"

Talin sighed. "I think you're very shallow, Lady Berwick, and please don't ask them. We enjoy very favourable trade relations with the Narans and little attention from their corsairs, so don't go opening your mouth and spoiling it."

"I'm not shallow; I'm interested in the customs of other nations, particularly those who might go about naked. Now, go make cow eyes at the Captain while I get ready. I've forty warriors to thrash before this evening's revels can commence."

"You're not thinking of…?" Talin let the sentence hang unfinished, but Bear knew what he meant. Her face darkened.

"I told you, Highness, never again. I've kept my vow. Gods know it hasn't always been easy." She brightened. "Anyway, I've seen the competition. I don't think there's any need to get…*worked up*. Why, it's hardly worth the effort of pouring myself into this damn armour. Don't worry I'll put on a good show for your guests, like the devoted friend I am. Now where did I put my gauntlets…?"

Growing up at Bear's Tooth, surrounded by mercenaries Alyda had learnt to speak Tamalak, Hadami, and Antian with equal fluency and she'd also picked up smatterings of a dozen other languages and dialects. Alas, Khusani wasn't one of them. It was therefore a relief to find that the Princess spoke excellent Antian. The letter from Commander Trease stated that she must show the Naran delegation every courtesy. Apparently, the Princess was interested in Antian culture and had expressed a desire to see a tournament before she returned to her homeland.

'Interested' wasn't the word Alyda would have used. Since her arrival, the Princess had asked a constant stream of questions. She wanted to know about everything. Nothing was too inconsequential, from what they fed the horses, to the type of stone used to build the keep. By the time it came to take their seats, Alyda's jaw ached from talking so much.

"The warriors will line up, twenty on either side of the rope, eighty feet apart. When the signal is given, the rope will drop and the melee will commence." Alyda felt like a bloody tutor.

The Princess, clad in billowing robes of orange silk, nodded and pointed to one of the knights. "Not all of them carry lances; surely they are at a disadvantage?"

Alyda shook her head. "Not after the first charge when many drop the longer weapons in favour of those that are easier to wield. It's a personal choice. The winner is the one who ends up with the most tokens, not the one who unseats the most knights."

"Are many killed?"

"Very few, Satvani Rhami." Alyda hoped she'd got the name and the title the right way round. "'Tis a dangerous game and accidents happen, but thankfully few are fatal."

"With all due respect, Captain Stenna, I find that hard to believe given what I have already seen. I think some warriors, if not already dead, will be maimed by the injuries they have received in other, supposedly less violent games than the melee. It seems, if you will forgive me…a little wasteful."

Every Courtesy. Alyda gritted her teeth and smiled, taking a moment to work out how best to frame an answer that wouldn't offend.

"I can see how the games may seem so to someone unfamiliar with our ways, but it is a traditional way of honing martial skills without waging war, 'tis healthy, good natured competition."

As soon as the words had left her mouth, fate conspired to make her a liar. From the tilt yard came the sound of a bone crunching collision, accompanied by a chorus of gasps and groans from the spectators. The Satvani flinched, her bodyguard reached for the jewelled hilt of her sword. Alyda saw the Princess give a tiny flick of her finger, the gesture enough to stay the bodyguard's hand.

"I think our ideas of what constitutes 'healthy competition' differ greatly, Captain Stenna." The Satvani lifted her veil and took a sip of water. Alyda could see why some thought the Hadami had originally come from Khusan. The woman had very similar features to her mother's people, save that her skin was much darker. Over her shoulder, Alyda spotted Prince Talin making his way through the crowd on his way to the stand.

When he arrived, Alyda got up and saluted. "Your Highness, may I introduce the Satvani Rhami, of the Kingdom of Nara." At least now the Satvani could direct her questions to him, and leave her alone.

"It's an honour to meet you at last, Satvani Rhami," said Talin, smiling politely. "I hope your business has been successful, and your visit to our kingdom a pleasant one."

"Thank you, Prince Talin. Business has indeed been very profitable for all concerned, both in the kingdom and Cathlan."

"Cathlan is in the kingdom," said Talin leaving no room for debate.

"Ah, yes of course, forgive me, Prince Talin," said the Satvani, "my Antian is very poor."

Alyda could feel the tension between the two princes. She preferred an open, stand-up fight; it was so much cleaner than politicking someone to death. Just then the Marshals took up their positions on the parade ground.

"I believe the contest is about to start, Highnesses," she said.

"Is magic permitted during the melee, Captain Stenna?" the Satvani asked.

Not more bloody questions. "No it isn't, Satvani. Void magic is outlawed here as it is everywhere, and for the purposes of tournaments, Fey items and earth magic are also forbidden."

"But how would you know if one of the knights had a charm or talisman on their person, surely earth magic is a subtle art and difficult to detect?"

Here we go. Alyda knew where this was leading. "Have you heard of the Arth Wards?" She asked the Satvani, knowing full well the answer.

Handy things those veils, but not foolproof; they allowed a person to hide a smirk, but not the twinkle in their eyes.

"Why, yes I have. They were created by the Djinn I believe, to protect your wonderful castles."

"Djinn?" queried Alyda. "Do you mean Fey?"

"Yes, I believe I do. I wonder—if Prince Talin would allow it—would it be possible to see a demonstration of the Wards?"

Talin hesitated for a moment, but then inclined his head politely to the Satvani. "Of course, Satvani. Captain Stenna, if you wouldn't mind?"

Alyda removed the Silver Spur and offered it to the Satvani. The moment it was in the Naran woman's hand, a shrill ringing filled the air and the Spur began to glow. The noise seemed to be coming from everywhere, so loud that the very air vibrated. The Satvani dropped the Spur. Alyda was ready for her reaction, and caught it before it hit the ground.

Much to everyone's relief, the ringing stopped as soon as it was back in her possession. Alyda waved away the knights who were rushing over to the stand. As for the Satvani, it was hard to gauge what she was thinking, but hopefully the fact that she wouldn't meet her gaze, indicated a measure of embarrassment that might curb her curiosity.

The Satvani's bodyguard was less reticent. She was staring intently at Alyda, her pale eyes narrowed to slits. Alyda didn't need to see her face to know what she was thinking. Her ready stance declared her hostility most eloquently. Alyda smiled.

"That's how we know no one has been foolish enough to bring in any magical items, or cast any enchantments within the Arth, without permission from Prince Talin or myself," said Alyda as she let the Spur flow around her boot heel.

"How fascinating," said the Satvani. "May I see the Ward?"

Alyda looked to Talin. He nodded for her to continue. "I'm afraid not, Satvani. It isn't something you can actually see; it's part of the fabric of the Arth itself." *And even if it wasn't, I wouldn't show it to you.*

"I understand," said the Satvani.

The competitors lined up, twenty on either side of the parade ground. Jamie was excited and determined to make a good show in his first senior competition; war was one thing, but doing well in the Melee could make his reputation.

Squires made last-minute adjustments to their knight's harness and weapons. Polyn handed him his sword, and wished him luck before she retreated to the earth bank. He saw that Iris Berwick was on the same side. The noblewoman was waving to the cheering crowds, but what drew his attention was the Guthland Warleader on the other side of the parade ground. The big Thane was with three other warriors, and his wife. Jamie's heart skipped a beat when he saw her. She looked over, gave him a slow smile and pointed him out to her husband. The Thane's jaw tightened. He eyed Jamie coldly and pointed him out to his comrades. *Dear gods.*

Jamie felt sick. *She's told him.* He didn't understand why she would do that, did she want him to die? Jamie looked to the stands. The Captain was talking with Prince Talin and some Narans, oblivious to the trouble he was in, and why wouldn't she be? He hadn't exactly bragged about tumbling the woman. He looked back at the Guthlanders. The Thane was glaring at him, Bethanglyn had gone. Jamie took a deep breath. So the Guthlander knew that he and his wife had fucked. To the Void with him, if he wanted a fight, Jamie would give him one. Resolved, he locked down his visor.

The senior Marshal bowed to the Prince. Talin nodded and when all the competitors were ready, the dividing rope was dropped. The crowd let out a thunderous cheer and the combatants charged each other.

Alyda missed this. She could take or leave the joust, but the Grand Melee made her heart quicken and long for more carefree times.

The early clashes were carnage, the fighting furious and dirty, much to the delight of the crowd. Alliances were made and broken on the spur of the moment. Two or more warriors would work together to unseat another and when the deed was done, would straightaway turn on each other. Tokens were taken and handed to seconds, who shouted encouragement, warnings, and insults from the safety of the earth bank. When the fighting permitted, they would race onto the field, dodging flying hooves, to gather dropped weapons and armour, or occasionally, to fight each other.

Alyda was finding it hard not to leap to her feet and roar her knights on; the enthusiasm of the crowd was infectious.

After the initial blistering exchanges, the group of forty was quickly whittled down to twenty, then fifteen. By this stage fatigue was beginning to take its toll on the warriors and their mounts, and soon only ten remained.

Alyda was pleased to see that three of the remaining fighters were hers, including Jamie. Bear Berwick was also still in contention, as was a knight from the Anvil who she didn't recognise. Of the five other fighters, two were independent knights and, surprisingly, three were Guthlanders. Althus would be happy that one of his had got this far and completely unbearable if she won. That possibility was crushed when the knight was knocked from her horse by a blow to the head that made the entire crowd wince. All hostilities between the knights of the Hammer were temporarily put aside as they took it upon themselves to avenge their fellow Guard and ride at the Guthani who'd dropped her. Their partisan reaction didn't go unnoticed by the Satvani.

"I thought it was every warrior for themselves, Captain Stenna?"

"Alliances will naturally form from time to time, but I assure you, by the end only one warrior will remain."

Despite her words she was proud that the Guards were looking out for each other.

The tide of battle turned with every breath. Alyda noticed that Talin was watching Bear Berwick intently, while trying to maintain polite interest in the whole melee. Her own composure was tested when Lady Berwick came up behind one of her knights grabbed his token while he was fighting one of the Guthlanders.

Rather than engage individually, the Guthlanders were openly working together. Alyda watched two more knights fall to their combined attack. She'd always thought the Guthani were undisciplined rabble, but after this she'd have to revise her opinion, they were good. Two of the three Guthlanders were using blunted spears, lighter than lances they were excellent weapons for punching riders out of saddles. Their Thane had chosen to fight with a broad-headed battle axe. Alyda knew from painful experience that it was a good weapon against armoured foes. Even with a blunted edge, a heavy axe could crush armour and break bones.

Toran, a Lieutenant from Alyda's command lance, spurred her mount at the Thane. He saw her, and calmly tucked a token he'd just taken into his belt. He wasn't quick, but his timing was impeccable. At the last possible moment, he twisted at the waist and swayed back in the saddle. Toran's sword whistled harmlessly past his face. The Guthlander's return swing caught her on the forearm. The axe skidded off her vambrace but there was enough power in the blow to send the knight's sword spinning from her grasp. She yelled and grabbed her arm. As she passed, the Thane snatched the token hanging from her saddle and held it aloft for all to see. For the first time in two years, Alyda wanted to be out there.

While she'd been watching the encounter between Toran and the Thane, Berwick had taken the token of another of the Hammer. The noblewoman rode past the stand, waving and blowing kisses to the cheering masses.

"The warrior in the blue armour doesn't appear to be taking the contest entirely seriously," said the Satvani.

"She's paying more attention than she appears to be Satvani," said the Prince. "She just likes people to think she's an idiot."

"Ah, she is lulling her enemies into a false sense of security?"

Talin raised an eyebrow. "Something like that."

While Berwick was playing to the crowd, the Guthlanders split up. Two rode wide, flanking Jamie. The Thane hung back. He was waiting to see which way her squire would go before committing himself. Their caution was a compliment to his skill, but she was concerned for her squire. Jamie was a brave and skilled fighter but this was his first senior melee, and the Guthlanders were taking the contest very seriously, too seriously some might say.

Jamie reined in his horse; the excited animal pranced on the spot, fired up and eager to run. When the destrier looked like she was about to burst, Jamie kicked her on and charged—straight at the Thane. When he was about half a horse length away, and much to everyone's surprise, Jamie dived at the Thane and tackled him out of the saddle.

"He has an interesting style," said Talin as Jamie and the Thane crashed to the ground.

"I have no idea where he learnt that," said Alyda.

Jamie landed on top of the Guthlander and punched him in the face. Metal rang against metal. Alyda felt her own fists bunch as Jamie hit him again before jumping to his feet and lunging for the token hanging from the Guthlander's saddle. *Nicely done.* Just as his fingers were about to close around the ribbon, the Thane's pony shied away. Before Jamie could try again, Thorgulsen grabbed his ankle and wrenched him off his feet. Jamie went down. The Guthlander dropped on his back with both knees, flattening the smaller man.

Jamie sprawled flat, winded. Thorgulsen got up, dragged Jamie to his knees by his surcoat and then punched him to the ground. Neither Thorgulsen nor the other Guthani made any attempt to take Jamie's token, even though his horse was standing nearby. The Thane retrieved his axe.

All eyes were on the Guthlander as he advanced on Jamie. So it came as a surprise when first one, and then the other Guthani were taken out of the contest.

Yelling a wild battle cry, Bear Berwick charged her horse into the side of one of the stout Guthland ponies, almost knocking the poor beast to the ground with her larger courser. The rider was thrown sideways and helped the rest of the way out of the saddle by a sharp jab from the lance Berwick had picked up.

The other Guthlander cast her spear at the noble-woman, but it flew wide. With barely a pause, Berwick returned the compliment and threw her lance—like a jav-elin. It hit the hirth square in the chest, punching her off her horse. The cheering died down to a stunned murmur.

"I haven't seen that before either," said Alyda. She looked questioningly at Talin. He avoided her gaze.

While Bear finished the hirth, Jamie managed to get to his knees. Thorgulsen rammed the butt of his axe into the squire's gut. He doubled, gasping for breath.

Alyda jumped up. "Marshall!" she shouted.

The Marshal nodded, and set off running across the parade ground, shouting for the Thane to desist at once. Thorgulsen either didn't hear or didn't care. He raised his axe above his head.

"Is this is normal?" The Satvani asked.

"No, it bloody isn't! Run damn you, stop him!" Alyda bellowed at the Marshal, furious that she was trapped in the stands and unable to help.

Jamie's head lolled forward. The axe whistled down.

Bear vaulted off her horse and charged towards the Guthlander. Alyda took in the distance between them. It was too far...

Impossible. Like the rest of the crowd, Alyda watched in amazement as Bear covered the ground between her and the Guthlander faster than was humanly possible. Skidding to a halt, she caught the axe-shaft, the blade inches from Jamie's neck. The crowd went wild and let out a cheer so loud, it scared the birds to flight. Bear grinned at the Thane who was struggling to wrest his axe from her grasp.

With her free hand, Berwick tore off his helm, and kissed him, full on the mouth. Spluttering, he snatched his axe from her and stumbled away.

Before the situation got out of hand, a crowd of Marshals came between them. The noblewoman and the Thane were escorted off the field in opposite directions. Bear was laughing and waving. The Thane was raging at the officials, and promising bloody murder. Semi-conscious, Jamie was carried off by Polyn and some of the other squires.

"Is this...?" asked the Satvani.

"No, it isn't." Alyda looked pointedly at Talin.

The veneer of innocence was almost flawless, but they both knew what Bear had done was beyond mortal skill. Alyda didn't need to ask why the Ward hadn't sounded, the flush in his cheeks told her. She was torn. Bear Berwick had just saved Jamie's life—by cheating.

After the shouting died down, tokens were counted and Thorgulsen was declared the winner. His temper had reduced to a vicious simmer by then, but he was still inclined to tell the cheating bastards where they could shove their prize. Beth and the Suvian begged him not to. Apparently, a show of good faith was required after almost killing the Captain of the Hammer's squire. Just to shut them up, he agreed.

Grubby peasants spilled onto the parade ground, all jostling for a view of the prize giving. Thorgulsen watched the other warriors file in front of the Antian Prince and his sycophants.

Bethanglyn fastened the clasp of his wolf fur cloak.

"There, now go—they're waiting," she urged.

"Don't rush me woman, the whelp can wait, and I'm in no hurry to get close to a filthy Searskin." Thorgulsen made the sign of the horns when he eyed the veiled figure standing beside the Prince.

"Aye. Just look at those beetle black eyes. You can tell she's laughing at us, even though she hides behind a veil. She finds our shame amusing," said Bethanglyn.

Thorgulsen growled. "A few hours in the company of my hirths would cure the sand demon of her insolence."

He made his way across the parade ground; the crowd of pig-eyed Antians parted before him. He smiled, knowing full well it was not a pleasant sight. Up close, the Prince had some bearing, he might have been fit to be a hirth, albeit one from a small, outlying stead where the pickings were thin. It was the woman at his shoulder who breathed the threat of steel.

The Captain of the Hammer stood eye to eye with him; her gaze hard and calculating. He knew the look. It was the same one that greeted him whenever he caught sight of his reflection. There was a challenge in that stare; one he'd be more than happy to call her on.

"Congratulations, Thane Thorgulsen," said Prince Talin as he handed him the prize.

Thorgulsen noted the lack of enthusiasm in the King's get. He grunted his acceptance. The 'prize' was a cast silver statuette of a stag. The only good thing about it was that it had weight enough to stave in a skull. Alas, the cunt in the blue armour was nowhere to be seen, and neither was that little, red haired bastard. He'd catch up with both of them sooner or later and finish what they'd started. Stretching their hides across his shield, and hanging their scalps from his battle standard would be a more fitting prize than the poorly fashioned piece of shit they'd given him.

When he returned to camp, he found Telvier waiting for him in his tent. Bethanglyn was not. The mercenary must have caught the drift of his foul mood, and was swift to agree that he'd been grievously insulted by the Antians.

"No mortal could have done what she did, not without the aid of magic. It was outrageous! The Prince or the Captain—probably both, must have been in on the deception."

Thorgulsen threw the stag on the table. "Like my wife, you have a gift for telling me that which I already know."

"Forgive me Thane; 'tis just that my sense of fair play has been grievously offended."

"I doubt that."

Telvier's lips stretched into a sly smile. "I have an idea how you might be avenged on them, *and* advance our other scheme at the same time."

"Does it involve killing any of those underhanded bastards?"

Telvier smiled. "Perhaps, at the very least you'll get to destroy their reputation. Honour means more than life to these soft headed fools, it will be a fair kick in their morale. Trust me, I have studied our enemy."

Thorgulsen snatched up his axe from where it was leaning against the table and smashed it down on the stag. The statue and the table exploded in a mess of silver and splinters.

Thorgulsen smiled. "It's a start I suppose."

After presenting the savage with his prize, the Prince went to watch the final of the joust. Bear Berwick had vanished and Jamie was in the infirmary, with, thankfully, nothing worse than a sore head and a cracked rib. Alyda would have liked to have a word with all of them, probably several, and none of them nice. Ruining the tournament's reputation was one thing—trying to kill her squire was quite another.

The joust was the last competition of the tournament, but the Satvani insisted on leaving without watching it. Duty bound, Alyda had to escort the Naran to her waiting caravan. It was an unexpectedly sudden departure, but she was glad to see the back of the Narans, particularly the Satvani and her incessant questions.

When they reached the huge canopied wagons, Alyda bowed. If she got this over with quickly, she might be able to catch the end of the joust. To her surprise, the Princess threw her arms around her waist and hugged her.

"Thank you for your hospitality, Ali," said the Satvani.

"Er…Thank you, Highness." Alyda replied, not sure if she should pry the woman off her or just wait until she was finished. The Captain of the Hammer wasn't in the habit of hugging strangers. After far too long, the Satvani let her go.

"Forgive my familiarity, Captain, but I feel I know you as well now, as I shall in the future."

Something hadn't translated from Naran to Antian, but Alyda let it pass. She just wanted to get rid of her. "Thank you, Highness. It's been a pleasure to meet you."

"Even though I have bored you with all my questions?"

Alyda was about to deny the truth, but the Satvani giggled and patted her arm.

"No need to answer, Captain Stenna, I own my faults. When you visit Nara, I will repay your patience, and your kindness."

Now Alyda was really confused. "Thank you, Satvani, but I don't think I'll have the liberty to travel to your homeland. A knight's time is not their own." *Which is why I'm here, and not watching the joust.*

The Satvani shook her head. "I am quite sure you will come, Captain Stenna. Zuharan al Nara has seen it, and he is seldom mistaken."

"I'm afraid I do not recall meeting the gentleman," said Alyda.

"You haven't, yet. My Lord is in Nara, he told me about you before I left."

Just go along with it. Alyda smiled politely.

The Satvani laughed. "I see by your face that I shall be leaving you with a mystery. Until we meet again, Captain Stenna. May the spirits bless you, and guard you in the darkness."

Alyda watched the Satvani's caravan rumble out of the Arth, the Satvani's odd prediction lurking like a shadow in the back of her mind. When they'd gone, she set off to the tilt yard. She hadn't gone very far when she met Nevenna coming the other way.

"I've missed it, haven't I?"

"Aye, that's what I came to tell you. Bergsten won."

Alyda clapped her on the back. "Well, I can honestly say that's the best thing I've heard all day."

Nev grunted. "Wish I could say the same. He might be one of ours, but Del was robbed."

"You would say that…"

For the whole of that night, it rained solidly. By noon the next day, the grounds of the Arth had turned into a bog, miring horses and wagons, sucking boots off feet and dampening any high spirits that had remained after the alcohol had run out.

Alyda was taking a short cut through the tented market-place. She was on her way back to the Arth after spending the morning organising the crews that were keeping the road clear. During the tournament the marketplace had been a thriving centre of activity. It was now a deserted, rain soaked island drowning in a sea of mud.

Alyda skirted the rut puddles that were the size of duck ponds, keen to get back to the Arth and get changed. She was soaked to the skin, and a little hung-over from celebrating Bergsten's win into the early hours. A peel of laughter rang out from the only ale tent still open for business.

Whoever owned *The Golden Hart* was making the most of the terrible weather and by the sounds of it, had caught a fair haul of stragglers, happy enough to drain the barrel dregs while they waited for the rain to stop. As she walked past the tent, someone called her name.

The last thing she wanted was to be dragged into a conversation with a drunken warrior she may have once met or fought with. But before she could wave and walk on, the rat-faced Suvian stepped out of the tent and planted himself in her path. He bowed extravagantly, wine slopped over the rim of his goblet, staining his kidskin glove scarlet. A familiar coldness flowed through her limbs when she saw that the Thane was also in the tent.

"Captain Stenna, please allow me to introduce myself," said the Suvian. "I am Captain Luca Telvier, Commander of Telvier's Free Company of Foot."

She remembered him—that wig was impossible to forget. Something told her this wasn't a chance encounter.

"Is there something I can do for you, Captain Telvier?"

"Indeed there is, Captain Stenna. Thane Thorgulsen—" he gestured to the Thane who gave the slightest nod of recognition, "—has a few questions he'd like to ask you. Alas, his Antian isn't very good, so he's asked if I could translate for him, if you wouldn't mind?"

Alyda noticed the laughter had died. Everyone in the tent was listening to the exchange.

"Very well, but I must be away soon, Telvier."

"You are most gracious. Isn't the Captain gracious, lads?"

The tent was packed with Telvier's mercenaries and Guthlanders. They all chorused their approval. She was being set up.

"The Thane would like to know why the Captain of the famous *Hammer of Antia* didn't take part in the tournament."

Here we go. Alyda's stomach tightened. The air was alive—charged with the promise of violence. If they attacked, she decided she would kill the Suvian first and then the Thane. If she was Void bound, she wasn't going alone.

"'Tis my duty to host the tournament."

Telvier made a show of translating, but it was obvious that the Thane understood perfectly well. The warlord looked at her as he answered the mercenary.

Telvier nodded, a sneering grin spread across his pox scarred face. "Thane Thorgulsen says that in his country, and please understand these are his words not mine, I am merely the messenger and as such…"

"Get on with it, Telvier," she said. Her fingers tingled in anticipation of drawing her sword. They would expect her to run, or go on the defensive. By the time they realised their mistake, the Thane and Telvier would be dead. She smiled.

"The Thane says; a true leader doesn't let their warriors fight while they watch. He also adds that only a…"

Alyda waved him to silence. "Enough. Save your breath for those who don't mind the smell." She turned to the Thane. "When and where, Guthlander?"

The Guthlander's moustache twitched. She imagined he must be smiling but the effect was lost under all that fucking hair. She stared into his pale eyes, trying to read his intentions. All she saw was ice.

"Dawn, tomorrow, the sword arena," he said.

"The miserable bastards! We can't let them get away with this." Nevenna ground her fist into her palm.

Alyda rocked back on her chair. "I'd like nothing better than to pay those fa'cachti another visit, only this time with the Hammer at my back, but then I'd have to explain to Trease why we pounded a delegation of Guthlanders after one of them offered me a challenge. I can't see that going down well, can you?"

"He wouldn't know about the challenge."

"*I* would."

"Ack, but it burns to let them get away with this. The honourless pig-fuckers," said Nev.

"I can't argue with that, and I'll stake a month's pay there's more to this than just a chance to make mischief. That fucking Suvian set me up."

"You don't think he's working for the Brotherhood do you?"

"No, they don't hold with mercenaries."

"I suppose we'll find out tomorrow. Shall I let everyone know to be ready, just in case there's trouble?"

"In case? Oh, there's going to be trouble alright."

Dawn broke, sullen and grey accompanied by a heavy drizzle. Talin took one look outside and decided that the best place for him was bed. He would have rolled over and gone back to sleep had Bear not burst into his room and told him about the duel.

He was angry that Alyda hadn't told him herself and annoyed that Bear sounded so gleeful at the prospect of a fight between Alyda and the Guthlander.

"I'm going to stop them," he said, and threw on his clothes.

Bear pulled a face. "Why in the name of the gods would you want to do that? I thought you liked her?"

"You can be fucking dense sometimes, Iris," Talin fumed.

"It's part of my charm. But listen Tal—Highness; if you stop the duel, you might as well cut your cock off for all that you'll ever get near the Captain. She'd never forgive you for shaming her." She threw him his boots. "Now please hurry, there's already quite a crowd ahead of us and I want to be able to see what's—"

Talin rounded on her. "Damn it, Bear, I'm serious. I won't stand by and watch her get hurt."

"I understand how you feel, but don't forget; it's what she does. If you interfere you'll lose her respect, and the respect of the Hammer."

"Fuck the Hammer! You've seen the size of that Guth-lander. Do you really think she stands a chance against him?"

"I do hope so, I've got a…I mean, yes! Of course. Now come on, or it'll be over before we get there."

The crowd was already three deep by the time Talin and Bear arrived. Guthlanders and mercenaries lined one half of the arena, the knights and squires of the Hammer the other. All he had to do was tell the Marshal to stop it. He was the heir to the throne, and not averse to giving orders, but he didn't, mostly because of the Hammer.

None of the knights seemed even the slightest bit concerned for their Captain. Most were watching the combatants preparing for the fight with an air of studied detachment. Some looked bored, and were hardly paying any attention to what was happening in the arena. Their attitude confused him, and caused him to pause. If they weren't worried, should he be?

The Guthlanders and the mercenaries weren't as reticent as the Antians. They were cheering Thorgulsen as though the fight was already won. Against his better judgement Talin decided to heed Bear's council, and say nothing—for the time being.

The Thane was arguing with the Marshal, while Kieran continued to school the juniors, infuriating the Guthlander even more. Alyda smiled within the darkness of her helm. It would soon be her turn to teach the pig-fucker a lesson and she couldn't wait.

"Pay attention, you lot!" Lorhine barked—startling the squires and pages to rapt attention. "You're not here just to watch the Captain win a duel; you're here to learn, so listen up. A suit of plate can weigh fifty pounds...on a good day. You will not always be mounted and therefore you must be able to carry that weight and fight on foot, like common warriors." There was a ripple of laugher among the youngsters. "You must be able to run in your armour, fight in it, even sleep in it. It must become part of you, a second, steel skin. The superior craftsmanship of Antian plate—the finest armour in the world—will enable you to effectively carry the battle to whomever, and wherever you are sent to enforce King Daris's will."

Lorhine was good. Alyda almost forgot why she was there. She flexed her fingers, worked them deeper into her gauntlets. Kieran gave her a sly grin and continued to instruct the youngsters. The Thane was sounding more enraged with every passing minute, which was exactly what she wanted. While she waited for Kieran to finish, she idly scanned the crowd. Prince Talin and Bear Berwick pushed their way to the front of the arena. Talin's face was as dark as a storm. She wondered if he was worried for her, and laughed at the fanciful notion.

"—The Captain will now choose weapons appropriate to the combat, taking into account her opponent," said Lorhine. "This is not a luxury you'll be afforded often, so you must make the most of it when it happens."

That was her cue. With great deliberation, she examined the weapon rack by the side of the arena. She turned, and very obviously looked over to the Thane before grabbing a stick that had been placed on the rack for this very purpose. It was a childish joke and, got the response she expected: The Thane turned purple with rage and everyone, including some of the mercenaries laughed their arses off. Alyda had a few practice swings with the stick before she tossed it aside and picked up a mace and a warhammer.

When they were both armed, the Marshal called them to the centre of the arena. "Captain Stenna, Thane Thorgulsen." He bowed to both. "You will fight until one of you yields, or you both decide 'tis a draw, or one or both of you are unable to continue, due to injury or death. Do you accept these terms?"

Alyda agreed immediately, but Thorgulsen shook his head.

"Before we start I want the Captain checked for magic," he said.

Furious, Alyda swept up her visor. "Do you think I'd dishonour myself and my Company by cheating?"

The Thane smiled, and leaned on his huge, double-headed axe. "Let's find out, shall we? Unless you have something to hide, something your Ward is keeping quiet about…?"

"I don't need magic to put you on your arse," she snarled.

The Marshal cleared his throat. "Captain Stenna, do you have someone here who can, er…*test* the Thane? Thane Thorgulsen, I gather you have someone who can detect such things?"

"Aye, Marshal, I do." He jerked his thumb at his wife.

Alyda saw the trap too late. They weren't just after her blood—they wanted her honour.

"Captain?" enquired the flustered Marshal.

Alyda shrugged nonchalantly, even though she was fuming. "The Ward will sound if the Thane has been foolish enough to use magic."

The Marshal muttered under his breath and turned to the Thane's wife. "If you would…" He threw up his hands. "… Do whatever it is you do."

Alyda focused her concentration and ordered the Ward to accept the spell the Guthlander was about to perform—*so long as it isn't a harming spell.* The court mages had drilled her for days on how to order the Ward with a thought when she had become Captain. It was always an unsatisfying experience because there was never the slightest indication that the damn thing had heard.

The thought occurred to her that the Guthani might not even bother to cast a spell. All she had to do was accuse her of using magic and that would be enough to ruin her reputation. The witch closed her eyes and began to chant under her breath. The air grew heavy, like the moment before a storm breaks. She was casting a spell alright. Alyda was uncomfortably reminded of when the Shadewalker appeared.

After several tense minutes the Guthani opened her eyes. "Captain Stenna has nothing of a magical nature about her person."

Thorgulsen's smile vanished. He fixed his wife with an icy stare. "*Are you sure?*"

Alyda didn't know exactly what they'd planned, but if the murderous look Thorgulsen gave his woman was anything to go by, the plan hadn't worked.

"Quite sure, husband," the woman said. As she turned to leave, Alyda saw her wink at someone over on the Antian side of the arena.

Talin turned to Bear. "Did she just wink at you?"

Bear looked suitably confused. "Who, Highness?"

"Don't make me waste breath on this. You know who."

The tiniest hint of a smile twitched at the corner of her mouth. "Oh, *her*. No I don't think so, Highness. She might have something in her eye, or a nervous affliction... or something."

"By Sest, I swear, Lady Berwick, if Alyda gets hurt because you've been acting like a bitch in heat, you and I will have a problem."

Alyda's visor locked into place with a satisfying click. She rolled her shoulders and waited. Thorgulsen adjusted his grip on his axe.

"Are you both satisfied that everything—*magical or otherwise*—is as it should be?" The Marshal asked, somewhat exasperated. Alyda and the Guthlander nodded their assent. "Thank the gods for that," said the Marshal brushing a palmful of rain off his balding pate.

He began to explain what they could and couldn't do to each other. Alyda had heard the speech a dozen times before and took the opportunity to get the measure of her opponent.

The Guthani was wearing the same heavy scale coat that he'd worn for the melee, but a different helm. This one had a mail aventail and bronze cheek plates instead of a full visor. It allowed for a broader field of vision, but less protection than a fully enclosed helm. Alyda had a far more limited view of the world though the narrow slit in her sallet, but she was used to it. The Guthlander was big enough and slow enough that she wouldn't lose sight of him in the small arena.

If Lorhine's lecture was anything to go by, she should be flattered by his choice of weapon. The haft alone must have been over five feet long, but it was the twin-bladed axe heads that earned her respect. Every gleaming curve, every inch of finely honed edge promised pain.

The Marshall cleared his throat, "On my mark…"

Alyda took a step back. She was sure he'd go for a quick strike and try to finish her before wielding the beast of a weapon took its toll on his strength. The Marshal raised his baton. After a last check to make sure they were both ready, he brought his arm down and backed out of the arena.

As she expected, the Guthlander rushed her the moment the baton dropped. Yelling a battle cry, he brought the axe over his shoulder in a gleaming arc. Alyda easily dodged the blow, but with unexpected speed, Thorgulsen swept it up and back round. The huge axe wasn't a weapon to block, it was one to avoid. She leapt back. The fine edge of the blade kissed the keel of her breastplate, striking sparks from the metal.

The near-miss focused her attention; she circled the Thane, edging back and sideways, careful to avoid the spinning blades. Mud squelched underfoot. One slip, one misplaced step and it would be over.

Ignoring the mocking taunts of the Guthlanders and mercenaries, Alyda made no attempt to attack, but continued to dodge around the arena until she'd turned the Thane so that his baying supporters were behind her. She let their insults wash over her as she bided her time, waiting for the right moment to strike. She didn't have to wait long. Something behind her caught Thorgulsen's attention, just for a second. It was enough. The moment he looked away, she hurled the mace at his head.

The Thane reacted quickly, and batted it away with the axe, just as she'd hoped he would. Alyda took a single, long stride towards him, swinging the warhammer underhand as she closed. The Thane had blocked his own line of sight with his axe, and wasn't quick enough to parry the lighter warhammer with his unwieldy weapon.

She could have driven the warhammer's lethal, rear spike through his jaw, and into what passed for a brain. But she chose instead to clip his chin with the flat hammer-head of the weapon. She'd already decided that she wasn't going to kill him if it could be avoided, she didn't want to mar the tournament with his death. His head snapped back, he staggered. She pressed her advantage and side-stepped right, pivoting on her right foot, which put her almost directly behind him. *You're mine.* She swung the warhammer against his unarmoured knee. The Thane howled. Alyda stamped on his calf. He dropped.

"Do you yield?" she growled, hammer raised, ready to deliver the killing blow.

The Thane rolled over and tore off his helm. His face and beard were streaked with blood that was welling from a deep gash on his jaw. A tense silence fell over the crowd as they waited for him to answer.

"I yield," he snarled through bloodied teeth.

Alyda lowered her weapon and stalked over to the Antian side of the arena.

Lorhine turned to the squires. "Observe and take note." The youngsters, who had been screaming themselves hoarse cheering her on, fell silent. "Size and brute strength are not enough to win out against an intelligent and skilled opponent. I hope you were paying attention. We'll be discussing this lesson in more detail on the 'morrow. Dismissed!"

It was over, just like that. A sudden flurry of blows and the duel—if it could be called such—was over and, Twins be praised, Alyda had won. It was not what Talin had expected, nothing like the practiced rituals that took place in the Royal Gardens and training yards of the 5th. Back home, the knights and nobles with honour to defend would posture with whip-thin blades and dance about until a hit was scored, or honour was satisfied by a particularly dazzling display of blade work. Fatalities happened occasionally, but were usually accidents and considered bad form. What he'd just witnessed was an entirely different beast. It was so… unashamedly violent.

At some point in the future Talin might be able to put into words the tremendous sense of relief he'd felt when Alyda walked out of the arena unscathed. Right at that moment, all he could do was stand there and catch his breath while she and her knights headed off to the Arth to celebrate.

He'd wanted to end the fight a dozen times, but Bear had begged him not to interfere, insisting every time that Alyda knew what she was doing. His friend had been right, although he could never tell her because he'd never hear the end of it.

"See? I told you there was nothing to worry about." Bear grinned, and tucked a bulging pouch into her doublet.

"Don't get all smug—you once thought that mare's piss was an aphrodisiac."

"At least *I* didn't drink it…"

They both laughed.

"I promise you this, Iris, when I'm king; I'm going to outlaw duelling—no matter how skilled my wife is."

The poppy juice Bethanglyn had given him took the edge off the pain, but it still took his breath away when she straightened his leg and eased his kneecap back into the socket. The pain lessened immediately, but his knee was swollen and didn't feel like it wanted to stay where she'd put it.

She pressed her fingers against his foot. "I can feel your heartbeat, the leg hasn't died."

"That's fascinating. Now splint it, and before you say I should rest it—don't."

"As you wish, but don't blame me if you cripple yourself."

He grabbed her by the scruff of the neck and dragged her towards him until her face was inches from his. "Why would I blame you for that, when I have so many other things to choose from?"

She glared, but held her tongue. Tempted as he was to wring her neck, he let her go.

"You got off lightly, Thane." Telvier purred.

Thorgulsen shrugged. He wasn't about to admit he'd come to the same conclusion. "What did you expect? Stenna hits like a girl."

"And yet she showed a remarkable…" Telvier began, and then caught the look on Thorgulsen's face. "Yes. Quite. She hits like a girl…who got lucky."

Thorgulsen laughed. He'd give Telvier his due; the man had the survival instincts of a cockroach. "That's what I thought, but I'm still going to kill her."

Hot water lapped around her ears. Alyda rolled the stem of the wine glass between her fingers and drowsily watched steam rise off the skin of the bathwater. Alone at last, she let herself wallow in the warm afterglow of victory. She still had no idea why the Guthlander had picked the fight, but she was sure she'd find out, this stank of unfinished business.

She took a sip of wine. The deep oak tones and hint of summer fruits washed over her tongue and filled her mouth with rich, velvety sweetness. The door creaked softly. Her eyes snapped open and locked on the hand curling around the edge of the door. Instantly awake, she reached for her sword… and then stopped when she saw the familiar ruby ring flash scarlet in the lamp light.

You must tell him to go! The voice of reason ordered. Talin came over to the tub. *No good will come of this…* She reached out, pulled him down to her, and kissed him.

Water boiled from the tub. The voice of reason drowned in the torrent. Without regret, Alyda acknowledged that this was one battle she was happy to lose.

Chapter Eight

Weyhithe Forest was burning. At least that was what its autumnal livery looked like to the King's Councillor. *Everything is burning.* Acid bile scourged Hyram's throat and his stomach cramped as he thought about the storm that was brewing. He stared hard at the flaming hues of autumn, tried to see the beauty, but all he could see was fire.

It was the end of September; the Autumn Council was in full session. The King, the Governors of Cathlan and Tamalan, and the kingdom's most influential nobles were gathered for the third and final time before Midwinter. Hyram hated every excruciating minute of every Council meeting. This one was no exception, but this time it was for other, more important reasons than his general loathing of the squabbling and back-biting that invariably attended these gatherings of sycophants and dullards.

Familiar footsteps echoed across the polished floor. He casually turned away from the window. Neither the master nor his apprentice showed the slightest flicker of recognition when their eyes met for the briefest of moments. Garian was helping an aged Duchess to her seat. Hyram was impressed with the boy's performance; he looked completely ordinary, utterly bereft of personality and invisible to the noble company. None of them would suspect what a sharp mind lurked behind those lustreless eyes. *Just as it should be.*

Hyram let his gaze slide across the chamber. He wondered who could be trusted, who was a true supporter of the King, and who he would have to kill, blackmail, or imprison. He could make a good guess, he knew these rogues of old, but he had to be sure before he acted. A good surgeon did more than guess when they had to cut out a diseased organ, and he was a good surgeon. He and the boy would observe the honourable Council members and wait for the masks to slip, which they surely would. If he knew one thing, it was that few people had the wit to keep secrets. Knowledge was currency and most people were spendthrifts. He on the other hand had always been a miser.

Feigning boredom, he gazed at the ceiling. His mind was awhirl with the schemes of kings and princes, but he couldn't deny the magnificence of the Council Chamber.

As a child, he was awed by its beauty and believed absolutely in the legend that the hall had been created using Fey magic. The only concessions to practicality were the seats that had been cut into the white marble walls and the magnificent rainbow-hued window. The ring of seats was broken by the King's dais and the massive Wildwood doors that were opposite the throne.

Hyram thought the doors must have been an afterthought; beautiful though they were, they marred the smooth perfection of the walls that rose to form the graceful vault a hundred feet above them.

In recent years the pale walls had begun to blur into indistinct, grey fuzziness long before they reached the ceiling. These days he was forced to rely on memory to conjure the detail of the roof, rather than his failing eyesight.

The room humbled him, which was rare. Humans failed, but this room with its doors that burst into bloom every spring, and the Rainbow Window that flowed like water would endure long after he was dust. It was small comfort, but growing old had taught him to be grateful for the little things.

The Governor of Tamalan was sitting beside the King, huddled in furs. Lady Tula was the very image of a kindly grandmother, except for the sword poking out from under her cloak. The seat on the other side of Daris, where the Governor of Cathlan should have been sitting, was empty.

Jerim's messenger had arrived bearing an apology from his Lord, but not the taxes that were due from Cathlan. They'd anticipated such a move and had planned for it, but as the time approached Hyram found his mouth was dry and his hands clammy. He never used to feel like this before indulging in a little play-acting. When had anticipation and excitement turned into weariness and dread?

"When you got old…" he muttered under his breath.

The King beckoned the nervous messenger over. "Tell my brother that because he is ill, I shall give him one month's grace to gather the taxes and deliver them here, in person. However; and this is most important, so listen well, sirrah. Tell him that my patience is not infinite. If he cannot cope with the responsibility of being our Governor of Cathlan, I will appoint someone who can."

Hyram saw several of the Cathlan nobles exchange knowing looks and smug, pursed-lipped smiles. The chamber fell silent; the messenger shuffled uncomfortably. Hyram marshalled his strength and hauled himself to his feet. *On with the motley.*

"Your Majesty, I must protest!" he barked.

A shocked murmur followed the echo of his words around the chamber.

Daris gave him a dead-eyed stare. "What about, Lord Costaine?"

"He's gone too far, Majesty! How many more times will you allow the Governor of Cathlan to flout your authority, and the authority of this Council? He makes fools of us all—"

The King leapt to his feet, fists clenched. "How dare you question me? If I choose to give my brother the benefit of my patience, it is none of your concern!"

Hyram felt the blood pumping through the veins in his neck as the eyes of everyone in the room bored into him. "Your Majesty, I must—"

"One more word, Costaine, and I swear I will banish you to the Northern Wastes. I have said all I wish to say on the matter; let that be an end to it." Daris turned to the messenger. "Take my words back to Prince Jerim with all haste."

The pale-faced messenger bowed and backed from the chamber.

"Does anyone else have anything they wish to say about the Governor of Cathlan?" Daris demanded. No one spoke. "Council adjourned." The King strode from the chamber, before anyone had time to rise and bow, leaving Hyram to endure the censure of his peers.

Hyram was unrepentant and argued his point vociferously, even though he felt that his labouring heart was about to burst at any moment. All the while, he was taking note of which way the blades were falling as was his apprentice who was standing mutely in the background, watching his master's performance. Later, when they got the chance to compare notes, they would compile a list of who merited further investigation, who could probably be trusted, and who was going to have an unfortunate accident.

His apprentice was the last to leave the chamber. Hyram didn't think he had the strength to get up and go even if he wanted to. As the last Council member swept past him, Garian turned to Hyram, and frowned. He shook his head and waited for the doors to close. Alone at last, he closed his eyes and waited for the iron bands constricting his chest to loosen.

Later that evening, Hyram again found himself in a tight spot, this time trying to squeeze down a narrow passage that he hadn't used in years. After almost choking to death on a mixture of dust and cobwebs, he considered the route was better suited to someone half, or perhaps even a third, his size.

Daris, Lady Tula, Commander Trease, and General Tyrus were already in the King's study when he got there.

Daris smiled. "Ah, cousin, there you are. So how did I do?"

You were average, I was bloody marvellous. The King's Councillor divested himself of a veil of cobwebs.

"Not bad at all, Majesty, if your noble lords' reactions to our little charade were anything to go by. Several of the Council are convinced I'll lose my head before the week is out. Indeed, some of your more…*faithful* subjects were quick to offer sympathy and assistance now that I'm no longer in your favour. Is there any wine? I've swallowed a century's worth of dust."

Daris waved absently at a decanter on the table. "That's good; I thought I might have overdone it. I can't believe people really believe that I'd give my brother a month's grace after all he's done. Have I been so indulgent?"

It was left to Trease to break the deepening silence. "Going on past leniency, I think most will accept it. What matters is that your brother believes it."

"Aye," agreed Hyram. "I'm sure we did enough to convince his agents, and Jerim is arrogant enough to swallow it."

"How soon can we be in position? I want to bottle him up in Cathlan, before he has the chance to move across the border in strength."

General Tyrus rocked on his heels, his small eyes narrowing to pinpricks as he stared into the middle distance, counting armies in his mind before he spoke. "Four days, Majesty. We'll pick up Mallebeck's Bowmen on the way. I thought it best to have them wait with the Fifteenth. Gursten's a good woman, very discreet."

Daris turned to Hyram. "I take it he has the full support of all the Cathlan lords?"

Hyram managed to compact the torrent of curses that sprang to his lips into a disdainful growl when he remembered the Cathlans' smug faces. "Naturally, Majesty. 'Tis all this, 'independent kingdom' nonsense he keeps spouting, they eat it up."

Tension drew Daris's shoulders into a hunch, signing his anger louder than words. His face was composed, but the mask didn't fool Hyram.

"Matlin; are the Third and Second in position?" Daris asked.

"Yes, Majesty, they're ready to board ships at Sallis as we speak. Shall I send word for them to embark?"

"Aye. If my brother has bought the support of Vanen Iceheart and her sea wolves, Vorbek and Costaine could be in for a fight before they even reach Carngarthe. Who else is ready to sail?"

"The Lowland Lancers and Lady Denholme's companies," Trease added.

Hyram wondered if it was wise to discuss his more *subtle* plans with the warriors present. Lady Tula had the wit to grasp bold schemes, but then she was an excellent game player, unlike the other two who were...*uncomplicated*. Lack of time made the decision for him. Tyrus and Trease could think what they liked and be damned. Hyram poured himself another glass of wine.

He cleared his throat. "About the Iceheart...Ulyan Redbear is backing this little uprising and, as you may know, he slew the Iceheart's family. I have it from a trusted source that none of her Wolf Raiders will try to take advantage of our ships should hostilities break out, and they certainly won't be helping Redbear. I've also heard she may take the opportunity to wreak a bit more vengeance on Redbear and those who support him."

"You haven't been making deals with pirates have you, Councillor Costaine?" Daris asked.

"Of course not, Majesty," said Hyram, trying not to overplay his innocence. *Less is more*.

Daris looked unconvinced. "That had better be the truth, because if I ever catch the Iceheart and her pirates, they'll hang for their crimes."

"Indeed, Majesty. Quite right too. I am informed she neither asked for, nor was offered anything except information on Redbear's whereabouts. I *am* sure that her hatred for him is stronger than her dislike of Antia. Which is why she's been told where Redbear's ships are to be found, and who his allies are."

Hyram expected the disapproval of Trease and Tyrus. They did not disappoint him. The Generals scowled at him, haughty disgust written on their faces.

"Oh, for Asha's sake! She would have found out anyway," Hyram declared. "There isn't a ship that sails between here and Guthland those bloody flying worms don't mark. This way it looks like we've helped her, not the other way around."

"I hope you're right, because you've wagered seven hundred lives on it."

Like all warriors, the Commander of the Royal Guards was as arrogant as he was small-minded. Normally Hyram would ignore his bleating, but he was in a foul mood after being mauled by the Council and snapped back. "D'you think I make decisions on the throw of a dice? Or do you forget that Merrin Costaine is my daughter?"

"I dread to think how you make your decisions, and yes, I often forget that Merrin is your daughter. She's been in the Guards since she was twelve; she's now twenty-eight. In that time I feel sure I have seen more of her than you have."

"Enough, both of you," Daris commanded. "Now is not the time." He tapped the table, drawing their attention to the map of the kingdom that was spread across it. "The Fifth can stay here and guard the city with the First. Stenna can bring my son back and then take over command of the defences from Corvinius." He jabbed the map. "I want the Fourth to stay at Gallen Arth for now. I need to know how many Free Companies are loose in Antia before I commit all of my forces. I need that information soon, Hyram."

Hyram bowed. "I've already sent out scouts."

Daris turned to the Governor of Tamalan. "Lady Tula, I need your warriors to meet us at Hainian Pass. If my brother intends to mount an invasion, that's where he has to come through. How many can you send and how soon?"

Her skin was as creased as old parchment, but when she lifted her face from the thick, fur collar of her cloak, her eyes shone as bright as snow in sunlight.

"Four thousand warriors are already on their way south, my King. After reading your letter I thought they might be needed. I hope I haven't been presumptuous?"

Daris smiled and inclined his head. "Not at all, Lady Tula, your insight serves our kingdom well."

The King might be pleased, but Hyram wasn't so sure. He didn't think it wise to let a descendent of the Clan Lords move armies around Antia. They had a taste for such things that should not be encouraged.

Daris folded his arms. "So that's almost five thousand at Hainian pass, and seven hundred by sea to Carngarthe. Hardly a mighty host. How many warriors have my lords of Antia promised?"

"We should have another eight to ten thousand in about eight days," said Tyrus. "Maybe less time, and maybe more warriors. I'm sorry I can't be more certain, Majesty."

The King fixed his gaze on the map. "If only I could be sure of all of my nobles. Damn Jerim for seeding so much division in the kingdom, after our parents almost killed themselves trying to unite it."

A knock at the door saved them from another uncomfortable silence. It was the King's valet. Listening in on other people's conversations was more than a habit for Hyram; it was a necessary part of his job. Although he didn't make a habit of eavesdropping on the King, he couldn't help but pick out Rufus Corvinius's name from the rustle of whispers. Just thinking about the man made his chest ache. The Captain of the 5th was at best a rake, at worst a buffoon who could play no part in their carefully crafted plans.

"If you will excuse me, Lady Tula, gentlemen—I have a message to send."

After Daris left the room, and he was satisfied that his fellow conspirators were otherwise engaged, Hyram ambled over to the slightly open door.

"Ah, Rufus…"

Hyram heard the King say.

"…I need you to send your best riders with a message for Captain Stenna."

"As you command, Majesty," the Knight Captain replied.

That wasn't too bad, thought Hyram. Not even Corvinius could make a mess of so simple a task.

Night turned to day while Garian and Lord Hyram decided which members of the Council warranted closer investigation and who they thought trustworthy. Garian had been surprised by how easily the nobles had been deceived by Hyram and the King's performance. It was hardly the most convincing acting he'd ever seen. But from what he'd overheard, it had been good enough to convince them that the King was once again showing leniency towards his brother.

What infuriated him was that so many of them had gloated over Hyram's supposed fall from the King's favour. He knew his master didn't possess the most endearing personality, but until today he hadn't realised just how many enemies Hyram had at court. It galled him to think that his master had to carry the shame of being rebuked by the King and that few would ever know the truth.

"Are you listening, boy?" Hyram barked.

"You want me to stay in the guise of librarian, keep my eyes peeled for any assassins, and if I find any, to deal with them quietly and efficiently. No fuss no mess."

Hyram narrowed his eyes. "Something of an over simplification. Let's hope for the sake of the kingdom you won't be as casual in the performance of your duty. Mark me well; as sure as night follows day, they will come. Don't let Olin out of your sight. He's second in line to the throne."

"Who's guarding the Queen and Prince Talin?"

"Don't worry about Talin. He's with the First, and Thea has her own bodyguards. In fact, don't worry about anything; you just concentrate on guarding the Prince. I'll worry enough for both of us."

The ghost of her body lingered after Alyda crept out of bed, but as stealthy as she'd been, the lack of her presence woke him. Talin opened his eyes. She was over by the washstand, braiding her hair. Tattoos that had been drawn by a skilful hand in shades of indigo and azure, danced across her back and down her arms. Half horse, half stag creatures leaped and chased across her skin, moving as she moved.

"What do they mean?" he asked, trying not to think about the erection waking between his thighs.

She tossed a finished braid over her shoulder. "What do what mean?"

"The tattoos; do they mean anything?"

She shrugged, strong fingers deftly weaving her hair into a second braid. "No idea. All I know is they're traditional. My mother knows, but if she ever told me, I've forgotten."

"Aren't you curious? They're part of your heritage—part of you."

Alyda gave him a wry smile. "To the Shemisana I'm a Tamalak, to the Tamalak I'm Hadami. I've never felt like either. Now, if you want to know *anything* about the history of the Royal Guards, I'd be happy to oblige."

"If they were on me, I'd want to know."

"That's because you're nosey." Her eyes sparkled in the flickering candlelight. "Do you like them? Or do you think they're barbaric, like most *proper* Antians?"

"I like them. But then, if you were covered in horse shit I'd like it."

"That's good, because you'd be surprised how often that happens."

"No, I wouldn't. I've been around you long enough now."

She dived onto the bed and sat astride him, pinning him beneath the covers. He wrapped himself around her and rolled over onto her, reversing their positions.

"Stay," he whispered.

She sighed. "I can't."

He didn't ask again, he didn't want to spoil the moment. She pushed him off and got up and finished dressing.

"Will I see you tonight?" he asked.

"Whenever you want, Highness. I'm at your service." She winked and tucked her boots under her arm before quietly lifting the door latch.

"I'll see you later…" He was about to add, "*My love*", but the door was already closing.

Night hadn't quite faded from the sky, the birds hadn't woken, and the foxes had returned to their dens. It was the still time, the frozen moment just before dawn broke and the world woke. Alyda loved being up this early and going to see her horses while it was quiet, but today it was not to be. The moment she set foot outside of Talin's rooms, Jamie waylaid her.

"I've been looking all over for you, Captain," he said, slightly out of breath.

"Why, what's wrong?"

"A messenger has arrived from the King."

"Sit down before you fall down," Alyda ordered the knight in russet and silver. The knight flopped into a chair. Alyda broke the King's seal and read the letter.

Captain Stenna,
You are to escort my son back to Weyhithe immediately. You will then report to Captain Corvinius for further orders. The First Company are to ride at once for Gallen Arth and await your return.

Daris.

Alyda peered over the letter at the messenger. Her mousy hair was plastered to her head, and she was sitting awkwardly on one arse-cheek, like she was saddle-sore. Hardly the kind of person Alyda would have trusted to deliver a missive from the King, however brief. Although thinking about it, she might have been the best the 5th had to offer.

"Well, that's short and to the point. What's your name, knight?"

"Dervla, Captain Stenna. Dervla Kellam."

"Did the King give you this, Dervla?"

"Aye, Captain, and he told me that it must be delivered to you with all haste. I haven't stopped since leaving Weyhithe except to change horses, not even to eat or sleep."

Alyda ignored her whiny tone. "And there's nothing amiss in Weyhithe?"

The woman winced as she changed position. "All was well when I left, Captain."

"Thank you, Dervla. Go report to the watch, they'll find you a bunk and something to eat."

The knight looked like she was about to faint, but climbed to her feet and gave Alyda a sloppy salute before hobbling from the room.

"Do you think we're going to war with Jerim?" Jamie asked.

"That's *Prince* Jerim, and I wouldn't be at all surprised. I just don't understand why the King wants to send the Company to Gallen Arth. The Black Lancers don't need our protection, and there's nothing else up there worth defending." She examined the letter. "I've never received orders directly from the King."

"Perhaps Commander Trease is ill?"

"If the Commander was ill, the King would have mentioned it." Alyda folded the letter and tucked it in her tunic. "Did she have a letter for Talin?"

"*Prince* Talin? No, I don't think so, Captain.

"Have a care, Squire Turlowe. Go wake Lieutenant Vysten. Tell her to sound the call to arms and when you've done that, fetch my armour."

Talin elbowed Bear in the ribs. She stopped mid-yawn and gave him a puzzled look, completely unaware of the noise she was making or that the officers of the Hammer were staring daggers at her.

Alyda shook her head; behind her, hanging above the fireplace, the great Sea Drake skull cast its baleful, empty eyed stare over the gathering. "…and the Company is to ride to Gallen Arth and stay there until I return from Weyhithe with further orders. I'll be accompanying Prince Talin back to the city. Lieutenant Lorhine; give this to Captain Vorsten." She handed Lorhine a letter.

Kieran addressed the Captain, but cast a pointed glance at Talin. "You're riding to Weyhithe without an escort?"

"It's heart-warming to see how much they care, don't you think?" Bear whispered to Talin.

Talin shushed her. He wanted to hear what Alyda had to say; see if she could shed some light on why his parent's hadn't seen fit to tell him what was going on.

"We'll ride with the Company as far as Kellimarsh Bridge where we'll be met by a detachment from the Fifth."

Kieran snorted. "So you are going without an escort."

Laughter rippled through the group. Talin was aware that the 5th weren't called 'Rusties' because of their russet and silver surcoats. More unkindly, it was because their weapons were said to be rusty from lack of use. Talin knew the Hammer well enough to know they were only joking, but he felt sorry for the red faced knight who had to stand there and endure their mockery.

"Mean bastards," said Bear, a note of genuine sympathy in her voice. "The poor thing looks like she's going to cry."

"Alright, that's enough," Alyda ordered. "You now all know as much as I do. Are there any questions?" There was a general negative rumble.

Alyda clasped her hands behind her back. "I don't know what's going on, but I don't think we'll have to go far to find trouble."

She avoided naming his uncle directly, but everyone knew who she was talking about. *What a family,* thought Talin, ashamed of the blood in his veins.

By midday the Company was saddled up and ready to leave the Arth. Dark clouds roiled overhead, and a dense brume had rolled in from the Chase casting all the knights as shadows. Talin shivered; ahead of him Alyda was giving some final instructions to the garrison watch commander. Behind him, Rann Lacgarde unfurled the Company standard. The bright scarlet banner blazed against the lowering sky. Bear rode over.

"Sest's teeth, you look glum," she said. "You should be happy; you're going back to civilisation. No more early mornings, no more drill, no more terrible wine,"

Talin shook his head. Without looking behind her, Alyda raised her hand and the order rippled along the column to ride on. "I thought I'd be here until Midwinter. Why didn't my parents tell me I'd have to leave before then? And why haven't they told me what's going on? I'm sick of being treated like a child."

Bear shrugged. "My parents never tell me anything either. Do you remember when I got back from that hunting trip to find the house full of eager suitors?"

"Was that when you stole your parents' carriage and threatened to marry that shepherdess?"

She grinned wolfishly. "No. It's the very last time I got *worked up*. Nobody was hurt, I hasten to add, but they haven't tried to marry me off since then."

They laughed; some of Talin's frustration ebbed away. "I know there's probably a good reason why they've summoned me home, but I wanted to stay here for Midwinter…with Ali.

"Ack, Midwinter's a long way off. I'm sure you'll be back in the arms of your beloved by then. Or, maybe they've filled the Arth with ugly princesses and have a Midwinter wedding in mind for you. Look on the bright side; whatever happens, you'll always have me," said Bear.

The road to Weyhithe threaded its way through neatly quilted fields, hemmed on either side by miles of dry stone walls. It would take three days at a steady pace to reach the city.

Alyda had made the journey a hundred times and would normally have enjoyed the leisurely ride, but not today. Something was wrong. It wasn't the looming spectre of war, she was a warrior—fighting was what she did. It was the King's letter. She knew it was stupid, but that damn note bothered her. She had no doubt that it was authentic, she knew the King's seal and his handwriting; her commission bore both. It was the content—so brief and unsupported by orders from Trease. It just wasn't right.

"Something wrong?" asked Talin.

She had forgotten that the Prince was riding beside her. His words broke into her thoughts. *Yes damn it, something is wrong.* She wanted to say. But as much as she wanted to talk to him about the letter—about her doubts, there was no way she could explain something as tenuous as a gut feeling without sounding as stupid as she felt.

She smiled. "No, Highness, everything's fine."

When they set camp for the night, Bear noticed that the Rusty had camped slightly apart from the Hammer. She didn't blame her; it couldn't have been easy putting up with the constant jokes about her company, even if they were true. Bear popped a pebble of Pel and decided to go over and try to cheer her up. If nothing else, it would give her something to do while Talin was off with Captain Stenna, supposedly exercising their horses.

"Dervla, isn't it?" Bear asked, startling the knight who was unsaddling her horse. The poor thing was in a bad way, she stank of fear.

"Oh, I didn't hear you." She tossed the saddle on the ground and let it lie where it fell. "Aye, I'm Dervla."

A knight sitting nearby who was watching shook his head on seeing her rough treatment of the saddle. Dervla didn't notice. The girl didn't look at all used to long hours of riding and was quite obviously worn out.

Bear smiled brightly, the warmth of the Pel spreading through her limbs, easing the tension building behind her eyes. "I wondered if you needed a hand with anything."

Dervla's expression hardened. "Why? Because I'm a Rusty and therefore incapable?"

"No, because you're on your own and you look done-in."

The knight sighed, her shoulder's sagged. "I'm sorry… you're right. I am tired, but I can manage, my Lady."

"Call me Bear. I think we've met before, possibly in Weyhithe, but I confess—I have a rotten memory for anything useful."

Dervla unpacked her bed roll and sat down. "Aye, you've seen me before. I've guarded the Prince's quarters on more than one occasion."

"Ah. Of course. Please allow me to apologise for anything offensive I may have done or said. I was probably drunk."

"No need to apologise. We Rusties can be relied upon to never see or hear anything. Ask the Hammer."

Bear laughed, so did Dervla, but there was flint in the knight's eyes, and sharpness in her tone of voice.

"You mustn't take their teasing to heart; they don't mean any harm. Their humour's a bit rough is all, like them."

"What, the Hammer?" Dervla chuckled softly. "Oh, I don't take them seriously, Lady Berwick, not in the slightest."

On the third morning out from Trelanlith, they reached Kellimarsh Bridge. As promised, an escort of twenty Rusties were waiting for them. Alyda wasn't surprised to see that the Rusties were lounging on the grassy verge next to the road while their fat horses grazed unchecked. Their officer looked up and made a half-hearted attempt to dust crumbs from his chin before coming over to greet them.

"Endis, isn't it?" said Talin.

The officer looked surprised. "Why yes, yes it is, Highness," he said and wiped his greasy hands on his surcoat before saluting. "Lieutenant Endis reporting, I've been sent to escort you to Weyhithe."

"What's going on, Endis?" Alyda demanded. The man already irritated her and she'd only just met him.

"I really don't know, Captain Stenna; my orders are to escort you and Prince Talin back to Weyhithe."

Alyda's sense of unease grew. The Hammer were about to head off without her, which alone was unusual, and the Rusties were being particularly sloppy, even by their low standards. It all added to her suspicion that something was wrong. Or was this Suvia catching up with her? *Is this how battle fatigue started?*

Although it had never happened to her, she'd seen perfectly able knights break after one battle too many. It was rarely talked about, but could happen at anytime to even the most hardened veteran. It was said that something—the barrier between them and what they did—broke, allowing fear and doubt to flood in. The anxiety this caused often ended in deep despair, even madness. Was that what was happening? She dismissed the idea immediately; she knew herself, it wasn't in her to break. There *was* something wrong; she just didn't know what it was yet. Until she did, she'd keep her doubts to herself, but take a few precautions just in case the unsettled feeling manifested into a more tangible threat.

While the 5th got ready to leave, Alyda let the Hammer stretch their legs and water their horses. She waited until Endis was talking to Dervla before taking Kieran to one side for a quiet word.

"Stay sharp on the way to Gallen, and don't take the main road. Head up toward Keeling Delve and take the road to Gallen from there," she said with a smile on her face, just in case they were being observed.

"Why, what's wrong?" Kieran asked, adopting a similarly casual attitude.

She shrugged. The sun was shining; the Hammer and the Rusties were exchanging friendly banter. Bear Berwick had decided to ride north with the Hammer and was saying goodbye to Talin. *Nothing's wrong, Kieran, I'm just going mad.* "Just indulge me, Lieutenant, and take the back route."

Chapter Nine

The sun was nothing but a smear of red and gold against the dark line of the horizon when Alyda caught sight of the towers of Weyhithe.

The Arth road was completely deserted and the main East Gate was closed. As they got closer, she noticed the postern gate was open and the patrols on the wall had been doubled, confirming her suspicions that something was amiss.

Endis rode ahead of the escort and spoke to the guards. Moments later, the main gates yawned open to admit them. They entered, watched closely by the knights on the wall. Once inside, the gates were closed and barred behind them. It was all very different from the last time Alyda had entered the city.

The main street was almost deserted. The traders and merchants had closed up early and the only people about were small groups of warriors whose colours she didn't recognise. They had the look of mercenaries about them, but that couldn't be. Free Companies weren't allowed into the city armed, let alone invited to perform guard duty or patrol the streets.

She casually adjusted her belt, bringing her sword hilt within easier reach. Her escort didn't seem concerned that the streets were empty or that unliveried warriors were hanging around. On the contrary, their jovial banter was a lively accompaniment to the clatter of hooves on the cobbles. Alyda had seen enough. She rode up to Endis and pulled across him, forcing his horse to stop.

"Alright, what's going on, Endis?" she demanded. "Who are those soldiers? Where is everyone?"

"Ah, yes, I forgot to mention. There was an outbreak of swamp fever. The King drafted in some mercenary companies to keep the peace…people were starting to panic. It's nothing to worry about; there weren't many fatalities up until we left."

"And you forgot to mention this? Have *you* come down with fever, Endis?"

His mouth twisted into a sneer. "It slipped my mind. I was more concerned with bringing our beloved Prince safely back to the city, like I'd been ordered. Of course, I'm sure you find that hard to believe of a *Rusty*." His gaze flicked over her shoulder.

Alyda went cold. "It seems I'm not mad after all," she said.

"W…what d'you mean?" A bead of sweat ran down Endis's forehead.

She ducked and half drew her sword, smashing the pommel into his face. A moment later, the world exploded in a blinding burst of light.

Talin could tell something was bothering Alyda. Her face had been set like stone for most of the journey, and the only time she'd spoken since they'd left Kellimarsh was to question Endis. The Lieutenant was an amicable fellow, more than willing to look the other way when Talin and his friends wanted to sneak in or out of the palace, but he didn't seem himself today. He looked nervous and on edge, and spent most of the time trying to avoid Alyda. He didn't blame him; she wasn't exactly hiding her contempt for the poor fellow. When they were nearing the Arth she pulled Endis over. The escort came to a halt, Dervla rode up beside him. She also looked worried.

"I'm very sorry, Highness," she said.

"For what…?"

If she answered he didn't hear her because right at that moment, Alyda smashed her sword into Endis's face. The Lieutenant rocked back in his saddle, blood pouring from his nose. Before her sword cleared the scabbard, a knight came up behind her and hammered a punch into the back of her head. She wasn't wearing her helmet and the blow felled her instantly. She slid from the saddle. Nua reared and danced away from her fallen rider, the other horses nearby shied. Talin spat a curse and reached for his sword, which was when he noticed that Dervla was holding a knife on him.

"Please—I don't want to kill you," she mumbled, waving the knife in her shaking hand.

Without hesitation, Talin straight-armed her out of the saddle. The knife flew from her hand, and she grasped ropes of air before vanishing over the side of her horse. Furious, he drew his sword and spurred his mount over to Alyda, but a group of Rusties cut him off before he could reach her. Outnumbered, he was quickly overwhelmed and dragged from his mount. He lashed out with his sword—kicked, punched; even bit, but eventually he was taken to the ground and disarmed.

Cursing, Endis swatted away assistance and stormed over to Alyda, blood pouring from his nose and mouth. He kicked her in the stomach. Talin heard her groan; she was alive at least.

"Fucking, cunt!" Endis spat.

"Don't you touch her!" Talin roared, earning himself a punch in the face.

"Get him on his feet and tie him up," Endis ordered.

When Talin was securely bound, the Lieutenant marched over and squared up to him. "Don't try and order me, *Highness*. I no longer serve you, or your bastard father. D'you hear me?"

"Touch her again, and I'll kill you." Talin didn't shout, but pushed enough murderous anger into his voice that Endis backed away.

"I'll do what I fucking please." Endis sneered. "Like you and that fat slut used to; whoring and drinking your way around Weyhithe while we had to guard you! Oath-sworn knights, treated like fucking nursemaids and never so much as a nod of thanks. You make me sick. I'll dance a jig when the Guthani—"

"Shut up, you fool," Dervla hissed. She glared at Talin and limped towards him, knife in hand. He wondered what being stabbed would feel like and braced himself to find out.

She didn't stab him; she slapped him across the face. It stung, but it was better than a knife in the guts.

"I owe you that," she said and turned to the knights clustered around Alyda. "Take her to the Captain. You two—" she flicked the tip of the knife at two of the Rusties. "—take the Prince to his mother's quarters. He gets there in one piece, or else you'll answer to Corvinius. Same goes for her, got that?"

The knights did as they were bid.

Endis spluttered angrily. He grabbed her arm and spun her around to face him. "Who the fuck died and left you in charge?"

"You did," said Dervla. Her arm jabbed forward, once, twice…three times.

Endis gasped. A fat gob of blood splashed on his boot. Dervla stepped back, the bloody blade grasped tightly in her shaking hand. The Lieutenant sank to the cobbles, clutching at the mass of quivering guts that were spilling from under his breastplate. Dervla looked at Talin like she'd just been damned to the Void.

"Don't look at me like that," she snarled at him. "More than a few of your ancestors earned their crowns doing worse."

Talin didn't answer. There was no arguing with an unsheathed blade.

She was lying on smooth stone, not cobbles, so she knew she wasn't in the road. She tried to move and discovered that her hands were bound behind her back. Her head was pounding so hard that her eyes hurt. Reluctantly, she forced them open.

A blinding pain knifed into her skull. When she could see past the tiny explosions of light, she saw that she was in the Council Chamber in Weyhithe Arth. The painful brightness was flooding through a ragged hole in the wall where the Rainbow Window should have been. Squinting against the glare, she tried to sit up. A wave of nausea swept over her, she fell back.

"Brawling in the street, Captain Stenna? Whatever happened to the fabled Guards' discipline?" It was Corvinius.

The Captain of the 5th was sprawled across the King's throne, surrounded by smashed bottles and broken glass from the window. Now that she looked she could see that the whole chamber was splattered with wine and blood, it also stank like a latrine. The moment she laid eyes on him all the little things that had bothered her since she'd received the King's letter made horrible sense. She would not have believed it possible, but she couldn't deny the evidence before her. Corvinius, an oath-sworn Captain of the Royal Guards, had turned traitor. *I almost wish I was insane.*

He was holding her sword. When he saw that she'd noticed, he grinned and tossed it to one of the Rusties who were standing near the throne. He gestured to Alyda with a curt nod. The Rusty stalked over to her and raised the blade above his head in a two-handed grip. Alyda fixed her gaze on Corvinius.

"No, you idiot, cut the rope!" Corvinius shouted before the blade fell. "You lot are a fucking embarrassment, you really are," he said.

The Rusty muttered something under his breath and cut the rope binding her wrists.

She sat up carefully; certain her skull would shatter if she moved too quickly. The knight backed away. She had a sly look around the chamber as she rubbed feeling back into her hands. She counted six Rusties in all. Five of them held crossbows, all levelled at her. She should have seen this. Somehow, she should have known. The Captain of the Hammer, scourge of the Brotherhood of the Redemption, had been fooled by a drunken game cock. Worse, she'd delivered the man she loved into danger, possibly death. Gods only knew what had happened to Talin and his family. She got up slowly, very aware of taut bow strings and the itchiness of fingers.

"What have you done with the Prince? You treacherous fa'cachta."

Corvinius laughed. "Tamalak is such an expressive language. Don't worry 'Lyda, His Royal Spoiltness is alive and well with his mother and brother."

"And the King?" she demanded.

"So many questions! Anyone would think I was the prisoner. Lucky for you, I'm in a good mood, so I'll indulge your curiosity. The King is riding to his death as we speak. I promise you'll be the first to know when his head is taken.

"How could you turn traitor? Do you even know what you've done, Rufus?"

"Oh, 'Lyda, you say the word 'traitor' as though it was worse than Void sorcery. All I've done is change allegiance. I haven't sold my soul to a demon, or feasted on the flesh of babes. I've swapped one master for another. Ack! You wouldn't understand. You get to ride off and play hero while I'm left to rot in this dump."

"I don't call fighting for my King and country *'playing'* and neither would any of those ancestors you're always bragging about."

Corvinius smiled. "Talk of ancestry is so amusing coming from a half-breed gypsy."

"Better half-breed than in-bred if you're what comes of a family fucking each other for centuries."

Corvinius clapped. "That's my 'Lyda! Always so erudite. Now shut up and listen. I didn't bring you here to fight with you."

"You broke your oath." Spots of light danced before her eyes.

"It's nothing more than a chain around my neck—around your neck. A gilded leash to keep the fiercest hounds in check, and have no doubt, that's all we are to them. If only you could see it, but you've been blinded by their lies. The myth of the hero, oath-sworn and honourable…it's a fantasy. Wrap it up in as much braid as you like; you're a killer, nothing more."

He snatched up a bottle and took a careless swig before tossing it across the room. It smashed, splattering red wine across the once pristine, white marble floor. She could hardly stand to look at him.

Corvinius strutted unsteadily before the throne, evidently enjoying playing to his captive audience of one. "Oh, I wish I could tell you that I've heard the call of destiny. I'm sure that would appeal to your naïve sense of drama, but I'm afraid my reasons for…*resigning my commission,* are terribly mundane. I want power and wealth. I want what they have. You wouldn't believe how much the Guthani and Prince Jerim are paying me, or what they've promised."

"Whatever it is, it isn't enough," she said.

"You think? Come now, does it really matter which prince rules Antia? They're both whelps of the same bitch." He laughed. "If only you could see your face; eyes blazing with righteous indignation." He stopped laughing. "Don't you *dare* judge me, Captain Stenna. Hate me by all means, but do not presume to judge me. In fact, you should be grateful to me. Because of my plan, *mine!* the lives of hundreds, nay, *thousands* of good Antian subjects have been saved. Do you know why?"

"Pray, enlighten me."

"When Daris finds out his beloved family have been captured he'll roll over like a whipped cur and beg Jerim to take the crown—anything to save them."

He staggered over and draped his arm across her shoulders. Her blood ran cold, she clenched her fists. The nearest Rusty saw her stiffen and raised his crossbow. Alyda relaxed. Not even a Rusty could miss from less than twelve feet away.

"I've missed you, 'Lyda," Corvinius slurred.

She shrugged him off. "I haven't missed you."

His mouth contorted into a snarl. "I have the keys to the kingdom!" he bellowed into the vault. "When the Guthani arrive on the 'morrow and drag that bitch and her get to Cathlan it will all be over, and I will have won! Me!" The echo of his treacherous confession reverberated around the chamber. It was an ugly sound.

"Have you got the guts to kill me, Rufus? Or will you get the Guthani to do it for you? You've never been one for getting your hands dirty. Despite all the whining, you've no stomach for bloodletting."

Half a dozen emotions flitted across his face before he shook his head, defeated. "I don't want to kill you, 'Lyda," he groaned. "Why do you think I sent orders for you to come back with the Prince?"

"Because you missed me?" she offered.

"Yes, damn you. I've missed you from the moment you left Weyhithe after the parade. That's when I knew I wanted you. I don't even care who your family are, or where you come from: I want you, 'Lyda."

"I'm touched. But is this really the time to discuss our failed relationship, given that you're trying to destroy the kingdom?"

Corvinius's face darkened. Bow strings creaked ominously. She was about to find out if she'd pushed him too far. He rounded on her. She braced for the bowshot, but it didn't come.

"If I want to talk about it, I fucking will. I'm in charge now! Not Daris, not Thea—me!" His expression suddenly changed from furious to confused. He turned away. If she didn't know better she would have said he was feeling guilty, or it could be that he'd lost his mind, in which case she was entirely fucked.

He paced, idly kicking at the broken glass scattered across the floor. "I know it's my fault, 'Lyda, I didn't give you the slightest hint that I cared. In truth, until you left last time I didn't think I did, but I know now. Jerim has promised me governorship of Tamalan. You can rule there with me as my Queen. Think of it; a Tamalak Queen in the Ice Halls after centuries of Antian rule. The people would rejoice."

He really is deluded. She had to laugh. "You don't know much about Tamalaks, do you? They dislike half-breeds more than you Antians do."

"Fuck them, then! You will rule by my side. I love you, 'Lyda."

She waited for him to laugh, but he didn't. This new sincerity was almost as disturbing as his treachery. Was it possible that he meant it? She was still alive; perhaps in his own twisted way he really did think he was in love with her. If nothing else, it was an opening and she would seize it. She had to turn his weakness to her advantage before the Guthani arrived. The very thought of feigning disloyalty disgusted her, but for Talin's sake—possibly the entire kingdom's, she had to try.

"I can't believe you tricked the King," she said, wincing at her clumsy attempt to appeal to his ego.

Corvinius didn't notice and rewarded her efforts with a smug grin. "It was embarrassingly easy; these things are when you're dealing with people as arrogant as Daris. The fool ordered me to take messages to you and Vorsten, and like a good little Rusty, I did."

"Only you changed them." It was hard keeping the contempt she felt for him out of her voice.

He sketched an extravagant bow. "I know it sounds like I'm bragging, but I am rather pleased with my forgery skills. I pocketed the King's seal for long enough to make a copy and nobody noticed a thing. You know, I think I may have missed my calling." He laughed alone. "So, with Daris's messages destroyed, and mine sent in their place, I watched our glorious King and heroic Commander ride off to Cathlan, straight into a trap." He smiled coldly. "It would have been remiss of me not to inform Jerim that Daris was on his way. I'm afraid the surprise attack probably wasn't much of a surprise."

"You've thought of everything," she said, unable to look at him in case he saw the hate in her eyes.

Oblivious, he continued with his tale. "Starting the rumour that there'd been an outbreak of swamp fever in the city was a stroke of genius. I even arranged for a few bodies to be found looking like they'd died of the disease. People are easy to control when they're scared, so when I ordered a curfew, not many objected. Those who did… were dealt with."

"You killed people just to give credence to a lie?" His callousness shocked her.

He shook his head. "No, not just for that. I killed some of my knights who were too stupid to join me and weren't worth keeping alive to ransom. I also dealt with some unlucky fools who were in the wrong place at the wrong time. Oh, and the Queen's favourite dog; just for the fun of it. You always said I didn't pay attention to detail. Well, I did this time. Aren't you proud of me? I ordered the curfew, dealt with the *issues* in the Company, and when I had the Arth locked down I took the Queen and threw the court leeches in the dungeons. Checkmate, I believe."

"Only when you trap the King. Someone will warn Daris."

"Who? The only ones who were inclined to that are either dead or in the dungeon and as you've seen, I have the city sealed. There are over two hundred mercenaries plus the majority of the Fifth controlling who leaves and who enters. Nothing is going to get by me. I only have to keep the city under curfew until the Guthani arrive tomorrow, then they'll take dear old Thea and her sons and leave me an enormous sack of gold." He looked at her expectantly. "You're surprised, I understand. You're not the only one who's underestimated me. That bastard Trease won't live long enough to regret passing me over so many times. Sweet Asha! I wish I could be there when they kill him.

I've asked that they take their time, make him suffer… and tell him why." He folded his arms.

I can't do this. There was no way she could phrase a lie plausible enough to convince him she was as faithless as he was. The very thought made her want to vomit. *Come on Ali, say something damn you!* "There's too much to take in. I…I need some time…" she mumbled.

"There isn't any time, you're either with me or—"

"Don't make me decide now. Not if you love me as you say you do." She was close to failing. She couldn't bring herself to say she'd join him; sure the lie would choke her.

"Teril!" Corvinius barked at the knight who had her sword. He shuffled forward. "See if you can take Captain Stenna to my quarters without fucking it up, and make sure she can't get up to any mischief. That *doesn't* mean kill her." He turned to Alyda. "I'll give you an hour, 'Lyda. Please, don't disappoint me."

"Is what he's offered you worth it, Teril?" she asked the knight as they walked through the ransacked halls. He answered her with a dig in the back with her own blade.

Corvinius's quarters were as much of a sty as the rest of the Arth, if not worse. *Only a sick animal lives in its own filth.* Corvinius certainly fit that description.

"Take off the armour, Captain, and don't try anything," said Teril.

"Don't worry, I won't. I've seen how eager you are to kill me. When I'm crowned Queen of Tamalan you will not be invited to the ceremony." She unbuckled her armour and tossed each piece on the rumpled bed. "Did you kill your comrades, Teril? Or did you let the mercenaries do it?"

His face reddened and he drew back her sword as if to strike.

"Shut up!" he shouted. "They should have surrendered, just…just shut up."

For all his threats, his hands were shaking. Teril was a traitor *and* a coward. If she could goad him a little more, make him come closer…

Before she had chance to try, the door flew open and another Rusty barged in, crossbow at the ready.

"What's wrong?" she asked, eyeing Alyda from behind a fringe of black hair. "I heard you shouting, d'you need a hand?"

"No, I mean…yes," he mumbled. "Tie her up, would you? She's to wait here for the Captain." Teril fled the room.

The Rusty pointed to a chair with the bow. "Take a seat, Captain Stenna."

"You know my name, who the fuck are you?" Alyda asked.

"None of your damn business. Put your hands behind your back, nice and slowly or I'll stick you like a pig."

When she'd finished tying Alyda's hands to the spindles of the chair, she came around in front of her. The crossbow hovered inches from Alyda's face. She didn't flinch; she wasn't going to be intimidated by a Rusty.

"I'll wager you aren't feeling cocky now, are you, Captain Stenna?" The crossbow drifted closer, the tip of the bolt a finger width from her eye. "I could kill you, and say you were trying to escape. Who's to say otherwise?"

Alyda tried to focus on the bolt. "Do I know you? I haven't killed a friend of yours have I?"

"No, although thanks to darling Rufus, I feel like I know you. He's called out your name more than once when we've been fucking."

"Ah. It sounds like your issue is with Corvinius. Why don't you do both of us a favour and put a bolt through his eye?"

The knight laughed, but the bow stayed where it was. "Maybe one day, when he's of no further use. You know, if I thought for one minute that you were going to join him,

I *would* finish you, and damn the consequences, but you're not going to, are you?"

Alyda didn't answer.

The Rusty smiled and put up the bow. "My name's Karla Lystrom, for what it's worth. We've never met, but I've seen you and the Hammer many times. I could never decide if you were the great warriors everyone said you were or just a bunch of big-headed, swaggering thugs."

Alyda allowed herself a slight smile. "A little of both, but I'll tell you this; any one of us would gladly lay down our lives to defend any member of the Guards, no matter what we thought of them."

Lystrom's smile faded. "Then you're fools," she said, and left the room.

Alyda waited until she heard the key turn before trying the ropes. They were tightly bound around her wrists, but the spindles were long and slender. She took hold of the dowels and pulled. The wood bent and was about to snap when she heard footsteps outside, and the key turn. She froze. The door opened.

Much to her surprise a librarian walked in. He cast a furtive glance down the hall before closing and locking the door behind him. As he turned, she saw that he had a blade in his hand.

So Corvinius has taken the coward's way out and sent someone else to do his dirty work. She wasn't going to sit there and wait to have her throat cut. She heaved on the spindles. One snapped, but the other stubbornly refused to break. She jumped up, her right wrist still tied to the chair. She swung it at the would-be assassin. He leapt back and caught the improvised weapon. Before she had chance to wrench the chair from his grasp and beat him to death with it, he cut the rope, freeing her wrist.

"Captain Stenna," he whispered urgently. "My name's Garian Tain. I work for Lord Hyram."

While the knight searched for weapons, Garian explained what had happened, carefully omitting that neither he nor his master had suspected the Captain of the 5th of anything more daring than an affair with Princess Matia. It was a mistake that had cost them dearly, and one he would much rather keep to himself. Stenna listened to his tale, while she ransacked Corvinius's room. After enough cursing to make a sailor blush, all she'd managed to find was an old hunting knife.

"Where's your master?" she demanded.

"He's in the dungeons with those they thought worth keeping to ransom."

There had been nothing he could do when the Rusties came for Hyram, but it didn't stop him feeling guilty that he was free and his master was a prisoner.

"They didn't kill him?" She sounded surprised.

"I don't think Corvinius has the guts to kill the King's cousin. The Queen and her sons are being kept under guard in her apartments. I think they're still trying to pretend it's for her safety, not that there's anyone left to convince."

"I don't suppose you've got a sword hidden under those robes, have you?"

"I'm afraid not. I've got a spare knife if that's any use?"

The knight snorted. "Knives are for eating with. I'll make do with Corvinius' pig-sticker for now." She flipped the blade in her hand. "What I'd give for a decent sword and twenty knights. Liberating all the prisoners isn't going to be easy with just the two of us."

Her arrogance didn't surprise him. Garian hadn't expected her to thank him for the rescue; the Captain of the Hammer wasn't renowned for her good manners, but he was irritated that she seemed to think she was in charge.

"Corvinius didn't consider us lowly servants worth rounding up," he said. "There are about half a dozen of the King's agents at large in the Arth. But we have to focus our efforts on rescuing the Queen and her sons. Everyone else is expendable."

Stenna raised an eyebrow. "Says who? We must free the other prisoners, as well as the Queen and the Princes. I won't leave them to the mercy of the Guthani. Trust me, with a few good people we can get them all out. The Rusties can't fight for shit."

"We can't risk it."

"I won't leave those people to be butchered, Master Tain. Don't look so grim, I know a way we can do this. I did a stint of training with the Rusties when I first joined the Guards. I learnt nothing of tactics, but I did learn the lay of this Arth. There's a tunnel under the dungeon."

"Aye, I know the one. It leads to the sewers."

"That's right. When the guards have been dealt with, you need to open the gate and get the prisoners down there. Once you're in the city sewers they'll never be able to track you."

"They're a maze right enough...So who did you say was going to deal with the guards in the dungeon?"

She winked at him.

"Just like that, eh?"

"It should be fairly straightforward for a resourceful fellow like you."

"One thing; how do we get into the sewer when the gates are all warded shut? Nothing can open them except the King or Corvinius."

"The rightful King, the Captain of the Watch *and* the heir to the throne. Prince Talin can open them."

As much as he hated to admit it, the knight's confidence was infectious, perhaps dangerously so. Nevertheless, he felt like his burden had lessened since he'd rescued her.

Hyram wouldn't agree; he could hear the old man now, ordering him to leave everyone except the Queen. If he knew what they were planning, he'd explode.

"If me and my people are going to try and rescue everyone in the dungeon, does that mean you're going after the Queen and the Princes alone?"

She didn't even pause to think about it before she answered. "Aye. Now listen; I need you to get a message to Master Armourer Bainley. He should be at his forge here in the Arth, if he isn't in the dungeons or dead. D'you know him?"

"Not personally, but if he's here I'll find him. Why do you need him?"

"Horses. Tell him we need four and that he's to take them west, to the wood on the edge of the water meadow, down by the rotten oaks. Tell him to wait for me there and tell him to hurry."

"He won't be able to get horses out of the city."

"He won't have to. His sister lives by Tyris Bridge. That's where you'll find him if he isn't in the Arth. So I hope those little legs can run because you might have to cover some ground." She grinned.

He didn't take offence at the friendly dig; truth be told, it was nice to see a smile. It had been a tense week of sneaking around and avoiding patrols while trying to work out what the fuck he was going to do with the limited resources at his disposal.

"Don't worry; I'll saddle up a cat if I have to go over to Tyris."

She laughed and clapped him on the shoulder. "Good man. We'll take the Queen and her sons out through the old boathouse and make our way along the river bank, under the curtain wall. That way we don't have to fight our way out of the city, or risk being spotted trying to swim the river."

"The old boathouse has a warded gate…" said Garian, and then he remembered. "Ah, Prince Talin."

Time would tell if she was over confident and his trust misplaced, but right now she'd given him hope, which was more than he'd had a few hours ago. Hyram wouldn't agree, he'd say she was reckless. When he thought about his master—that his life depended on their actions—Garian was suddenly seized by doubt. "What happens if you fail?"

She looked him in the eye, her gaze steady. "I won't."

"But how will I know that you've succeeded?"

Despite the voice of his mentor ringing in his ears he wanted her to give an answer he could believe. He'd failed Hyram and Prince Olin once already; he couldn't fail them again.

"Corvinius will be here any minute. It must be what? Almost seven? I'll be at the Queen's apartments in an hour. That's when you need to be in the dungeon with your people."

"And I'll know you've freed the Prince and opened the gates how?"

"By trying them. I'm sorry, Master Tain, 'tis the best I can do. You'll have to have a bit of faith."

"Faith, eh? Not something I go in for much in my line of work."

"D'you have faith in your comrades?"

"They're as skilled and as well trained as any knight," he answered proudly.

"Then there's no reason we should fail. I have never lost a battle and I don't intend to start by letting Rufus Corvinius and his fucking Rusties beat me."

"Beat *us*, you mean, and I hope that's confidence not arrogance talking, Captain Stenna."

She grinned. "It's a little of both, Master Tain."

Corvinius arrived soon after they'd finalised their plans. Alyda was sitting on the chair, holding the rope behind her back. Now that her headache had gone and her anger had cooled, she noticed how drawn and dishevelled Corvinius looked. *A sick animal...*

"I'm sorry about this, but you didn't give me a choice. I can't trust you, 'Lyda. If I had a soul stone I'd damn well make you join me."

"That would satisfy you? Knowing that I was only with you because you compelled me with magic?"

"Yes, it would," he said earnestly. "Have you decided?"

She didn't answer.

"You don't owe the King or Trease anything. Antians have oppressed your people for centuries, why fight for them? Live for yourself, 'Lyda, as they have done."

"I can't," she said. It was an honest answer amid all the subterfuge.

Corvinius unsheathed his dagger. "You're a stupid, stubborn woman. You could be queen of your own kingdom, but instead you're choosing to die, and for what?"

"For my honour and my oath, Rufus. If you weren't such a self-centred fa'cachta you'd understand."

Anger flashed across his face. He took a two handed grip on the dagger. "I'm glad you said that—you've reminded me why I need to do this. Even though I know I'm going to regret it when I'm sober." He raised the knife.

Tain had been hiding behind the bed curtain, and had been slowly creeping up on Corvinius since the knight entered the room.

"No you won't," said Tain, and cracked him over the head with a chair leg.

Alyda leapt up and caught Corvinius before he hit the ground. Tain relieved him of his weapons.

"Neatly done, Master Tain."

"You've no idea how much I've wanted to do that."

"Oh, I think I do."

Tain listened at the door. After a few tense minutes he gave her the all clear. She slapped Corvinius across the face. It took a few attempts to bring him round but eventually he opened his eyes. He groaned when he saw the knife at his throat. "I knew you'd be my downfall."

"Do as you're told, Rufus and you'll live to hang another day," said Alyda.

The Arth was swathed in shadows and as quiet as a tomb. Alyda strode confidently along the corridor, arm-in-arm with Corvinius, a dagger pressed against his ribs.

She'd given him his sword back after tying it discreetly into the scabbard. She'd also had to swap the hunting knife for the spy's smaller blade. She wasn't happy about that; if Corvinius tried to break free or raise the alarm, she'd be hard pressed to stop him with a fruit knife. She'd have to trust that Corvinius's well-developed sense of self-preservation would win out over any altruistic desire he might have to warn his knights.

"You really are full of yourself, aren't you, 'Lyda? Do you honestly think that you and that little, *torch cul* can liberate the Queen and her brats? Two of you, against three hundred?"

Alyda had to laugh; it was either that or knife him. "Since when have any number of Rusties or mercs been a match for a real knight?"

"I wasn't going to kill you, you know," he confessed.

She pushed the blade against his ribs. "Shut up, Rufus because have no doubt, I *will* kill you."

She took a deep breath and tried to look at ease as they entered the corridor that led to the Queen's apartments. There were two guards outside. One was slouching by the door, the other was taking a piss against the wall. Like their Captain, they'd obviously been enjoying the contents of the wine cellar. A dozen empty bottles lay strewn across the floor.

"Remember what you're doing, Rufus, or—"

"You'll do something unmentionable to me. Fear not, my love; I know my part." He cleared his throat. The guards saw him, and jumped to attention.

"At ease, Toral," said Corvinius to the shorter of the two.

This would be easier than she'd thought, they both looked drunk. The one he called Toral was as wide as he was tall. By the way he was ineptly juggling his sword and bow it looked like he spent as much time in the practice yard as she did in the scriptorium. While the guard unlocked the door, Alyda kept her eye on Corvinius. If he was going to try to warn them, it would be now.

"I do hope the Queen isn't still snivelling. We don't want her looking a mess when the Guthani arrive." Corvinius grinned at Alyda.

Toral puffed out his chest. "She wailed a fair bit when they brought in that little shit Talin. By the looks of him he'd had a bit of a kicking, but she soon shut up when I told her. You know me, Captain, I won't put up with any nonsense."

Alyda kept hold of Corvinius until they were inside and she heard the door lock behind them. Talin was standing in front of his mother and brother. His face was bruised and his shirt torn and blood stained. A broad smile lit up his face when he saw her. Alyda put her finger to her lips and gestured to a braided cord dangling from the curtains. Talin ripped it down and used it to bind Corvinius's hands behind his back before shoving him into a chair.

"What do you think you're going to achieve, 'Lyda? You'll never get out of the Arth," said Corvinius.

"We got past you," she said, and then turned to Talin. "Talin, you must command the Ward to open the sewer gate so that Garian Tain and his companions may pass through. Do it now—and while you're at it, revoke Corvinius's ability to command them."

"The Ward, of course." Corvinius laughed. "If only I'd thought of that. Too much wine I suppose, but it doesn't matter; you'll never be able to avoid all of the knights between here and the sewers. Not even the heroic *Captain of the Hammer* can fight her way through two hundred warriors."

"Shut up, Rufus, or I swear I will end you right now." Alyda hoped he believed her.

"And if she doesn't," Talin added, "I will."

Corvinius smirked, but held his tongue.

Talin closed his eyes and touched the wall. A short time passed before he opened them again.

"It's done. We need to get out of here, Ali. I overheard the guards talking; the Guthani are coming. They intend to use us to force my father to abdicate in favour of my uncle."

"That cannot be allowed to happen," Thea croaked. Her eyes were red rimmed and puffy from crying.

"I know. Don't worry—I have a plan." Alyda suddenly remembered who the sniffling woman was and bowed. "Forgive me for being brusque, Majesty."

"No need to apologise, Captain. As for you," Thea turned to Corvinius. "You will pay for what you have done. There's a cold place in the Void reserved for traitors like you."

"There aren't any traitors like me, and please; spare me your peasant's view o' the Void and who warrants entry. If killing to get what you want is a criterion for admittance, your husband and his ancestors will surely be there ahead of me."

The Queen recoiled, stung by his words. Talin looked close to punching the smug grin off Corvinius's face. Alyda stepped in and grabbed the disgraced knight by his shirt.

"You can plan for your future when the rope's around your neck, right now we have to get out of here, and you are going to help us."

His mother and Olin locked themselves in her bedchamber; Talin positioned himself behind Corvinius, who they'd sat in a chair opposite the door. Alyda was standing next to the door with her back to the wall and the traitor's sword in hand. She signalled Corvinius; the knight said nothing. Talin showed him the blade and gestured at the door with its tip.

"Toral," Corvinius shouted with little enthusiasm. "Get your arse in here. The old bitch is sick."

That was it. Talin grabbed Corvinius by the hair; he was going to cut the bastard's throat. Alyda gestured furiously for him to stop as the key turned in the lock. Much as he wanted to draw the knife across Corvinius's throat, he let him go.

The short knight ambled in. Before he'd taken two paces into the room, Alyda swung her sword, and hacked into the side of his neck. The blade bit deep. Blood sprayed across the room. The knight gurgled a cry and fell, clutching his throat.

The second Rusty was standing open-mouthed in the doorway. By the time she managed to drag her eyes away from her dying comrade, it was too late. Alyda spun on her heel, sidestepped and thrust her sword between the plates of the knight's cuirass. She gasped; Alyda grabbed her arm and pulled her onto the blade. The dying guard squeezed the trigger of the crossbow, the bolt buried itself the ceiling. Alyda dragged her inside, and kicked the door closed.

Talin had seen people die in the lists and he'd witnessed two executions, but he'd never seen killing like that. The woman he loved had just slaughtered two people in front of him without breaking a sweat, without a moment's pause. He knew that was what she did, but to see it, to hear the bubbling rattle of a man choking to death on his own blood, and that smell; like honey mixed with hot iron... Disgusted and on the point of heaving, he tore down a curtain and covered the twitching corpses.

Corvinius didn't look even slightly aggrieved that two of his knights had been butchered in front of him. The bastard was smiling at Alyda.

"Get your mother and brother," she said to Talin as she wiped the Rusties blood off her face.

The shadows were kind to Garian and his accomplices as they made their way to the dungeon to do the exact opposite of what Hyram would have wanted. He wasn't sure how Stenna had convinced him to do the right thing, for the wrong reasons, but like when he rescued Suli, it felt good. If only it could offset some of the wrong he'd done for the right reasons—*for the good of the kingdom*, but he doubted that.

He led the unlikely group down the unguarded stairwell to the cells. With him were a pastry cook, two scullery maids, a pantry boy, and a footman. All of them were agents; all had been playing those roles when Corvinius had staged his takeover. Garian was playing himself. Having ditched the robe he was dressed in nondescript, dark shirt and breeches. He might very well die, but it wouldn't be because he tripped over the hem of that bloody liability.

He reached the bottom of the stairs and signalled for the others to wait. He could hear snatches of conversation coming from the guardroom. After listening for a few minutes he edged closer and stole a look inside. Two armoured guards were sitting at a table in the middle of the room; a third was warming herself by a brazier in the corner, they weren't Rusties. Opposite the stairs was a weapon rack. A corridor stretched off to the left.

Bloody mercenaries. He'd have preferred to take on a group of out of shape Rusties, but six against three was still good odds. He signed to his comrades how many there were and how they were going to attack them. One of the scullery maids spanned and loaded a heavy crossbow. Garian unhooked the handbow from his belt and did the same. They crept down the stairs while the others waited.

Garian mouthed, "*One, two, three.*" On three they stepped into the room, picked their targets and let fly. Garian's bolt struck the knight by the brazier in the back. The slender shaft snapped with a loud crack as it hit the steel cuirass she was wearing beneath her surcoat. The scullery maid fared little better. Her bolt struck one of the seated guards in the face, scoring a bloody gouge in his cheek before flying past and shattering against the wall.

The warrior roared, grabbed a mace off the table and jumped to his feet. Cursing, the other guard flung the table aside and snatched up an axe. Garian dropped the bow and drew his knife as the one he'd hit ran at him swinging a battle axe. The rest of the agents charged down the stairs.

The cook ran over to Garian and blocked the mercenary's blow with her sword. The blade locked against the hook of the axe, but the mercenary was quick and twisted her weapon, pulling the cook off balance and within reach of the dagger she had in her offhand. Too late, Garian saw the blade. All he could do was shout a warning, unable to get at the mercenary because the cook had come between them. The mercenary ripped the blade up, into the cook's stomach, two hard jabs that spilled her guts. The cook went down and died in a spreading pool of her own blood and entrails.

The mercenary stepped over the body and took a swing at Garian's head with the axe, at the same time slashing at his stomach with the dagger. He jumped back; narrowly avoiding both attacks, but caught his heel on the bottom step and fell backwards. The mercenary had him. Garian watched the axe descend, but as she closed for the kill she slipped in the cook's blood.

Garian seized his chance and rolled aside. The axe whistled down and struck chips of stone from the step where his head had been. He rolled back, and using his body weight to add strength to his arm, stabbed the knife into the unarmoured hollow of the mercenary's knee. She howled in pain and fell forward, tearing the knife from his grasp. Before she had a chance to recover, he leapt on her back, grabbed her head, and smashed her face against the steps until she stopped moving.

Heart pounding, he turned to see how his comrades were faring. The pantry boy and the footman had one of the other mercenaries cornered. The wiry pantry boy was ferociously quick with the rapier he was using. He darted in and feigned an attack while the footman, who was armed with a poleaxe he'd taken from the rack, thrust at the mercenary's body. There was a high-pitched screech of metal against metal, but the poleaxe failed to pierce the fluted breastplate. However the force of the blow slammed the mercenary against the wall, where the footman pinned him long enough for the pantry boy to step in and open his unprotected throat.

Across the other side of the room, one of the scullery maids went down with the side of her head smashed in. The other maid avenged her by stabbed her killer in the face, dropping him instantly.

As suddenly as it had begun, the fight was over. The scullery maid tossed the sword she'd been using and positioned herself at the bottom of the stairs where she spanned and reloaded the crossbow. Garian searched the mercenaries. When he found the keys, he rushed to unlock the cells.

Roused by the sound of fighting, the prisoners were hammering on the doors, begging to be released. In the first cell he unlocked he was surprised to find a handful of Rusties. They all looked like they'd taken a beating. A grey-haired knight followed Garian to the next cell, while his comrades hunted for weapons.

"Is this a full-scale attack or a daring rescue?" he asked.

"It's only us, I'm afraid."

The knight sighed.

Garian unlocked the remaining cells; he was searching for one prisoner in particular, but it was so crowded he couldn't find him.

He was starting to worry that he wasn't there when a familiar figure barged out of the last cell.

"Are they safe?" Hyram demanded. The King's Councillor had a black eye and his velvet robes were ripped and stained, but other than that he seemed his usual amiable self.

"You're welcome, and yes it's good to see you too, sir."

"Don't be glib, boy. Are they safe?"

"Yes…I think so."

The Spymaster narrowed his eyes. "You only *think* so? This had better be bloody good."

"It is. I'll explain on the way out," he said as he tried to usher his master over to the sewer entrance.

The scullery maid called over. "We've got company on the way, sir. I'd say several and armoured."

Garian hoped Stenna had succeeded or this would be a very brief escape. "My Lord, if you could make your way down the stairs *now*." Garian shouted over to the pantry boy who was holding the door to the sewers. "Fingal! Hurry up and get 'em down."

He took a deep breath and tried to relax. Saving lives was as good a way to go as any, but it hurt to think he'd never see Suli again. Hurt worse than a knife in the gut. A little longer to think about it, and he had a feeling that it might not seem like such a good idea.

"Well, I must say, this is a poor rescue..." Hyram muttered, dagger in one hand, mace in the other. "Do you know how long it's been since I tackled anything more dangerous than a mature cheese?"

"Asha's paps. My Lord, you must go! We can hold them long enough for everyone to get out, but you have to leave now!" said Garian.

Hyram opened his mouth to protest when the grey-haired Rustie stepped forward.

"With all due respect, sir, the Fifth guards the royal residences. We'll hold them for as long as we can, but I fear it may be little more than a gesture of defiance. The sewers are Ward locked. No mortal force can open them."

Garian sighed. "How hard can it be? The Wards will be lifted. You can all escape; we'll stay and cover you."

The knight didn't look convinced. "Well, I'm pleased to hear that, lad. Now go, and let us do our job. We'll show this scum what real knights are, even Rusty ones."

There was no point arguing, Garian threw up his hands. "Very well, I don't have time for this. Lock the door behind us, and good luck."

The knight raised the axe in salute. "Please tell our families; I'm Lieutenant Leo Ternis..." He pointed to the other five in turn "...Fredrick Ghentz, Luta Stornitz, Mishal Lumov, Kyrin Morrill and Kieran Delrich. Please tell them..." The old knight scratched his chin as he hunted for the right words. "Tell them we didn't betray our oath."

"You forgot me!" A young girl peered from behind Ternis, eyes bright with tears.

"I haven't forgotten anything. This rascal is my squire, Gabriella Aldred. She's in dire need of more training, so I'd be most grateful if you could take her with you."

"No!" the girl protested. "I want to stay."

"We need to hurry, sir," called the footman, backing down the stairwell.

"Go now," said the knight and pushed his squire towards Garian.

"I'll tell them," he said. He'd already forgotten their names, but the girl knew. Stenna would probably say something meaningful to the old warrior, something stirring. He had no words of comfort for those about to die, what was the point? The Rusty marshalled his people at the bottom of the stairs. Garian shouted for the remaining agents to fall back, and he set off towards the sewers, making sure his master was with him.

Hyram took the girl gently, but firmly by the arm and led her down into the darkness. "Did you know I once saw two Guthani Sea Drakes fighting during a thunderstorm?" Hyram's voice echoed in the dank passageway. "Of course you don't. Let me tell you what happened…"

To Garian's great relief when he reached the bottom of the stairs he saw people filing through the open grate and into the murky waters of the castle sewers. Stenna must have reached the Prince. He had no way of knowing if they'd escaped, but at the moment he had more pressing concerns. Shouting erupted from above, swiftly followed by the clash of steel. He and the other agents hurried the prisoners along. When they were all through, he closed the grate. The huge locking clasp fastened over the bar beneath the water with a dull clang.

Chapter Ten

"Why are we bringing him with us?" said Thea, and cast a venomous glare at Corvinius as Alyda herded them along a narrow passageway.

"We might need him as a hostage, Majesty," said Alyda, tied by etiquette to answer the Queen even though she was more concerned with getting them out than having a discussion about Corvinius. She'd decide what to do with the miserable bastard later. "I've arranged horses for us," she said, hoping to change the subject. "They'll be waiting near the water meadows."

"How will we get out of the Arth?" Thea asked.

"Do you know the old boathouse? The one behind the orchard, next to the little chapel?"

"Of course, but it's…ah, yes. Talin can lift the Ward on the gate." Thea smiled for the first time since they had been freed. "I know a short cut to the chapel. It's not a secret passage as such, but few people use it these days. Come—let me show you."

The Queen set a brisk pace and led them down an even narrower passage to what looked like a dead end. She urged them on and into a cunningly hidden service corridor.

"I often come this way when I want to avoid people," Thea confided.

The Queen's knowledge was a surprising boon. Alyda had no idea the passage existed, and she knew the Arth reasonably well. She hoped Tain was sharing their good luck. She hadn't heard any alarms, which was as close to a good sign as they were likely to get.

Candles flickered in niches set in the walls on the way to the chapel. Centuries ago, when the Arth had been a more modest fortress, this had been the only chapel to Ashania and Sestrian. Like the seed of a pearl, it was now hidden within the great fortress that had grown around it. Alyda listened at the ancient Wildwood doors until she was satisfied that it was empty.

They crowded into the modest chamber. Candlelight bathed the room in a warm glow and draped the sanctuary in deepening shades of amber. A row of simple wooden benches ran either side of a narrow central aisle. The stone floor was strewn with clean rushes and sweet scented herbs. It had been worn into softly undulating hollows from centuries of use. At one end of the room was an ancient altar stone on which were a pair of silver candle sticks shaped like the branching antlers of a stag. Alyda tipped a nod towards the altar. It didn't hurt to hedge one's bets and they still had a way to go before they were out.

"I wonder who lit the candles?" said Olin.

The door that led to the orchard was across the aisle, opposite the one they'd just used. While the others caught their breath, Alyda opened it a crack and stole a look outside. The only movement was the gentle sway of fruit laden branches. The sweet smell of apples made her stomach growl. After checking the wall was clear of patrols, she ushered the fugitives across the shadowed orchard.

When they were halfway across, a bell began to toll somewhere in the Arth. Thea froze; Alyda grabbed her wrist and ran her over to the boathouse gate that was set in the curtain wall. Talin shoved Corvinius in front of him;

Olin hitched up his robe and ran ahead of them all. They flattened against the wall, hardly daring to breathe.

Alyda quickly realised that it wasn't the Ward, just a mundane alarm bell, but an alarm nonetheless. The walkway above them remained clear, and there weren't any sounds of pursuit coming towards them from the Arth or the chapel. It didn't mean they were safe; the bodies in the Queen's apartments might have been found, or perhaps Tain had been caught. Either way, the Arth was on alert and they had to get out now. Alyda took hold of Corvinius, while Talin commanded the Ward to unlock the gate.

"You'll never make it," Corvinius whispered. Even in the darkness she could tell he was smiling.

"You should be grateful that I brought you with us. The Guthani wouldn't thank you for losing the Queen."

He leaned closer. "And how would you like me to show my gratitude?"

She drew Tain's knife from her boot. "By shutting up or dropping dead, either will do."

Flaking warts of rust crusted the gate's hinges, but when Talin addressed the Ward and tugged the metal bars, it swung open easily. Once they were all inside, he pulled it closed and it locked in place with a hollow clang. He asked the Ward to make sure it stayed that way.

The rotted decking was beyond any magic he could invoke. Spongy and threadbare, the planks were slippery with fungus and spattered with bird droppings. The pale ghost of a sunken row boat lay just beneath the waterline, and starlight shone through the pockmarked roof.

The building looked like it was about to slide into the Wey, but the gate would hold out against an army if the legends about the Wards were true. Talin didn't find the knowledge particularly comforting. Right then he'd kill for a ball of Pel.

"Over here," said Alyda and proceeded to pull off some panelling on the side of the boathouse. Although she was being as quiet as she could, the noise of straining wood sounded horribly loud.

"Why are we going this way?" his mother asked her. Talin was pleased that she sounded more like her usual assured self.

"By working our way along the curtain wall we'll avoid having to swim the Wey, Majesty. It'll take a little longer to reach the water meadows, but I think it's our best chance of getting away without being seen."

Alyda didn't sound particularly happy about having to explain her plans, even if it was to the Queen of Antia. He empathised; he'd been on the end of his mother's habitual interrogations many times. No matter how critical the situation, he knew she wouldn't move unless forced or convinced that they were taking the best route.

"Are you sure we wouldn't be better off swimming the river here?" Thea asked as if to prove his point.

"Yes, Majesty," said Alyda. "The river's fast and deep here and there's no cover on the opposite bank. Even if we all made it across we'd more than likely be spotted. The water meadows have tall reeds that we can use for cover and they're bordered by Tyris wood. They'll be a damn—." Ali coughed. "They'll be much easier and safer to cross than the river."

Talin grinned. He could hear his mother give a tiny worried sigh, but she nodded her assent.

The ledge at the base of the curtain wall was about four feet wide and overgrown with wiry shrubs and snagging brambles. It was just about passable if they went in single file.

Corvinius glanced over his shoulder at Alyda as she shoved him ahead of her. "How long are you going to keep me alive, 'Lyda?" he whispered. "How long before you decide I'm of no further use and just slowing you down?"

She didn't answer. She had no desire to get drawn into an argument with Corvinius.

He laughed softly. "I don't think you know. I'm sure the Queen and her get are also wondering why I'm still alive. Why aren't I dead 'Lyda? Why aren't I in that, *'cold place in the Void'*, dear old Thea has lined up for me?"

Why not indeed. Alyda tightened her grip on his arm, and let him feel the point of her knife against his ribs.

"Because I want to see you hang, Rufus. I want everyone to know what you've done and see you swing for it. I want you to hang until you rot off the fucking rope."

"Now don't hold back, 'Lyda my love. You know what I think? I don't think your childish notion of honour will let you kill an unarmed prisoner, least of all me. Could it be that you still have feelings for me?"

"Trust me, that's not a wager you want to make, Rufus."

She was sure that she could end him in a heartbeat if he tried anything, but he knew her well enough to know that she wasn't given to killing in cold blood. She was an oath-sworn knight; her honour meant something to her, even if it meant nothing to him.

Pain in the arse though he was, Corvinius wasn't her only concern. Even though she made allowances for the Queen and her younger son, their progress was painfully slow. Not only were they far too noisy, but they had to keep stopping every few feet to help Thea, who kept tripping over her heavy gown and catching it on brambles. If they didn't hurry up, it would be daylight before they reached the woods.

Eventually they came within sight of the West Gate Bridge. Alyda gave a sigh of relief, they were almost there.

As they clambered over a particularly dense patch of undergrowth, Corvinius stumbled. Alyda lost her grip on his arm. It was the moment he'd been waiting for. Her stomach lurched as she watched him hop his legs through his bound wrists, and angle his body towards the water. She leapt on him and hooked her arm around his neck as he made to dive in the river. Planting her feet, she threw herself back, towards the curtain wall, dragging Corvinius away from the water's edge. They fell, Corvinius landed on top of her.

Hot blood gushed down her arm as his weight drove him on to Tain's knife. The traitor gasped; their eyes met. She twisted the blade, up, deeper and held his gaze as he died.

She pushed the corpse off her and put her back against the wall, steam rising from her blood-drenched arm. Someone, probably Trease, had said killing should never be too easy, and never too hard. In this case it had been very easy, and that shocked her.

By the time Talin had struggled past his mother and brother it was all over.

"Are you alright?" he asked. He had the same horrified look on his face as when she'd killed the Rusties earlier.

"Aye," she said, and wiped the knife on her breeches.

"We should throw him in the river," said Thea. Her voice was surprisingly cold. For all her tears, it seemed that the Queen wasn't as delicate as she looked.

"That's not a good idea, Majesty," said Alyda. "He might float downstream into the river gate. We don't want them to start searching up-river for us. We need to keep them in the dark for as long as we can."

She looked around for somewhere they could hide the body. The ledge wasn't ideal, but it would have to do. "We'll hide him in the undergrowth. He won't stay hidden for long." *Not when the rats get at him.* "But we'll be far from here by then," she said with more hope than certainty.

Thea didn't balk from piling stones and dirt onto the still warm corpse, but Prince Olin was shaking like a colt. When they set off again he kept glancing over his shoulder at the rough mound, as though he expected Corvinius to climb out of the make-shift grave and come after them. Alyda felt sorry for the boy, but she had no words of comfort to give him. He'd have to find the key to unlock his courage by himself, or learn to live with his fear. All she could do was get him and his mother safely away from here; the demons in his mind were his alone to conquer.

Passing beneath the West Gate Bridge was going to be the most dangerous part of the escape. It wasn't as busy as the East Gate, but there would still be more guards concentrated in the barbican than along the wall. Alyda tried to hurry them along, but they were only as fast as the slowest member of the group, which in this case was a middle-aged woman completely unused to scrabbling around in the undergrowth. Alyda didn't like looking after civilians, not even—or perhaps particularly, royal ones. She served them best on the battlefield. All this sneaking about was a job more suited to Tain, wherever in the Void he was.

When they were safely hidden in the shadowed arches of the abutments, Alyda called a halt so that the Queen could rest. She was quietly grateful when, of her own accord, Thea took off her heavy over-gown and hid it between the bridge supports. She looked cold in her thin under-gown and petticoats, but they might move a little faster now that she wouldn't be caught on every thorn they passed. While his mother and brother rested, Alyda took the opportunity to speak to Talin.

"The river veers off soon, and the water meadows are about two hundred feet beyond the bridge. If we're spotted, I want you to lead them into the woods. If Bainley's there, get the horses and ride north. If not, head north through the woods, follow the river as far as you can. Don't try to find your father; the west will be crawling with mercenaries and Guthlanders."

Talin plucked a leaf from her hair. His fingers brushed her cheek, rousing altogether inappropriate feelings given their situation and what had just happened.

"If you think I'm going to leave you, you'd best think again," he said.

She laughed softly. "You're such a pain in the arse, Highness."

Beyond the bridge, Alyda led them along the ledge until it widened out and became part of the watery reed beds that pushed the inky flow into the depth of Tyris Wood.

Wading across the waterlogged ground was hard going for all of them, particularly the Queen. When they finally reached the trees and solid ground, she and Prince Olin collapsed in a heap, exhausted and shivering in the cold night air. If Tain hadn't found Bainley they'd have no choice but to head out on foot. Looking at Olin and his mother, Alyda didn't imagine they would get very far. Neither looked to have much walking left in them.

Leaving Talin on guard, Alyda went to find Bainley. She looked back at the Arth. Torches skipped along the parapet, but there was still no sign to indicate they were onto them. Without Corvinius, there was nobody to give the orders, nobody with wit to organise a proper search. *Rufus.* In the old days, knights were soul bound to serve, it seemed so primitive, so unnecessary and yet after what damage he had wrought. *Damn you Rufus.*

She put him from her mind, and carried on looking for Bainley. She wasn't concerned that the armourer wasn't waiting to meet them. It would have taken time for him to get to his sister's farm even if the spy had found him straightaway. Of course, she had to consider that he may not have found him at all.

After half an hour of fruitless searching she was about to head back to the others and tell them the bad news when she heard a horse snicker a greeting. She ducked down until she saw Bainley's familiar, barrel-shaped outline loom from the darkness. He was leading a group of horses.

"Ali!" he exclaimed in a loud whisper when she showed herself. "Asha's paps! You're like your father, you are. You don't ask favours often, but gods, when you do…" He threw his arms around her.

"I'm glad to see you, sir," she answered when he let her go and she could breathe again.

They led the horses over to where the others were waiting.

"You're lucky your man caught me. I was just shutting down the forge for…well, I don't know how long. Hmm… anyway, a few minutes later and I'd have gone."

Alyda looked at the horses. "Only three?"

"Aye, and I cannot guarantee these beasts at all, but they're the only ones my brother-in-law could spare. They need the matched pair for the cart."

"I'm grateful to you and your family, Trell."

The armourer waved his hand dismissively. "Ah, 'tis the least I could do. You're the daughter of one of my oldest friends, and I know you'd do the same for me."

"True enough. I'll see your family right for these."

"No need to worry on that score. Bless her heart, but my sister's a grip like death when it comes to her purse and property. She wouldn't give over a cheese rind without seeing coin first, but as I'm her only brother I got a good deal." He winked. "Hmm. Anyway, here they are."

Bainley peered at the shadowy figures in the darkness. They didn't come forward and Alyda didn't offer to make introductions.

"They look fine. There's something else I need to ask you and it's no small task…"

Bainley raised an eyebrow. "Hmm. Let's hear it. Although I must warn you, my Free Company days are long gone. I'm fit enough to swing a hammer, but I've not done any soldiering for many years."

"No offence, but if you get into a fight, we're fucked. Avoiding trouble is what's required. I need to you take a message to the King."

Bainley listened while she explained the meat of what had happened without directly telling him the people with her were the Queen and her sons. The creases on his brow deepened as the tale unfolded. She felt guilty asking him to take on such a risky mission, but she didn't have a choice. She couldn't rely on Tain getting out and she couldn't leave the Queen and Princes and go herself.

Bainley scratched his balding head, he didn't look happy. "Hmm…well now. Nothing for it, I suppose. The King needs to know right enough. I'll have to go tell Nessa and the girls. They're at my sister's; we're all heading off north until this blows over." He smiled tightly. Asking him to perform an even more dangerous task was a poor reward for helping her. *Hard as iron, cold as stone, Ali.* She took the reins from him. "I'd tell them to leave tonight if I was you. Guthlanders will be here on the 'morrow."

"Aye? Can't believe it. We'd planned to set out as soon as I got back, because of what the 5th were up to, Nes isn't going to be happy when she hears this."

She nodded; anything she said now would be cold comfort.

"I wasn't sure if you'd need any supplies," said Bainley, "so I put some food and spare cloaks in the saddle bags just in case."

"Thank you, Trell, I owe you."

Bainley chuckled. "Aye you do. You can buy me an ale or five when we're back in Weyhithe and this bad business is done. Hmm…speaking of which, I'd best be going. Good luck to you, Ali, and to your friends." He inclined his head to the shadowy figures before heading back the way he'd come.

When he'd gone, Alyda gave the Queen the reins of the most docile looking animal.

"What an excellent fellow, I'm sure I've met him before. Tell me, how do you know him?" The Queen's tone was more questioning than conversational.

"I've known him all my life, Majesty. He served in my father's Free Company."

Thea patted the dark bay cob. "Forgive my caution, Captain Stenna. I find that I'm a more suspicious person today than I was yesterday."

"I understand, Majesty."

"So, where do you think we should go from here?" Talin asked.

Good question. And one she'd given a great deal of thought to as they'd made their escape. "Ill-equipped as we are, I think the closest and safest place we can reach is Gallen Arth where the First and the Fourth should be."

"Not Trelanlith?" asked Thea.

"No, Majesty. Corvinius forged a letter from the King and ordered the First to Gallen."

"Is there anywhere else worth considering?" Talin asked, as he helped his brother onto one of the horses before climbing up behind him.

"No, not really. It's too risky to go across country to try and find the King, and there'll be Guthani warbands hunting for you on the 'morrow." She didn't add that the King might already be dead.

"I trust your judgement, Captain Stenna," said Thea. Alyda thought it best not to tell her the full extent of Corvinius treachery. She bowed to the Queen.

"If we keep off the main roads and stick to hunting trails and back routes, we'll avoid search parties and be at Gallen in less than two days."

"Then let us make haste, while we still have the night on our side," said Thea.

It took three of them to lift the sewer lid, but eventually the rust and accumulated filth relinquished its grip on the iron grate.

Garian was the first out. Keeping low to the ground, he did a quick sweep of the area before deciding it was safe for the others to climb up. He was relieved to have got them here after taking a few wrong turns in the confusion down below. He was used to solitary trips through the sewers not leading dozens of angry and scared civilians.

The square was in the poorer quarter of the city and too close to the tanneries for any but the lowest vagrant to set up home there for long. The air was rank with the stench of rotted fat, piss, and dung, but it was like perfume compared to the smell of the sewers.

Garian sent the footman to watch the entrance to the main street. The other agents shepherded the bedraggled survivors into a derelict building out of sight of any passing patrols.

Hyram detached himself from the group and steered Garian out of earshot. The King's Councillor fished a chain from the folds of his robes. It had a chunky signet ring dangling from it. Garian saw the old man's hands were shaking as he struggled with the chain's clasp. Hyram was grey, and sweat beaded his forehead. After mumbling a few curses he pulled the chain apart and slid the ring off.

"Here, take this." He pressed the ring into Garian's hand. "Those who need to, know it's mine."

It was gold, comfortably heavy, with two diamonds set in the shoulders of the mount. Blunt claws gripped a polished carnelian engraved with the King's griffin. It was a grander version of the ring Hyram had given him on his fourteenth birthday. Garian threaded it onto the leather thong he wore around his neck and tucked it into his shirt.

"You must find out what has happened to Thea and the Princes," commanded the spymaster. "I know Talin lifted the Wards, but that doesn't mean they escaped. When you've done that, you must go to Daris. Pray gods it's not too late. He must know what has happened here, is that clear?" Garian frowned. "Crystal. Aren't you coming with me?"

Hyram laughed. "Ye gods, boy! My days of haring across the countryside are long gone. No, I shall remain here and cause as much trouble as I can for that treacherous bastard Corvinius. I'll send Fingal to Daris tonight, just to make doubly sure the information gets through."

"Don't worry, I'll reach the King."

"Of course you will—and I'll see you when we've cleaned up this mess. Now get going, time is our enemy." He snorted. "One of many!"

He watched the boy disappear into the winding maze of streets, a dark scrap of shadow flitting between buildings. Hyram could just about remember the locations of three or four safe houses dotted around the city. He'd split the group and send them off with his agents. They were an unwelcome burden, but he couldn't leave them to make their way alone in the city, some of the noble escapees weren't bright enough to find their arses with both hands. When they'd gone on their way, he'd head over to Swift Street and a rather ordinary looking tailor's shop.

The merchant who owned it was highly skilled with a pair of shears and like all talented artisans, measured twice and cut once. If anyone could get to Corvinius and deal with the treacherous bastard, he could. He could also make very flattering robes for those with a fuller figure.

Hyram leaned against a wall and waited impatiently for the pain in his chest to ease. Sitting there, rubbing the ache from his arm, he was struck with an uncustomary pang of regret when he realised that he hadn't thanked the boy for rescuing him.

It had started to rain, but Alyda was much happier now that they were putting some miles between them and the city. The narrow hunting trail didn't look like it had been used in a while, which was also good. The rain beat a steady rhythm on the leaves, and from across the valley she caught the occasional glimpse of rosy light spilling from cottage windows. As night drew on and they rode deeper into the forest, the only illumination was the moon, shredded into slivers by the thinning canopy.

They rode through the dreary night and the monotonous drizzle. Alyda was grateful for the cloaks Bainley had packed. She wondered if he'd set off yet to find the King, wondered if Nessa was cursing her name for drawing her family into this mess. Her thoughts turned back to Corvinius and the devastation his treachery had wrought. Now that a few hours had passed, the only thing she regretted about his death was that she hadn't killed him sooner.

It was almost midday when she decided it was safe enough to call a halt. They found a sheltered dell with a trickle of a stream running through it. It wasn't the best campsite, but it was out of sight of the path.

While his mother and brother stretched their legs, Talin helped Alyda with the horses.

"So what's for lunch, roast duckling? Beef stew?" he asked brightly.

"How about stale bread, hard cheese, and a couple of apples." She looked over to his mother and brother. "How are they doing, Highness?"

"Better than I would have thought, but I'll be happier when we reach Gallen Arth—and why are you calling me 'Highness'? We don't need to hide our affections."

"I'm not trying to hide anything," she said, even though that was exactly what she was trying to do.

"No? My mother doesn't call my father *Majesty*, you know."

"She's his wife and a Queen. I'm neither, and…it's just better if we observe protocol." This wasn't a conversation she wanted to have right now, or ever. This kind of talk smacked of plans for the future. When it came to her relationship with Talin—*the heir to the throne*, there was no future.

He smiled. "Why, Captain, you're not ashamed of me, are you?"

Alyda checked her horse's hooves, flicked a wedge of mud from under its shoe as it hungrily tore at the grass.

"No, of course not," she said and moved on to the next horse. "But I need to keep my mind on my duty."

"Then I command you to stop frowning and smile at once. There, how's that? I keep forgetting you warrior-types like being ordered about."

She laughed at that. "I'm a Knight Captain. I like *giving* orders. I'm sorry by the way. I should have listened to my instincts instead of leading you into a trap back there. I knew something was wrong the moment I read that letter."

"There's no need to apologise. If we hadn't gone back to Weyhithe my mother and Oli would now be in the hands of the Guthani. I should be thanking you for saving them."

"That isn't necessary, *Talin;* it's what your father pays me for."

"That may be, but when we reach Gallen Arth I insist on showing my gratitude personally."

She made sure that his mother wasn't looking and gently cupped his crotch. "I look forward to it."

They ate the last of the food Bainley had packed and set off again. The Queen's mount didn't want to go anywhere, so Alyda rode beside her to encourage it to get going.

"It's good to hear them laugh," said the Queen, "especially Olin. This has all been very hard on him."

Alyda looked at the brothers. *It is good,* she thought. *Talin's face lights up when he smiles.*

"You have quite charmed my son, Captain."

Alyda wasn't expecting that. She felt her cheeks redden. "It has been a privilege to help mentor him. He's a fast study and—"

"That isn't what I meant."

Alyda was acutely uncomfortable. There was nothing she could say without entering very awkward territory and so she tried to change the subject.

"If we can maintain the same pace we've kept thus far, we should arrive at Gallen Arth before nightfall tomorrow."

The Queen smiled and graciously let the previous conversation die. Alyda took the opportunity to ride ahead.

"You have to be firm, let them know you're in charge and not to be trifled with, but you also have to be calm and reassuring." Talin was trying to instruct his brother in horsemanship from over his shoulder.

Olin wrinkled his nose in disgust. "Easy for you to say, you like the brutes and they don't make you sneeze. What if we're attacked? I'll probably just fall off and break my neck. Make sure you hold onto me, and warn me if you're going to make the bloody thing run."

Talin felt sorry for Oli. He spent his time in libraries, not the practice yards. Court scholars gushed effusively about his academic talents, but living rough wasn't a skill that could be learned from a book.

"Don't worry, I won't let you fall. We'll soon be at Gallen Arth, where I hear they have a fine library."

Olin laughed. For the first time in days he looked something like the annoying little brother Talin knew and loved. He ruffled his dirty blonde hair.

"Actually, it's quite small, but then you probably wouldn't know that, unacquainted as you are with our own magnificent library. That's the room with all the books, in case you were wondering." He sniggered. "Lady Vorsten did send me a rare copy of '*The Moon and the Stag*' last Midwinter. It's in old Tamalak, but I got through it easily enough. It's a…" Olin looked round at him and frowned "…You're not remotely interested, are you?"

"I can't say I share your love of books, little brother."

Olin giggled. "I know what you do love though, or should I say *whom*?" He stared pointedly at Alyda.

Talin cuffed his ear. "The sooner you're back in one of those, 'book rooms', the better, methinks."

That night, Alyda and Talin hunted up a meal of blackberries, wild mushrooms and a fistful of hazelnuts that the squirrels had missed. Alyda wouldn't have minded eating the squirrels rather than their leftovers, but without a bow they could perch in safety and mock her from the tree-tops. Before darkness fell, Thea and Olin turned in. Huddled together on a bed of bracken beneath their borrowed cloaks they were soon asleep.

Alyda took the watch after Talin; the early hours of the morning that the Tamalak called the *gralc mai* which roughly translated meant 'little death'. These dead hours belonged to the Lord of Shadows; when sleep was at its deepest, when those abed had a little taste of death and those awake struggled to remain so. It was also the best time for an ambush, so she kept her sword unsheathed and her wits about her. To give her something to do other than conjure monsters from the shadows, she re-braided her hair.

Being alone in the dead of night was also when the grim thoughts she'd been able to ignore during the day clamoured loudest for her attention.

The worst was that she didn't know if the Hammer had got through to Gallen. The thought that her comrades might be injured or dead, knotted her guts. Then there was the King. If he was dead, she was guarding the sole ruler and her heirs. Tonight the world was made of blades. One slip, one wrong move and they would be undone.

The next morning Alyda roused the Queen and Princes and gave them a handful of blackberries she'd managed to scavenge before they set off.

It was cold and damp; a biting wind followed them along the trail, twisting flurries of fallen leaves into swarms that danced in their wake. They'd gone as far as they could on the hillside paths and now had to drop down into the heavily wooded valley.

The brothers remained in good spirits, despite the privations. Alyda could see that they were close by the way they talked to each other, even though there were almost ten years between them. She wondered briefly about her own brother, and if her family even knew that war was coming. At least in Bear's Tooth they were as safe as anyone could be.

Unlike her sons, the Queen looked ready to drop, despite the sleep she'd had. It was unfortunate, but they had to push on for as long as Alyda could keep them in the saddle. They were so close; allowing them to rest longer would be a false kindness.

As dusk approached it began to rain more heavily. The horses' heads went down; their ears flattened to their skulls as they tiredly plodded along the boggy path. The closer they came to Gallen Arth the more people they began to encounter.

Alyda pulled her cloak around her in an attempt to hide her blood-stained clothing. Not that anyone was giving them a second glance thanks to the weather. Everyone they passed was more intent on getting out of the rain than staring at the dishevelled group riding towards the Arth.

The fugitives reached the main road through the forest without incident. It ran from the village of Kellimarsh to Gallen Arth and was far busier than Alyda would have expected on such a miserable day. A man and a woman were sitting under a tented shelter by the side of the road. Tendrils of smoke drifted up from their campfire. They were scrubbing pots and plates with grass, cleaning up after what smelled to Alyda like the best meal in the world.

"Hello there!" she shouted over to them. "Tell me, d'you know why there are so many people on the road? Is anything amiss that a group of travellers ought to know about?"

The woman cast a glance at the man before coming over. "I'm surprised you don't know." She wiped her hands on her apron and eyed them suspiciously.

Alyda smiled and waited for the rest of the tale. When she'd made them wait long enough, the woman continued.

"Bunch o' mercenaries been lurking hereabouts. Up t'no good, waylayin' travellers, they say."

"Mercenaries? Any idea who they were?"

"No, and we're not hangin' around t'find out in case they come back now that the knights have gone back to the Arth. I'd head north if I was you. We heard the knights ran 'em off south, down past Galegallen, towards Kellimarsh."

"Did the knights engage the mercenaries?"

The man came over and put his arm around the woman's shoulder. "Don't think so, 'leastways, not that we've heard. The knights came out o' the Arth an' chased the mercenaries south. We've come from Redburn, we were on our way to Keeling Delve, but I think we'll be straight back home if there's wrong 'uns about."

Alyda nodded. "Aye, I think you've got the right idea."

The woman unfastened her apron. "Some folk are headed to the Arth, but I think that's a bit over-blown. My advice is: don't go south if you can help it. Keep yourselves clear o' the trouble."

If only. "Thanks for the advice," said Alyda.

Weariness gave way to relief when they reached the edge of the forest and were greeted by the lights of Gallen Arth shining out of the darkness. The ancient keep was surrounded by a moat that had been excavated by humans on three sides, and carved by nature on the fourth. The mighty Galerun River flowed protectively around its rocky base. Alyda told the others to wait while she approached the outer gatehouse, the first of the Arth's formidable defences. The moment her horse's hooves touched stone, torches flared into life, and a handful of guards appeared from the shadows and levelled crossbows.

"Who goes there?" Came the challenge from the darkness.

This is going to surprise them. Alyda cleared her throat. "Her Majesty, Queen Thea, Princes Talin and Olin, and Captain Stenna of the First." The guards kept their bows trained on her; their caution was reassuring given that mercenaries were roaming the area. The one who'd issued the challenge stepped from the shadows. "What's the watchword?"

"Black Griffin," she answered.

The guard put up his weapon.

Once inside, the Queen and Prince Olin were quickly whisked away by Lady Vorsten and her servants. Alyda and Talin were escorted to the Riverside Hall by what looked to be most of the Hammer, who had flocked to the gate as soon as word got out who had arrived. Alyda learned from a dozen hurried conversations on the way to the hall that the Hammer had reached the Arth safely and had helped the Black Lancers chase off the mercenaries. Had they gone the other way, the tale might have been different. She thanked her stars that she'd trusted her instincts on that one.

Mugs of spiced beer appeared and promptly vanished while they waited in the Great Hall for the Captain of the 4th to arrive. Alyda was tired but she had to brief Cassian before she slept. Talin had already fallen into a chair by the fire and was well on his way after a mug of beer.

She would have liked nothing more than to curl up beside him, but she stayed on her feet and well away from the seductive warmth of the fire. Even standing, she must have started to drift off and found herself jerked to sudden wakefulness when the hall doors burst open and Cassian marched in, followed by Kieran, Nev and a relieved-looking Jamie.

"Ali! I've just been speaking to the Queen. She said Corvinius has turned traitor, what's going on?" The Captain of the Black Lancers halted abruptly when he recognised the man sitting by his fire and snapped a salute. "Forgive me, Highness, I didn't recognise you."

"That's perfectly understandable, Captain Vorsten. I barely recognise myself. Captain Stenna, if you would be so kind as to brief Captain Vorsten…" Talin slurred.

"Certainly, Highness." She clasped Cassian's proffered hand. "It's good to see you, Cass, but the news isn't good."

After she'd briefed Cassian and their officers, Kieran explained what had happened after they'd parted ways at the bridge.

"Aye, Captain, they'd found a nice little place to set their ambush. It would have been a tough old fight if we'd taken the main road. Although, 'tis a shame they didn't stick around. They must have legged it as soon as they got wind that two companies of knights were out looking for them."

"Any idea where they went?" Alyda asked.

Cassian toed a log back into the fire. "South, somewhere. I've sent scouts out to search, and to offer the shelter of the Arth to the locals in case they come back. I was going to hunt them down, but after what you've told us, I think it best if we secure our position here."

"Aye." She stifled a yawn. The warmth was working on her, fogging her senses. She was just about drained of all but the most basic ability to function and remain awake. She knew they were still in trouble, but her fatigue-deadened senses felt nothing even close to alarm. Cassian on the other hand, was a study in concern.

Ali Stenna refused to rest until she'd gone over everything with him and the senior knights. Cassian was impressed by the calm, unemotional way she related the ghastly details of what had happened. She was so like Trease in that respect.

He was most dismayed to find out that the blood on her clothes was that of their fellow Knight Captain. A day earlier he would have challenged anyone to a duel for even hinting that a Captain of the Guards, even a rake like Corvinius, could betray their oath.

Whatever happened, the stain on their honour wouldn't easily be removed after this.

When his unexpected visitors were settled, Cassian returned to his own quarters to find Beria pacing, anxious to find out what was going on.

"So that's why the mercenaries came; they were after the Hammer. Oh, Cass, why did Alyda have to bring the Queen here?" Beria twisted a curl of dark hair around her finger.

"Asha's sake, Beri. Sometimes your inner voice forgets its place, my love."

"I'm sorry, but I can't pretend I'm happy about this, even if 'tis treason to say so. Ali Stenna has brought danger to our door. I know you don't want to hear me speak like this, but I can't be anything other than honest with you. I really wish she hadn't brought them here." She sighed. "I know that makes me a terrible, selfish person, but I can't help it. When it comes to you and Tomas, I am."

He was dismayed by her bluntness, but couldn't be angry with her, not when he looked at her sincere, beautiful face. He pulled her to him and held her.

"Everything's going to be alright. We're safer here than anywhere in Antia."

She looked up at him, her dark eyes shining with tears. "Do you think it makes me a traitor to think like this? Am I a wicked person?"

Cassian kissed her. "Gods, no! It makes you a fierce, protective mother, and a devoted lover and I can't fault you for either. But don't forget: I've sworn an oath to serve the King and protect the kingdom—with my life if necessary. My oath to *you* is that I'll never let any harm come to you or Tomas…" He smiled to reassure her, even though he felt the brush of cold wings against his heart. "…and that I'll love you forever."

Beria rested her head against his shoulder. "I knew you were a bloody knight when I married you. It was exciting then, but ever since Tomas was born I've been terrified that I'm going to lose you both. I told myself I was stupid, that it was a foolish notion, but I can't help seeing danger lurking in every shadow. They get so bad sometimes, these dark thoughts, this terrible overwhelming fear. I just want to scream or bang my head against a wall. Anything to stop thinking these dreadful thoughts…" She started to cry.

I am such a blind bastard. How could he have failed to see that she was in pain? "Why didn't you tell me?"

"I didn't want you to think I was insane or worse; that I was weak. I wanted to be strong like you… only I'm not, and I hate myself for it. Dear gods, how I loathe myself sometimes, but I can't lie—I would damn a hundred kings and a thousand kingdoms if it meant you never had to fulfil your oath."

Chapter Eleven

There wasn't a deep enough pit in the Void for that worthless piece of shit Corvinius to hide in. Thorgulsen fumed silently while his hirths and Telvier's dogs tore Weyhithe Castle apart searching for the Queen and her sons and the bastard who had betrayed him.

Thorgulsen executed the knights who hadn't the sense to flee. Their bodies were piled in the castle's bailey; those who they hadn't strung up on the battlements by their guts as an example of what happened when you crossed a Guthlander. The screams of those yet to die rose above the flames that were hungrily devouring the castle, but not even the ferocious blaze could match the intensity of Thorgulsen's anger.

Telvier pranced out of the smoke ahead of two of his mercenaries. They were dragging a steelskin between them. They dropped the battered knight at his feet.

"We found this wretch hiding in a garderobe." Telvier dug the toe of his boot into the knight's side, eliciting a pitiful groan.

"What's your name, Steelskin?" Thorgulsen commanded.

"Frannel, s…sir," she stammered and dared a glance at Thorgulsen through her blood-matted hair.

"D'you see your friends up there, Frannel?" Thorgulsen gestured to the disembowelled bodies hanging from the battlements.

The trembling knight whimpered. There was suddenly a strong smell of piss. "I'll take that as a yes. If you can't tell me what that whoreson Corvinius has done with the Queen and her sons you will join them. Do you know this?" Thorgulsen felt nothing but contempt for the Ant, lying there in her own water.

"My Lord, I…I don't think Captain Corvinius betrayed you." One of the mercenaries lazily kicked the knight in the gut. "Please, I beg you, for the love of Asha, hear me out!" she squealed.

Thorgulsen raised his hand to stay the beating.

"I…I found the guards dead in the Queen's apartment and… Captain Stenna was gone. I think she got the Queen out and freed the prisoners in the dungeon."

Even though the knight was a snivelling coward, she was the first person to tell Thorgulsen anything even vaguely interesting since he'd got here. She'd also mentioned the cunt who'd dislocated his knee and damn-near broke his jaw. If there was a chance to meet up with the Captain of the Hammer and repay the compliment, he was interested.

He grabbed the woman by her ragged surcoat and dragged her to her knees. "Where would Stenna take them, Steelskin? Would she take them to Trelanlith?"

"No, sir, I don't think so, not Trelanlith. Captain Corvinius sent the Hammer t…to Gallen, b…but it was a trap. Only she didn't know that—she'd go there. 'Tis less than three days' ride from here. That's where she will have gone. I'd stake my life on it."

Thorgulsen smiled humourlessly. "Funny you should say that." He turned to Telvier. "Has *he* arrived yet?"

Telvier opened his mouth but his words were lost when at that moment, it sounded like all the bells of the city rang out at once. It was painfully loud, but from behind him came a voice that was perfectly audible over the din.

"You called, I came. The question you should be asking is: how much will my services cost you?"

Thorgulsen dropped the Steelskin and spun on his heel, axe in hand, ready to strike. When he saw what was behind him he took an involuntary step back.

Floating about two feet above the ground was the ghostly form of the sorcerer. Grey robes swirled around a whip-thin body, stirred by an unearthly breeze no one else could feel. A heavy cowl was drawn low, obscuring its face. The damn thing was an illusion, but even the ghost of the sorcerer was enough to set the Ward off.

"I will not enter this thrice-damned place. We will conduct our business elsewhere, but first, tell me what you want, barbarian?"

"I want you to bring me the Queen of Antia and her sons. They're probably within another Arth, or soon will be. Can your power reach them through a Ward?" Thorgulsen's flesh crawled, and the hair on the back of his neck bristled, but he wouldn't show fear in front of his hirths or Telvier.

The sorcerer gave a dry, rasping laugh. "You doubt my power? You were right, Luca. This one is amusing...and stupid. You should have asked for the King's head. Alas, it is too late now."

Thorgulsen shot Telvier a dark look. The Suvian shrugged innocently.

"I should turn you inside-out and let the dogs feast on your innards for your insolence, but never let it be said that the Obsidian Prince is needlessly cruel to dumb beasts. I can reach the wench and her get, even if she was within the Ice Halls of Tamalan. To perform this... insignificant deed, I will need a human spine and five, fresh human hearts. In addition, I require a chest of gold, the weight of…a Guthani Thane. *You* in fact. Not an ounce more or less, or we're back to the turning you inside-out and feeding you to dogs scenario. I include you in that, Luca Telvier. Do you agree to my terms?"

"Agreed," said Thorgulsen.

"So shall it be." The image of the sorcerer faded.

"Get this dog out of the keep, and find me four more. Shula!" The Thane bellowed at one of his terrified hirths who'd been watching while the sorcerer had laid down its terms. "Go get the chests we took from the treasury. Take them outside and post a guard. Telvier—you're with me."

The next morning, Thorgulsen ordered his people into a square near to the ruined Arth and insisted that Telvier join them. The Suvian reluctantly complied—the pig was paying his wages even if he was bartering away the spoils. A half-dozen hirths guarded the chest of gold that had been carefully weighed against their lord. Four beaten and bound Steelskins lay nearby. They looked terrified, the shadow of their fate written on the Guthlanders' blood splattered faces. The unfortunate Frannel had been savagely beaten. Telvier felt neither pity nor anger towards her, or indeed any of the Ants. His hate was reserved for the Guthland pig who had bargained his gold away.

The Suvian paced aimlessly while they waited for the sorcerer to arrive, his restless gaze often drifting to the chest. He'd thought employing the Obsidian Prince to find the Queen would be a stroke of genius, a marvellous short cut. The last time he'd made a pact with the Void-spawned bastard he'd made a handsome profit and it had been so very easy; a sack of gold in exchange for a Fey trinket. "*Call on me anytime,*" he'd said. He hadn't mentioned that he would ruin him if he did.

I should have made the bargain myself, thought Telvier bitterly. That lackwit Thorgulsen had asked for too much. Damn the sorcerer, and damn Thorgulsen. Between them they would make a pauper of him.

Telvier smiled at him. *Man looks like a fucking skull in a wig.* Thorgulsen gave Telvier a nod and took a swig of the brandy Beth had brought, but declined the food. The smell of burning human always robbed him of his appetite. Beth's laugher intruded on his thoughts. She was talking with the hirths while they waited for the sorcerer.

He knew her game. Bringing the food was an excuse—she'd come to gawk at the demon. Fucking woman was drawn to trouble like a fish to water. One day she would go too far and burn for her wickedness and there'd be nothing he could do to save her.

They'd been waiting for about an hour when the air in the centre of the square began to shimmer and the temperature suddenly dropped. There were no warning bells this time when the Obsidian Prince stepped out of the air. Without a word of acknowledgement he extended a skeletally thin hand, as black and shining as his namesake, towards the chest. The heavy wooden box shimmered, grew pale and insubstantial, and slowly vanished.

"Excellent, although you were a little generous," the sorcerer hissed. "I shall forgive you this time, barbarian. I find your brutishness endearing, you would have made a fine, savage pet. Now give me the spine."

"Don't you need to know where you're going?" Thorgulsen asked.

The sorcerer made a rasping noise that might have been laughter. "Aren't you the inquisitive one? Fear not, the path I walk will lead me unerringly to my prey. It may take a little time, but I will find them before the day is out. You haven't wasted your stolen gold."

Thorgulsen shrugged, the mockery of a monster didn't offend him. He spat on Frannel. "You do her, Telvier. The coward's blood would shame my blade."

Telvier sighed and took off his gloves. A knife dropped from his sleeves. He grabbed the unconscious knight by the hair and opened her throat. Indifferent to the Steelskin's dying agony Thorgulsen watched the knight feebly struggle for breath as her blood gushed across the flagstones and her face bleached. When she stopped twitching, Telvier hacked out her spine.

For all that he knew what he was doing, it must have been a while since he'd done any real butchery; the peacock was sweating like a pig when he'd finished.

Do him good to get his hands dirty. Thorgulsen smirked, while Telvier dug through the ruin of the knight's back and pulled out her quivering heart. Wiping sweat from his face, he accidentally anointed himself in her blood before dropping the grisly relics at the sorcerer's feet.

When they saw their fate, some of the other prisoners found the courage to fight, but it was far too late. Thorgulsen gave the order and his hirths slashed the Steelskins' throats. Before the bodies cooled, they cut out their hearts and tossed them at the feet of the sorcerer alongside the other ghastly tribute.

The sorcerer fell upon the organs, and one after the other, sucked them dry. When he'd slaked his thirst, he raised his arms above his head and began to chant. The eerie, inhuman voice and the strange words all preyed upon the most ancient fears locked deep within Thorgulsen, a shiver ran down his spine. In contrast, Bethanglyn's eyes were shining. Thorgulsen saw her mouthing the aberrant words under her breath.

Still chanting, the Obsidian Prince turned his shadowed face towards her. She flashed him a brazen smile. Thorgulsen weighed the axe in his hand and wondered which one of them he'd like to kill the most.

The sorcerer ceased chanting. For a moment nothing happened, and then the air above the bloody spine began to run like water on glass.

"I'll see *you* again," he said to Bethanglyn before stepping over the spine and vanishing into the watery nothingness.

Thorgulsen didn't like magic but there was no doubting its power. *What about the price?* He was an ambitious man, but when he considered the question: *how far would I go?* The answer was:—*not that far, not again.* If only he could say the same of Bethanglyn. Thorgulsen broke the spell of silence that had settled over the square by slapping his wife across the face.

He turned to Telvier, who took a cautious step back. "Round up your people, we're leaving this midden. Gathorl! Gather the warband and send the scouts ahead to this, Gallen Arth. I want whatever the Void-spawn leaves."

He was consumed with rage and guilt when Corvinius had taken over and imprisoned Hyram, but that was nothing compared to how Garian felt watching Weyhithe burn, knowing there was nothing he could do to save it. A few hours earlier he was about to sneak back into the Arth, when he encountered another of Hyram's agents, wading through filth beneath one of the garderobes. She was called Jarel, and what she told him saved him the trouble of climbing up through the slimy shithole, as she'd just climbed down it.

A cobbler by trade, she'd stayed in the Arth as long as she'd dared. When the Guthani began to kill indiscriminately, she decided it was time to get out with what little information she'd been able to glean. She told Garian that the Guthlanders had ransacked the Arth when they couldn't find the Queen or Corvinius. As the skinny cobbler cleaned herself up, she explained how she'd heard that the knights guarding the Queen had been found dead in her apartments some time during the previous evening, but that was all she knew. The Guthlanders' murderous rampage aside, Garian was reassured that Stenna had succeeded in getting the Queen out of the Arth. The agents wished each other luck, and then went their separate ways.

That had been hours ago. Now he was sitting on a rooftop, watching his city burn. He desperately wanted to stay in Weyhithe and hunt down the bastards who'd torched his home, but he had his orders. With a heavy heart, he turned his back on the conflagration.

When he could go no further by rooftop, he climbed down into an alley a few hundred feet from the East Gate. The moment his feet touched ground, a group of mercenaries rounded the corner.

"Hey, you!" One of them shouted at him in Suvian and drew her sword.

"Stay where you are, I want to talk to you!"

Without wasting breath Garian unhooked the small crossbow, spanned it, dropped a bolt in the notch, aimed and squeezed the trigger. The woman fumbled her weapon and staggered, dumbly clutching at the shaft sticking out of her chest. Her three companions charged past her, yelling obscenities at Garian. He dropped the bow and ran.

There were many who could run faster than him, and a good few who knew the city better, but he was a damn sight faster and more knowledgeable than the mercenaries chasing him and soon lost them in the guts of the city.

With his blood still pumping from the chase, he turned a corner and ran straight into another group of mercenary scum who were busy looting a half loaded cart. Lying in the road nearby were the bloody bodies of the family the cart must have belonged to. As soon as they saw him, the mercenaries stopped what they were doing and drew their weapons.

"Wrong time, wrong place, boy..." one of them snarled in Antian and advanced towards him.

There were four of them, all armed and armoured. He was about to turn around and run back the way he'd come when a door opened behind him and another one stepped into the street carrying a large trunk. When he saw Garian he sighed, put the trunk down and unhooked the axe from his belt.

"Whatever you've got, hand it over and we'll let you go on your way. Isn't that right, Dario?"

"Like you let these people go?" Garian spat.

The one called Dario shrugged. "They wouldn't play nice." He laughed. "Don't make the same mistake, boy. Drop the knife and hand over your purse and you can run along, unless you want to stay and play? Pretty lad like you, who knows? Play nice and I might end up giving you *my* purse."

Garian drew his knife. The mercenaries closed in. He backed up against the wall, trying to keep them all in view. They stopped. Their smiles faded, their eyes widened.

Garian wasn't arrogant enough to think he'd inspired such a swift change of attitude. They were staring at something above him.

He desperately wanted to know what it was, but daren't risk a glance, not while they were within striking distance. A shadow passed over him; he felt a whoosh of air and ducked instinctively. When he looked up he understood why the mercenaries were afraid.

The beasts were sickeningly fast and the uneven contest was over before the mercenaries had time to scream. When they'd finished, one of the seven foot tall monsters raised a dripping, dagger-clawed hand and pointed above him. Garian looked up to see Suli clinging to a drainpipe, smiling down at him. He'd never been so pleased to see anyone in his life.

She dropped the last six feet and landed lightly beside him. She wasn't wearing traditional Vodoni dress today, but practical buckskins. A knife was hanging from her belt, although with her companions, he doubted that she'd need to use it.

"You did so well to get away from the first lot," she said, and kissed him.

"How long have you…? I mean are they…when did you…?"

"Not long, and they're my cousins. When we saw the smoke we came as quickly as we could. It took a while to find your scent in all this mess *and* because you don't actually use the streets. You go under them and above them, but not often *on* them. You're a strange fellow, Garian Tain; did I ever tell you that?"

"Yes, I think you did." Garian refrained from commenting on the two hulking shapeshifters that were snuffling about the pile of corpses not five feet away. *And she calls me strange.* He returned her kiss with interest.

"We need to leave this place quickly. There's something here that we do not want to run into," said Suli.

He would take her at her word; whatever it was must be pretty bad for her to say that. "Lead on. I trust you and… your friends know a way out of the city?"

Suli looked expectantly at the shifters. The shaggy beasts sniffed the air and exchanged a look. Their feral yellow eyes glowed in the light of the fires licking at the nearby buildings.

They seemed to come to an agreement, although it was hard to tell, their conversation was conducted in grunts and sniffs. The male nodded to Suli before he and his companion loped off the way Garian had come.

"Let's go," said Suli and took off after them. Garian followed.

The Children of the Moon made escaping the city seem easy. Garian and Suli clung to their massive backs and the two shifters flowed up the wall faster than he could have run the distance on the flat. Minutes later they were on the other side. If anyone saw them, they didn't dare try to stop them.

When they were safely down, the shifters bounded off ahead. Garian and Suli were forced to sprint just to keep them in sight. On all fours, they could almost be mistaken for animals, but when one or other of them stood on their hind legs to sniff the air or peer into the distance, they were clearly more than mere beasts. Garian could see elements of wolf and cat in their facial features, but no animal ever looked at a person with eyes like theirs.

In spite of the circumstances of their reunion, he was overjoyed to see Suli. He was still distraught that Weyhithe was being sacked, like everything else he'd loved; it was being destroyed by an act of wanton brutality.

He had a sudden desire to keep running, to go somewhere far away with Suli and never look back. He was suddenly afraid for the girl running by his side.

"*Don't love nothing, and then nothing can hurt you.*" That's what Minchin, one of the older boys in the orphanage had told him. Then as now, he understood what he'd meant.

For a moment—a heartbeat, he regretted that he'd wandered into the wrong inn and let a blue-eyed girl strip him of his defences, because just for a moment, with Weyhithe burning behind him, he felt as vulnerable and helpless as a five year old boy grieving for his murdered mother.

A few miles from Weyhithe, the shifters disappeared into a stand of trees. Garian and Suli took the opportunity to catch their breath. They returned a short while later in human form. Garian guessed that they must be brother and sister by how similar they looked. They were the same height; both had the same sandy coloured hair and very similar features. Like Suli's mother, it was their eyes that he found most disturbing, even in human form. They were too bright and a little too large—hunter's eyes. The male smiled a toothsome grin, displaying the tips of sharply pointed canines.

"Garian, I'd like you to meet my cousins," said Suli. "This is Pytre."

The male stood forward and tipped him a nod.

"And this is Lhazinia."

The female smiled. "Garian Tain; the King's man. We're pleased to meet you."

"And I you. Thanks' for the help back there."

"Don't mention it, we're kin. Family look out for family, isn't that so even amongst the Gadji?" Lhazinia asked.

He snorted. "In theory."

He spared no detail when he told them what had happened. They took it in, but neither they nor Suli showed the level of concern he would have expected. He concluded that rather than a lack of empathy it was probably because they were nomads and didn't have strong ties to any one particular place. He shouldn't have been surprised that they didn't feel the loss of Weyhithe as keenly as he did. They were more concerned that mercenaries and Guthani were roaming the countryside, and it was quickly decided that Lhazinia would go and warn the Charaval.

"These are ill tidings for all, not only the Gadji," said Pytre.

Garian grunted his agreement. He was bone weary and the thought of what he still had to do was daunting, even for him.

"What's wrong, Captain?" Suli asked.

"Nothing." There *was* something, but he was reluctant to ask more of Suli and her family.

"I don't believe you. What is it, Garian?" She pushed him towards the inevitable request.

"Suli, Pytre; do you think you could track the Queen?" He asked quickly so that the question wouldn't stick in his throat.

The shifter raised his eyebrows and smiled a perfect, white-toothed smile. "The mortal hasn't been born who I cannot track, cousin."

"I know I'm asking a great deal of you and your people... you've already done so much..."

Pytre rested his hand on Garian's shoulder. "We're your people now. You are family, Garian Tain, and really, it's not much of a task."

"Thank you, both of you." As much as he was grateful, he felt uncomfortable being obligated to anyone, but this was too important to let pride get in the way.

"I'll catch up with you when I've found her; it may take a few days. Tell 'Zia where I've gone when she gets back, and be careful." Pytre kissed Suli on the cheek and set off at a jog, back towards Weyhithe.

Unlike the shapeshifter, who looked like he could run all day and night without tiring, Garian was dead on his feet, but he still had to find the King. "I'd better be going too... do you want to come with me?" he asked Suli, trying not to sound as desperate for her to say yes as he was.

She gave him a kiss. "Try stopping me."

Chapter Twelve

Gallen Arth was like an old dog sleeping through its dotage. It either didn't mind, or hadn't noticed Kilner's presence. Some of the other Arths, like Trelanlith, were positively hostile and jealously guarded every drop of power, but not Gallen. Here essence dripped like honey from the deep well of its untouched reserves and he drank his fill. Kilner liked Gallen for that reason, and because the great, high walls and huge, drum towers made him feel safe.

It was a pity that he'd have to leave soon. He didn't like travelling or being out in the wilds. He feared the creatures that hunted in the dark forests and lonely moors, and now they were saying there were brigands and mercenaries abroad to add to the danger. He was capable of defending himself if he had to, he was a mage after all, but the very thought of violence made him feel ill. Kilner did not like conflict. If only he had enough coin so that he didn't have to work. *If only I could turn rocks into gold and had my own personal well of earth essence…*

"Ah, there you are, Master Magus—just the person I was looking for."

The voice jolted Kilner from his daydream, but he had the presence of mind not to turn around. Pretending not to have heard her, he put his head down and continued at a brisk pace in the opposite direction. He thought he'd got away when he reached the Guest Hall, until a heavy hand slapped down on his shoulder. Groaning inwardly, he turned to face Lady Berwick.

"If I didn't know better, I'd swear you were trying to avoid me," she said, a wry smile on her face.

"You're right: you don't know better. Now leave me be or…" the mage mumbled and made to go inside.

She palmed the door closed and casually leaned against it. "Or?"

Kilner took a step back; his knees were already turning to water. "Just leave me alone. I can't help you. How many times must I tell you before it sinks in?"

"Can't, or won't?"

"Can't! I've told you: you are what you are, what you were born. It cannot be undone, you're g… going to have to learn t…to live with it," Kilner stammered. "Or not. I don't care, just leave me be."

"I still think if you tried you could do something to at least help me keep control." Her smile vanished. "I'm tired of drugging myself just to get through the day, just to feel…human."

Kilner felt sorry for her, even though she'd hounded him from the moment she arrived with the other knights, he wasn't made of stone. "I can't, I'm sorry. I'm not as young as I was. It's too risky and…I just can't. Earth magic doesn't work like that. I must use what I'm given, we cannot destroy—only…well, I can't take it out of you, and if I tried to change your pattern, I'd most likely end up killing you or worse, killing myself—and I will not risk either outcome, so please, stop hounding me."

She looked downcast. Kilner really did feel sorry for her, but the risk was too great…for him.

"Is it money? I can pay," she said brightly. "I've got pots of gold."

It was as though she hadn't heard a word he'd said. "Money can't buy me my life back! I'm not a...a sorcerer. I don't have power over life and death, I ca—" Without warning an excruciating pain ripped through his body. Kilner fell, paralysed and in agony, unable to even scream.

Berwick caught him as he collapsed. "What is it? What's wrong with you? Reese! Speak to me!"

He could barely think, let alone speak. All he could do was send a weak pulse of power into the Arth to warn it about what was trying to break through, what had burned his very spirit. Before unconsciousness claimed him, he heard the Arth Ward scream.

Alyda was halfway to the door, sword in hand before she was even awake, dragged from deep sleep by the Arth's deafening Ward. She looked around and tried to remember where she was. Constable's room. The barbican. Gallen Arth. She hadn't bothered getting undressed when she'd fallen onto the cot and ran from the room and down the stairs, in search of what had set off the Ward. She glanced out of the arrow loops, expecting to see an army massing, but all was quiet.

In the bailey, knights and civilians were running in all directions, hunting for the source of the disturbance. Over by the Guest Hall, she saw Bear Berwick kneeling beside a prone figure.

When she got closer she recognised the earth mage. He was as pale as death, but trying to speak. "What's wrong?" she demanded.

"He just collapsed, and the Ward started ringing," said Bear, her eyes shining in the torch-lit darkness.

"I...I'm alright," the mage gasped and raised himself onto his elbow.

"I know you..." Alyda said. "Reed isn't it?"

"Close enough," he groaned. "Listen, Captain—a sorcerer is trying to get into the Arth. In the name of all that is holy—*you must not let it in*."

Alyda's blood ran cold, she shuddered. "Where is it?"

He reached out his shaking hand and touched her sword. "Now you can hurt it, like her Ladyship here, but the spell won't last long, so hurry!" Kilner fell back, exhausted, leaving Alyda no wiser as to where the demon might be.

Bear craned her neck, tilted her head as though she'd heard something. "It's near Tal," she said, and tore off towards the Keep Tower. Alyda followed.

The Obsidian Prince perched on the broken spar of a dead dragon's wing bone while he waited for the hunting spell to find the human Queen. He held a trinket he'd made over a thousand years ago. It had survived in the mortal realm all that time. The flower was fashioned from Yorl—the metal of magic, formed of raw earth essence. It had been a gift for his lover. *Such a long time ago.* Back when his dragon had flesh on its bones.

He'd modelled the flower after one of the thousands that had grown in his lands, it was a perfect blossom— the most beautiful he had ever grown. Now the flowers were gone. In their place was the nightmare landscape of the Void, the demon haunted realm that terrified mortals, and filled their simple minds with fear. Writhing mists caressed the bones of the dead that littered the cindered ground. The sky was a monotonous grey, the air tasted of ash and sulphur as befitted the home of the damned.

Pained by memories of what had once been, the Obsidian Prince spent some of his hoarded power and made the Yorl flower bloom once more. It unfurled twirling stems and tiny buds and turned from a hair pin into a crown of radiant silver flowers, but that was all. It had a simple pattern and could grow no more. A crown made for a human princess, long since gone to dust.

Damn them, damn them, damn them… he scourged his mind with the oft chanted litany.

"Are you still damning them for death?" The shade asked.

"My own brother did this to us. He broke our covenant, and condemned you to death. My own brother…"

The shade drifted through the dragon's bones. "We've talked about this before. The Carmine Prince did the right thing. He freed me; death is a gift not a curse."

"You were always so forgiving. How could he? *My own brother.*" If he could remember how, he would have wept.

"You should leave them alone, leave all of this," she whispered. Her voice was the same, but he could never see her face; it was just shadows and memories. He let the crown change back into a hairpin.

"He took it from a dead girl and sold it to me. Forged a link, damn his eyes. I should have flayed the filthy creature for even looking at it."

"I wish I'd destroyed it. It's over, my love. Leave the humans, stop existing like this."

The sound of his laughter vibrated the bone cage of his chest like a swarm of angry wasps. He wasn't sure if there was anything left inside him except blood essence and hate.

"Don't blame me, blame them, stupid animals. *Freedom,*" he spat. "Did they ask you if you wanted the freedom to rot, to age, to die?"

"I accepted it, it was right. Things had to change or…"

"No they didn't!" he raged. "No. They didn't. The world was perfect, beautiful, and will be again. I can feel it; the storm is gathering, the gods are stirring."

Even though he couldn't see her face he could feel her eyes dripping pity. She was always so kind, so wise...*She is dead*. He was alone, had been for a millennia.

The ethereal hound bounded from Between and crouched at his feet. Trailing behind it was a pulsing strand of scarlet which would lead him to his prey.

The Obsidian Prince placed the flower on the dragon's bones and wrapped the throbbing vein around his fist. With a casual flick of the wrist, he dismissed the spell. The spectral hound howled and flew apart like smoke. The sorcerer girded himself in spells of protection and stepped over the maggot-infested spine and into Between.

The trail led the sorcerer to Gallen Arth. As he drew closer, he could feel the furnace heat spilling from its burning heart.

The Prince revelled in the savage tide; it had been so long since anything had warmed him. *Stupid mortals.* They'd been lazy, or had forgotten how to use the power. If his pattern hadn't changed he would have shown them how to shape a Ward, how to harness the power of the earth, but it was too late for that by a thousand years, and a thousand terrible deeds. Now, merely approaching the heart of the Arth would flay his spirit and consign him to oblivion. *Ah, but what a magnificent way to go.* The thought sent a thrill of pleasure running through his withered flesh.

As he floated Between he sifted through the writhing mass of patterns in the Arth, a hungry spectre lurking on the edge of life. *There.* The red cord led to a particular maggot squirming amid its kin. He pushed through the veil between the mortal world and Between, and slipped into the Arth like a shadow. He held his breath, waiting for the alarm to wail, and battle to be joined, but the Ward did not wake to his presence; his spells had succeeded in hiding him.

Other than his quarry, there were only a handful of noteworthy patterns within the Arth. One in particular caught his attention.

"A dirt mage, how delightful," he hissed. He should take the Queen and go, but it had been such a long time since he'd matched power with a mortal mage, so long since he'd felt the cold rush of blood. The Obsidian Prince sent a vicious barb of energy at the dabbler; an introduction delivered in the sharpest terms. The barb struck. The mage's pattern writhed in agony and vanished. He laughed. Whoever they were, they immediately cloaked their essence rather than accept his challenge. *It isn't like the old days,* he concluded with regret.

The weight of ages fell on him like a tombstone. The Clan mages and his misguided kin had been fools to choose death over immortality. Their knowledge and skills had been lost and all that remained of the Great Art was illusion. They would surely weep to see their magic debased by the likes of this worm, too cowardly to muster even a token defence, let alone an attack. If he hadn't a task to perform he would have taken great pleasure peeling this pathetic excuse for a mage to its core.

Just then, a tiny throb of magic pulsed into the Arth. He laughed a curse as the Ward woke and lashed him with its terrible scream.

Talin thought he'd have to let Oli win the game of Stones he'd been badgered into playing. He was therefore surprised to find he had to play his best game just to stay on the bloody board.

"Do you think we'll be home for Midwinter?" Olin asked as he slid another stone into an attacking position.

"Er…yes, of course—at least you will be. I'll be at Tre-lanlith." Talin was struggling to concentrate on the game and talk at the same time; he'd no idea his brother was this good.

"Ah, yes. Juliana told me you'd commissioned a gold-smith to make a special gift for someone. I wonder; is it a Midwinter gift? Or a promise of betrothal?"

"Juliana should concentrate her energies on being a good lady-in-waiting instead of a gossip. Does anything happen in the Arth that your friend doesn't know about?"

Olin laughed, his hand hovered over a stone. Too late, Talin spotted the danger, but there was nothing he could do about it now. After a moment's indecision, Olin changed his mind and moved another stone.

"I don't know what has happened to Juliana," said Olin. "The soldiers took her away, she was crying. I suppose they killed her."

Talin was shocked. It wasn't like his brother to be so cold, so matter of fact about what might have happened to his friend. "You mustn't think that, Oli. I'm sure she's fine."

"It's alright Tal; if she's dead, she'll go to Sestrian and I'll see her again when I die. It's your move, by the way."

It was clear that his brother had been more affected by what had happened than anyone had realised.

"I yield, little brother. That was a bold attack, well done."

Olin laughed. "Thank you for letting me win, but you made it a little too easy. You're going to have to put up a bit more of a fight to fool me these days."

Talin opened his mouth to bluff a lie when the Ward began to scream. Startled, Olin leapt up. The board and game pieces went flying. The door to their mother's room burst open. Talin was up in an instant, sword in hand. He barged past the Queen's maid who'd opened the door and into the adjoining room. His mother was sitting up in bed; she looked alarmed, but unhurt.

"Lock the door and do not open it until I tell you," Talin ordered the maid before rushing back into the other room.

"Oli, get that!" he shouted, pointing to an old axe hanging on the wall. Olin was shaking, but did as he was told.

"Stay in here and hit anything that comes through that door that isn't me."

Olin nodded vigorously. Talin threw open the door to the hallway. Two knights were standing outside, back-to-back. The tallest of the pair raised his visor.

"You should stay within, Highness," he suggested firmly.

Talin was about to protest when the other knight shouted a warning to her comrade and pointed down the hall. He didn't see anything unusual at first, but then he noticed the air was shimmering like heat haze, roughly twenty feet away. To the amazement of all three, a shadowy figure appeared through the shifting wall of air.

The figure was tall, almost skeletally thin and dressed in flowing grey robes. Talin took a step into the hallway but one of the knights shot out an arm and pushed him back. The robed figure extended its arm towards them with a languid flourish. The air crackled, a rippling cone of air coalesced at its fingertips. It flicked its wrist.

The twisting cone flew at the knights and struck them with bone-jarring force, hurling them against the wall at the end of the hallway. Talin was thrown back into the room. He hit the floor hard, his head slammed into the table. White light exploded.

The Obsidian Prince had prepared himself for the Ward to attack when he entered the Arth, but aside of the shrill warning, nothing else had happened. In the past he'd fought the formidable magic of the Wards many times, but there was no fire this time, no dragons or griffins, no immortal warriors. There was only the pitiful alarm.

Two mortals defended the door to the Queen's chamber. He wove a spell of air. When he raised his hand, they braced. *As if they can resist me.* He released the spell and smashed them against the wall. A swell of malevolent joy rose within him, he had cast a harming spell, and the Arth had done nothing. He smiled. *I'm going to enjoy this.*

Bear took the last flight of stairs three at a time. Stenna had fallen behind, but she couldn't wait; something terrible was close to Tal and the Queen. In the corridor outside of the Queen's chamber two knights were lying in a heap against the far wall. Between her and them was a tall, hooded figure. It turned to face her. She felt a primal rush of fear and revulsion as she locked eyes with the creature. The stench made her gag. *Nothing living smells this bad.*

"Well, well, an Unmaker. Not quite what I expected." Its laughter sounded like metal scraping stone. "Come, pup—let's see your fangs."

"I won't be drawn by the likes of…whatever you are. And do you ever bathe? You smell like a cesspit." Bear drew her sword and advanced.

"Why, look! It's going to attack me with a sword. What other tricks have they taught you? Can you sit up and beg? Roll over perhaps?"

Whatever it was, it knew her true nature, but she wouldn't let it provoke her.

"You refuse to reveal yourself? Have it your way, foolish creature. If you wish to mimic your masters, you shall suffer like them."

The Obsidian Prince summoned his powers and warped the air around him. Twisting its pattern to suit his purpose, his magic hammered the air into a blade and he hurled it at the werebeast. The creature was almost upon him when the blast struck her in the chest, and sent her flying back.

She hit the wall, cracking the masonry and slumped to the floor. She did not get up.

"Too easy."

He walked towards the Queen's chamber, his prey within reach. The sound of footsteps echoed up the stairs. "More fools charging to their doom." He sighed and prepared to destroy the stairwell...

A shiver ran down his withered spine. He lowered his hand. "If it isn't the *demon slayer...*" he hissed at the woman who charged into the corridor. When she saw him she skidded to a halt. One look at the Unmaker and the broken humans should have set her feet to flight. But she held her ground, her pretty emerald eyes blazed with anger. She was not what he'd expected. "How did *you* slay one of the Order? You're just a child, an un-tempered blade...and who gave you an imbued sword? You could hurt someone."

"Funny you should say that, *demon*," she said.

There was confidence here, steel in her voice. The sorcerer extended his hand towards her. "Bravely said. Come, child—let us play."

Alyda charged but the minute he raised his bony hand, she knew she wasn't going to reach him. A moment later, it felt like she'd run into a wall. An invisible force enveloped her and squeezed the air from her lungs. She couldn't draw breath, couldn't move. She fell to her knees, stars dancing before her eyes. The sorcerer took a slender dagger from his robes and glided toward her.

"So here you are, come to save your Queen, but who will save you, bright eyes? I think I will take them, to remind me of you. Don't worry, I'll let you keep them long enough for you to watch me feast on your heart, and this time, no one will save you."

The crushing pressure increased, her ribs felt like they were about to break. The sorcerer stopped. From behind her she heard a low, rumbling growl. Alyda managed to crane her neck round. It was Bear. She was crouched by the wall, her inhuman eyes shining with an inner light. Ensnared, Alyda could only watch as Bear underwent a horrific transformation.

The noblewoman's armour flexed, the metal groaned. Claws burst from the huge paws that had been her hands and long yellow fangs tore through the skin of her elongating jaw. Armour straps snapped, rivets burst, and the metal shell buckled and fell away. What emerged from the debris was a creature that bore little resemblance to the woman it had been scant moments before. The beast let out a roar and charged the demon. A blur of claws and fur, it leapt, missing Alyda by inches.

Bear swung a huge taloned paw at the demon. It threw up its arms, the heavy swipe snapped bones. The sorcerer screamed and staggered back. Bear crouched, ready to leap again. The sorcerer thrust out its hand. An icy blast of air struck the shapeshifter, slamming her against the wall.

The invisible bonds that had been squeezing the life out of Alyda fell away and she hit the floor. The sorcerer shouted something in a tongue Alyda thought she recognised. The air behind it began to shimmer.

Bear leapt again, this time her claws tore into the wounded sorcerer's chest, spraying the corridor with ichorous blood. It stumbled back into the shimmering wall of air and vanished. When Bear pounced again her claws slashed empty air. She roared her fury; her great shaggy head swung round and her baleful gaze fell on Alyda.

When he opened his eyes, Talin was somewhat alarmed to see Olin standing over him with an axe, and then he remembered what had happened.

"Tal! Thank the gods, you're alive!" Oli cried. It sounded like all the demons of the Void were loose in the corridor.

"What hit me?" Talin groaned, tentatively feeling the egg-sized lump on the back of his head.

"Something threw you back and you hit your head on the table. When I saw you were hurt I locked the door. I didn't know what else to do."

"You did the right thing." Talin got up, unlocked the door and opened it a crack. He expected to see the skeletal creature, but it was nowhere in sight. Instead he saw Bear, and she had changed.

On seeing his friend transformed, he guessed what had happened to the creature, but there was little cause for celebration. There wasn't a body in the hall, and Bear was stalking Alyda, who was on her knees with a sword in her hand.

"Bear, no! Ali, please don't—" Talin ran into the hall and put himself between them.

"I don't want to hurt her, Talin…" Alyda warned.

"I don't want either of you to get hurt." He raised his hands and edged towards Bear. "Bear listen to me," he pleaded. "It's me—Talin. Try to remember who you are."

"Never mind try!" Alyda snapped.

Bear snarled.

As if the situation wasn't bad enough, two terrified-looking guards appeared at the top of the stairs. When they'd recovered from the shock of seeing a shapeshifter, they levelled their crossbows at Bear.

"Lower your weapons!" Talin commanded.

The guards exchanged a look of confused resignation, and put up their bows.

"Bear, *Iris*. It's me, Talin. For the love of Asha! Snap out of it."

Talin slowly inched closer, keeping his hands raised. Bear gave a low rumbling growl that he felt more than heard. She took a step towards him. Alyda got up, drew back her sword. This was the worst situation he could possibly imagine. Two of the people he loved most in the world were on the verge of killing each other.

"It's alright, Iris…" said Talin in a soothing voice.

Bear glared at him, her lips peeled back in a snarl, but Talin was sure he could see the ghost of the woman in the beast's features. For several tense minutes she held him with her sulphurous gaze before lowering herself onto what was rapidly becoming a hairless, human elbow.

In a matter of minutes the beast was gone and Iris lay naked and shivering on the floor. Guards swarmed up the stairs and the injured knights were taken to the infirmary. Talin got a blanket and covered Bear and then went to check on his mother and brother. When she'd recovered, Alyda told the Watch Commander what had happened. It was about then that Talin noticed that the Ward had stopped ringing.

When he'd seen his mother, he came back to see how Bear was doing. Everyone else was keeping a wary distance from the noblewoman.

She opened her eyes and groaned. "Did I hurt anyone I shouldn't have?"

"I don't think so. The creature's gone; was that you?"

"Aye. Filthy thing, it stank like a pile of rotten offal. Reese said it was a sorcerer. I'm not sure if I killed it. It's all a bit of a blur. I know I hurt it."

"I'll have them organise a search, hopefully its dead…if they can die. Are you alright?"

"No. I'm cold, I feel sick, I stink of sorcerer and I've wrecked my chances of bedding anyone in this Arth." She laughed. "I'm sorry, Tal."

"You have nothing to apologise for."

"No?" She shook her head. "It's been years since I let the monster out, but there was no other way. I couldn't stand against it as a human." She tilted her chin towards the guards on the stairs. "Look at them. Look at the way they're staring. They're all terrified of me now. They think me as much of a monster as the damn sorcerer. Who knows? Perhaps I am."

Talin was ready to deny her claim, but the guards *were* staring and some who'd just arrived were making the sign of the horns as they listened to their comrades' tale.

She grunted. "See? Just like the old days. Now if you will excuse me, dear Prince. I need some clothes, some Pel and some ale—lots of ale." Bear got up and, wearing nothing but a smile and a blanket, strolled across the hall and down the stairs. He wished there was something he could do to help her, but there wasn't. Gods knew he'd tried often enough.

In her dreams Alyda was hunting for the sorcerer, but whenever she got close it would disappear.

She opened her eyes and rolled over. She was still dressed in the same clothes she'd been wearing for the past week; the smell was less than pleasant. Her boots were beside the cot and Jamie was by the fire, stirring what smelled like a pan of spiced tea.

She sat up—and immediately wished she hadn't. Her head started pounding. Added to that, her ribs were sore and her back was as stiff as a poker. She very much wanted to lie down until the pain went away. She pulled on her boots and got up.

"How are you feeling?" Jamie asked, pouring her a mug of tea.

"Like a sorcerer beat the damnation out of me." She rolled her shoulders and stretched her aching limbs; everything just about worked.

"It sounds like quite a fight."

Alyda grunted. She didn't want to talk about it. She was still angry that she'd been taken down so easily. *Demon slayer*, it had called her. She laughed.

"Something funny, Captain?"

"That…thing called me a child. I bloody felt like one. If Iris Berwick hadn't been there we wouldn't be having this conversation."

"There's been a lot of talk about Lady Berwick. People aren't happy that there's a shapeshifter in the Arth."

"I'll tell Cassian to throw her out, and the next time a sorcerer turns up those doing the complaining can deal with it. Idiots. Did you find me any armour? I think I could do with some just to hold me together."

"Yes, Captain, it's here." He went over to the corner and dragged a sheet off the armour stand.

"You packed my parade armour?" Alyda laughed, surprised to see her best armour gleaming on the stand.

"Well, our orders were so vague, I brought as much as the quartermaster would allow me to put on the cart. I didn't bring the spur though; sorry, Captain."

"No matter, you did well. Sweet Asha! I'm going to look like a Suvi general strutting around in that on the battlements. Wipe the oil off, and find me some clean clothes. I'm going for a walk on the wall—clear my head."

There was a door leading straight out onto the wall walk from the room in the Barbican. She stepped outside and squinted against the dawn as the first rays of sunlight ploughed golden furrows in the forest canopy. The sweet aroma of her tea scented the crisp morning air.

While she walked off her headache, she took the opportunity to assess the Arth's defences. The curtain wall was a good sixty feet high, ten feet thick at the top, and wider at the base. Its roots were deep, anchored in stone that would take months to tunnel through, even without the added complication of the moat.

She paced the width of the walkway. There was room to fight and it was wide enough to withstand a bombardment. The Arth didn't have a drawbridge; an indication of how long it had been since war had visited the heart of Antia. It had been replaced years ago by a gently arching stone bridge that connected the Arth's great barbican to a second, smaller gatehouse on the far side of the moat.

The lack of a drawbridge was a weak point, but the gatehouse and barbican were well defended. They both had two sets of heavy oak doors and two iron portcullises. Alas, only the inner gates of the great Barbican could be Ward-locked.

Magical or otherwise, it remained a mighty fortress that would daunt all but the most determined attackers. She wondered how determined the Guthani were, and if they were on their way. As she looked down, she saw a group of hunters leave and head into the forest. Clad in dull greens and browns with longbows slung over their shoulders, they quickly disappeared among the trees. They would be the eyes and ears of the garrison, watching the roads and trails for sign of enemy forces.

She hoped they wouldn't have cause to loose the warning arrows—the last thing she wanted to see were the trailing red ribbons, arching above the canopy, but after last night that was a wildly optimistic hope. A shadow of doubt crossed her mind. It was a strong keep and she had two hundred reasons why assaulting it would be nothing more than a declaration of suicide. *But what if we can't hold?*

A cold wind cut along the wall and blew the shadow away. *There's no need to worry.* This was what they did, what they were good at. *Hard as iron, cold as stone.* If the Guthani came for the Queen, they would only find death.

"I don't think I'll need the cloak, Jamie." Alyda adjusted a buckle on her cuirass. She felt much more comfortable now she was back in armour. Jamie looked a little disappointed, but hung the cloak back on the stand. There was a knock at the door; she bid whoever it was to enter. An Arth guard came in and saluted.

"Captain Stenna; there's a knight just arrived, says he's from Weyhithe and that he'll only speak to you."

"Weyhithe?" she asked, immediately suspicious. "What's his name, who sent him?"

"He won't tell us. He just says he from the Fifth."

She made her way through the angry sea of scarlet and black to the cause of their disgust; a lone knight in russet and silver. It was Teril. When he saw her, he saluted. She didn't return it.

"Give me one good reason why I don't hang you from the gate right now?"

The crowd edged closer as eager as she was to hear his answer. He looked scared, rightly so.

"I…I came to bring you this…" he stammered, and offered her an oilskin wrapped bundle.

She took it from him, felt the familiar weight and unwrapped it. As she'd guessed it was her sword.

"To answer your question, no, it wasn't worth it, Teril. stammered. "I just didn't want to end up in the river with the others who refused to join Corvinius. I know now, knew then if I'm honest, that just being alive could never make up for betraying my oath…my comrades. It's been eating away at me ever since, that's why I had to find you, give you that…" The knight shuffled nervously.

Alyda examined her sword before buckling it around her waist. "It's the dead who deserve your apology, Teril. You'll be tried for treason; you know that, don't you?"

"Aye, Captain. But with all due respect, whatever you intend to do with me you had best get to it, because there's an army hard on my heels."

The senior officers of both companies gathered in Cassian's office to hear what Teril had to tell them. When he'd finished, the room fell silent as the knights digested the grim news. Alyda glared at the Rusty.

Teril shrank beneath her scrutiny. "I...I know what you think of me, but believe me, you don't loathe me any more than I do."

"Don't bet on that," said Lorhine. An affirmative rumble passed through the gathering.

"You haven't redeemed yourself," said Cassian. The Captain of the Black Lancers was sitting at his desk, Alyda was standing beside him. "But if what you've told us is true, you've gone some way towards removing the stain on your honour. Take him away."

For the next few hours, the officers thrashed out the details of what they could do to strengthen the Arth's defences in the short time they had before the Guthlanders arrived. When they were done, every knight had a task and set to it immediately. On her way out, Cassian called Alyda over. She had an idea what was coming.

"Ali, we have to settle the matter of overall command."

"It's your garrison, Cass."

"But you're Captain of the First. You have rank on me."

She knew him well enough to know that wasn't the only reason he was offering her command, but waited for him to spit it out without her prompting.

"And then there's Beri and Tomas. I'm not sure...I'm not sure I'll be able to make decisions objectively with my family here. I—"

"I understand. I'll take command."

As she expected, he looked relieved. "Thank you, Ali. I suppose you think I'm shirking my duty?"

"No, Cass. I think you've thought about this long and hard and come up with the right decision. Anyway, I damn well should be in command." She grinned as his face fell into a confused frown. "Well, I do have the nicest armour."

The hall was thronged with knights and civilians waiting for the officers to delegate duties. Jamie sat quietly amid the chaos waiting for the Captain. With its glorious stained glass windows and ornate plasterwork the hall reminded him of home. It had been such a long time since he'd been back. He wondered how his parents were, if they knew that war was coming.

"Don't look so worried, Jamie lad, we're in the strongest Arth in Antia." Lorhine's cheerful voice broke into his thoughts.

Jamie straightened up. The Lieutenant looked relaxed, almost happy—but then this was what the Hammer lived for—wasn't it?

"I'm not. That was my thinking face, not my worried face. I'd say that Bear's Tooth was the strongest Arth. It's smaller, but much harder to attack."

Lorhine smirked. "And that opinion has nothing to do with it being the Captain's home, eh?"

"Not at all, sir, it has to do with it being halfway up a mountain with sheer cliffs at its back."

"It's also in Tamalan, not Antia," Lorhine countered.

It was technically on the border, but Jamie didn't think it wise to argue with the Company Second-in-Command. He changed the subject.

"I've never been in a siege—have you, sir?"

Lorhine rubbed his bearded chin. "Aye, a couple of times, but only from the other side. I'll tell you this: it's a damn sight easier keeping the bastards out than it is trying to get in."

"There are only two hundred of us, d'you think that's enough?"

"If we were talking about two hundred ordinary warriors, I'd say no. Two hundred of the finest knights in the world? Aye, lad, that's plenty. And don't forget the Arth guards and there'll be some handy civilians come in from the villages, plus all the support staff. Nobody can swing a hammer like a blacksmith. That's easily another two, maybe three hundred. More than enough to see off a bunch of pig-fucking Guthani and merc rabble." Lorhine grinned and slapped him on the back. Jamie noticed that the smile didn't quite reach his eyes.

A stiff breeze tugged at the edges of the plans, but between Alyda and the chief engineer they managed to keep hold of the drawings. They were discussing the placement of defences while the carpenters and engineers assembled the heavy weapons that were kept in the Arth and until now, had never been used in anger.

Everyone else with a strong back was out clearing the trees and scrub that had encroached on the killing ground. The vast open space fanned from north to south along the eastern half of the Arth. The Galerun guarded the west along with the walls that rose above the river as high and sheer as a cliff face. It was no Bear's Tooth, but if she had to hold out anywhere else, this was the place she'd choose.

Alyda and the chief paced the bailey, dodging the steady stream of refugees that were trickling through the gate. They had come with their possessions piled on everything from hay ricks, to hand-carts. Tired and bewildered, vicious arguments flared over nothing, as worry and uncertainty caused tempers to fray.

When she was a child, people had flocked to Bear's Tooth to hide from renegade Clan warbands. Today, as she looked at the faces of the refugees, she saw the same expressions of fear and confusion, the same haunted look in their eyes. *Tamalan, Suvia, here. Nothing ever changes.*

Not all the refugees were cowed, some, like the blacksmith cursing his way through the crowd were always going to react to upheaval with hostility and aggression. Alyda knew his type: just as scared as the next person, but unable to control it. The moment their eyes met, she knew that if dissent was voiced, he'd be part of the chorus, if not the choir master. It might be anything from a lack of privies, to the enemy hammering on the gate. But if a complaint was going to be made, she'd bet gold that he'd be one of those making it.

He drew up next to her, looked her up and down. "Nice armour," he said, more as an accusation than a compliment.

"Aye, it is," she replied.

The blacksmith leaned on his cart, sweat gleaming on his bald head, dark eyes peering from beneath bushy, black brows. "Where can I set myself up?"

"I've no idea," she said, matching the sharpness of his tone before returning her attention to the plans. "Ask a guard."

There was nothing to be gained from weighing balls with the man. She'd given him someone to focus his ire upon, now hopefully he'd be less of an arse to everyone else who crossed his path. She seemed to have gauged it right judging by his mutterings as he walked away.

No idea, she says. Now why doesn't that surprise me? Bloody knights, couldn't find their arses with both hands without a squire to help 'em…

Thea sat by the window trying and failing to embroider a silk kerchief Lady Vorsten had kindly given to her. The light was excellent; the tower sat atop the old castle hill on the northern side of the bailey and soared above the shadows cast by the imposing curtain wall.

The rooms were pleasantly furnished and blessedly quiet. They were modest compared to her apartments in Weyhithe, but comfortable. She had insisted on staying in the guest quarters even though Lady Vorsten had generously offered to vacate her own rooms. She wouldn't dream of evicting Beria and her family, but she would not forget the offer.

Beria was a most gracious hostess, particularly given the unexpected nature of their arrival. She had done her utmost to accommodate them in every way, while trying to hide the worry Thea could see was gnawing at her.

Her heart went out to the girl; she understood what it was to be a parent of young children, the constant worry over everything from a high temperature to a grazed knee. As the mother of princes, she had the added fear of assassin's daggers, poisoned food and murderous uncles to contend with. Fear had become part of her life from the moment Talin was born—part of the price she'd paid for falling in love with the heir to the throne.

The current heir was restlessly prowling around her room, armed and armoured for battle. She was shocked and proud to see how much he looked like Daris. He'd grown up this year, but she thanked the gods that both her boys were with her and safe.

Oli was happily burrowing into a pile of books. Unlike Talin, he was a sensitive child. He hadn't once mentioned the sorcerer's attack, or their captivity in Weyhithe. His conversation, on the rare occasions that he spoke at all, revolved around whatever he was reading. She was worried for her youngest; he wasn't like Tal and Daris who put their heads down and ploughed through things. Olin hoarded experiences like a miser hoarded gold.

Her thoughts strayed from her work and she stuck herself with the needle. A speck of blood bloomed on the white silk. *The first drop of rain before the deluge?*

"Mother?"

She looked up. Talin had obviously been talking to her, but she hadn't heard a word he'd said.

"I'm sorry, Tal, what did you say?"

"I said, when the time comes, I intend to fight with the knights."

"Would that be because of any knight in particular?"

"I can't say she isn't part of the reason. Do you object?"

Like any mother, she wanted her son to be happy, but she wasn't just any mother, she was the Queen of Antia. His relationship with the knight was not in the best interests of the kingdom; princes married princesses, forged alliances. If this was just a fling like all the others she wouldn't care, but she knew her son. He was in love with Captain Stenna, or at least, he thought he was, which amounted to the same thing. Of course, she couldn't tell him that she objected and that he must end the relationship. That would only harden his resolve and drive him further into the arms of his lover. It would also make her a terrible hypocrite.

She did not forget that she was the daughter of a minor noble house. Although their love was as strong today as the first time they'd kissed, she couldn't escape the truth that if Daris had married a Guthani princess, this wouldn't be happening. Could she sit by and watch Talin make the same mistake? Could she in all conscience stop him?

She forged a smile. "Object? No, of course not, Alyda is your father's favourite knight. But I do object to you fighting. You are the heir to the throne." She put down the ruined sewing.

"And what kind of king would I make if I watched while others fought to protect me and my family?"

"I don't want to argue, Tal." She was finding it hard enough not to burst into tears. The world had turned hard and she felt as fragile as glass.

Talin sat beside her and put his arm around her. "Father wouldn't—*isn't,* watching men and women die in his place."

Thea's gaze was drawn to the horizon, to where the jagged line of the forest met the sky. The thought that Daris might be lying dead somewhere out there, pushed her tears to breach the dam of her resolve and they flowed hot and swift down her cheeks.

"Just be careful. I may have already lost my husband; I will not lose my son." She took his hand. "Never mistake being brave for being heroic," she said, trying to keep the anguish that was tearing her heart to shreds from shaking her voice to pieces. "One is born of necessity; the other is a foolish notion, and I did not raise you to be a fool."

They had done as much as they could; now, like they'd done a hundred times before, they had to wait. If Teril was telling the truth they wouldn't have to wait for long. With some time to kill, Alyda decided to go and see the Hammer. On the way to their barracks, she passed groups of civilians who'd gathered in the bailey waiting to be assigned a duty.

Some kept busy cleaning weapons, others searched for courage in the bottom of a bottle. Many sat and stared into the camp fires, as though trying to divine their future in the flames.

Alyda yawned; she'd get some sleep as soon as she'd seen the Company. She'd had to order Cassian to go and rest, but she understood what was driving him. He not only faced a battle to protect his Queen, but also to save his family.

Her father had done the same when Bear's Tooth was attacked on the day she was born. He'd gone into battle knowing his wife was about to give birth alone, somewhere in the hills. Year's later he'd told Alyda it was the best and worst day of his life. Her mother never spoke of it.

The next few days were going to be hard if the Guthani came, and although she relished the challenge of command, at times like this, she missed the easy companionship of her fellow knights.

She paused in the doorway of their barracks to steal a glimpse of the life she'd left behind when she'd become Captain. Rann was sitting cross-legged on the floor, gruffly instructing his squire how to sharpen a sword *the Company way*. Della was on her bunk, quietly playing a tin whistle. Nevenna was beside her, cleaning her armour. Some knights were reading, some prayed, others slept. War was coming—it hung over the Arth like a cloud, but the barracks was a haven of calm, the eye of the gathering storm.

She heard footsteps behind her and turned to see Kieran with a keg under his arm. When he saw her, he cleared his throat loud enough for those inside to hear.

"We've been here a few times, eh, Captain?"

"Aye. And we'll be here a few more before we have to settle the butcher's bill."

"Do you want me to assemble the Company?"

"No. It's an informal visit."

"In that case, would you care for a wet?" He patted the keg.

Alyda grinned. "I thought you'd never ask."

It was still a wonder to Cassian that something so small could so completely disarm him. He could have sat there all night, watching Tomas sleep. The feared Captain of the Black Lancers, completely at the mercy of a one year old. If his knights could see the idiot smile that was plastered across his face they would, quite rightly, laugh themselves sick. One of his braids drifted into the crib. Although he was fast asleep, when it brushed against his hand, Tomas grabbed it.

"Come to bed, Cass," Beria called sleepily.

The Knight Captain gently uncurled his son's fingers from his hair and kissed him goodnight. He stirred, but didn't wake.

Cassian sat on the bed. "He's got a good strong grip. He'll make a fine Lancer," he said to Beria who began un-braiding his hair.

"You're so handsome," she whispered and kissed his neck.

A thrill of excitement ran through his body at her touch. After they'd made love with quiet, ardent passion they lay in each other's arms. Sleep eluded them both.

"What's wrong? Why are you looking at me like that?" he asked her.

Beria had an intense look of concentration on her face. "That portrait doesn't do you justice."

"Oh, I don't know. She got the crooked nose right—and the scar on my chin. Thin, pointy face, pale as a dead fish. I think it's an excellent likeness."

Beria slapped him playfully, and nestled against his hairless chest. "It's your eyes. Painters never get eyes right, especially yours. She gave you cold eyes and they aren't, they're alive and warm and…Oh, Cass. I'm so afraid."

Alyda returned to her quarters to find Jamie asleep on the floor. Her spare sword was lying next to him, along with a heavy file and some blade oil. He'd been busy; the old blade was shining like it had never been used. She carefully stepped over him. She'd moved out of the barbican and into here. It was a smaller room, but it had everything she needed. The room in the barbican was now full of archers, baskets of stones and pots of oil.

She grabbed a blanket off the bed and threw it over her squire before taking off her gauntlets and unsheathing her sword. She propped the naked blade against the bed and lay down. She didn't bother taking off her armour; the scouts had reported that a large force of Guthani and mercenaries were on their way and would reach them around dawn if they kept their current pace. It was bad news, but at least they'd had a warning. She closed her eyes.

It wasn't uncomfortable sleeping in harness; she'd done it many times before and in much less pleasant surroundings. She went over the list of everything that needed to be done, and measured it against what they had managed to achieve. It balanced well.

She yawned and pushed aside all thought of war and sieges, and pictured instead the high mountain pastures near Bear's Tooth. She made the season of her dreams summer, and the horses grazing on sweet grass, fat and playful. The sky she painted was brilliant azure, speckled with the lightest brushstroke streaks of cloud. With the image fixed in her mind, she was soon fast asleep.

Chapter Thirteen

Was that blood? *His* blood? He held up his hand, it was twisted and broken. A crooked black claw against the grey Void sky. Something that tasted sharp and metallic dripped into his mouth. He was bleeding. The Obsidian Prince laughed.

"Who did this to you, brother?" hissed the Prince of Bones.

Although he couldn't see her from where he was lying, her sibilant voice was as unmistakable as the faint hollow clinking of tiny bones that accompanied her speech.

"Oh, I think you know what it was. Surely you can smell the unmistakable aroma of an Unmaker." He groaned, relishing the sharp pain of breath ripping through his torn lungs. It had been so long since he had felt this alive.

"Of course we can smell it, but what happened? You know full well that you are currently the only one with a connection—the only one who has named and is named because of your slave whore's gift."

She knew that he was broken or else she would never have dared to insult the woman whose love bound him to the mortal realm. *The flower.* Panic gave him strength and he sat bolt up. It was where he'd left it on the dragon's bones. He fell back onto his shattered elbow, the agony was exquisite. The Prince of Bones glided towards the hairpin, her fingernail garb rattling around her fleshless body as she moved. She reached towards it, the bony digits of her fingers questing like antennae before withdrawing into the sleeve of her robe.

"Go on, touch it—end it all, go back to the essence," he joked as his blood soaked into the hungry ground. She snapped round to face him, her white eyes blazing. If she still had eyelids, she would no doubt have narrowed them.

"I'll never give up this form because of a *human's* magic, especially not that of your pet," she hissed.

Her venom fed him, gave him the strength to smile. "It's not human magic. This is the gods' will. That's why it would turn you to charcoal if you touched it. Be assured; I'd use your bones to write a most beautiful eulogy in your honour.

"How amusing. I wonder if you will still be laughing when I've told you why I'm here. The Order has sent me to seal your realm. You will not join in the Sharing."

She tilted her bony jaw to emphasise her triumph. He thought it a fair attempt, considering she didn't have any skin.

"You have been to the mortal realm three times and brought us nothing of our own, just let us lick the crumbs from your fingers—and this time you almost brought an Unmaker back with you. What would have happened if it had followed you here?"

"You would have had to use some of the power you've all been hoarding and fight for your existences, like the old days. You should try it, it's invigorating." He coughed up a slimy clot of black blood.

"You're a fool," she hissed. "You have such power and you waste it! While we have to search through millions of dirty little human minds to find one that might be open to our influence, you have a link and you squander it. You are banished and thrice damned! You will never partake of the Sharing again. You are cast from the Order, and your realm will be sealed when I leave."

"Tell me, sister; how long before another is singled from the herd to feed the hunger like poor dear Azure? Will you be next? For all the hissing we both know you are as weak as a newborn. That is why they sent you to me. If I take you, they lose nothing. How long do you think you can sustain yourself on what you have left?"

She drifted over, planted a bony foot on his chest, and pushed him back to the ground. "Longer than you."

He lacked the strength to sit up, but he sensed when she left had his realm. He turned his head; fascinated by the new perspective that the inability to move had given him. *Agonising pain, incapacity and banishment. Such a busy day.* The spine lay nearby, still fleshy, still alive with writhing maggots. *Still alive.* He inched his hand towards it, tendons straining. *Too far.* He tried again; something tore in his arm but he moved a fraction closer. He laughed; *this might take a while.*

The villagers had fled, but Thorgulsen burned the village of Galegallen to the ground all the same. It wasn't merely an act of spite, although he enjoyed it. Even in Antia, where the winters were mild, rebuilding their homes in the snow would teach the peasants to respect and fear their new masters. Cold and hunger were useful tools to keep skraglings in line, but that wasn't why he was here. He had come to make the crows fat.

The few peasants they'd winkled out of their hovels had babbled about evil magic at the keep. The sorcerer hadn't shown up with the Queen in a sack, so he had to assume the demon had fucked up—not only that, but the Ants would know he was coming. Thorgulsen spat in the mud, all that gold, wasted.

"Pity they've gone," said Gathorl, "the Ants will be more biddable when we've skinned a few more of 'em."

Thorgulsen shrugged. "Be content, the wretches from here and the other villages will have fled to this, Gallen Arth. They'll huddle there together like flies on shit, sharing fleas and talking up their fears while they wait for us. The crying of bairns and handwringing of the olds will wear at the nerves of their warriors and every tear stained face will remind them of what they have to lose." He grinned. "And then, when they behold our cold eyed hirths and red handed mercenaries, what store of courage they've hoarded will vanish like morning mist. Mark my words; they'll beg us to take the Queen and her get in exchange for their lives."

Gathorl nodded. "Aye. I've waited behind the palisades more'n once, forced to listen to the young 'uns bawling and hating it for putting me on edge. Wains give voice to what we pretend not to feel, eh?" The hirth winked.

"You can't pretend anything, Gat. We can smell the shit in your pants when you go into battle," one of the hirths chimed in, to the amusement of all.

On the ride to Gallen Arth it began to rain heavily, making the day as piss-dreary as the country they were stuck in. Thorgulsen warmed himself with the image of the knights begging to surrender, and of him handing the Antian Queen to Redbear. He was keen to be done with this and return to Guthland, ships laden with slaves and booty. He'd return a wealthy and influential man, the Dragon Throne but one corpse away.

Behind him, six hundred hirths and two companies of mercenaries were warming up for the fight, their voices raised in jagged laughter, their rough songs promising death and glory. The Irregulars' war engines and their knowledge of the Steelskin's tactics would set the edge to the formidable weapon he wielded. He just hoped Trenham was a more able commander than the idiot Suvian.

Telvier had avoided him ever since the worm-sack of a sorcerer had failed to bring him the Queen. He'd have strangled the rat-faced little prick with his own guts long before now if his rabble didn't take so willingly to butchery. Thorgulsen smiled to himself. If nothing else, dreaming of tormenting Telvier was an amusing distraction from thinking about the inglorious task that lay before him.

A slender blade of light severed the earth from the sky just as they reached the recently cleared tree-line. Rising from the mist that covered the open ground was Gallen Arth. Thorgulsen was impressed. Unlike Weyhithe, this place hadn't been born of womanish fancy. This was a keep birthed from the hard experience of war. The castle's forbidding walls soared above the trees, crowned by five huge towers that speared into the sky. The walls were sheer, save for strategically placed arrow loops. It had a moat, a double barbican, and four huge towers anchored the corners of the curtain wall. The fifth tower was taller than its siblings, its turret graced by a night black standard. His gut clenched when he saw the scarlet banner of the Hammer hanging beneath it.

A thousand warriors could hold that keep for years, if they had food and water to supply them. It was built to crush the will and break the bones of any force set on attacking it. Even now, he could feel it testing the strength of his determination. But the Ants didn't have a thousand warriors or the guts to stand.

At most, there were two companies of Steelskins cowering within and they were more used to playing games of war than making orphans. Confident that he was mere hours from accomplishing his mission, Thorgulsen sent his herald over to the Arth.

An icy chill ran through Alyda as she watched the Guthani crowd into the tree-line. When the hordes were packed in tight, shield overlapping garish shield, they began to sing. Hammering sword hilts and axe hafts against their shields, they beat out a primitive rhythm and announced their intentions to the garrison. Alyda spat a curse when she saw the Irregulars' standard amongst those of the Guth-landers.

"That treacherous bastard," growled Lorhine. He and a dozen other knights and squires were with her on the roof of the barbican. He'd shaved his head except for his twin braids, revealing intricate blue spirals tattooed around his skull. Usually hidden by hair, they declared his Clan her-itage.

Alyda shrugged. "He's a mercenary. It's not personal."

"With all respect, Captain, I think he's an honourless turd. He was fighting with us a few months ago."

Alyda laughed. "Aye, and he'll remember how well we schooled the Suvians, and that he's the one about to face us now," she said, loud enough for those in the gatehouse to hear and take heart. Battles were won or lost on the strength of an army's morale. She had to nurture the spark of courage in her warriors, turn it into a flame strong enough to sustain them when the dark tide swept towards them.

After about half an hour of wailing and shield beat-ing, the noise died down and a lone rider trotted out of the trees on a shaggy little pony. The rider was waving a flag of truce. When he reached the bridge he halted. The Grey Beard was wearing bronze scale armour and red and orange striped trews. He looked remarkably composed, to say there were a hundred bows bent upon him.

"Know me and hear my words!" His voice carried clean and clear on the brittle air. "I am Garuld Snowfoot, Herald and Talespinner of Thane Kasper Thorgulsen, son of Thane Brandar Thorgulsen, Warleader of his people. Thane Thorgulsen seeks to discuss terms with the Commander of this castle. What say you? Before your gods, and upon your honour."

Alyda tipped Lorhine the nod. He climbed up between the crenels.

"The Commander of the garrison will meet to discuss terms with your leader, upon her honour and before the gods," he bellowed.

The herald bowed and trotted back to his lines.

Alyda turned to Jamie. "Saddle Lyco."

Three knights rode out of the shadows of the gatehouse. Trenham knew them. They were the tip of the spear, the point of the blade, the hard, striking face of the Hammer. Front and centre was Alyda Stenna, clad in mirror bright plate, a fiery plume in her closed helm. To her right, making the tall captain look slight by comparison was Rann Lacgarde, the Company Standard Bearer. He had his visor up and was grinning like a broken bottle; he carried the company colours and a spiked ball and chain draped across his saddle. Third was Kieran Lorhine, Second-in-Command of the Hammer. Even with his head shaved, those black, killer's eyes were unmistakable. *So this is what it's like to see them as enemies.* It was much less appealing than viewing them as comrades.

"That armour is magnificent!" said Telvier, his voice a breathy mix of appreciation and avarice. "It must be worth a small fortune."

The Thane bestowed him with a frosty glare. Trenham laughed.

"She's overdressed for the coffle," the Thane snarled.

"What?" Trenham was sure he must have misheard.

Now it was Thorgulsen who grinned. "You heard me—or did you think I was just going to let them go?"

"I…yes, well… under escort and unarmed, but not…" This wasn't what he'd expected. The game had changed somewhere and he'd missed it or worse; just assumed they were playing by different rules.

"I'll tell you what I'll do, Trenham. We'll draw lots for the armour—and for who goes first on the officers. If you're lucky you might be near the top of the list."

Telvier coughed. "I'll pass on the officers if I can have two draws on the armour…?"

The knights came to a halt and waited. If he didn't know better he'd swear they'd come to accept Thorgulsen's surrender and after what he'd just heard he almost wished it was that way round. Ali Stenna raised her visor and nodded curtly to Thorgulsen. A sly smile twitched the corner of her mouth.

"Thane Thorgulsen. How's the jaw?"

Thorgulsen's fist tightened around the axe haft. This could turn sharp, certainly would, if they knew what Thorgulsen had planned for them. Trenham didn't rate their chances against those archers' dead-eyeing them from the wall. Wisely, neither did Thorgulsen and he relaxed back in the saddle.

"It's fine—unlike Weyhithe which I have reduced to smouldering rubble. How are the Queen and Corvinius?"

She didn't answer.

Thorgulsen continued. "These are my terms: hand over Queen Thea and her sons and you and the garrison will be allowed to live. If you do not hand them over, I will destroy this Arth and kill every man, woman, and child within and still take the Queen and her sons. Many lives are depending on your decision, Captain Stenna. Don't let your pride kill them; this is not a fight you can win."

Arrogant bastard. Thorgulsen could have been more provocative, but not by much. Fire burned in Stenna's eyes and for a moment Trenham thought she was going to draw her sword and set to, but she didn't. She turned her attention to him.

"I didn't know you were in the business of killing children, Trenham. You've gone down in the world."

He wanted to explain that he'd thought Thorgulsen was going to offer a better deal, but he couldn't. He couldn't even warn her of the fate Thorgulsen had in mind for them. What should have been a straightforward surrender now balanced on the point of a blade—one that cut whichever way it fell.

"Just surrender, Captain Stenna," was all he could say that wouldn't break his contract, or perjure his conscience beyond redemption.

She gave him a disdainful look and turned to Thorgulsen. "Will the garrison be treated as honourable prisoners of war?"

Thorgulsen smoothed his long moustaches. "Life should be enough for someone who is in no fucking position to bargain."

Lacgarde growled—Lorhine's hand clamped around his sword hilt. Trenham was sure he could hear the creak of taut bowstrings and got ready to slide down the side of his horse and ride like fuck for the trees. Alyda raised her hand and stilled the bladed air. "I'll need time to consider your offer," she said.

"You have one hour," replied Thorgulsen.

Trenham couldn't believe it. This wasn't how it was supposed to go. They were supposed to negotiate, the outcome would have been more or less the same, but the Antians would have had safe passage as honoured prisoners, not sold into slavery.

Thorgulsen's orders were to capture the Queen, all he had to do to achieve that was sweeten the pill, but he'd fucked it up. Telvier knew it too; his fellow captain gave him a resigned shrug. Like him, he'd seen the look in Alyda Stenna's eyes when she turned for the Arth. There would be no surrender. Bemused, Trenham began to recalculate his plans.

Cassian was waiting for them in the bailey when they got back. "What did he have to say?" he asked.

Alyda had clenched her jaw so hard against her anger that her teeth ached. She took a breath and let the anger go. "Nothing that we didn't expect. Hand over the Queen and he'll let us live, don't and… You know the rest. We have an hour before we tell him to go fuck himself."

Without waiting out the hour, Alyda ordered the call to arms to be sounded. What she didn't tell Cassian was how relieved she was. She couldn't have given the Queen up, no matter what the Guthlander had promised. That he'd promised nothing had made it easier to reconcile.

The children, elderly and sick were moved into the cellars beneath the Riverside Hall. They were large and deep and would offer the best protection from any heavy missiles that might be loosed at the Arth. The hall backed onto the west curtain wall, but the gate would be the focus of any attack.

Ropes had to be dowsed in water to stop them burning from hauling basket after basket of stones up the wall. Fires were lit at intervals along its length and pots of tar and oil set over them to boil. Archers took up positions behind the battlements, smoothing arrow flights and waxing bow strings. After some debate, the ballistae were positioned on the wall and towers and their bases weighted with sacks of rocks and river sand.

In the bailey, against the rise of the keep hill, forges were erected and blacksmiths set to work. North of the hill, the stables were full to capacity with the restless mounts of both companies. Engineers worked furiously to finish assembling the two huge trebuchets. Alyda had them positioned opposite the barbican on the far side of the bailey. Dozens of large clay pots were stacked beside them. The pots were filled with jagged stones and sealed, ready to hurl at the enemy from the mighty catapults. They were called 'beehives' because of their shape and the nasty sting they delivered.

Alyda was in the Bailey with Cassian, waiting for the last grains of sand to trickle through the hourglass. She looked around. Nothing of the domestic remained. The tents and livestock, washing lines and children were gone. The Arth was now fit for battle, sharp and deadly, a towering grey monster with teeth of steel and bones of stone.

Cassian handed her a flask. "We've enough stores to feed the Arth for a month, including the refugees. The horses probably two, maybe three, weeks. Thank the Twins we don't have to worry about water."

She took a swig from the flask. It was brandy and burned all the way down. "Aye. Those wells are a blessing." *If only supplies were the worst of our problems.* "We're in good shape." She said. It wasn't entirely a lie.

"How long do you think we can hold?" Cassian asked.

She handed the flask back and let her gaze travel across the Arth as she watched the ghost of a battle that had yet to take place. "If they storm the walls they could take us in hours. If they come in waves...I don't know, perhaps a week? Much will depend on how long it takes them to get through the gates. Can we Ward-Lock the ones in the outer gatehouse?"

"No, nor the outer gates of the barbican, perhaps once, but no longer. I think when they built the bridge, the magic was damaged."

"No matter. We won't have to hold out for long. Relief's probably already on its way."

Lyco snorted; she patted his neck to calm him. All the horses were fired up, they could sense the tension building. "If for some reason help *is* delayed, is there another way out that isn't on the plans?"

Cassian sighed. "No. It's either over the walls or through the gate, unless you can fly."

Griga, Cassian's Lieutenant coughed.

"What is it, Grig?"

The Lieutenant stepped forward and saluted. "Sir, Captain Stenna, I couldn't help overhearing." She lowered her voice. "There is another way out, under the Queen's Tower. There was a boat landing there, but it kept flooding, so Captain Mardyn had it filled in."

Alyda looked across to the tower on the north east corner of the Arth. "Who knows about it?"

"Not many," said Griga, "it hasn't been used in years, but the cellar's dry, so I'm guessing the tunnel might be useable."

"I want it cleared. Have people you trust on it day and night until it's open, and nobody else must know about it. I mean it Griga—this rests on your head."

The Lieutenant saluted and left.

"For what it's worth, I understand." Cassian said when she'd gone.

Alyda wished he didn't. She'd feel less guilty if he was angry and unreasonable. "We can't let the Queen and the princes be taken, Cass. If they are, they'll be used to make the King surrender and we'll lose the kingdom to Jerim."

"It's alright, Ali," he said.

Will you say that when they come to kill your child and your woman? For the first time in her life, the responsibility of command weighed heavily on her shoulders.

"I won't lose," she said, as much to herself as to Cassian.

"*We* won't lose. We're in this together."

He was right of course; it just didn't feel like it.

Kilner let his spirit sink into the earth and float on the rivers of energy that spilled from the Arth and webbed the world in a net of power. He drifted beyond the castle, out beneath the forest, delighting in the bubbling presence of tiny sprites like the ones he used in his performances.

There was something else close by, something *much* more powerful, and far more dangerous. The slumbering elemental slept, wrapped in the roots of the forest. The magician steered his spirit away—even asleep it could destroy him if he strayed too close.

Like a fish kiss on the skin of a lake, a pulse of magic rippled from the heart of the Arth. He could almost taste the raw essence as it washed over him. This far from the source it was like warm honey.

It was very different in the heart of the Arth. In there it was a raging inferno, a volcano of magical essence that would destroy him if he got too close. *Power consumes power.* The thought that he was so close to something so awesome terrified him. He froze, afraid to move. He might have stayed like that for hours, paralysed by fear, but something tugged at his consciousness, drawing him back to the world of flesh.

It was never pleasant returning to his body. The first painful breath that had to be dragged into dusty lungs, the heaviness of ungainly limbs chaining his lighter-than-air spirit had little to recommend it. He opened his eyes to see the Captain of the First's Squire standing before him.

The lad grinned. "Finally. I thought you'd died in your sleep. Captain Stenna wants to see you."

Gathorl tapped the last grains of sand to the bottom of the hourglass. "Time's up, my Lord. Shall I send Snowfoot over to find out what they have to say?"

Thorgulsen spat into a glowing brazier. The flames hissed. "No need, they've given their answer. I knew the Steelskin was arrogant, I didn't think she was insane."

Trenham didn't know how Thorgulsen could be surprised after the offer he'd made the Antians, but he held his tongue. Like it or not, he had a job to do and arguing with his employer wouldn't make doing it any easier.

The Thane sat by the table on a fur heaped chair, brawny elbows making space amongst maps and candles. He looked at Gathorl. "When will we be ready to attack?"

The hirth opened his mouth, but Trenham saw his chance and cut in, earning a sour look from the old warrior.

"I think it would be wise to build some earthworks, Thane Thorgulsen. It'll take two days at the most to raise some banks. If you look at the plans I've drawn up you'll see what I had in mind. The ground here is perfect for it." Trenham unrolled a sheaf of plans on the table.

Thorgulsen brushed them aside. "I don't have time to waste building walls to protect your precious machines. We'll attack as soon as we're ready—today. I'll let you use those...what do you call them, crawlers? Get them up to the moat with the ladders and bridges, as fast as you can. My hirths will finish the job and we can all get out of here."

"If you let me throw up some earthworks, more of your hirths will survive to scale the walls. It's over three hundred and fifty yards from the trees to the Arth."

Thorgulsen looked up slowly and fixed him with a hard stare. It might work on Telvier, but Trenham wasn't as easily cowed.

"We signed a contract, Trenham. Must I show you the part where it says you will obey my commands? Or have you decided to break a Free Company contract?"

Trenham took a deep breath before answering. "I would never break a contract. I just want to get the job done as efficiently as I can. Give me a day; it will save time and lives."

"Enough. This has already taken longer than I can spare, damn that Steelskin bastard to the Void. Now go do the job I've paid you for, or I'll find someone who will."

It was pointless to argue, Thorgulsen's face was as hard set as dung in the sunshine. Trenham swallowed his frustration, rolled up his plans and left.

"The lad's right," said Gathorl when Trenham had gone. "That's a big old killing ground they've made for us. Makes sense to throw up some earth banks."

"Do you think I'm a fucking dullard?" Thorgulsen snapped. His old friend didn't deserve his ire, but he was annoyed. "I know it makes sense, but we don't have time. This whole plan, this 'bloodless victory' has already gone to shit and will go worse if Daris beats Jerim before we capture his Queen. We need to take her quickly and damn the cost."

"If I were Daris, I wouldn't give the stink off my shit for her. You can always find a wench able to sire an heir or two; crowns are a mite harder to come by."

"Which is why we need to take her sooner rather than later, while Daris is still unsure of victory. If he knows the Queen and his sons are prisoners it'll take the fight out of the bastard, especially when Redbear sends him a few

pieces to encourage his surrender; an ear, a hand, a tit—
something he'll recognise."

Gathorl chuckled. "Aye, true enough. These Ants are a
soft lot. Lucky for the Queen she isn't wed to a Guthlander."

Thorgulsen sat back and regarded the old warrior
with a critical eye. "Wouldn't you surrender to save your
woman?"

"You've met my wife. Why do you think I still drag
these old bones on campaign?"

Thorgulsen grinned and smoothed his beard. "So it's
not because I inspire unwavering loyalty?"

Gathorl gave a gap-toothed grin. "Aye. That too, my
Lord, that too."

"But you could do it if you wanted to?" Alyda was trying
not to lose her temper, but it wasn't easy.

"Well…er…no. As I have already explained, it's not that
simple. I can't just 'cast a spell or something', as you put
it. My abilities don't work like that…it's much more com-
plicated. If there was anything I could do, I assure you, I
would do it."

Reese plucked at some lint on his robe to avoid her
gaze. She wanted to slap him; a blind woman could see he
was lying. "You cast a spell on my sword the other night."

He shuffled uncomfortably. "Well, yes. And I would
be happy to do so again, but you see, the enchantment I
placed on your blade merely enabled it to hurt the Void
creature. If you think there are more Void creatures out
there 'tis worth doing, but against ordinary humans it's
pointless, I'm afraid."

This was getting nowhere. "Why can't you do something like the damn sorcerer did? Blast our enemies from
the field, or use those fire things you had at Trelanlith and
set them ablaze?"

Reese looked horrified. "Captain! I know you speak from ignorance rather than wilful malice, so I will not take offence." He sucked in his gut and stuck out his chest in a bid to affect an air of gravitas; it failed. "I am an earth mage—not a filthy sorcerer. I do not use blood magic, nor do I warp essence or twist the weave and the weft of the world to suit my will."

She slammed her fist on the table. "Why the fuck not?"

He shrank back in his chair.

"Damn it, Reese, I'm trying to save lives—yours included. Make an effort, man."

"I'm s…sorry, Captain," the mage stammered, "I c… cannot help you."

She couldn't waste any more time on this. The man had a coward's heart and wouldn't do anything. Not even to save his own hide.

"Just go, Reese. You've been most…informative."

The mage smiled weakly and hurried towards the door. He paused on the threshold. For a moment she thought he'd changed his mind. "I wonder; might it not be better to surrender, Captain?"

The look she gave him conveyed her thoughts on the matter. He turned red, swallowed hard, and scuttled out.

It was only after he'd left that she noticed the child. He couldn't have been more than five. Filthy, and as thin as a rake, he was wearing ragged clothes three times too big for him. She'd no idea how long he'd been there, but he was playing with the feather in her helm, brushing the plume against his dirt-streaked face and smiling as the delicate fronds tickled his skin. He opened his eyes, saw that she was watching him and dropped the helm. Quick as a flea, he bounded for the door and was gone. She laughed. A minute later, the first volley of stones rocked the Arth.

Trenham's first task was to destroy the gatehouse and the barbican, but leave the bridge intact. His second was to provide cover for the warriors to get the bridges and ladders up to the moat. No doubt his third task would be to sprout wings, fly over the Arth and piss fire onto the Ants. He'd brought all twelve of his new trebuchets. Two had been damaged on the journey and needed repairs, but the other ten were in good working order.

They were not the biggest examples of their type, but they were more than capable of raining destruction down on the Arth. He'd worked like a dog and saved everything he'd earned for two years to buy them, but even with the favourable price he'd got from old Kon Stenna he still had a sizable loan left to pay the Free Company Council.

Only a few short weeks ago, before he'd taken this damn contract, he'd been eager to test them in battle, but the shine was now well and truly tarnished. He could derive little pleasure from using them against someone he respected and admired and, worse still, was the daughter of the man who'd made them. It was a cruel co-incidence, and one that he'd probably come to regret. He kept trying to convince himself it was only business, but it didn't sit right.

Trenham's mood didn't improve when upon returning from his pointless meeting with Thorgulsen, he found Telvier in his tent.

"I'm no seer, but I guess by your sullen mien the audience with the Thane didn't go well," Telvier purred. His desire to gloat breaking through the thin veneer of sympathy he was trying to project.

Trenham wasn't interested in gossiping with the Suvian. He'd only use whatever was said to try and wheedle his way back into the Thane's favour. Telvier's reputation for backstabbing preceded him. Fellow Free Company Captain he may be, but he was not to be trusted.

"You've fought with the Antians before, d'you think they'll surrender?"

"Possibly. Eventually." Trenham feigned interest in some maps on his desk in the hope that Telvier would take the hint and leave. He didn't. He nosed around the tent, further irritating Trenham.

"What about bribery?"

Trenham laughed. "Corvinius is an exception. Coin isn't the currency these knights deal in."

"No, perhaps not, but I'll wager their families will be happy to pay up if it means getting their kin back in one piece. We could make some coin if we were allowed to ransom the surviving knights. Damn that Guthani oaf to the Void! He's going to ruin me; I've been forced to empty the prison yards to fill my ranks *this* year. I need to make on this contract or next year I'll only be able to afford to enlist old people with wooden spoons. Some of these knights will have wealthy families, it's such a waste." The mercenary fanned himself with the enormous ruffles of lace at his cuffs. "Why can't he kill peasants to slake his bloodlust? I have debts to pay! You know how it is. Which reminds me; I must congratulate you on your fine trebuchets. I do so admire your ambition, and bravery. Those things must have cost a fortune."

Trenham continued to look at the maps, and let the silence lengthen. The Suvian eventually got the message.

"Well, as much as I'd love to stay and banter, I must away. Got to stop my rabble getting too drunk while they're waiting for your lot to soften up the Ants. Let's hope Thorgulsen will—*at the very least*, allow us the pleasure of the garrison before he guts 'em, eh?" Telvier winked conspiratorially before sauntering from the tent.

Trenham felt the need to bathe. The Suvian might wear fine clothes and affect the manners of a gentleman, but underneath the silk he was no better than the murderous gutter-scum he employed. He poured himself a glass of wine and downed it in one. He was starting to think this was a bad contract.

The trebuchets pounded the Arth late into the afternoon. Trenham had managed to confine his thoughts to the job at hand and direct his crews to destroying the gatehouse. The ballista on the towers hadn't been idle during their attack and had put one of his engines out of action, but in the long range battle of heavy weaponry, he was winning.

As dusk rolled purple across the sky, the attackers had cause to cheer when the defenders finally abandoned the battered, outer gatehouse. Emboldened by the withdrawal, Telvier's warriors formed up, eager to attack. Trenham didn't share their excitement; he didn't trust the Antian's uncharacteristic retreat and went over to speak to the Suvian before he sent his fighters in.

"Ah, Herick! Have ye come to watch my lads finish off the Ants?" Telvier smirked. He'd changed his outfit again, and was now wearing a fine cuirass of polished steel.

"Actually, Luca, I was going to suggest you hold off. Let me take out the gates from a distance."

The Suvian laughed and fluffed his lace cuffs. "You really are too cautious! Look at the damage you've done. I really don't think we'll have any trouble getting in, the Ants have retreated." He grinned, gold teeth winking in the fading light. "Time is money, dear fellow! They aren't paying me by the day." He took another pull on the silver flask he was waving. "I must say, your crew's aim is rather good, but then I suppose it is a big castle. Cheer up, we're almost done. Now if you would excuse me, 'tis time to unleash the hounds."

Trenham let him go. Telvier was so desperate to win his way back into the Thane's favour he'd throw his fighters at the Arth no matter what he said.

Chapter Thirteen

The Suvian marched over to his company, drew his rapier, and with a flourish, gave the order to attack. The mercenaries swarmed from the trees in a ragged wave, dragging a rough-hewn battering ram with them. Telvier stayed where he was; safely out of ballista range. Trenham shook his head. This would not go well. The heavy ram was swinging wildly in its shoddily constructed cradle that ploughing deep furrows into the road as they dragged it along. When they reached the bridge, Trenham halted the bombardment.

Kiri, the Irregulars' Second-in-Command, sucked her teeth. "Not a single defender left on tha' walls. I 'spected more from tha' Ants."

Trenham shook his head. "I'm not so sure they've given up. This is too easy."

"Easy?" She gave a throaty chuckle, her dark eyes mocked him. "I'd hate t'see your idea of tough. You underestimate yourself and overestimate tha' Antians. They've taken a poundin'. 'Tis enough to break even—"

Trenham pointed to the Arth.

As soon as Telvier's company set foot on the bridge, the gatehouse portcullis rattled up and the gates were thrown open. The mercenaries stumbled to a halt as the Hammer and the Black Lancers charged across the bridge and out of the gatehouse.

The knights had mounted up in the Bailey while the defenders made a show of pulling back from the gatehouse. The moment the wheel of the ram carriage touched the bridge, the signal was given for the defenders hiding in the gatehouse to throw open the gates and raise the portcullis. The other three sets of gates had already been quietly opened during the bombardment.

- 335 -

Without doubt, there would be some who would question her decision to ride out. They would argue that the gatehouse was un-defendable, that it was better to sacrifice it without loss. Technically, they were probably right, but Alyda knew there was more at stake here than bricks and mortar. They needed an early victory. The defenders—particularly the civilians, had to believe they could win if they were going to stand and fight. She settled into the saddle, reins gripped in one hand, sword in the other. Now all she had to do was deliver that victory.

The swifter, less heavily armoured Lancers led the charge, followed by the Hammer. The 1st rode straight at the main body of mercenaries. The Lancers split, half riding round either flank of the attackers. While one of the Hammer doused the ram with oil, the rest attacked the startled mercenaries while the Lancers raced to cut off their retreat. Poorly trained, half drunk and scared to death, Telvier's company ran as though all the demons of the Void were chasing them.

Alyda took no pleasure from slaughter, but there was something deeply satisfying about dealing with the scum who'd put Weyhithe to the torch. She would have liked to have pushed the advantage surprise had granted them and carry the fight into the enemy camp, wreak all shades of havoc upon them, but they had to stick to the plan. They would ride down this scum and destroy Trenham's engines—the bastard himself if he got in her way.

Trenham's heart sank. He'd seen this before in Suvia, only this time, he was on the receiving end. Because Telvier and Thorgulsen had rushed the assault on the gates, his crews and trebuchets were now vulnerable. The Hammer scattered Telvier's fighters without even slowing their charge before turning their attention to his engines. Cursing, Trenham pulled on his coif and strung his bow.

The Irregulars' trebuchet crews drew swords as the tide of steel flowed towards them, but there was no way they could fight it out with the heavy cavalry and Trenham ordered the retreat. They didn't need to be told twice.

The knights didn't pursue the crews; they set about wrecking his trebuchets. It came as no surprise that they knew exactly which ropes to cut and pins to smash to cripple them. Ali Stenna turned to face him. He plucked a shaft from his quiver.

She raised her visor. "Nothing personal!" she shouted, a wolfish grin on her face.

He nocked an arrow, loosed. She slammed down her visor. The shaft flew wide.

When the Guthani finally got themselves in some sort of order and were ready to attack, the Black Lancers' herald gave a short blast on his horn. Immediately, the knights stopped smashing the trebuchets and spurred their mounts back to the Arth. Guthani and mercenaries flooded from the trees, screaming for Antian blood.

When they were roughly halfway across the open ground, the Lancer's herald gave another blast. Trenham wondered if it could get any worse when a dozen huge clay pots arced over the Arth walls. He groaned. Apparently, it could.

The pots hit the ground and exploded into hundreds of jagged shards. The fist-sized rocks that were inside them ripped through the attackers, killing and maiming dozens. The counter-attack stalled. Trenham looked across the field—not a single Antian was down. Their archers had returned to their positions on the curtain wall and were picking off anyone foolish enough to come within range of their longbows.

Stunned and bloodied, those Guthani and mercenaries who were able, staggered back to the woods, pursued by the mocking laughter of Antians. Trenham sighed and slackened off his bowstring, conflicting emotions trapping his feelings somewhere between despair and admiration.

Victory seeded thunder in the voices of the garrison and a wave of exultant cheering washed over the Hammer and the Lancers when they rode back into the bailey. Alyda sucked the blood-charged air through the breathes of her helm, but only let go of the hard knot of tension that nestled in her guts when she'd counted back in, every warrior who'd ridden out.

After exchanging savage oaths with her knights, she briefed her officers and then went to her quarters. She was tired, but confident that they would not be attacked again that night. The Guthani and mercenaries would hopefully be too busy arguing over who was to blame for that shambolic attack. She shouted for Jamie, expecting him to be waiting for her—but he wasn't. She knew he'd got back unscathed; he was right behind her when they rode in. Cursing his untimely absence, she entered her room to find a crackling fire burning in the hearth, food and drink on the table and Talin reclining on the bed.

He smiled at her. "I sent Jamie and the little one away. I didn't think you'd mind."

"Little one?" She enquired confused, but happy to see him. She unbuckled her sword belt and tossed it on the couch.

"Aye, your little shadow; the child who's been following you around. I found him hiding under the bed."

Alyda shrugged. "You've lost me, I...Oh, d'you mean that little imp I caught playing with my helm? No, I don't mind in the slightest, but Jamie would be useful about now." She reached for the clasp on her gorget.

"As I'm the one who sent him away, I feel I ought to act as your squire."

"I think that's fair."

"Fair, you say? You're very honoured. Few people are privileged enough to have a prince do this." Talin unbuckled her cuirass.

She shrugged out of the armour and pushed him back onto the bed. He lay there smiling while she took off her sweat-soaked arming jack. A slow smile spread across her face. "You're most gracious, Highness. Now, what was it you said about showing your gratitude when we reached the Arth…?"

It was fully dark before Trenham sent his crews out to retrieve the damaged trebuchets. He had to hand it to the Hammer; the bastards had done a thorough job. His people would have to work through the night to repair the damage.

The next time he turned them on the Arth he wouldn't stop until the gatehouse was a memory. He didn't understand why they'd taken the risk of attacking, just to put them out of action for one night. He stowed his bow and stripped off his mail. The sooner they got started the sooner they'd be done. Alyda must have known the engines could be repaired. For all that the attack had been daring, they had only won a respite, not a reprieve.

At sunrise it began to rain stones. Alyda wasn't surprised; the only way to permanently put a trebuchet out of action was to destroy the main timbers, but that hadn't been an option. She had hoped it would take them longer to make the repairs, but the sortie hadn't been in vain. The trebuchet's volleys were neither as numerous or as concentrated as they had been the previous day and the mercenaries were making a more cautious and more importantly, slower, advance across the field, protected under crawlers.

She remembered discussing their effectiveness with Trenham and Althus back in Suvia. They were simple constructions comprising a wooden frame covered in fresh cow hides and dowsed in water. They could protect large groups of warriors from arrows and other light missiles, while allowing them to approach defences carrying cumbersome scaling equipment instead of shields.

She pulled on her gauntlets. Talin rolled the quilt around himself another turn, but didn't wake. She wanted to kiss him, but she let him lie. Today would be a long, ugly day; he'd need all the strength sleep could give him for when it was his turn to take his place on the wall. She had to leave this quiet haven, angle her mind away from gentle thoughts and plan for the misery they would stamp on the bones of the bastards massing outside.

Alyda, Cassian and their officers crouched behind the battlements on the barbican to watch the advancing Guthani. Stones ricocheted off the walls, gouging great chunks from the masonry and shaking the building to its foundations. It was strangely liberating knowing that at any moment a well-aimed boulder could smash her to pieces and that neither skill nor will could save her. What scared her was making a bad decision. The bombardment eased. She peered over the wall at the crawlers.

"Have the wall commanders been briefed?"

"Aye, Captain," Cassian shouted above the thunder of a stone smashing into a nearby section of wall. "I've put some veterans in with the volunteers to steady them up. We've three groups in reserve and half the Lancers ready to mount up."

"Good. Keep a watch on the river side. I doubt they'll attempt to cross the 'Run, but they may try to dam it upstream. We need to be ready for that." She clapped him on the shoulder. "Look on the bright side, at least the stones will stop when the crawlers get closer."

Cassian swept his gaze across the ranks of enemy fighters. "Aye. That's when the real fighting will start."

Chapter Fourteen

"Hoy, Snowfoot!" Skani bawled at the Talespinner. "Hurry up you sluggard, we're forming up. D' you still have my dagger?"

Garuld Snowfoot patted the ornate hilt of the dagger sheathed at his hip. He'd considered selling it to pay his dicing debts, but he knew it would break the big fool's heart. He'd either win the sword to match it, or lose it back to Skani at some point, but he wasn't going to tell him that.

The Talespinner nestled his behind into a tangle of tree roots. He was in no mind to hurry; he hadn't broken his fast yet. He flipped the oatcakes cooking on the hot stones at the edge of the fire. He'd made a half dozen, which was more than he would eat, but he knew Skani would come snuffling around like a pig in an orchard when he smelled the food.

"When will you give me the chance to win it back?" The hirth hung his shield on a branch and squatted down beside the fire.

Snowfoot shrugged and turned the cakes.

"You know, for a Talespinner, you don't say much."

"You don't pay me, Skani Felar. I'm saving my voice for those who do." Snowfoot pulled a hot cake from the fire and offered it to the hirth. Felar accepted it with a grunt of thanks.

"The fucking Ants in their nest. Why don't they come out and fight like real warriors?" Skani sprayed a mouthful of crumbs into the flames.

Snowfoot poked at the fire. "To be fair, they did come out, if only briefly. But to answer what I think you're trying to ask; it's because they lack all sense of drama and have no concept of true heroism and, mostly, because we significantly outnumber them. They aren't like us; they probably think it's stupid to meet us on the field when we are at least four times their number. Whereas we would see it as an opportunity to win fame and a glorious death were our situations reversed." The Talespinner scarfed down an oat cake. "Hard to fathom, I know."

Felar snorted and helped himself to another. "I hate this fucking country and I really hate these Arths. Stinking stone rat holes. It would shame my shadow to cower behind those walls rather than stand shoulder-to-shoulder with my brothers and sisters on the open battlefield." Felar wiped his mouth with the back of his hand and shook the crumbs from his moustache.

Snowfoot smiled as Skani carefully rearranged the little brass beads threaded into his greying yellow beard. *Hirths: always so vain.*

Unlike his shield brother, Garuld thought Antia was a beautiful country, one that had already provided the inspiration for a dozen new songs. When they were back home, he'd live well for months on the booty he'd earned and the tales he'd spin of this adventure. For Skani, being in Antia granted him an opportunity to have something new to complain about. Gods love him, but he was the kind of person who would never see the glory in a sunrise, merely the spots before his eyes.

"So when your turn comes to go against those walls with the arrows falling like rain, you'll stroll along in the open, instead of getting in a crawler, eh?"

His friend's mouth fell into an angry pout. He really shouldn't tease Skani. Funny though it was, it was far too easy.

"Aye, damn right!" Skani narrowed his eyes. "And don't try t' confuse me with twisting words, Garuld big ears. I see that glint in your eye; I'm wise to your tricks, Raven's Son.

Snowfoot chuckled. *Is Skani finally learning?* It had only taken ten years and a few sacks of coin for the lesson to sink in.

Snowfoot swatted his friend's suspicions away with a casual wave. "No, no, I was just curious, but seeing as you're so confident—will you wager the sword that matches my nice dagger on it? Because I think you'll scamper inside after the first beehive explodes next to you. If you've still got legs to scamper with."

Skani frowned, unsure. "And if I win, do I get my dagger back?"

"Of course, and the most priceless possession you own… your honour. Unless you're scared…?"

"You're on! A hirth fears nothing! Although…the dagger is smaller than the sword—there must be something more you can throw in. My honour is mine to win or lose; what else will you add?"

"How about a warrior's funeral?" Snowfoot threw back his head and laughed. "I can't believe how easy it is to trick you, Skani. Will you never learn? I'm surprised you aren't dead or walking around naked and weaponless, I really am."

"Shut up, fatty, I'd have done it," the warrior protested. "These Ants don't frighten me." He looked both embarrassed and relieved.

"They *should* frighten you." Snowfoot hunkered closer to Skani, drew down his brows and lowered his voice. He spared a nervous glance over his shoulder, to confirm the presence of unwelcome and unseen guests. It worked every time. Skani was drawn in, as wide-eyed as a child. "Tis said that the pale knight is a Fey who drinks the blood of children and can kill with but a look and that Stenna is the battle-born daughter of the Mountain God and cannot be defeated and…" He let the pause lengthen. "…Who are *you* calling fatty? Face it Skani, you're twice the man you used to be—and not in a good way."

"Bah!" Skani thumped his stomach. "'Tis pure muscle! My Gardu says I have the body of a god."

"A slightly chubby, past his prime god, maybe." the Talespinner chuckled.

A horn blared, summoning the warriors to arms. Snowfoot doused his fire and donned his coat of bronze.

Felar grabbed his shield, slung it over his shoulder. "Come, old friend—time to make the worms fat, one way or the other."

"Aye. I hear you brother." The Talespinner felt the weight of his armour drag on his shoulders. Time was he wouldn't even notice he was wearing it. He was getting old. These days his love of fighting was more often outweighed by the desire to sit by a fire, eating oatcakes and telling stories.

It was bright and cold, the air as sharp as flint. Sunlight glazed the battlements, turning steel to silver and bronze to gold. The glorious weather seemed at odds with the bloody promise of the day. Talin shivered. He wasn't sure if it was because of the cold or because he was scared witless. The knights of the Hammer and the Black Lancers gave no sign that they were in the least perturbed and were exchanging crude banter and brave words as the enemy edged closer. Nevenna tapped the butt of her halberd on the stones and gave him what he imagined was supposed to be a reassuring smile.

"How many do you think are in those things?" he asked as they watched the crawlers slowly approaching the moat.

The herald squinted against the sun's glare. "By the size of them I'd say maybe… thirty warriors, Highness."

"I count twelve."

Despite his mother's pleas, Talin had joined the fighters on the wall. There were twenty knights in his unit, plus militia. The civilians were easy to distinguish from the career warriors; they were the ones wearing mis-matched armour and who looked as nervous as he was. His gut told him fighting was the right thing to do, but his bladder wasn't convinced.

Their orders were straightforward enough even for him to remember: hold the wall. His unit was on the right of the barbican. It wasn't where the fighting would be heaviest, but he was embarrassed to see that when he joined them, a handful of the Hammer quietly replaced some of the civilians in the group.

Bear had promised she'd be there, but as ever she wasn't where she was supposed to be. The fat cow was probably snoring her face off in a Pel-induced slumber, but he wished she was there—or that he was with her. This time last year he would have been. Hard to believe how much had changed in a year; most of it for the better, but not this. This was bloody terrifying.

The Sergeant-at-Arms counted off the range markers as the enemy came on. An icy shiver ran through Alyda, her muscles twitched in anticipation of action. The Sergeant signalled that they were in range.

"Loose," she ordered, and the ballista sang. Bolt after bolt tore through wood and canvas, flesh and bone, crippling the crawlers in the vanguard. Warriors who escaped the wreckage were nailed to the ground by a storm of arrows.

The effectiveness of the Antian ballistae did not go unpunished and after a few near misses, the bow mounted on the east tower took a direct hit and exploded in a shower of riven timbers and smashed bodies.

The first battered crawlers reached the moat. Alyda took her place in the line as bridges were extended across the water. Defenders hurled rocks from the walls, smashing planks and breaking bodies. Archers had their pick of targets and thickened the air with shafts. This slowed, but didn't stop the advance.

Iron hooks bit into the Arth side of the moat. Guthani swarmed across the planks. Screaming war cries, they hoisted scaling ladders over the crushed bodies of fallen comrades. Alyda shouted herself hoarse urging the defenders to stand firm, willing them to hold the line. The gatehouse was shaking in time to the rhythmic pounding of a new battering ram as it was driven again and again into the portcullis.

A shout went up. Guthlanders had gained the walkway east of the barbican. Clad in shining bronze, shields strapped to their backs, they hauled themselves over the wall bellowing to their gods for blood and victory. Alyda slammed down her visor, the clasp locked into place. It had begun.

The scarlet plume in her helm drew the Guthani to her and into the teeth of the First. Time slowed when the first attacker came within reach of her blade. She sidestepped a spinning axe and thrust her sword at a bronze helm that appeared above the wall. Her blade found its way into an ocular. There was a spray of blood and the helm dropped from sight. Something bright arced towards her; she swayed back. The whistling blade bit stone, bowing its wielder before her. She hacked through the offered neck and moved to meet the next attacker.

Talin had almost died in the first bloody exchange when his sword snagged on a fellow defender's armour. Frozen with fear, he'd closed his eyes and braced for the blow that would send him to the Void.

Instead of the cruel kiss of steel, he felt a rush of air and heard the ringing clash of metal. He opened his eyes to see a spiked buckler locked against a sword inches from his head. The buckler twisted the blade away, swept back round and smashed into the face of his attacker. Blinded by her own blood, the Guthani fell backwards over the wall clutching her bleeding face. His saviour was Bear. She winked at him, gore streaked buckler in one hand, falchion in the other.

"Sorry I'm late, Highness. I couldn't find my gauntlets anywhere."

The Antians fought with a fury borne of desperation and held the Guthani at bay for hours, but as the day wore on Talin could see that the tide of battle was beginning to turn against them.

The sun was slipping below the horizon when the battering ram smashed through the gatehouse's outer portcullis. Pressure eased on Talin's section as the Guthani concentrated their attack on the damaged gate. Exhausted, he leaned on his sword and watched the attackers drag the ram into the passage. He was grateful that he couldn't see the mixture of oil and tar being poured on them from the room above the passage, or see the torches being dropped. It was enough to hear the agonised screams and see flames blast through the portcullis facing the Arth.

As the fire took hold, two ropes uncoiled from the windows above and either side of the gate and two unarmoured figures dressed in hunters' green descended. Without a backwards glance at the inferno, they sprinted across the bridge, grabbed the ropes that had been lowered from the barbican walkway, and climbed up. Behind them, burning hands clawed at the spiked and chained portcullis before charring to stumps. Thick black smoke quickly enveloped the gatehouse. The screaming stopped.

The bronze wave continued to pour over the wall. Alyda's sword work was economical, blade thrusting snake-fast into faces and throats. Kill or maim, it was all the same to her, so long as they fell back.

Every foot of wall was contested as though it was the most precious piece of ground in the world. The sun went down and the knights fought on. They were a grinding, tearing beast that chewed flesh to meat and bathed the walls in ruin.

Despite their efforts, Alyda knew that one big push from the Guthani—a breakthrough anywhere on the wall would finish them. Night sank its teeth into the horizon. Exhaustion sapped strength and will, but they fought on until horns blared from the enemy camp recalling the attackers.

They had survived.

Alyda put her back to the battlements and gulped air into her hungry lungs. The bottom of the wall in the bailey was piled with corpses. The fire in the gatehouse was still burning, and the air stank of cooked flesh, but they'd kept the Guthani out.

When the last of the enemy fighters had withdrawn, Alyda watched light bloom amongst the trees on the far side of the killing ground. Dozens of workers armed with picks and shovels scurried from the woods, and began to dig long shallow ditches and mound up the earth.

She should have been flattered that they were raising bulwarks, but it felt like a poor reward for not buckling under their first real assault. She rubbed grit from her eyes, a task made easier now that her visor had been torn off. The dried blood on her face served as a reminder of how close she'd come to losing her head. It wasn't just skill that kept you alive in battle, luck played its part, and she was damn grateful for all that she'd had.

After briefing the wall commanders, she made her way to Cassian's office. The Riverside Hall had taken a beating, but the lower levels had remained completely intact. Exhausted civilians and warriors slept where they could, bundled up in blankets and facing a restless night beneath the sky-pocked roof. Glass crunched beneath her boots, rainbow-hued shards all that remained of the windows. She yawned a sigh, the hall could be re-built. Those who had died were gone forever.

A gaggle of children darted around Kilner. They were being chased by another of their number wielding a bright red feather. The little ones squealed with delight as they charged around the cellars while the adults listened fretfully to the thunder above. Kilner found a quiet nook and hunkered down, jealously marvelling at the resilience of children.

Before the last attack he'd tried to lighten the dour mood in the cellar. He'd performed, pulling clouds of jewel-winged butterflies from his sleeves and transforming faded silk kerchiefs into bunches of roses. It worked, for a while. His audience had laughed and gasped and, for a short time, forgot they were afraid. The first booming impacts pounded fear back into them and not any amount of butterflies could dispel their terror. Kilner stopped his performance and let the butterflies fade.

He'd learned to live with guilt over the years, but from time to time it reminded him of its presence, like now. He could have sent sprites onto the battlefield to confuse the enemy; he could have summoned a fog, or rain, any number of small, but potentially useful magics to confound the enemy. But the truth that Captain Stenna had so quickly discerned was that he was a coward. He was afraid that the sorcerer might still be out there, waiting for another chance to attack him.

"Magic's wasted on you." Those were the last words his father had said when he left him at the grove, a few months after his powers had manifested. That he was right had never eased the sting of his words. He could clearly remember his tutor; tall and imposing, bathed in dappled sunlight. He was so happy that day, he'd dreamed of a new beginning at the Grove. He wouldn't be clumsy, stupid Kilner any more. Useless in the fields and no good in the workshop—he would be a mage. Then he saw the look of disappointment on the woman's face when her gaze settled on him, and he was crushed.

It was a painful memory, one he didn't wish to examine any further. A shadow fell across him; he looked up to see the child with the feather standing before him, staring at him with large sad eyes. Habit drove him to wave his hands and reach behind the boy's ear, from where he produced a quarter crown. The mage offered it to the surprised child. The boy's impish face split into a grin. He snatched the coin and thrust the feather into Kilner's hand. Before the mage could decline the exchange the boy was off running back to his friends with his prize.

It had been a while since Cassian had beaten out dents in his armour with his sword pommel. He was pleased to see he hadn't lost the knack and quickly softened the uncomfortable crease in his breastplate. Chunks of black enamel flaked off, exposing the bare metal, but he'd worry about rust after they'd beaten the Guthlanders.

Alyda's herald hissed a curse as Griga helped her into a chair. The sheen of sweat on Lieutenant Vysten's pale face and blood spots on the bandage around her leg explained her ire. The echo of the axe blow that had dented his cuirass made Cassian's ribs ache. Griga looked to have escaped injury, for which he was thankful. The grey-haired Lieutenant was due to retire this year. He now felt guilty that he'd asked her to stay until Midwinter. Guilty, but not regretful. He needed his right hand for one more battle.

Alyda blew in like a hurricane; her energy straightened all three of them, and chased away the creeping lethargy that was stealing into his limbs. Sometimes he doubted that *she* was human—never mind what they said about him. Her gore splattered armour spoke of a hard day of fighting, but her eyes were bright and her cheeks flushed with a healthy glow. He could endure days, weeks, even months, of war; it took a while to wear him down. Some rare few seemed to thrive on conflict and grow in the midst of battle as though nourished by hardship; people like Alyda. She paced the room, hands clasped behind her back, casually kicking bits of rubble as she passed.

"We've lost the gatehouse, but I expected that. What matters is we didn't sell it cheaply. Most of the ballistae are gone, and one of the trebuchets has been damaged. We need to reposition the working one, now that they've seen where it is."

"I'll have the damaged one salvaged if it can't be repaired," said Cassian. He eased himself back into his armour, pleased with the repair. Alyda stopped pacing and turned to her Lieutenant. "How many of the Hammer did we lose, Nev?" She asked.

Nevenna grimaced as she repositioned her leg. "Thirty-three dead, another three probably won't last the night."

Though she hid it well, he could see that the news rocked her. She clenched her jaw and nodded. "How many Lancers, Cass?"

"Twenty-eight," he said, the number didn't match the depth of his sorrow as each face loomed large in his mind. Griga sighed.

"Both companies are still above half strength: that's good. Cass, I need you and half the Lancers ready to ride tomorrow, along with half of the Hammer. I can't strip the walls of our presence. Twins know, I'd love to put us all on horseback, but we need to support the civvies. I'm waiting for Malby to get back to me with how many of them are still fit to fight." She lowered her voice. "I want you to move your family, the Queen and the princes over to the Queen's tower. Do it quietly and do it soon.

Cassian wasn't surprised but he was torn. He felt an overwhelming sense of relief, but also that he'd failed the garrison. He looked at Alyda. He saw no conflict there, no guilt. Her oath was to the King first, the kingdom and its people second. An oath that was probably much easier to keep when your family were in another country. That she was planning to save *his* family was a gift that he couldn't have given himself without destroying his honour. *Was that why I asked her to take command?* The thought appalled him. Shame weighed in on top of guilt. He was angry with himself and with Alyda for enabling his cowardice. There was a knock at the door, it was Alyda's squire.

"What is it?" she asked.

"A delegation, Captain. They want to speak to you. I told them you were busy, but they insisted. Shall I send them away?"

She rolled her shoulders. "No, let them in, we're done for now. Tell Kieran to meet me by the barbican in ten minutes."

Griga left with Jamie but Cassian hung back. He had to speak to Alyda, to voice his discomfort.

"Before you say anything, Cass, I've made my decision, so just accept it, she said before he had chance to speak. "That will be all."

Am I so easy to read? His embarrassment grew. He stiffened, anger rising from several unreasonable and unnameable sources.

"I said that will be all, Captain Vorsten." Her tone made it clear she would brook no discussion.

The simmering pot of his fury boiled over. "You outrank me by a blade's width, Alyda. Do not abuse the privilege… not even to help me. My honour will only stand so much." Even as he said it he knew it was a lie. He was so grateful he could have wept, which only increased his anger. Alyda folded her arms and leaned against his desk. Did she know that she'd saved and damned him in the same breath? She smiled. *Yes, she knows.*

"Just do your job, Captain Vorsten. We'll discuss any points of honour after we've beaten the Guthani."

"That was hard," said Nevenna when Cass had left.

"But necessary. How's your leg?" Alyda didn't need to be told that she'd offended Cassian. The murderous look on his face when he stormed out had said it all. Perhaps she should have given him the chance to talk it through, but she was tired and the outcome would have been the same. *Diplomacy has never been your strong point, Stenna.*

"Gedthis says no riding, but its sound enough to stand on."

You should be in the infirmary."

"I can't lie in the sickroom taking up a bed. I'm best where I can be of some use, here or up on the wall.

Her herald looked like death, but Nev knew her limits.

"How's he doing?" Alyda didn't need to say who she meant.

"Good, once he got over his nerves. Don't worry; not much is going to get past Lady Berwick."

"True, but if you do decide you're fit enough to go back up there…"

"Of course." Nevenna got up and limped out. Alyda could see a group of people massed outside of the office. *That'll be the delegation then.* She thought about wiping some of the filth off her armour, but decided against it. Let them see the marks of her craft. It might make them think twice before they annoyed her. She took off her helm. The plume was gone, as well as the visor, but it had done its job and kept the contents more or less intact.

She wasn't at all surprised that the first person through the door was the blacksmith. He had the same disgruntled expression on his face as the first time she'd met him. *Man looks like he was born frowning.*

He stepped forward, drew a breath and jabbed a calloused finger in her direction, ready to deliver what she imagined was a well-rehearsed speech.

She raised her hand, halting him before he hit his stride.

"I take it you are the representative of these people? What's your name?"

The smith lost his momentum. "I, er...yes. I represent these people and most others trapped here. My name's Smith, just Smith'll do."

Alyda had the measure of the man. There was a Smith in every town and village in Antia, probably the world. Someone who believed so surely in the rightness of their opinions that they felt it was their god-given duty to share them, loudly, and often. He folded his arms. *Some fools never know when to stand down.* So be it. If he wanted a fight he'd come to the right person. Fight was all she had in her today.

"It's like this, Captain: we want you to make terms with them barbarians. We see no reason why we should die for...for other folks." Smith's gaze slid sideways. The fearless representative of the people knew how close he was to speaking treason. It was an open secret that the Queen was in the Arth.

"You must go out there and make terms before we're all killed. It has to be done, Captain Stenna, everyone is agreed on it." He paused, chest out, chin up, ready to counter whatever argument she offered. If only she gave a shit about what he had to say.

"I'll tell you what I must do, Smith. I must do my duty to the King and the kingdom, as must we all, including you." Her voice was calm, her tone measured, though that was far from how she felt, standing there covered in the blood of friends as well as enemies. She was hungry and tired. She wanted to eat and sleep, and get ready for the next attack, not waste time arguing with this feckless cunt.

"Is it your duty to see babes and old folk slaughtered?" Smith demanded. His cronies sparked up at that and mumbled supportively.

"You were offered shelter here in the King's Arth. Neither you nor anyone else was forced to take it. Any who wish to leave may do so. But mark my words: the Guthani will kill anyone who tries to leave now."

Smith's mouth twisted into an angry sneer. "Then surrender! Make terms! How many more must die before you admit defeat? The King isn't here—he doesn't need saving, we do! Isn't it a knight's duty to protect the innocent? Or don't common folk like us count?"

Luckily for him she had enough self-control to ride out the anger his words provoked.

"I didn't see you fighting today, Smith, so don't talk to me about dying when you aren't willing to spill a drop of blood in your own defence." She let her gaze travel over the group. "Do any of you think you would have been spared if you'd stayed in whatever miserable shitholes you came from when the Guthani rode through? At the very worst you've lived a few days longer than you would have; at best you've been given a chance of surviving this."

The other delegates shuffled back against the wall, distancing themselves from their leader as the air turned sharp and cold. Smith opened his mouth to speak, but Alyda beat him to it.

"Go or stay. I don't care which, but if you stay, you will not question my actions or make demands like this again or I'll have you thrown in a cell with the other traitor. Listen well, Smith; I don't tell you how to shoe a horse, or mend a cook pot, so don't try to tell me how to fight a fucking battle. Now get out."

The colour drained from Smith's face. He stormed out of the room, the other delegates following close behind him. When they were gone, Alyda sank into a chair.

Jamie was grinning. "Looks like someone found out he wasn't the meanest dog in the yard."

Alyda didn't give a damn about winning a pissing contest. That Smith might be right was what rankled.

Alyda didn't remember falling asleep, but woke abruptly as a ball of fire burned a trail across the night sky before crashing into the Arth. Horns sounded the call to arms and were answered by the chant of armour as defenders ran to take up their positions. She got up, shook sleep from her leaden limbs and drew her sword.

She ran outside the Great Hall and straightway had to leap aside as a burning bail of hay tumbled across the bailey and smashed into the doors of the hall. Clouds of sparks swarmed into the night seeking to take root in thatch and timber, but worse was to come.

Before she could drag the hay away from the door, another missile splattered against the wall, showering her with gobbets of pulverised flesh and blood. She looked up. Shreds of human flesh and bone were dripping in thick clots down the wall. Terrified cries filled the darkness, as those less inured to such horrors realised what was being hurled into the Arth along with the burning hay.

Delivered less than an hour ago, Redbear's parchment was like a knife in the gut. The Iceheart had allied with the Antians. And no matter what Redbear said, his Warprows didn't stand a chance against the Raider's drakes. All hope of victory now depended on beating Daris on land where the Guthlander's gave up a sizeable advantage.

"You've run the Ants to ground, now let's call them out and be done in time to help our kinsman celebrate victory, eh?" Hanser beamed. Thorgulsen wanted to punch him.

As well as the message from Redbear, Hanser had brought two hundred mounted warriors, proving it was possible to be both useful and a prick.

The tide was beginning to turn against Jerim's little uprising, and that left Thorgulsen with some hard decisions to make. He could stay and take the Queen, but if he did, he risked being cut off should the war go against them. He could abandon the siege and go support Redbear in Cathlan, but it might already be too late and if it wasn't, his kinsman would want to know why he hadn't taken the Queen. The last, most practical option was to head back to his ships docked at Pridmore and go home.

Neither of the last two choices held any appeal, not because they lacked strategic merit, but because choosing either would mean Stenna had won, and that bothered him. In fact, now that he thought about it, he realised it bothered him more than letting the Queen escape or abandoning his kinsman. He was so close to ripping the guts out of that fucking castle, he could taste it. *So close to winning.* His heart quickened at the thought, something that hadn't happened for a long time. Before he hung her, he'd have to thank the Antian for re-igniting his lust for battle.

"They won't just come out, Hanser. You're going to have to get off your nags and go get them."

"Eh? Impossible." Hanser took off his magnificent dragon crested helm, and admired his reflection in the polished metal. "I told Redbear: we don't fight on ships and we don't fight on foot. We are horse warriors."

"Can your horses climb walls?" growled Thorgulsen.

"No, of course not—"

"Then they're no fucking good to me."

"If I might interject my Lords…?" The Priest had arrived with Hanser and had been sitting quietly at the back of the tent, pretending to read his prayer book while taking in every word that was said.

"Do you know how to get horses up walls?" said Thorgulsen.

The Priest coughed a laugh. "The only way that springs to mind would be in a catapult, but I'm not sure Thane Hanser would approve."

Hanser's eyes bulged. "I see now why the Brotherhood has few friends outside of Suvia."

The Priest offered a contrite bow, but his eyes were as sharp as broken glass. "'Twas a jest, Thane, merely a jest. As to the problem of horses and walls; I overheard Captain Trenham discussing the matter, he had some interesting ideas…"

"Bethanglyn." She rolled over. She was still in bed, but surrounded by a heavy, grey mist. A dream then; a dull one.

"Bethanglyn." It wasn't Kasper, but she knew the voice. She closed her eyes, willed herself to sleep again. This dream was wrong.

"Hear me, Bethanglyn!"

It isn't a dream. Her eyes flew open. She was in bed in the tent. A few feet away, the air shimmered like water. Wary, she got up; cold nipped at her bare skin and raised gooseflesh. The wall of shimmering air turned iron grey. No. *Not a wall, it's a window*. She stumbled back when she realised she was gazing into the Void. Her skin tingled, she could almost taste the power that lay beyond the portal, and then she saw him.

"Help me…" the sorcerer breathed and reached out to her.

She recoiled from the steel-eyed demon who was lying amid bones on the black ground. He was a monster, and yet…he needed help; her help. *There's power in that, Beth, bargains to be made.* The tent flap lifted. She spun, afraid that Kasper had returned, but it was only the wind.

Kasper.

She had believed he was the one who would lift her out of the mire. Her grandmother had killed the lamb and had seen in its steaming guts that a power would take her far from Guthland's shores. When she met him—the brash, ambitious young hirth with fire in his ice-blue eyes, she thought he was the one. As she stepped through the portal and into the Void, she realised her expectations had been too modest.

When the fires had been brought under control, Talin dragged his weary carcass over to the Queen's tower where his mother and brother had been moved. Other than the royal fugitives, the tower was empty. It smelled of damp and disuse. He stank of smoke and death.

When he entered, Olin looked up from his book and grunted. Their mother was sitting by the fire, staring into the flames. She'd been crying.

"They're dying because of me. I can't stand it, knowing that I am the cause of all this misery," she said.

Talin went over and held her, as much to find comfort as give it. "This isn't your fault, this is our uncle's doing," he said.

"Oh, my darling boy, it *is* my fault. If you could trace the thread of this back far enough you would find that it leads to me. I allowed myself to be ruled by a fool's heart and that selfishness was the seed of this nightmare." She smiled wearily at him. "I just couldn't give him up. Oh, Tal. I miss him so much."

There was nothing he could say; she was distraught, sick with unfounded guilt and worry for his father. The only thing he could do, the only comfort he could give was to hold her.

Eventually, she retired to her room, wrapped in a blanket of misery too thick for him to penetrate. He banked the fire up and sank down beside it. For all that he'd had his fill of flames, he was cold, and dark thoughts were keeping sleep at bay. Olin closed his book and came over and sat beside him.

"I think I hate the Guthani, Tal," his brother whispered, flame shadows tattooed his boyish face with writhing patterns. "It's like something alive, crawling inside me. It makes me feel sick just thinking about them. Do you think it's possible to hate too much?"

"I don't know, brother, but if there is a limit, I've not reached it yet."

They toiled through the night to control the fires while the Void rained down on them. When the flames were doused and the trebuchets fell silent, Alyda slid down beside the well and fell into an exhausted asleep.

She woke at daybreak and cursed Trenham for what he'd done. They'd saved the Arth, but on seeing it in the cold light of day, she wondered why they'd bothered. Something squirmed against her back. She looked round to see the child she'd taken to calling Flea, huddled against her, fast asleep. She scooped him up and carried him over to the Great Hall.

Nobody had claimed the boy when she'd made enquiries about him, and he didn't speak as far as she could tell. He might have just become separated from his family in the confusion, but more likely he was one of the castle rats; a by-blow or orphan given food and a place to sleep in exchange for chores. Either way, he was going to the cellars.

On the way over he woke up and fixed her with a steady gaze. His huge brown eyes were old beyond his years; they were the eyes of a child who had seen too much. Alyda was tired; her feelings deadened by exhaustion, but even so, she probably should have felt some small measure of guilt for the misery that accompanied the practice of her bloody trade. Should have, but didn't.

"Not you again!" said the housekeeper when she unbolted the cellar door and saw who Alyda had brought her. Thank you, Captain. He's such a rascal. I can't keep hold of him; he's as slippery as an eel,"

Alyda went to hand him over, but the boy threw his scrawny arms around her neck and clung on. As gently as she could, she extricated herself from his limpet grasp and quickly passed him over to the woman who enfolded the squirming child in her doughy arms before he had chance to escape.

"Don't let him out again," Alyda ordered more sharply than she intended.

The woman mumbled an apology to Alyda's retreating back.

She couldn't wait to get away from the cellars, and those anxious faces peering out of the gloom. *They're all going to die.* Her inner voice whispered. She stopped at the top of the stairs, took a breath. She was tired, that was all. Everything looked bleak when you were exhausted. They would hold; reinforcements would come, and she would not let the civilians die. Yesterday that had been a statement of fact, a solid truth she could put her back against and face the fight with certainty, with conviction. Today it sounded more like a prayer.

When she was back in the bailey she looked up at the ancient walls. In time, the smoke-black and bloodstains would be nothing more than a memory. The walls would remain; a towering monument to the fragility of human life. *Tired, that's all.* She went to the well, drew a bucket of water and poured it over her head. The shocking cold stole her breath, but drowned the nagging voice of doubt. Walls were just walls, and while she had breath in her body this place would not become a tomb.

Chapter Fifteen

"Their dead are rotting three deep down there and they still have warriors who have yet to draw their blades."

Alyda shrugged. "There are always more dogs than lions."

They were on the roof of the barbican, peering through the smoky haze rising from the husk of the gatehouse. Dozens of untouched crawlers were lined up halfway across the field before the earth bulwarks. Behind them, scores of Guthani warriors were forming up and another battering ram, bigger than the last, was being wheeled onto the road.

"Still nothing from the scouts?" Alyda asked, even though she knew the answer.

Cassian shook his head. "Nothing at all. I don't think help is coming, Ali. Or if it is, I think it will arrive too late. They're bound to break through on the next attack."

"What do you suggest? That we surrender?"

"No, but …" He threw up his hands. "Aye. Maybe. It's over, Ali. There's nothing to be gained standing on the wall any longer."

Cass looked dour when he was happy, right now he was the embodiment of despair. She laughed.

"Something amuses you, Alyda?"

"Sorry, Cass. I'm just tired." She composed herself. "You're right, there's nothing to be gained standing on the wall. We haven't nearly enough bodies to hold back an assault—*up there*." She grinned, gave him a moment to catch her drift. "We're the best damn cavalry in the world, we should play to our strengths, don't you think?"

Cassian shook his head. "There are less than a hundred of us and what would be the point? Even if we went out and wrecked the trebuchets again, or halted the attack, we're still going to lose. Today, tomorrow, it's over. You have to accept that, Alyda."

"If you were anyone else, I'd say just do as you're damn well told. The truth is, I need another night. I need the cover of darkness to get the Queen and your family out of here. I'll ask for terms tomorrow, and before you say anything, don't worry. I have a plan to save the rest of the garrison. I won't see innocents slaughtered if I can help it, but I can't lie; it does depend on the Free Companies. Now we both know they're a bunch of backstabbing bastards, but I have faith in their laws and what's more, I understand them." She laughed, knowing how horrified her father would have been for a whole second before he laughed with her.

"What if the Free Companies don't play their part? What if your plan fails?" he asked.

"Then I've got a lot of innocent blood on my hands."

Cassian's face was all angles; his thin lips were drawn in a knife straight line, his brow was a deep 'V' of concentration. He shook his head. She didn't blame him; this was a hard circle to square. Logic demanded that she sue for peace now, and let kings and princes squabble over power. Her duty as a knight was to save as many people as she could, but that was at odds with her duty as a Royal Guard Captain, oath-sworn to serve the King.

No one ever said it was going to be easy, but damn, she never thought it would be this hard. And then there was Talin. The very thought of him made her face burn with shame. *You're not serving the King and saving the Queen, you're saving the man you love.*

"That's hard, Alyda."

"You know as well as I do that innocents get hurt in war. I swear, I'll do everything in my power to get them out of this, and that means stopping the attack today, giving those fa'cachti a taste of steel that'll make 'em think twice. They can't be enjoying climbing over their dead bloating in that moat. If we hurt them today they're more likely to accept terms tomorrow."

Cassian rested his hands on the wall and stared hard at the stone between them. "I refer you to my earlier comment; there are only a hundred of us fit to ride."

"I refer to you mine; we're the best damn cavalry in the world, and look here." Alyda directed his gaze to the earth bulwarks. "Look at where they've positioned those banks. They haven't considered that they might be attacked on the field; they're just there to protect them from arrows and the trebuchet."

"Either I'm being dense or...?"

"See how the warriors are packed between the moat and the walls, they're like sheep in a pen."

The ghost of a smile flicker across Cassian's face. "They are hemmed in. If we rode along the moat..." he said.

She nodded. "Hit hard and fast, use their numbers against them."

"Wolves among the sheep, eh? Getting back will be... interesting."

"But not impossible. They aren't expecting a ground attack. Speed and surprise will be our allies."

After what felt like an age, Cassian nodded. "As you say, Captain Stenna, we should play to our strengths. I'll tell the stables to saddle the horses."

In her mind, Alyda fought the battle a thousand times. It went perfectly to plan right up to the point where they turned back for the Arth. Try as she might, she could not see a way through the bristling field of spears closing in around them. So be it. Live or die, Talin and his family would be taken to safety, Nev and Griga knew what to do. *Oh, but where were those fucking reinforcements?*

"Have you been avoiding me?"

She turned. Talin was standing at the top of the rubble strewn stairs.

"No. I thought you'd know where to find me; this roof's become my second home. Anyway, I'm glad you're here. I've got something to tell you…"

"I know they'll try to use me if I'm taken, but with Oli and my mother safe, I'm resolved to deny them any advantage. If I fall into their hands I know what I must do."

Alyda shook her head. "No. The people—your mother, they'll need you."

Talin laughed.

"What's so funny?"

"You are."

She smiled and kissed him. It was a while before they parted, both lost in the pleasure of the moment, far from the reality of their situation.

"I'm sorry, Tal. You can't ride out with us for a dozen reasons you already know. No one will think any less of you, least of all me."

"I don't give a screw what people think of me. I just can't bear the thought of you being out there without me."

"Please, just do as I ask." She didn't add that although she couldn't command him she could order her knights to lock him up with his mother until after they'd gone.

"Very well, Captain Stenna, I will do as you ask. You know, not so long ago I wouldn't have been so obedient, not for anyone. What have you done to me?"

"Nothing you didn't enjoy."

"Just promise me you'll be careful," he said.

She didn't have an answer so she pulled him close and kissed him again.

Tomas gazed up at him, his bright blue eyes full of wonder. The joy of the moment was made more precious by the thought that this might be the last time that he held his son.

It had been the happiest day of his life when Beri told him he was going to be a father, and such a shock when, nine months later, Tomas arrived. He looked like his mother, thank the gods. His eyes were the same shade of blue and he had her thick, dark hair and her adorable, angry pout. Tomas grabbed his chin and giggled. Cassian kissed him before handing him to his nurse. The girl was on the verge of tears, but somewhat hypocritically, Beri had already scolded her for sniffling. She bit her lip, curtsied and left the room. When the door closed, he and Beri rushed into each other's arms. He held her close, as tightly as he dared, she smelled of roses.

"No matter what happens, never forget; you and Tomas mean everything to me," Cassian whispered, his voice thick with emotion.

"Stop that, you foolish man. You're going to make me cry." She pushed him away and tugged the scarf from her hair. "Here, take this for luck." She tied it around his arm. The delicate blue silk looked incongruous against the battered armour.

Cassian smiled. "Do you remember the first time you did that?"

"How could I forget? It was at the joust in Weyhithe, you almost broke your neck. I thought it the most miserable luck. I'd finally plucked up the courage to give that handsome, if rather serious looking knight my favour and he's gone and got his head knocked off."

He laughed, the memory of the impact still eluded him, but waking up in the infirmary to see her beautiful face staring down at him was as clear as though it had happened yesterday, as was the angry lecture that had followed.

"I remember waking up and you telling me that I'd been sloppy, reckless, and stupid."

She laughed through tears. "Well it was true, you were reckless." She gripped his hands, they were both shaking. "You can't be reckless today. You see, Tomas and I will be riding with you. Anything that happens to you, happens to us, so you must be careful."

A cold certainty gripped his heart. No matter what sweet lie he told her, no matter what promises he made, he felt sure that he would not return.

He couldn't stand watching the knights preparing to ride out. So rather than hang around in the bailey, Talin climbed up onto the wall walk. While he was up there, he talked with the others who would be staying behind to defend the walls.

Most were civilians; people from all walks of life and possessed of every shade of character, rank, and occupation. They had forged strong bonds during the brutal fighting, and now bakers stood shoulder to shoulder with dressmakers and veteran knights, all proud to call each other comrade.

Talin was humbled by their courage and felt profoundly guilty for all the years he'd wasted taking his life of privilege for granted. He swore that if he survived he wouldn't spend another hour in idleness—not that Alyda would allow him to sit on his arse even if he wanted to. *Alyda.* He thought of the short time they'd had together and the promise of the years that that lay ahead, and how close they were to losing everything.

Bear hailed him and came over. "You ready for this, Highness?" she said, her bloodied buckler hanging from her belt, the heavy falchion casually resting on her shoulder.

"No, but I don't suppose that's going to change anything. How about you?"

She shrugged, gave a wry grin. "Oh, you know me."

"I know you could leave if you wanted."

She yawned and scrubbed at bloodshot eyes. "Aye. Over the wall and gone like a fart in the wind. Lucky for you, I've decided to stay. Purely for selfish reasons, you understand. I mean, without me you'd only go and get yourself killed and I'd lose a drinking partner."

He sighed. "Are you ever serious?"

She gave him a sideways glance. "I think you know when I'm being serious."

"I don't know how to do this, Iris. People are looking to me for reassurance, can you believe it?" He laughed.

"No, not really, if I'm honest." She laughed and punched him on the arm. "I don't think anybody knows how to deal with this, Tal. People like Alyda just hide their fear better than most. You'll do alright. I've been watching you; I've seen how you are with people, like up here, just now. You've lifted their spirits, made them smile, and forget for a moment what in the Void's going on, and that's a bloody good trick at a time like this. My advice is, don't think about it too much. Just keep doing what you're doing. You know thinking isn't one of your strong points."

"You just did that thing again: being nice and a bitch in the same breath."

"Yes, Highness, I know."

"I could have you executed."

"No you couldn't…"

An hour after they were ready to ride, the first volley of stones hammered into the Arth. Alyda held Lyco steady while they waited for the bombardment to ease. When the stones stopped falling, the weary defenders returned to their posts. The Guthani were massed on the far side of the moat, and a new battering ram had been dragged to the bridge ready to assault the barbican. Archers on the wall loosed at the ram, but their arrows failed to penetrate the thick cowhide screen.

The ballista could have pierced the mantlet, but Alyda had ordered them not to loose just yet. She wanted the ram closer. Cassian was at the head of the Black Lancers, Beria's scarf tied round his arm. Alyda felt a sharp stab of guilt. Cass would have surrendered; he would have saved the garrison and not put everyone through this…

Enough!

"Hard as iron, cold as stone…" she whispered.

They had to ride out, flatten the enemy and return. Something they'd done a thousand times before. Her fingers tightened around her sword hilt. She lowered the visor of her borrowed helm, gathered her reins and signalled the Guard Sergeant in the winch room. Battle standards were unfurled; they ripped and snapped in the sharp wind. The portcullis bared its fangs and the gates yawned open. Horns blared and the sound of thundering hooves echoed in the barbican as the Hammer and the Black Lancers rode out.

The knights drove their mounts over the bridge, and ploughed through the mantlet protecting the ram, trampling those beneath it. Swords flashed and the trapped ram crew were quickly dispatched. Alyda led the knights left, between the moat and the nearest earth bank.

A sea of shocked faces turned to see the wrathful knights bearing down on them. Some of the attackers scrambled up the banks; others dived into the corpse-choked moat. Crushed together in the narrow defile, most could only raise their shields or couch a spear as the Hammer and the Lancers roared towards them.

Let them know fear, thought Alyda as she drove Lyco on, *let them feel despair.* She spared a glance over her shoulder. Defenders piled out of the Arth and heaved the ram and its carriage into the moat, clearing the way for their return. She laughed.

This is what you were born for, said the voice in her head.

It was right.

A group of battle-hardened Guthani formed up, interlocked their shields and set their spears. Alyda heeled Lyco in the flanks. The world whipped past in a speeding blur. They smashed into the Guthani, splintering shields and crushing warriors into the dirt. Alyda saw a destrier impaled on a sheaf of spears. It fell screaming, taking its killers and its rider with it to the grave.

Death surrounded her, sharp and bright, eager to claim its dues. *Not yet you don't.* The Guards hurtled along the moat, hacking a bloody swathe through the penned attackers. When they reached the end of the earth bank, Alyda looked back at the destruction they'd wrought and it filled her with a savage joy. *Just as it should be.* They'd punished the enemy's arrogance, and stalled their advance. Now, with speed and a little luck, they'd get back to the Arth before the enemy had a chance to rally. She amended that to *a lot of luck* as the trebuchets were turned towards them.

The first volley of stones missed and crashed into a group of mercenaries mustering in front of them. The second hit some of the Lancers and some Guthani. After that, Trenham's engines fell silent.

They rounded the end of the earth bank—a trail of mangled corpses behind them. Cassian's gaze fell on the trebuchets. Despite his orders, despite Beria's plea, his blood was up and the damn things were unguarded, just begging to be attacked. Before his horse had taken a dozen strides in their direction, he came to his senses and signalled for the company to turn back and follow the Hammer. The trebuchets were *too* tempting. As they wheeled away, he saw the trap and bellowed a warning as the mounted Guthani burst through the brush screens cunningly hidden in the tree-line.

The Guthani poured from the woods and around the trebuchets. Cassian saw one of ponies bolt and run in front of the engines. The ground gave way beneath it, and they vanished into a pit, suffering the fate that was meant for them. He thanked whatever gods had granted him the sense to pull up, and at the same time cursed his impetuous heart.

Like the Lancers, the Guthani cavalry wielded slender-bladed spears. Instead of swords they had long-handled axes strapped across their backs and painted shields hanging from their saddle bows. They were led by a warrior in shining mail and a dragon-crested helm.

The Hammer didn't try to attack his engines, even though he'd left them wide open. Instead they'd scythed through the hirths who were waiting to cross the moat. Trenham was angry and his pride was dented. His machines weren't as important a target as the Guthani. That mis-calculation had cost them, but it wouldn't change the outcome.

The knights had dealt a savage blow to the warriors by the moat, but they wouldn't live long enough to enjoy their victory. He should be pleased, it was almost over, but he wasn't. If anything, he was ambivalent. In contrast, Thorgulsen was murderously furious. He didn't blame him; his woman had gone missing and he'd just watched his hirths being pulverised.

"You were right about them coming out, but wrong about their choice of target," Thorgulsen growled. "Many of my hirths will be sleeping in the Void tonight because of that mistake."

"I told you the Antians weren't predictable."

"You talk out of your arse, boy. You said they would attack your fucking engines. I was looking forward to seeing them and their fat nags impaled in those pits. Now that lackwit Hanser get's to finish the job. I'm not happy, Trenham and that is never a good thing." The Thane gave him the dead eye and walked away.

As if I give a fuck. The Guthlander was in danger of thinking he could bully him like he could Telvier. That could prove to be a costly mistake—for all concerned.

Trenham checked his quiver before pulling on his coif. He didn't know what Ali Stenna was up to. It might be nothing more than a final act of defiance; a glorious suicide, but his gut told him there was more to it. Whatever her plan, it was doomed. Hirths were blocking the road ahead of the knights, and Hanser's cavalry was closing in behind them. This whole sorry mess would soon be nothing more than a footnote in some poorly scribed history. He should be pleased, but truth was, he liked his enemies far more than he liked his employer.

A unit of hirths had formed up in their path. Alyda bellowed her orders at Della, who relayed them with a trilling blast on her horn. All the knights, including the Lancers, increased their speed. Lyco's footfalls echoed the thunder of her heart as they hurtled towards the Guthani.

At the last possible moment, just before his long stride took them too close to manoeuvre, she turned sharply to the left. The destrier pivoted on his powerful hind quarters and sprang away, followed by the Hammer. The Lancers mirrored the manoeuvre and split right. A handful of horses skidded in the mud, lost their footing and went down, delivering their riders to the enemy, where death was waiting, sharp and swift.

Alyda took the Hammer around the Guthani and charged for the road to the Arth. Cassian took the Lancers towards the bulwark.

Kilner couldn't bear to be in the cellars a moment longer. The knights had ordered everyone to stay inside and keep the doors bolted, but he had to get out. Eventually he made enough of a fuss that the housekeeper who held the keys was only too pleased to be rid of him. Outside, under the blessed open sky, he was rewarded by the kiss of a cold breeze.

The gut-twisting panic eased, his heart stopped pounding quite so hard. The air reeked of death, but it was a huge improvement on the stink of fear and ceaseless, pitiful crying that had driven him from the cellars. He just wanted the fighting to stop, but the bloodthirsty bastards wouldn't be satisfied until everyone was dead. As he stood in the bailey, pondering his fate, a warrior fell screaming from the wall. She hit the ground, bounced—burst, and broke on the jagged rubble.

Kilner almost fainted. He had never seen death so raw, so visceral. He wasn't safe here, but he couldn't go back down into the bowels of the Arth and wait to die with the others. He tried to gather shadows and hide himself, but his mind wouldn't hold the spell. Another body plunged from the wall and smashed into the gore-drenched ground.

Fear set his feet to flight. He ran blindly across the bailey, desperate to flee the mayhem. He collapsed behind the keep tower and crawled between the buttresses. He could see the stables from his hiding place. He wondered if the horses knew that their riders were probably dead. More likely they didn't care and just wanted to get away from this madness, but like him, they were trapped. He thought about trying to climb the west wall, take his chances in the Galerun, but he didn't have much of a head for heights and he didn't like water—all those fish... He shuddered. Something soft caressed his chin. Startled, he looked down to see that he was still clutching the scarlet feather.

It was beautiful, so delicate, so out of place amid all the ugliness. He wondered what kind of bird it had come from, something exotic from a distant land. He'd always wanted to travel, to see the world beyond Antia's tame borders. There were so many wonderful places he'd read about and dreamed of seeing, and now he never would because he was going to die here.

It isn't fair! Hadn't he always been careful to avoid the slightest whiff of danger? He'd never even allowed himself to fall in love because he was too afraid to risk his coward's heart. All that sacrifice, the denial of a life half-lived, and he was still going to die a violent and untimely death. It was too much. Kilner broke down and sobbed a flood of tears.

By the gods' good grace, they had beaten the enemy to the bridge. Cassian called a halt before the ruined gatehouse. The defenders on the barbican were screaming for them to get inside. He looked at Griga. She had lost her helm; a cut on her forehead bled fingers of scarlet down her face.

"What are your orders, Captain?" she asked, leaning heavily on her pommel, her spear slick with Guthani blood.

The Lancers were less than a hundred paces from the Arth. Beria and Tomas were waiting for him...*So close.* Through the heaving sea of spears, Cassian saw the Hammer's standard fluttering above the jagged tide.

"We stay and hold the bridge," he said.

The Black Lancers were valiantly trying to hold the bridge, but the Hammer was cut off. Alyda was cut off. *Where did the fucking cavalry come from?* Driven by helpless rage, Talin fought like a man possessed and tried to drown his fury in the blood of the enemy swarming over the wall. He hacked wildly, blindly swinging his sword at whatever came before him. Something heavy fell across his back, taking him down.

An arm flopped beside his head; he was pinned under a body. He struggled to throw it off. A hirth saw him, raised his axe and charged. Nevenna hobbled between them. The Guthani yelled his fury and swung. She raised her halberd, but the injured knight stumbled and mis-timed the block. The Guthani's weapon struck her polearm and bounced off at an angle, shearing through her neck guard before burying itself in her shoulder. She screamed and dropped her weapon. Blood sprayed from the terrible wound, her right arm fell useless. Snarling a curse, she spat a mouthful of blood in her attacker's face. He recoiled.

The dying knight grabbed the horse tail plume on his helm, and dragged him towards her. Off-balance, the Guthani stumbled, clawing at the strap fastening his helm. With the last of her strength, the Knight Herald threw herself back off the wall, taking her killer with her to the Void. Talin crawled from under the corpse and picked up the halberd.

At first, the dreams that came to Kilner were a jumble of meaningless images. But as sleep dragged him deeper under its thrall, they began to change. He was in a vast, empty land of dark, rolling hills beneath a grey sky. Under his feet, a web of silver shone through the short, purple-tinted grass.

His dream self calmly watched the argent tendrils quest towards him. He didn't move. Something was there with him, something unseen, but a comforting presence all the same. The tendrils latched onto his feet, and quickly flowed over his entire body, covering him in a silver filigree web. The web pulsed. It was alive.

The vein-like strands swelled and ran together until he was completely encased in a shining metallic skin. *I'm not afraid.* On the contrary; he felt safe, unassailable within his new, steel skin. It rippled and flowed, distended and hardened into layers and plates of gleaming metal; a suit of impossible armour more fantastical than any real harness ever could be. He raised his hand; saw the reflection of a scarlet flame burning atop the inhuman helm. It reminded him of something, but he couldn't recall what it was.

This isn't right, this isn't me. As soon as he had the thought, the armour flew apart like rose petals caught in a storm. The silver skin rippled. He looked at his new form. *Yes. This is right,* he thought, and flexed his claws.

Kilner woke with a start. His heart felt ready to burst from his chest. He was filled with an overwhelming sense of urgency, a need to act that was more pressing than anything he'd ever felt before. He didn't panic. He knew what he had to do; the Other had shown him—opened his mind to all that was possible. The mage closed his eyes, freed his spirit from his body and plunged into the essence flow. For the first time in his life, Kilner wasn't afraid.

At the first touch of the slumbering elemental his courage faltered. There was so much power! He would be consumed, destroyed before he got close enough to—

The Other was with him.

It didn't speak, but its presence alone was enough to reassure him, to hold him to his course. He hovered on the edge of the maelstrom, just a little closer and he would be gone. It wasn't too late to pull back; nothing was forcing him to proceed. The Other had only shown him the way. But if he did go back, they would never stop. *But what if it doesn't work?*

The elemental was a shadow of what it had once been, and held together by nothing more than a vague memory. There *was* a mind somewhere within the mass of energy, a consciousness buried deep within the furnace, and only one way to reach it. He had to let go. It was all he'd ever had to do…and finally, he did. Kilner let go of his essence and became one with the elemental.

As the pattern of his spirit began to unravel, he visualised what he wanted, and drove the vision like a knife, deep into the slumbering creature's mind. A heartbeat later, Kilner Reese ceased to exist.

Rayna checked the picket line for the third time in an hour. She'd lost her good sword and the wound in her shoulder ached like the Void, but it was thinking about Big Janni that darkened her mood.

She kept seeing him snatch the shaft from his neck, unstoppering the wound that fountained blood over both of them. She'd reached out—snagged a link of mail, but she lost him, and he fell back, into the stinking cess pit of a moat. And then he was gone. Just like that, the putrid water swallowed him. She'd miss Janni, miss his company on cold winter nights, and miss his laughter...*Bastard archers.*

She slumped down against a boulder and cursed the day she'd signed up for this ill-starred venture. The pickings had been slim, and the fighting too hard. The sooner they were done and away the happier she'd be. Rayna closed her eyes; if nothing else, sleep was free. The horses would wake her if anyone came near.

The dense forest dulled the din of battle and soaked up the spiky sharpness of metal striking metal, but the screams of the wounded and the dying scratched at her consciousness and kept her awake. The trees had an odd way of distorting noise; they made it sound like the fighting was getting closer. She opened her eyes. Maybe it was. Maybe reinforcements had come to save the Steelskins. She sat up; palms flat either side of her. The ground was trembling.

She scrambled to her feet; that was no army—it was an earthquake. The ground heaved beneath her. The terrified horses ripped the picket line out of the ground and galloped into the forest. The mercenary tried to run but the ground was shaking so violently that she fell. A nearby hillock cracked and split, throwing up dirt and rocks as it erupted.

The shaking was so powerful that a pair of beech trees started to slide down the flanks of the shattered mound. She scuttled back on her arse; the ground flowed around her like water. The beech trees trembled and creaked ominously, branches snapped and crashed down around her.

She yelped as a thunder-loud crack ripped the air and the trees split along their entire lengths...and snapped open like a pair of giant fans. Pulpy fibres within the trunks swelled like the veins in the wings of a new born butterfly... No. Not *like* wings—they were wings. While she struggled with the stunning realisation, a massive bony head shook itself free of the clinging earth at the base of the hill.

As grey as stone and crested with jagged scales that were veined and flecked like marble, the head looked like that of a giant lizard. The scales ran down the back of the huge skull and formed a ridge along the length of its muscular, earth coloured back.

Rayna wanted to run, but her legs were trembling so much she couldn't take a step. The huge head swung in her direction, a breath of dirt bathed her face. It opened its eyes. Dappled gold and green, like sunlight shining through leaves, the great orbs held no pupils, but were a constant hypnotic swirl of colour. It blinked and tilted its head from side to side, as though trying to decide what she was. Rayna was quite certain she knew what *it* was.

The dragon's dream was over. It arched its back, and spread its wings, flexing each spine like a finger. One at a time it heaved its massive feet free of the earth and took its first steps in a millennium.

A small but insistent thought had roused it from its slumber and given it purpose for the first time in a long time. It couldn't remember the name it once had, but there was a memory buzzing on the edge of its thoughts, like a...something it couldn't remember.

It lurched forward, trying to recall how to move and how to keep its spirit within the rock and earth that with every passing moment, was turning into its body. It had been a long time since it had existed in the world of flesh and bone, an age since the Other had shaped its pattern.

It stopped and tried to catch the tail of a long forgotten memory. There were great trees reaching up to an azure sky, and the shining people worshipping their Shining God. It was a pleasant memory, it wanted to see more and almost slipped back into the dream, but the tiny buzzing thought stung it again, as angry as a wasp.

I remember.

For the first time in a long time it had a task to perform. It also remembered that it wanted to travel.

They were deep in the shit, and the bridge was a hundred angry warriors away. Alyda could see the Black Lancers in the distance. Faithful Guards to the last, they were fighting to hold the bridge and keep it open for them, but there were just too many Guthani. Rann hacked his way through to her; he was bleeding from a dozen wounds, but still had the colours and was grinning like a demon.

"Well, Captain, it looks like the time's come t'pay the butchers' bill!" he bellowed over the din.

"I'm not ready to settle my account just yet!" Alyda yelled back and touched her spurs to Lyco's flanks. The snorting destrier plunged into the mass. She wasn't about to give up, but trapped as they were, she had to admit this might indeed be their last ride.

Although she was a warrior, she'd never much thought about dying, when she had, this was how she'd imagined she'd go. If today was the day, so be it. No one could have asked for a better life or finer career. Her only regret was that she hadn't met Talin sooner. These thoughts flashed through her mind in an instant, but their impact was profound. The battle was raging bloody fury all around, but she had found the calm eye of the storm. And if death wanted her, it would damn well have to fight to take her.

The Lancers scythed down the living and ploughing under the dead, but for every Guthani they killed, two more took their place. Cassian had to order the retreat before they were overwhelmed. There was no way they could hold the bridge, not now that the Guthani had rallied. And yet, the scarlet banner still flew above the swarming mass on the road. *Guards do not abandon their own.* Beria would never understand, but he hoped she would forgive him.

Lyco lashed out with his iron-shod hooves and barged warriors aside with his massive shoulders, but the press of bodies was closing in around them. A mercenary grabbed his bridal. Alyda hacked a warrior in the face, as another speared her in the thigh. She heeled Lyco in the flank, bringing him face-to-face with the warrior clinging to his bridle. She slid her foot back, heeled the destrier again—hard. He kicked out. There was a loud crack, the warrior fell screaming. Lyco reared and plunged, the warrior didn't get up.

She swept her sword around and struck the spear wielder across the head before he had a chance to stab her again. He fell back clutching his bleeding face. A sharp pain ripped through her thigh. A wave of nausea washed over her, her vision blurred. The noise of battle grew distant...

A peel of thunder tore through the forest. Lyco ripped the reins from her hands and tried to bolt, almost throwing her. The trees on the edge of the woods by the road exploded, and unbelievable though it was, a dragon stepped from the shadows of history and onto the battlefield.

The massive creature casually surveyed the bloody field until its eyes lit on the trebuchets. It threw back its head, let out a deafening roar and pounced on the machines, its massive wings flattening trees and warriors alike. The des-triers' prey animal instincts finally overcame their training and when the dragon leapt, they bolted in the opposite direction through the awestruck Guthlanders and back towards the Arth.

Thorgulsen had never seen a true dragon before. He might have appreciated its grace and majesty a little more if the fucking thing wasn't killing his warriors in its haste to destroy Trenham's engines. Worse, its arrival had given the Steelskins a chance to escape. *First Beth, now this.* He'd had worse days, but he couldn't remember when.

Thorgulsen ordered his hirths to attack the dragon. Those Irregulars who were able had scattered when it had leapt at the trebuchets. They now gathered outside Trenham's command tent. Many were in shock, a few were wounded. The rest were putting on armour.

"I knew this was a bad contract," Kiri muttered. She flopped down; a long, arrow-thin splinter was sticking out of her forearm.

"You might have mentioned that before we signed up," said Trenham, as he slammed more arrows into his quiver.

His Lieutenant gritted her teeth and pulled the splinter from her arm. Blood teared down her wrist. She bound the cut with her torn sleeve. "You're not thinking o'having a go at *that* with a bow are you, sir?"

"Yes!" He dashed the quiver on the ground. "No. Fuck! I should just aim one at myself; put me out of my misery."

Kiri shook her head and wiped her bloody hands on the grass. "I wouldn't do that if I was you. Tha' way your luck's runnin', you'd miss."

Everyone dived for cover when the dragon ripped the throwing arm off one of the trebuchets and hurled it. Tren-ham watched his profits tumble end-over-end, across the field before it slewed onto the road and smashed a group of hirths into oblivion. A knot of scarlet-clad knights took advantage of the chaos and charged towards the Arth. He wasn't sure, but he thought one of them was Ali Stenna.

A dozen Guthlanders paid with their lives for every foot of ground the Black Lancers gave. It just wasn't enough.

By the time the dragon arrived the Lancers had been driven back into the shell of the ruined gatehouse. Then all fighting stopped. Deadly enmity was momentarily forgotten as all combatants fell under the dragon's spell, and stared in open-mouthed disbelief at the mythical creature come to life. Something stirred in Cassian's blood, a memory, a sense of familiarity. *Kinship*. He shuddered, dragged his gaze from the beast.

The Guthani cavalry were being rallied by a warrior in a dragon crested helm. He raised his spear and quite unbelievably, charged at the beast. The attack on the gatehouse faltered, impetus fleeing with the horse warriors who followed their leader. Strength and hope renewed, Cassian gave the order to charge.

When his innate belligerence overcame his instincts, Alyda was able to steady Lyco's wild gallop. Dozens of Telvier's mercenaries were fleeing the field. Many of the Guthani seemed to have forgotten the Antians and were instead running to attack the dragon. Alyda didn't know if they were brave or stupid. Whichever it was, she was grateful. Hope had sprung from a most unexpected source, but they weren't out of trouble yet. Not all of the Guthani had broken off the chase, and several groups continued to pursue them up the road.

"Typical heavies, always late." Cassian shouted when the Hammer joined up with the Lancers on the bridge.

Alyda answered, but her words were lost when, having finished destroying the trebuchets, the dragon noticed the humans attacking it. The beast let out a sky-splitting roar, and swept dozens of Guthani aside with a casual flick of its tail.

Alyda and Cassian ordered their knights inside while they waited by the ruined gatehouse for stragglers. Rann was one of the last to make it back. He came charging up the road, covered in blood, a swarm of Guthani in his wake the ragged banner of the 1st clutched in his hand. Alyda thought he looked like Ataghenach, the Tamalak war god, and on a day like today such a visitation would not have surprised her.

"D'you have any idea where our saviour came from?" Cassian asked as the knight thundered past them.

Beyond the rubble-strewn ruins, the Guthani paused to lock shields, mindful of the archers on the wall.

"Not the slightest, but as long as it's attacking them and not us, I don't care if it came from the Void."

"I'm with you there," he said, just before a spear split the difference between them.

"Time to go I think," said Alyda, and kicked Lyco on.

As the knights turned for the Arth, a flaxen-haired hirth darted from behind the shields. Yelling a war cry, she hurled her axe. A moment later she was dead, feathered a dozen times before she hit the ground. The axe continued on its deadly path and struck the left hind leg of Cassian's horse, snapping bones. The horse let out a scream and crashed to the ground. Cassian rolled clear and was quickly on his feet. He drew his sword, took a two handed grip, and dispatched his crippled mount.

Emboldened by his comrade's reckless bravery another hirth came from cover and cast his spear at Cassian. He too was rewarded with a swift death, but not before he threw his weapon. Alyda shouted a warning. The Captain of the Lancers raised his sword to block. His breastplate lifted a few treacherous inches. The spear sparked off his sword blade and buried itself in his gut. The archer's redoubled their efforts and loosed a blizzard of shafts at the Guthani. Cassian fell to his knees, clutching the spear. Alyda turned back and put Lyco between the Guthlanders and the wounded knight.

"Cass! Take my hand," she yelled, reaching down to him as spears and arrows laced the air around them.

The pale knight yanked the spear out and stared, dazed and confused, at the bloody blade in his hand.

"Captain Vorsten!" Alyda bellowed. "Give me your fucking hand!"

Cass blinked, refocused. He dropped the spear and reached up. She grabbed his wrist just before he passed out.

The unconscious knight's weight threatened to drag her from the saddle. Alyda wrapped her legs around Lyco. Her injured leg burned, but she managed to haul Cassian up, and over the saddle.

"I've got you Cass, I've got you," she said and was about to turn for the gate when a spear flew from behind the shield wall and struck Lyco in the chest.

No! The warhorse reared. Alyda threw herself across Cassian. The Guthani cheered and closed in for the kill. Lyco's blood bathed the cobbles. Alyda bellowed her rage and frustration. *So close, so damn close!* Cassian groaned. She couldn't give up. Summoning what strength she had left, Alyda reined Lyco around and dug her spurs in his flanks, hating herself for doing so. The destrier snorted foamy blood, but put his head down and ploughed towards the Arth.

The air sang as archers loosed volley after volley into the Guthani. Something hit her helm. The ringing impact lit stars before her eyes. She drove Lyco on, willing him to stay on his feet. The warhorse stumbled, but he did not fall; bloody—minded determination keeping him moving. Alyda could feel consciousness starting to slip away. The gates opened. She wrapped the reins around her fist and locked her other arm around Cassian. The world grew dim and distant…

Talin led the charge out of the gate, but was quickly overtaken by Bear. The great black horse staggered towards the barbican, blood pouring from its chest.

Jamie led a group of yelling squires past Talin. Rann Lacgarde was still mounted and charged past them and slammed into the Guthani, smashing a hole in their shield wall that the archers took full advantage of. For the second time, Bear broke her vow. Snarling, the woman became a beast and followed Rann into the knot of Guthani on the bridge. The pursuit slowed.

Before he could take the reins from Alyda, a hirth charged him. Talin stabbed him in the chest and kicked him over the side of the bridge. Another took his place. The black horse stumbled past them.

"Hold on, Captain!" Jamie shouted as Lyco staggered towards the barbican.

"Jamie!" A strangled voice shrieked in terror. He spun round. It was Hedden. His fellow squire was under a ferocious attack from a Guthani with an axe and shield. Jamie wanted to help the Captain, but Hedden was no match for the Guthlander he was up against. Cursing, Jamie fought his way through the press toward his fellow squire. Just as he reached him, the hirth beat down Hedden's defence and hacked him in the gut. Hedden fell.

Jamie bellowed and launched a flurry of savage blows at the Guthlander. She stumbled back, her guard dropped. Jamie brought his sword down against her shoulder, smashing bones and sending brass scales flying from her hauberk. She fell. Jamie brought his sword up and round in a slashing arc and split her skull. He wrenched the shield from her arm and slung it over his back before dragging Hedden towards the barbican. The squire was screaming, trying to hold his guts in. Before Jamie could get him inside, Hedden fell silent. *So close.*

Something hit Talin in the face, denting his visor. Blood filled his nose and mouth. He fell, stunned and choking on top of the Guthani he'd just dispatched. The tide of bodies closed over him. He couldn't breathe, couldn't get up, he was being trampled, kicked... As panic set in, strong hands grabbed the back of his cuirass and hauled him out of the crush. His rescuer half-dragged, half-carried him into the bailey and propped him against the wall of the barbican, where he saw it was Lorhine who had saved him. Talin tore off his battered helmet and gulped air. Lorhine shouted something at him, but all Talin could hear was a loud ringing in his ears. Without waiting for a reply, Lorhine ran back into the barbican. Talin got up to follow, but his legs had lost all strength and he fell back against the wall.

Just then, Lyco stumbled out of the shadows of the barbican and into the bailey, blood streaming down his chest. Knights ran to close the gates as the Guthani tried to force their way inside. Outside on the bridge Talin could see Lacgarde, surrounded but still fighting. A blood chilling howl rose above the tumult and a huge hulking shadow loomed up behind the foremost attackers. The pressure on the gates eased allowing them to be closed and the portcullis to be lowered.

They passed from darkness into light. Hands reached up and gently lifted Cassian off Lyco's trembling back. Alyda looked up; focused. They were in the bailey. Lyco plodded on, his breath coming in ragged gasps, his lungs working like bellows. Alyda laid her head against his neck, and listened to the thunder of his mighty heart. Slowly, like a passing storm, it diminished to a whisper. When the destrier fell, she had neither the strength, nor the desire to jump clear.

Flea could hear the Bear rending flesh and snapping bones beyond the gate. It didn't sound very nice. He watched them carry the wounded knights away, but they left the black horse where he'd fallen in the middle of the bailey. His thick legs were folded beneath him, the tip of his armoured nose rested on the ground. He could have been asleep, if it wasn't for all the blood. Flea crept over to the dead giant.

Clouds had already veiled his angry eyes. He reached out and stroked the horse's corded neck. It was hot; the fur velvet-soft, except where his fingers found the hard ridge of an old scar. He traced the knotted flesh with the tip of his finger to where scarlet streams branched across the horse's chest and etched zigzags in the dirt. Flea watched the patterns crawl ever more slowly across the ground until…they…finally…stopped.

The dragon's name hovered tantalisingly on the edge of its memory. It chased it like a cat chasing a moth, discovering as it did all manner of fascinating memories it had long forgotten or indeed, had never known. As it examined these thoughts, each in its turn, it ripped apart the trebuchets.

When it finished its task the dragon knew it was pleased that the terrible weapons had been smashed into kindling. It noticed more of the little flesh things—the *humans*. They were all around it. There had been a time when it had talked with humans, but that had been long ago.

Today, it would have ignored them, but then a bright sharp pain blossomed in its foreleg. The dragon who-almost-remembered-its-name, immediately remembered something important: *what magic has made, it can undo*. A powerful rage swelled within its fiery heart and it smashed them aside. But that wasn't all. The dragon felt an altogether new sensation, something it was sure it had never experienced before. It knew that this entirely new, but not entirely unpleasant sensation was called *fear*. The dragon-who-wanted-to-travel decided it was time to be elsewhere and launched into the sky. Humans and trebuchets were soon forgotten as it revelled in the joy of flying as though it had never flown before.

Chapter Sixteen

It was pure bad luck that the mercenary had fled from a dragon only to run into a shapeshifter. The warrior's neck had snapped like wet wood and he now lay cooling at Pytre's feet, a surprised look frozen on his face. *If only there was more time.* Pytre crouched beside the corpse to watch what was happening on the battlefield. The Guthlanders were such perverse creatures. They supposedly revered dragons, but what did they do the moment they laid eyes on one? He gave a throaty chuckle and stretched out in the long grass beside the kill.

The Guthlanders threw themselves at the elemental, but the beast was oblivious to their presence. It was wholly intent on destroying the war machines. *Blood, fire, and silver.* The shapeshifter sat up, dug his talons into the dead mercenary's hide and sniffed the air. Yes, there it was— faint, but unmistakable; the sweet smell of Yorl.

He tracked the slender thread of scent to the leader of the horse warriors and the spear he wielded; finely crafted and shining with the subtle light of magic. A ripple of excitement tightened his balls as he watched the spear spin through the air and strike the dragon in the leg. It didn't penetrate deeply, but stung enough to anger it.

The elemental roared its fury and lashed out with its huge claws, sweeping the horse warriors across the field before launching itself skywards.

Pytre's keen eyes marked its passage through the towering cloud stacks until it was nothing more than a dark speck against the vault of heaven.

On the field, a warrior with the arrogance of a pack leader ordered the body of the horse warrior to be taken back to their camp. As pleasant as it was, lying in the long grass with a fresh kill, Pytre had to go. He licked the blood from his claws before padding silently into the forest.

They built the bier for Thane Jorun Hanser: *Dragon Slayer,* out of Trenham's smashed Trebuchets. It seemed a shame to waste all that good, seasoned wood. The pyre was eight feet high and strewn with what flowers they could find; Hanser's dead horse lay at the warrior's feet.

Thorgulsen knelt before the utter, fucking waste of his time and effort, and inspected the scars on the back of his hands. When he'd pretended to pray for what seemed like an appropriately respectful length of time, he got up and threw a handful of coins onto the body. Quietly cursing Hanser to the Void, he went to find the mercenary captains and the Priest.

For once the sell-swords looked like they'd earned the fortune he was paying them. Trenham's face sported a livid bruise and Telvier was wigless, his shaved pate gleaming with sweat and his usually spotless attire grubby and blood splattered. Neither was happy to hear what he had to tell them.

"We need to get this over with now, it's gone on long enough," argued Trenham.

The mercenary was touchy today; but then, he'd just seen his profits turned into expensive firewood.

"I must agree with my brother captain. I mean a dragon! Really, it's too much. I'm sure my contract does not cover fighting mythical creatures. And surely one has to actually *slay* a dragon in order to be called a *Dragon Slayer?* Not that I wish to speak ill of the dead, but the cursed thing flew away." Telvier laughed mirthlessly and examined a tear in his cuff.

Thorgulsen shrugged and smoothed his moustaches. "They're saying that it flew away to die. Anyway, it's out of my hands. Thane Hanser must have full funeral rites performed before the sun sets tomorrow, 'tis the law."

"Then burn him tonight, for gods sake!" exclaimed Trenham.

"I can't. Tonight the Heroes' Song must be sung, and we must feast with his spirit before he goes to join the ancestors on the 'morrow." Thorgulsen noted the ill-concealed disgust written on their faces. He couldn't blame them, but the law was the law. He might as well declare himself renegade and cut his throat as break it.

He leaned across the table and whispered. "If it was up to me I'd throw the glory-seeking prick in the shit pit, but he's one of Redbear's shield brothers and a hero, and must be treated as such. I must do as the law commands. Don't worry: we'll kill the Steelskins later, they aren't going anywhere."

The flesh of Alyda's thigh was pulled tight in a neat, five inch long, line of stitches. A loop, a knot, a flash of a knife and Gedthis was finished. He got up, wiped his hands on his filthy apron and threw his tools into his bag.

"She's lost some blood and her knee may be broken; other than that, I don't think she's too badly off." He arched his back to stretch tired muscles. "I'll come by later. When she wakes up, tell her to stay here and rest. You never know; she might listen."

Jamie closed the door behind the surgeon. The sound of screaming echoed from the other rooms in the infirmary.

"Lyco didn't roll on her," Jamie said, his voice hoarse from shouting. "Even though he was dying he took care of her. She was the only person who could ride him…"

The brash young warrior was gone, leaving only the boy, struggling to come to terms with his grief. On impulse, Talin put his arm around him as he would his brother. Jamie wept.

"Hedden, damn him. He died in my arms. I was too slow, couldn't save him, he shouted to me, but, I…I couldn't…"

After a while he stopped crying and straightened up. Too embarrassed to look Talin in the eye, he mumbled something about guard duty and rushed out. He had no reason to feel ashamed; Talin had seen the boy fight like a Void-spawned demon trying to save his friend. He wanted to tell him that it was alright to cry, that no one could be as hard as iron or as cold as stone, all the bloody time. Well, perhaps there was one person who could.

For a moment, he wondered if he really knew Alyda. He leaned over and to erase his doubts as much as anything, kissed her. She stirred, but didn't wake.

"Don't ever scare me like that again," he whispered before curling up beside her and falling asleep.

Alyda opened her eyes, tried to focus on her surroundings. The parchment coloured walls were spotted and smeared with blood; it stank of vinegar, vomit, and piss. *Must be the infirmary.* Talin was asleep beside her. Dark circles ringed his eyes; he looked exhausted, but thankfully, very much alive.

She shuffled to the edge of the bed and carefully sat up. Her thigh was sore and she could feel the pull of the stitches beneath the bandage, but her knee was worse. It throbbed like a heartbeat, and had swollen to fill the knee cop of her armour. She took a breath and flexed her leg. A dozen sharp pains sang out in chorus, but it just about worked. She counted herself lucky, until she remembered Cassian and Lyco, and gods only knew how many others.

She stared at the wall, and tried to find the calm centre of her being where pain couldn't touch her, and dark thoughts couldn't distract her from what she had to do. Hard as iron, cold as…*as what?* She leaned over and kissed Talin. He stirred, but didn't wake.

Using her sword for support, she climbed to her feet. The moment she put weight on her injured leg she wanted to sit back down. The pain wasn't unbearable, but it was damn close. Gritting her teeth, she went to find Cassian.

Griga was slumped against the wall outside Cassian's apartments. Alyda gave her an enquiring look. The veteran knight shook her head. It was all she needed to know, too much. Alyda took a deep breath, knocked and entered. The Vorsten's nurse dipped a timid curtsy and continued to pace up and down, rocking their sleeping son in her arms. Beria was sitting at her husband's bedside, she didn't look up.

As pale as the sheets, Cassian was unconscious, his breathing shallow. A bright rose of blood had blossomed on his bandages. Beria was sobbing quietly into her lap. Alyda felt like she was intruding on private grief. She cleared her throat, searched for something to say, some words of comfort that could convey to Beria the depth of her sorrow, but what words sprang to mind sounded trite, empty. There was only one thing she could do, one unassailable mark of respect that she could give which Cassian would understand.

She saluted.

Cora kissed her tears from Master Tomas's cheeks and half-fell into a curtsy when Captain Stenna barged in. The knight looked as done in as all the others who'd come to pay their respects. But Cora would have been hard pressed to say Captain Stenna felt anything close to the same measure of grief as the rest of them. Hulking great knights had wept like babes when they'd said farewell to Captain Cassian, but that Stenna was as hard as iron. Cora scrubbed a tear away and rocked baby Tomas as much to comfort herself as him.

After not long at all, the knight hobbled out, and not a word of condolence offered to Lady Vorsten. She'd just saluted and left.

Maybe that's how they were up north, but it was cold, and plain bad manners if you asked her. The knight well deserved her reputation of being as hard as the steel she wore. Cora felt not a twinge of guilt when she considered that it was the wrong captain who lay dying.

Frozen with fear, Beria had watched the surgeon work on Cass and when he finished, he destroyed her.

"He is dying," he said. He continued to speak, but his words thereafter were inconsequential.

Hours later, with death drawing closer with every heartbeat, she could still hear the leaden echo of the surgeon's pronouncement: *He is dying, he is dying, he is*…Dying. She cried quietly and continuously as she gently combed out Cass's braids and washed the blood from his face.

She wanted to wail her grief to the heavens, to scream like a beast until her lungs bled and she could scream no more, but she couldn't do that. Cass would be embarrassed; he wasn't one for loud, emotional displays.

He hadn't woken since they'd brought him back to her, but she was sure he could hear her. So she held his hand and quietly berated him for being a stupid, wonderful man and told him how very much she loved him, her heart breaking with every word.

When Ali Stenna came to say farewell, Beria was struck by a sudden and unreasonable flash of anger. She knew she was being unfair, but she couldn't even bring herself to look at Alyda. She kept her head down and willed the knight to go, and leave them in peace. Not long after she'd left, Cass opened his eyes.

Beria bathed his icy cheeks with hot tears. "Hello, my love," she whispered.

He smiled weakly and mumbled something, but she couldn't make out what he was trying to say.

"I understand my darling, it's alright. Tomas and I are safe. You can let go now, Cass. My beloved, my heart..."

He must have heard her because he smiled. A breath later, death stole the light from his eyes.

Several large boulders had smashed through the ceiling of Cassian's office and lay scattered across the floor. Bone weary, and sore, Alyda righted a chair and sat down. She tossed her sword on the table and put her head in her hands. *We can't beat them, not even with the help of a fucking dragon! We've lost...I've lost.* That was the cold hard truth she couldn't stomach. She'd never lost a battle while she'd been in command. She didn't know what to do.

Failure had never been an option, now it was almost a certainty. She'd been so sure they could win, so sure help would come, but that had been before Cassian had died, before Rann, before Nev and Lyco. Her world, everything she had been so sure of, was suddenly as solid as smoke and all her plans seemed as fragile as glass...

Enough! She surged to her feet, snatched up her sword and hammered blow after blow into the table. She hacked chunks out of the wood until she was too tired to lift her sword.

Her anger spent, she leaned against the table. Her knee hurt worse than ever and she'd added a dozen new notches to her blade, but she'd thrown off the black wave of doubt that had threatened to overwhelm her. Her mind was once again focused on the task in hand.

Hope might fade, but she could always rely on bloody-minded fury to keep her going until the job was done. Talin and his family would get away and she would save the garrison from being slaughtered by that pig-fucker, Thorgulsen. *It will work.* She had to hold onto that thought, even as everything else crumbled.

Night's shadows were kind to the Arth and hid its terrible scars, but darkness couldn't mask the stench of death. Smith was on corpse clearing duty with another blacksmith—a woman called Kater who'd come from Galegallen. She moaned a bit, but at least they understood each other. They'd tied scarves over their faces but the fatty, sweet stink of rot still managed to worm its way into his nostrils.

"I don't see why we're doing this," Kater grumbled, angrily shoving a dangling leg back onto the cart that they'd piled with bodies. "I mean, who's gonna bury us?"

Smith shrugged. "Someone…or no one. Does it matter? An' we're doing this because we aren't dogs waiting to die. We go on; we do what decent people do."

"I'd rather be getting pissed. Look at this one." She dragged a huddled body from between the buttresses of the keep tower and dropped it by the cart. Smith toed the corpse onto its back. He was a short, dumpy fellow, dressed in a shabby robe. There didn't look to be a mark on him from what he could see. The only thing of note about him was the feather clutched in his hand.

"Must have died of fright," Smith offered, "weak heart or something." Even with the scarf he could see Kater's face twist into a sneer.

"Bloody coward if you ask me. He could have died on the walls, taking a few of those bastards with him, instead of down here."

"Aye well, it takes all sorts. C'mon—let's get him loaded. I want to get this lot into the pit and limed before the rats get at 'em."

As they loaded the body, the feather fell from the dead man's hand. Smith went to grab it, but a sighing breeze snatched it away and tumbled it playfully across the bailey.

"An elemental or a dragon?" Garian asked again. Pytre wasn't being clear; he seemed to be using the terms interchangeably.

The shapeshifter gave a lazy smile, displaying the overlong canines. "Forgive me Garian. 'Tis an elemental whose essence has been woven into the pattern of what you think of as a dragon."

Garian still wasn't sure he understood. "And it just flew off? Did you see where it went?" He pressed. He'd work out what it was later; all that mattered right now was that something with a taste for Guthani was loose in Antia.

Pytre smiled, obviously amused. "It went up, quite high."

They were hiding in a copse on the west side of Gallen Arth. Before them, the Galerun flowed unsullied by the filth and debris that clogged the moat on the other side of the huge outcrop of rock. Suli finished coiling the rope, and handed it to Garian. Now that night had fallen it was time for him to scale the curtain wall.

"Suli, I don't mean to sound ungrateful, but are you sure this, 'secret place' of yours is safe enough to take the Queen?"

She smiled, but something was troubling her. He knew how to read people and it was obvious that she was keeping something from him, and that was worrying. In the short time they'd known each other neither had kept anything from the other, at least, he hadn't kept anything from her. She smiled nervously and flicked a strand of sun-kissed hair over her shoulder.

"Oh, it's very safe, but I fear I might be endangering my own people by helping yours."

"You know I'd never betray your secret," he said. "The Queen and her sons don't need to know where we're taking them—in fact it's probably better if they don't know."

She shook her head. "You might not be so sure when I tell you where it is, but promise me you'll give me chance to explain?"

He nodded. "Of course, my love."

She took a deep breath. "Our sanctuary is in the Void."

"You'd better explain."

It was fully dark by the time she finished telling him about the place she called the Valley of the Moon.

"So, if this place is part of the Fey realm, does that make you…?"

She smiled. "Fey? It's such a poor description, like 'the Void'—and it will take much longer than we have right now to explain it to you. I'll tell you everything I know when this is over, I promise."

"Very well, but it's a lot to take in. You said there are sanctuaries like this all over the world, so how is it they haven't been found?"

"People have found them; they just keep quiet so that they don't get burnt for being sorcerers or demons. Which is why you must keep our secret."

Garian gave her a reassuring hug. "I'd rather tear out my tongue than betray you, love. Trust me; I'm very good at keeping secrets, it's what I do."

Lhazinia returned from scouting the Arth. She told them there were only two groups of six patrolling this side of the keep.

"I doubt they'd hear an angry bear crossing the meadow, given the noise they're making themselves," said the shapeshifter.

"That's something, but there's every chance they'll see me when I'm climbing."

Lhazinia and Pytre exchanged a knowing look.

"Leave it to us," said Pytre, and they slipped into the darkness.

About half an hour later, they returned.

"It is done," said Lhazinia. "We'll keep watch in case more turn up, but you'd better get going now."

Suli squeezed his arm. "Are you sure you're going to go in alone? They might kill you before you get the chance to tell them who you are. Let my cousins go with you."

Garian shook his head. "No. If Pytre or Zia come with me, they'll set the Ward off."

"I can climb, let me come."

"No. I don't know what's happened in there, which is why I need to go alone. You and your cousins have led us safely to the King and back, already more than I could ask, but sneaking in and out of places like this is what I'm good at. I'll be alright, I promise." He smiled and flicked a strand of hair from her eyes. "Wait here, I'll be back before you know it."

"You'd better be, or we'll come looking," she said, and kissed him goodbye.

The icy waters of the Galerun froze the marrow in his bones, but he warmed up quickly once he got out and started climbing. The stone at the base of the wall was smooth and tightly jointed, but higher up, where wind and rain had nibbled at the edges of the blocks there were abundant points of purchase.

Being short had its advantages and disadvantages when climbing. He had less weight to carry, but sometimes he had to overreach to find a decent hand or foot hold. He only slipped once, after mistaking a bird's nest for a hand-hold in the poor light. Hanging from one hand gave him an excellent view of the surrounding countryside, but it wasn't something he wanted to make a habit of.

A huge hall had been built directly against the curtain wall. Once he was over the parapet he was on the roof, or what was left of it. The slates on the northwest end were almost intact, but nearer the south end there was more hole than roof, which forced him to pick his route care-fully across the bones of what remained.

The stench emanating from the Arth made his stomach lurch—and he'd waded through the sewers of Weyhithe. He stopped breathing through his nose and crawled to the edge of the roof.

Lime dusted grave pits shone in the darkness, and doz-ens of horses roamed loose amongst the rubble. Most of the buildings at the south end of the Arth had suffered heavy damage. Great bites had been taken out of the cur-tain wall on the south and east sides of the keep. The outer gatehouse was little more than rubble, but the inner barbi-can looked surprisingly intact.

Beyond the Arth was the pyre that the shapeshifters had mentioned. It was surrounded by flickering torches, but was as yet unlit. The unlikely sound of singing floated across the black gulf between the Guthani camp and the Arth. Garian had read about the elaborate funeral rites of the Guthlanders, he'd just never imagined they'd perform them in the middle of a battle. Whoever they were, they must have been important.

He'd seen all he could from the roof. He had to go down and find Stenna or the Queen, or whoever was in charge if Stenna was dead and hope they gave him the chance to explain who he was before they killed him. Hyram's ring and the letter he carried should be enough to convince her Majesty he was who he said he was, if he could get to her.

He climbed down the side of the building furthest from the barbican. When he heard the tell-tale sound of people clanking towards him in armour, he flattened himself against the curtain wall. He stayed in the shadows, partly from habit, and partly because he didn't want to be killed by a nervous sentry before he had chance to explain himself.

He recognised Stenna straightaway, she was limping heavily. The knights halted by a well. Garian sheathed the knife that had found its way into his hand. As he did, one of them looked in his direction and drew his sword.

"Who goes there?" the knight demanded.

Garian raised his hands and stepped from the shadows. "Captain Stenna—it's me, Garian Tain. I have a message for the Queen."

The spy was less than forthcoming, if not exactly evasive, but Alyda let it pass. She was anxious to find out what was in the damn letter Tain had given to the Queen, desperate to know if reinforcements were on their way.

"So how did you get past the patrols on the other side of the river?" she asked, while they waited for Thea to finish reading.

"They were dealt with," he said.

"I know you!" Olin piped up. "You're the librarian."

Garian bowed to the Prince. "Upon occasion, Highness. More often I'm a cartographer or herbalist."

Thea folded the letter. "Captain Stenna, I would speak with you alone."

The Queen waited until everyone else had left before handing her the letter. "You must read this."

She read it quickly and then again, more slowly, in case she'd misread it. She hadn't. The brief hope that had sparked to life when Tain arrived was cruelly extinguished with a few drops of ink. There would be no reinforcements. The King's army was engaged with a larger force and he couldn't spare anyone to raise the siege at Gallen Arth. She snapped to attention and handed the letter back to the Queen.

"Everything has been prepared, Majesty. With respect, I think it would be right to take Lady Vorsten and her son with you."

"I agree, Captain. Please send her over."

Thea paused, bit her lip. Surely there wasn't anything else? Alyda waited, but the Queen didn't add anything, so she made to leave.

"Captain—"

Here it comes. "Majesty?"

"There's something I must ask you, Captain Stenna. Something I have no right to do, but I know you'll understand why I must."

The small group gathered in the cellar of the tower. The Queen was with her youngest son, a reluctant Beria Vorsten and her baby. Garian hadn't expected to be taking anyone other than the Queen and her sons; the extras were an added inconvenience, but with his travelling companions he doubted they'd encounter any trouble they couldn't handle or avoid.

He'd made a point of telling Stenna he was taking them north towards Cathlan. It was a necessary deception in case she was taken alive; she'd understand. They were actually going south to meet Suli and her cousins before heading off to the Vodoni's secret valley. That was a whole other pain in the arse he could have lived without. He loved Suli, trusted her with his life, but he'd feel a damn sight happier when he'd seen the place for himself. Right now, he'd settle for getting away from here. The place was a tomb.

When Lady Beria refused to leave, Alyda asked Talin to try and convince her to go. He failed and in the end had to order her to come with him. Even then, he had to just about drag the grief stricken widow to the cellar where his mother and Oli were waiting. Although that was hard, telling his mother that he wasn't going with them proved to be much easier than he'd anticipated. She accepted it with surprisingly good grace and bid him farewell without any of the fuss he'd been expecting.

Alyda was waiting for him in his mother's quarters while he said goodbye to his family. When he got back he found her sitting by the shuttered window, a single candle spluttered on the book strewn table. She looked tired, which was hardly surprising, but at least they'd be together for however long they had left. He went to kiss her, but she pulled away.

"What is it?" he asked, confused by her coldness. "What's wrong?"

"You have to leave the Arth, Highness," she said flatly.

"I told you, I'm not going. Please, let's not argue about this. I said I'm not leaving you again no matter what, and I meant it." He reached out to her, but she shrugged his hand away.

"Highness, Talin. You don't have a choice. Your father has ordered it. Please don't make this difficult; time is against us."

He chuckled. "You're wasting your breath, Captain Stenna, and if you think giving me the cold shoulder is going to make me go, you're wrong I'm—"

"I don't love you," she blurted. "I've been trying to tell you for days, but…well; I never got the chance to speak with you about it."

He laughed. "You are such a bad liar; promise me you'll never gamble—you'll lose your shirt. Not that it would be such a bad thing…you being shirtless." He probably shouldn't joke, but her clumsy attempt at lying only confirmed that she loved him, and that made him happier than he had a right to be given the trouble they were in.

"No, Highness, it's true. We had fun, but it was a dalliance, nothing more."

Talin folded his arms.

"It's true, damn you." She stood up. "I'm telling you now because I want to part with you honestly. I don't have to convince you to leave—I can have you tied in a fucking sack and dragged out of here, and I damn-well will if I have to."

What power to intimidate she had was lost on him. He'd take a knife in the heart from her hand. *She loves me.* It was wonderful, not least because he loved her too. He knew he was grinning like a fool, but he couldn't help it.

"Tell me again that you don't love me."

She locked eyes with him and held his gaze, willing him not to turn around. Willing herself not to glance at Bear, who was sneaking up behind him. When Talin went to say goodbye to his mother, she suggested that Bear hide behind the bed curtains, like Tain had done in Weyhithe. Unsurprisingly the shapeshifter moved quietly. Which was a blessing; Alyda didn't want to have to fight Talin to get him out, not unless she had to.

"Well, Captain, I'm waiting. Tell me you don't love me," he said. He was still smiling.

"I'm sorry, my love," Alyda whispered.

Before he had chance to answer, Bear hit him across the head with the cosh. He fell into Alyda's arms; she kissed him, before Bear hoisted him over her shoulder.

"If I'd known you'd have me beating up my best friend I'd have stayed outside with the Guthani. He's going to be very angry with me for doing this. I shall have to grovel for months."

Alyda didn't have the heart to laugh. "Tell the Queen I tried, but I'm just not a very good liar. She'll know what you mean."

The smile faded from Bear's face. "Of course. Is there anything else I can tell anyone?"

Alyda shook her head. "No, he already knows."

Bear headed to the door. She paused before leaving, her unconscious burden groaned. "It was an honour knowing you, Alyda Stenna. For what it's worth, I think you're the best thing that ever happened to Talin."

"Goodbye, Iris. Take care of him for me."

When Bear had gone Alyda slumped against the wall, numb to her core. The Queen had been right about one thing—she had no right to ask her to perjure her heart and tell Talin she didn't love him. She'd never seen it before, but there was a line between duty to one's sovereign and duty to oneself. The Queen had asked her to sacrifice one for the other. She'd tried; she was a Royal Guard; duty and honour always came first, except this time.

She'd been right to send him away with the truth instead of a lie. He'd be furious when he came round, but at least he'd know she loved him, and that was important; it was all they would ever have, and that hurt more that she'd thought possible.

She flexed her neck, cracked the small bones with a quick, right left twist and rolled her shoulders. It did little to untie the knots in her tired muscles, and nothing to ease the pain in her leg. She sighed a laugh. She was as broken and battered as the Arth, but like the old keep, she was still just about standing and would damn well stay that way until the job was done.

When dawn came, Alyda and Lorhine watched from the barbican as a Talespinner went and stood before the unlit pyre. He began to recite something that could have been a prayer or a long winded poem for all Alyda knew. The warrior laid out atop the pyre was dressed in gleaming scale armour, shield beneath his head, shining spear clutched in his hand. A slaughtered horse lay at his feet. It was depressing to see the hundreds of warriors lined up on the field, but also grimly satisfying to see the gaps in their ranks.

"Shame about the pony," she said to Kieran.

He grunted in agreement. "Shame the Thane they're fixing to burn isn't that pig-fucker Thorgulsen."

"Aye, but it's given us more time to plan and…" She stopped herself saying, *"For Talin to get away."* She'd have to be careful; she couldn't afford to let tiredness trip her.

Alyda told Jamie to round up the survivors and bring them to the Great Hall. She waited impatiently as a hundred and twenty children, old people, and injured, crept or were carried from the cellars to join the sixty or so remaining able-bodied fighters.

It hurt that there were only a handful of the Hammer amongst them, but it wasn't unexpected. They'd led the defence, standing front and centre on the wall, they'd borne the brunt of the attacks, and carried the fight to the enemy. *And gods, I miss every one of them.*

She'd never felt like this before, her hands were trembling. She stamped her foot, sending shockwaves of pain through her knee. Anything was better than surrendering to the wave of sorrow that was threatening to engulf her. She couldn't dwell on her loses, she had to stay focused on saving the living; the dead could wait a little longer.

Lurking at the back of the gathering, still grumbling, still with a sneer nailed to his face, was Smith. Alyda was glad the ornery bastard had survived, but it would be a cold day in the Void before she told him.

She cleared her throat. "I'll keep this short: you must be sick of hearing my voice by now. I know I am." A ripple of weary laughter passed through the crowd. "The Queen has commanded that I ask for terms of surrender. I have no doubt they will be accepted," she said, knowing full well it was more of a hope than a certainty. "You have endured hardships that few Antians ever have, that few even could. Your strength and your courage will be long-held as shining examples of those virtues, and I am humbled and honoured to have fought beside you."

When she finished, her knights snapped to attention and saluted. Alyda felt a lump rise in her throat as the rest of the garrison did likewise. She returned the gesture.

In contrast to the bleak mood of earlier, an excited murmur followed the weary survivors from the hall. Jamie stayed behind, his face set in an angry frown.

"What's on your mind, Jamie?" she asked.

"When the Guthani find out that the Queen isn't here they'll kill everyone: the old, the children—and it will not be swift."

That he of all people doubted her was another blow. Understandable perhaps, but it still felt like a kick in the gut. "You need to trust me, Jamie. I won't let you or the others down."

He nodded solemnly, but for the first time since she'd known him, she could see that he didn't believe her.

The Guthani lit the pyre when the setting sun kissed the horizon. There had been no further attacks. Alyda found a bottle of wine and took it up onto the roof of the barbican. She drowned a few sorrows and watched the Pyre burn deep into the night.

She woke just before dawn, slumped between two merlons on the roof of the barbican. It was raining, smoke coiled from the blackened remains of the pyre and drifted across the battlefield. A flock of crows took to the air and began to scribe lazy spirals above the Arth. The birds called shrilly, summoning more of their kin to the banquet. But the battle wasn't over just yet. She still had work to do.

She groaned, and tried to stretch the stiffness from her leg, but only made it hurt more. Cursing, she rubbed sleep from her eyes. Everything ached, including her head, thanks to the wine.

"You never could take your drink, Stenna." She laughed and tilted her face to the leaden sky; let the rain wash her doubts away. She'd fixed a plan in her mind, burned the details into her brain as she'd watched the Guthlander go up in smoke. She was certain it would work, not least, because it had to.

By mid-morning her leg was too painful for her to walk and she was forced to direct those of her officers who were left from a chair in the Great Hall. Jamie had made a small fire in a cooking pot and was boiling a pan of chai over it. He sheltered the flames from the rain that was pissing through the roof with a Guthani shield that he'd found somewhere.

"I need something for this." She gestured dismissively to her knee when Gedthis arrived.

He grunted, put down his bag and started unbuckling her leg harness. When he saw her stiffen and grip the chair arm, he got out a knife and cut the straps and then with uncustomary gentleness, eased the armour off. After carefully cutting open the leg of her breeches, he probed the mottled mass of swollen flesh where her knee should be. She swallowed a scream. *Hard as iron, Alyda, hard as... fuck! This hurts.*

Gedthis sighed. "You've made a mess of this, Captain. It's probably broken, but it's impossible to tell until the swelling goes down. You must keep it up. I'll get a—"

"Gedthis," she interrupted. She wasn't sharp; he meant well, but she didn't have time to listen to the whole speech. "I need to walk on it, not for long, and not far. Can you splint it or something?"

"I don't—" He was all set to argue until he saw the look in her eye.

"Yes, Captain..." he answered, resigned.

Muttering to himself he rummaged through his box until he found what he was looking for. He held up a small jar.

"Thistle Whelk poison. They use it to paralyse their prey; we use it to numb a localised area. It lasts for about four hours—more if you don't move much. Will that be long enough?" he asked as he applied the sticky ointment to Alyda's knee with a bone spatula.

She laughed through the pain. It was better than screaming. "More than enough I should think, Ged."

Gedthis carefully put the lid back on the jar and stowed it in his box. "You really shouldn't walk on it though. Even if you can't feel the pain you could do long-term damage."

The idea of anything being long-term struck her as particularly amusing and she let out a loud, unfettered laugh that degenerated into an infectious chuckle. Soon the sour faced surgeon was giggling like a child, quickly followed by Jamie.

"Why are we laughing?" Jamie asked when he managed to catch a breath.

Alyda and Gedthis looked at each other and laughed even harder.

When they eventually composed themselves, Alyda wiped tears from her eyes, and turned to Jamie. "Go find Pol; I need her to take a message to the Guthani."

"Out of the question. Kill the girl, tie her carcass to her horse and send it back. That shall be my answer. I can't be fucked to write anything." Thorgulsen tossed the scroll on the table.

Telvier winced a smile, and brushed past Trenham. "Indeed, Thane, most succinct, but might I suggest you refrain? If Queen Thea and her sons kill themselves as the note suggests they might, everything we've done, everything we've lost—" He looked pointedly at Trenham. "... will have been for nothing. Heroic deaths notwithstanding, I don't think Prince Jerim or Lord Redbear will be pleased with any of us."

"Fuck them," Thorgulsen snarled, hating that the Suvian prick was right. He also hated that the Antians were still making demands when they should just admit defeat and accept their fate. *What more did he have to do?*

"I hate to say this, but I agree with Telvier," said Trenham. "If we go in and slaughter everyone and the Queen dies, it won't matter if Jerim wins. He and Princess Matia will be fighting constant rebellion in Antia, and they'll not thank you for that."

"What does the Steelskin mean by, '—*having the surrender administered by the Free Companies*'. I don't understand all this word weaving. What ever happened to I win, she loses and I decide what happens?"

"I think Stenna wants assurances that you won't renege on any agreement you make," Trenham answered. "If the articles of surrender are written and witnessed by the Free Companies there's no chance of that happening."

"No? What if I decide to go back on my word, Free Company contract or not?" The Thane smiled humourlessly.

"Then every Free Company in Antia and beyond will be obliged to hunt you down," said Telvier, "an open contract as it were. 'Tis how we maintain our high standards."

Thorgulsen smoothed his beard. "I'm past caring; I want this finished one way or the other. Get yourself and your scribe ready, Trenham. Tell the Steelskin I'll meet with her captain."

There was no way Alyda could get her leg armour back on. Even though her knee was now pleasantly numb, the whelk poison did nothing for the swelling.

Jamie and Kieran helped her mount Nevenna's horse, a chestnut called Tuva. Alyda looked over to Lyco, still lying where he fell. She threw her cloak over her leg before riding out with Kieran and Jamie. She was pleased to see defenders stagger up to the wall and defiantly brandish weapons as though they were ready to fight again.

Thorgulsen and the two mercenaries were waiting in the middle of the field surrounded by bloating bodies, clouds of flies, and bickering troupes of carrion birds. The Thane looked well rested, his armour unsullied. Trenham and Telvier at least looked like they'd been in a fight. She swallowed hard and pretended sitting on a horse didn't hurt, pretended she didn't want to rip the Guthani's heart out.

"I have decided to agree to the terms you have requested," Thorgulsen said when they pulled up. "I will allow your garrison to leave under escort and command of Captain Trenham. I shall take the Queen and her sons with me."

"Thank you, Thane," said Alyda. Her heart was pounding so hard she was sure they'd hear it.

"I'll have the terms drawn up," Trenham offered unprompted.

She nodded and turned for the Arth.

"One more thing, Captain Stenna," said Thorgulsen. She halted, tried to look bored rather than panicked.

"You want the Free Companies to draw up and administer these *'articles of surrender'*. As I said, I will agree to this, but I also need assurances."

"What do you want?" she asked.

"I want it written in these *articles* that if any part of it is not held to by the Antians—and that includes the Queen cutting her throat to thwart me—that you will bear the responsibility *personally,* and forego any protection granted by the articles of surrender. Do you agree?"

"Can he do that?" Alyda heard Telvier whisper to Trenham. The mercenary nodded.

"Of course, Thane. We'll need three hours to prepare the wounded to travel."

"You have an hour," said Thorgulsen before heading back to his camp.

Telvier flipped Alyda a salute and trotting after the Thane. Trenham was slower to follow. He looked like he wanted to say something. She didn't wait to find out what it might be and rode back to the Arth. *That's the first part done.* It didn't go exactly to plan, but nothing ever did.

It took less than an hour for the garrison to gather their meagre belongings and assemble in the bailey. Thanks to Gedthis's ointment, Alyda was able to stand on her injured leg. *Not long now.* She told herself. Just a few more moves and then the game would be over and she would be able to rest. It stopped raining; shafts of sunlight pierced the clouds.

The survivors milled in the bailey, hardly daring to whisper while they waited nervously for the Guthlanders. Alyda swallowed hard and ordered the gates to be opened. So much blood had been spilled to keep them closed, opening them felt like a betrayal of all those who'd died.

A flock of geese arrowed over the barbican, wings flashing black and silver against the grey. She ordered the knights to lay down their arms and stand with the civilians, she limped over to Lyco to wait for the Guthlanders.

Smith peeled away from the group and came over. He had a bag of tools slung across his back. "They'll kill us all when they find out she's gone."

So much for keeping it a secret. She sighed. "Didn't we already have the conversation about you not telling me how to do my job? Don't worry, Smith, it's taken care of. How did you find out?" she asked, for want of something to pass the time while she waited for the Guthani.

He shrugged. "Only one guard on the tower this morn, no faces at the windows and mystery visitors in the night. You did at least remember to keep a candle burning in the Queen's room, but you didn't open the shutters. What can I say? I sleep poorly and I keep my eyes open."

"I'll remember to open the shutters next time."

"There won't be a next time, will there?"

Alyda shrugged. The last thing she needed right now was an argument with the Peoples' Champion. "You'll get out of here alive, Smith—you all will."

"Playing the hero to the end, eh? What about all those who are dead because your fucking pride wouldn't let you surrender?"

Alyda laughed. It was either that or punch him. "Come now, Smith, don't get all soft and sentimental, you'll make me cry."

"This isn't funny. People have died here, ordinary folk in the main, but do you know who'll be remembered?"

She looked him in the eye, tried to span the gulf between their worlds with a glance. Luckily for his sake, it was an impossible task; she wouldn't wish her nightmares on anybody. "I can't help that, Smith, and neither will I pretend to be meek and humble just to satisfy your fantasy of what a knight should be."

Smith flushed. "I don't want you to be anything. Why should I care?"

"I've no idea, as odd as this may seem to you, fathoming the workings of your peasant brain isn't high on my list of priorities. But you *do* care, and given the chance, you'd swap places with me in a heartbeat. Only life didn't give you that chance and that's why you're so damn bitter. You get to live out your days in whatever nameless dump you call home, mending pots and pans until you drop dead, or get too old and feeble to do anything other than beg for scraps in the street. Me? I get to die here, playing the fucking hero. It's not fair, in more ways than you've considered, but that's just the way it is."

Smith snorted and paced before her, caught somewhere between fury and embarrassment. "You've got me wrong. I despise your kind, and do you know why?"

"I could hazard a guess, but why don't you tell me anyway?"

"As long as there's stories told to bairns about heroic idiots, there'll always be fresh meat willing and eager to die to fill the storyteller's songbooks and keep kings and queens on thrones."

"Don't you ever get tired of being wrong, Smith? Has nothing ever moved you enough to risk your precious hide? Tell me I'm wrong; tell me you think there's something, anything—any*one* worth dying for. I'll wager the only important person in your life, Smith, is you."

The colour bled for his face. He clenched his fists. For a moment she thought he might hit her. *Just try it.*

"You make me sick." He growled and stormed back to the others.

"Goodbye, Smith."

The Irregulars were the first in. Alyda wondered whether they were impressed with their handiwork or horrified. She didn't give a damn which it was; they just had to help her with this last, most vital part of her plan to save the garrison and then they could all rot in the Void.

Trenham came over with his company accountant in tow. She was carrying a bundle of parchments and a writing slope. Alyda remembered her from Suvia. She was a singer and had a nice voice, but nothing compared to Nev. She could do with Nevenna's strength right now, her insight.

Alyda took her time reading the articles and provisions of the surrender. When she was sure every detail was as it should be and identical on all three copies, she added her signature to those of Thorgulsen, Telvier and Trenham.

Trenham gave two of the copies to his messengers. From her days in her father's Free Company she knew that they'd ride with all haste to the Free Company headquarters on Careth to register the contracts. They wouldn't take the same route or stop, save to change mounts. It was a reassuring, and often necessary precaution.

"Herick," she called after Trenham. He stopped. "Do me a favour?"

He smiled. "Certainly, if I can. You know when the dust settles, I'd like—"

"Kieran has my sword, but he's bound to be searched. Could you return it to my family? You know where they live."

He narrowed his eyes, gave her an appraising look. "What have you done, Ali?"

"It's a simple enough question, Herick. Yes or no?"

"There's no need to be like that."

"There's every need."

"Alright," he said quietly. "I'll do it."

Too late to feel bad now you greedy bastard, she thought, but kept her opinion to herself.

"Is there anything you want me to tell them?"

"Aye. Tell my father not to sell you any more fucking trebuchets and…tell them I love them."

"I will, and I'll look after this lot too. You have my word."

"I'll hold you to that."

Trenham immediately ordered the Irregulars to take up casually defensive positions around the survivors, bows at the ready, arrows nocked. Telvier's company rolled in soon after. The Suvian tipped his brocade and feather-festooned hat to Alyda. Last to enter were the Guthani.

A Talespinner announced Thorgulsen, who rode proudly through an avenue of cheering hirths, basking in their applause. He dismounted near Alyda, but his eyes searched the knot of survivors.

He turned to Alyda. "Where is the Queen?"

This is it. The moment she had been dreading and anticipating in equal measure had finally arrived. Her plan hadn't gone exactly how she'd wanted it to, but as her mother said when she taught her and Karl to play stones; *"Every good player understands the meaning of sacrifice."*

She smiled as Thorgulsen's grin faded. "I'm afraid Queen Thea will not be joining us."

Before the last word had died on her lips, the Thane slammed his fist into her face. Her leg gave out and she crashed to the ground.

"Search that fucking rabble and find the Queen!" Thorgulsen bellowed at Telvier and Trenham.

"As for you," he snarled at Alyda, "we have been remiss; we must do this properly, no? You should hand over your sword? Isn't that how *honourable* knights do things?" He kicked her in the stomach. She barely felt it through her armour, but she was struggling to see past the little points of light exploding before her watering eyes. She spat a mouthful of blood into the dirt.

"I threw it in the moat rather than let it be sullied by you, you miserable pig-fucker. If you want it, swim for it!"

The Thane kicked her again. This time she felt it. The air rushed from her lungs. While she lay there gasping for breath, a fight broke out amongst the garrison. She saw a flash of red hair. *Jamie.* Some of the Irregulars leapt into restrain her squire. If she'd had any breath she would have ordered him to stand down. Stupid boy was going to get himself killed.

"They're going to kill her!" he yelled, just before Kieran grabbed hold of him.

Thorgulsen barked something in Guthani and she was hauled to her feet. Her surcoat was torn from her and the straps on her armour were cut. Piece by piece, Thorgulsen threw her plate to the Guthlanders. A hirth helped her to the ground with a kick to her uninjured knee and her wrists were bound behind her back.

"You're a skinny wench without all that tin, Stenna, here—let me help you."

The Thane reached down, coiled her braids around his fist and dragged her to her knees. A dull pain ran down her leg. Cheered on by his hirths, Thorgulsen drew his knife, and hacked off her braids. She fell. The Thane held his trophies aloft for all to see before throwing them at Jamie's feet.

"There you go boy," he growled, "something on account. I'll send you the rest when we've had our sport."

Jamie tore free of Kieran's grip and launched himself at the Guthlander who was standing ready, knife in hand. Alyda tried to get up, but something hard hit her in the side of the head and sent her sprawling face-down into the dirt. She looked up to see Kieran punch Jamie in the back of the head, dropping her squire like a stone. Kieran grabbed him and threw him over his shoulder. In the same motion he scooped up her braids, tucked them into his belt and fixed the Thorgulsen with a knife-eyed stare.

Telvier daintily sniffed a sprinkle of snuff from the back of his hand. "Time for you to leave perhaps?" he suggested to Trenham.

For the second time that day, Trenham agreed with the Suvian. He ordered the Irregulars to move the Antians out. There was nothing he could do for Ali Stenna. She quite literally, had signed her own death warrant. He'd make sure her people got away safely—not because he owed her anything; their account was square, but the Irregulars had a reputation to maintain. That explanation might satisfy Kiri, but in his heart he knew it was a lie.

He marched the garrison away from the Arth in double time. Behind them, the cheering Guthani dragged Ali Stenna to the gates of the barbican, where they threw a rope through the bars of the raised portcullis.

He understood why she'd sacrificed herself, but it sat ill with him that she was going to die and he couldn't save her. Even if he had the numbers to overcome Telvier's cutthroats and the Guthlanders, he couldn't violate the Free Company Charter. To do so would condemn his entire company and he couldn't do that, not even to save someone he liked.

Death when it came would be a welcome release. She'd seen the Queen and the garrison safe, now she wanted the Guthani to just get on with it.

Thorgulsen's snow-pale eyes glared at her from beneath his heavy brows. He folded his arms. Was he waiting for her to say something? Perhaps he thought she'd beg for her life. If so, she hoped he was holding his breath. He barked something in Guthani. A course noose was fastened around her neck. Her blood ran cold, pumped ice through her veins. She shivered.

"Any last words, Steelskin?" he sneered.

She looked him in the eye;—saw the hate burning within those pale orbs, and smiled. "You lose."

Thorgulsen gave a sharp nod to the hirths holding the other end of the rope. The noose tightened. Panic gripped her as the rough cords bit into her neck and slowly closed her throat. Fighting for a breath she couldn't draw, she was hoisted off the ground. Her lungs began to burn. Thunder roared in her ears, her head felt like it was going to burst. The world turned scarlet.

A cheer rang round the castle when they hung the Steel-skin. Garuld would sing of how she'd whimpered like a whipped dog at the end. At least, that would be the version he'd sing for Kasper Thorgulsen. The yarn he'd spin in the inns and halls beyond the Thane's lands would be different. Then he would sing of how the knight had looked Thorgulsen in the eye and laughed in his face before he killed her. Neither was the truth, not quite.

She had only smiled at the end, but for the sake of drama he would embellish that small detail, sew a little more colour into the tapestry. He didn't think it would anger her spirit. The Talespinner pulled off his helm and ran his hand though his hair before wandering into the Arth to listen to what tales the stones had to tell him.

Chapter Seventeen

"I'll never forgive you for this, Iris!" Prince Talin hissed at Lady Berwick who was dragging him along the narrow trail.

"I know, Highness, but I gave Lady Ali my word that I'd see you safe and as I have mentioned before—she scares me more than you do."

"She's going to die, Bear, they all are."

She sighed, and shook her head. "I know. I'm sorry, Tal."

Garian was keeping an eye on the Prince and his friend in case Lady Berwick misplaced her loyalty and let him go. If she did, he'd run straight back to the Arth and he'd have to go get him, and he did not want to go back there. Garian didn't blame the Prince—he'd have done exactly the same thing if Suli was there, but then, he wasn't the heir to the throne.

"When will we be turning north, Captain Tain?" the Queen asked.

"We aren't, Majesty. The fighting near the border is too fierce." *And balanced on a knife's edge.*

Thea frowned. "But you said…You lied to Captain Stenna?"

The last thing he wanted was to explain his actions. He had more pressing concerns, like keeping her and her sons alive, but he couldn't duck answering his Queen.

He kept his voice down. He didn't want the Prince to hear; he was angry enough. "If the Captain is taken alive, they'll try to find out where you are, Majesty. If she doesn't know she can't tell them, and—if pressed, she'll tell them a lie that she believes to be the truth. It was a necessary deception."

"I understand. So where are we going, Captain Tain?"

"We've been offered sanctuary in a place known only to the Vodoni. It's very safe, Majesty. We should be there by nightfall." He bowed. "If you would excuse me, I need to check the trail."

Before she could question him further, he dropped back and scanned the trail behind them. He knew it was clear; Pytre and Lhazinia were circling the group as they moved and nothing would get past those two. He'd just wanted to avoid having to answer any more bloody questions. As much as it had been necessary, it didn't feel right abandoning all those people. He rarely felt guilt over what he did because it was always for the greater good, to protect the kingdom. He just couldn't forget the look on Stenna's face—of seeing the moment when the knight's hopes had died.

It took less time for the Steelskin to stop dancing on the end of the rope than Thorgulsen would have liked. When she went limp he ordered them to let her down. The hirths let go of the rope, it whipped through the portcullis. She hit the cobbles and lay there, as still as a corpse. He wasn't about to let her off so easily, and ordered one of the hirths to loosen the noose. A moment later, she coughed and gasped for breath.

"You had me worried for a while there, Steelskin." Thorgulsen laughed with his hirths as the knight fought her way back to life. "Send for the Priest," he ordered.

The Priest picked his way carefully through the debris on the bridge. Thorgulsen noted how he held his robe clear of the filth with one hand, and pressed a kerchief over his nose and mouth with the other. Crossing the body-choked moat was not a pleasant experience, not even for a man who was as intimately familiar with death as the Priest.

"Of course I've heard of him; his work for the Brotherhood is well known...in certain circles," said Telvier, as though Thorgulsen was interested in his prattle. "I've never had the pleasure of meeting him in the flesh. I must say, his taste in clothes is rather drab. A good cut, and expensive cloth but the colour is... uninspiring."

Thorgulsen shook his head. "You're worse than a fucking woman."

"Fucking women is precisely why I care about my appearance, Thane. In nature the male with the finest plumage attracts the most luscious mate."

"Male sea drakes look like flying turds. The females are iridescent."

"He has such a kindly face, don't you think? almost saintly—like the Eklesiasti himself," Telvier smiled.

Thorgulsen thought he looked particularly ordinary, as befitted a spy and assassin. His hair was close cropped and greying, age and overindulgence had comfortably, but not excessively, rounded his belly. He saw them and waved.

Telvier flourished his handkerchief. "I must say, this is a rare privilege. It isn't often I meet anyone with a worse reputation than my own."

Thorgulsen laughed.

"Ah, Thane Kasper," said the Priest, dabbing his forehead with the neat white square. "The gods have smiled upon us; his eminence will not forget your co-operation."

"Not at all, Priest. The information you gave me was good. Now I need to you to work your—" Thorgulsen was about to say 'magic' until he remembered what the Brotherhood thought about it. "...use your skills, to find out where the Queen is."

"Of course, of course. It is the least I can do. Captain Stenna has been a most awkward fish to land."

"I imagine the bounty his Holiness has placed on her head must be quite substantial to tempt *you* out of Suvia," Telvier purred.

Thorgulsen watched them size each other up like two vipers meeting on a path. The Priest's mouth curved into a tight smile.

"And this must be the poor misguided wretch." The Priest went over to the Steelskin and toed her onto her back. He sighed heavily and shook his head.

"Call me old fashioned, but I like to hang people *after* I've questioned them, not *before*."

Thorgulsen shrugged and smoothed his moustaches. "She annoyed me."

The Priest prodded her bruised throat, she gave a ragged cough. "So it would seem. How long do I have?"

"Until this time tomorrow at the latest. After that it won't matter what she knows."

The Priest frowned, his lips distended in an ugly pout. He wiped his hand on her shirt. "That really isn't very long. I may have to be *unsubtle;* results therefore may be less than precise."

"Do what you have to."

"Very well. If you could have her taken to the dungeon, I'll get started right away."

Alyda was dragged down a narrow flight of steps. The hard edges scraped her shoulders, her head bounced from one foot-hollowed depression to the next.

The dank old dungeon hadn't been used for its original purpose in years, but it still retained some vestiges of a prison. A sliver of daylight squeezed through a narrow slit cut high on the wall—impossible to see out of even if she'd been on her feet. Seized by a sudden urge to vomit, she rolled over and retched blood and bile onto the slime-sheened flagstones.

A large fireplace stood dormant on the same wall as the stairs she'd just been dragged down. Set in the floor by the hearth was the rusted ring of a trapdoor. The room was cut in half by an old iron grill. Piles of crates and old barrels were stacked on the far side of it.

Flea poked his head out of the broken side of one of the crates and looked at her. Her heart sank. He shouldn't be here; shouldn't see this. As though sensing her displeasure, he ducked back inside the crate. She prayed that he stayed there.

Time passed. She drifted, semi-conscious, through dreams and nightmares until slow, deliberate footfalls echoed down the stairwell, bringing the world back into painful focus. She recognised the polished shoes peeking from beneath the hem of the black wool robe. It was the one Thorgulsen had called, Priest.

"*This* is their dungeon?" the Priest sighed heavily. "No rack, no implements—primitive. I'll have to improvise." He walked over to the fireplace and slid a poker from the dusty rack by the hearth.

"You there…" He pointed the poker at one of the Guthani who'd brought her down. "Get a fire going, and bring more torches. And you—" He waved the poker at the other one, "get some rope and tie her to that." He gestured to the grill dividing the room.

Alyda was hauled to her feet and shoved against the grill. The hirth began to tie her, but the Priest muttered something in Suvian and huffily shooed her away.

"Not like that, you fucking oaf," he snapped, oblivious to the venomous glare the hirth gave him.

Alyda didn't have the strength to fight when he ordered her stripped. He explained in great detail to the bored looking warriors exactly how he wanted her bound and why. She knew the speech was for her benefit and pretended not to listen. A cold breeze squeezed through the narrow window. She shivered. The Priest gave a smug little grin, like he'd personally ordered the wind to blow.

"Yes it is a little chilly down here, isn't it? Forgive my terrible manners, Captain Stenna. My name is Alden Barziner, you might have heard of me? No? No matter. Some people call me Priest, perhaps you've…No? Ah, well, never mind. You know, I've been following your exploits for quite some time, ever since his Eminence asked me to…*redeem* you. I'm only a lay brother of the Order, but, and I do not wish to sound boastful…" He gave an empty chuckle. "I have a gift, a way of helping sinners unburden themselves. I tried to lighten your mortal load in Weyhithe when you returned from Suvia. Alas, my agent failed me. So I was forced to come myself, do the job properly." He brushed a strand of hair from her face; let his fingers trail across her cheek.

She refused to flinch. He smiled, evidently conscious of her effort.

"This has been quite a trial for me. I have a weak chest and the damp Antian climate does me no good at all. But now that we've finally met, in the flesh as it were, I cannot tell you how glad I am that I made the journey. Oh, listen to me! Chattering away and you're shivering like a newborn lamb. Don't worry, *Alyda*; I'll soon warm you up." The smile vanished like it was never there. He walked over to the fire and thrust the poker into the growing coals.

Alyda fixed her gaze on the wall above the fireplace and ignored the clank and scrape of metal. She forced herself to explore the landscape of cracks and fissures, the mottled patches of multi-hued damp that had colonized the dripping walls. There were a dozen shades of green, pale yellows and shining black. Barziner drew a blade from his sleeve.

Her gut reaction was to fight the ropes. He made a satisfied noise in his throat. She took a breath, stopped struggling. *Hard as iron, cold as stone. You are the Captain of the Hammer. You will not give in to fear!* The Priest came over, leaned against the grill beside her, so close she could smell the vinegary tang of wine on his breath. *Don't look at him.* She fixed her gaze on the wall above the fireplace, caught the gleam of steel out of the corner of her eye. *Do not fucking look!*

"Captain, you and your knights were very brave; no one could have fought harder for their people. It was a truly heroic effort—given how these things are measured. But you've done enough." He leaned closer, his hot breath washed against the inflamed skin of her neck. *Don't look...*

"If you tell me where Queen Thea and her sons are, I give you my word—I'll send you back to your company, alive, and intact. There is a small matter of confessing that you're a witch, but all that I require for that is a signature. I'll even take care of that rather painful looking knee for you. I must say, you show remarkable strength even to be standing on it." He dropped his voice to a whisper. "A good *and* bad thing,—being strong. Trust me; no one knows this better than I. Now, what say you?"

Her throat was raw and swollen. Just breathing was an effort, but she managed to find breath enough to hiss,

"Never."

He laughed; it was a hard, ugly sound. "That's exactly what I thought you'd say! I'm in the wrong business. I should have been a fucking seer. Oh, this simply won't work. There you are, a little battered and bruised, but still a very handsome woman. I have to confess, 'tis quite a distraction."

Without warning, he slashed her across the face. It was such a casual act of violence, little more than a reflex that it took a moment for the pain to register. When it did—when the blood began to flow—it burned. She roared an animal cry of agony.

"That's better." Barziner wiped the blade on his robe. "Now, if you would excuse me for a little while, Alyda. I must speak with Thane Kasper. While I'm away, I'd like you to consider what else I can take from you, as I have your beauty. Hopefully it will encourage you to be sensible and tell me where the Queen is."

For the first time in her adult life Alyda felt helpless. She fought the ropes, wild with pain and impotent rage. Time passed and her anger ebbed with her strength, leaving her drained. Her cheek throbbed and she desperately wanted to shift position and take the weight off her injured leg, but she couldn't move an inch.

The bar of light in the narrow window turned black. The hirths were talking quietly by the fire. For the most part they'd ignored her after Barziner left, so it came as a surprise when one of them came over and tipped a water skin to her mouth and gestured for her to drink. The cold water stung her ravaged lip, but quenched her raging thirst. Speaking was too painful, so she nodded her thanks. The Guthani said something she didn't understand before re-joining his companion by the fire.

Alyda would have fallen asleep had she not heard Barziner's steady footfall on the steps. He came in carrying the handle of a woodsman's axe. His affable smile twisted into a grimace when he saw a splash of water on the floor in front of her.

"Which one of you did this?" he snarled.

"I did," growled the Guthani who'd given her the water.

"I ordered you not to even fucking look at her, let alone give her a fucking drink! What next?" He gestured grandly. "A comfy bed and a feather quilt? Go, get out! And send someone who can follow simple orders."

The hirth strolled from the dungeon. Seeing him lose his composure was a small victory, but she'd take what she could get. Barziner forced a tight smile, but the flint in his eyes betrayed his anger. Perhaps he was angry enough to kill her? She hoped so—her dead were waiting and she was eager to join them.

"Please, forgive my outburst, Captain. It was most unseemly, but as you can see, these are less than ideal circumstances, and I do not thrive in chaos." The remaining hirth muttered something under her breath, earning a sidelong glare from Barziner. "Now, where were we, Alyda?"

She gathered her strength; she just needed to push him a little more. "I was about to tell you...to go fuck yourself." Was that enough?

"Bravado! How delightful." He wagged his finger and shook his head. "You're trying to provoke me, but I'm afraid it won't work. Only incompetence riles me to murderous levels of fury and you're playing the part of 'helpless prisoner' with consummate skill. Now, where is the Queen?" He flexed his fingers, took a firmer grip on the axe handle.

Alyda stared over Barziner's head, and fixed her gaze on the wall. A cluster of mould had spread across the old stone mantle; it looked like branching antlers, grey as old bone. Barziner rested the axe shaft on his shoulder.

"I imagine that strong legs are very important for a captain of cavalry. Now, where is the Queen, Captain Stenna?"

No, not just grey. The tips of the antlers were tinged with yellow...

Barziner drew the shaft back.

Above the antlers was a sky of shining black…
There was a soft whoosh of air.

The icy water shocked Alyda back to consciousness. She spluttered, coughed, every ragged breath was agony. She had no idea how much time had passed since Barziner had shattered her leg. That it was still dark outside was all she knew.

The pain was breath-taking, worse than anything she'd ever experienced and she couldn't escape it. Not unless she gave him what he wanted, but as much as it hurt, she wasn't remotely inclined to tell him where the Queen was. If anything, every blow he'd landed had only hardened her resolve. She just lacked the strength to tell him.

She watched Barziner dip a strip of cloth into a bucket of water and wrap it around his hand. He made a fist. Humming tunelessly, he went over to the fire and pulled the glowing poker from the coals. Steam hissed.

He came over, waved the poker in front of her face. Heat washed over her. "Those tattoos are very interesting; are they Hadami or Clan? No answer? I know you have a voice, you screamed loud enough earlier." He sighed dramatically. "Very well. Now: where is the fucking Queen?"

The captured weapons and armour had been piled in the bailey. Thorgulsen's hirths had first pick of the spoils. After much grumbling at the poor quality and worthlessness of everything, Skani chose a heavy flanged mace and a plate gauntlet for his share. A silver cloak clasp had caught Snowfoot's eye. It was in the Antian style, quite plain but well made. On the back it bore the inscription, 'To Hedden, our beloved son.' He thumbed the blood off and dropped it in his pouch. He'd also dug a scarlet surcoat out of the pile of plunder. The velvet was torn and filthy, but it was edged in thick gold braid. The Talespinner started to strip it from the velvet, but changed his mind and stuffed the whole thing in his pack.

"I'm not sleeping in here tonight," Skani declared as another agonizing scream ripped through the Arth, "not with that going on, bed or no bed. ''Tis enough to give you nightmares."

Snowfoot raised an eyebrow. "Unlike cleaving skulls with an axe from dawn to dusk?"

"That's different and I use a sword, not an axe. So come on—what have you heard, Garuld Big Ears?" The hirth grinned at his shield brother.

"I suppose it's better than '*fatty*'. As to your question; I think this little adventure is drawing to a conclusion. It's going badly in Cathlan."

"Oh," said Felar as he tested the balance of the mace with a few practice swings.

"Don't get too excited will you?"

"You haven't told me anything yet. *Badly* could mean anything. Stop building it up and just tell me. I'm not getting any younger."

"Isn't that the truth…" The Talespinner grinned, and put his back to a huge chunk of wall that had crashed into the bailey. "The Antians have blockaded the ports. Well, *the Iceheart* has blocked the ports. The Steelskins couldn't out-sail a dead cat, let alone a Guthlander. The long and the short is that Redbear's trapped in Cathlan. My guess is we'll be moving out in the next day or so, either to Pridmore, the ships and home, or gods forbid—marching to Cathlan. Try to keep it quiet will you?"

Skani's laughter was cut short by another scream, swiftly followed by another. Snowfoot thanked his ancestors that he wasn't the one being tormented by the Void-hearted Priest.

"That fucking screaming's giving me a headache." Skani shoved a dented tankard into his bag before shouldering it. "I'm off back to camp, are you coming?" He set off towards the gate.

Another scream shattered the silence.

"Aye, wait up," said the Talespinner, and hurried after his friend.

Trenham didn't dare slow the pace until he saw the lights of the monastery shining in the darkness. He'd let the garrison survivors rest long enough to stop anyone collapsing. The wounded, the old and the bairns had been put on carts. He didn't care if they sprouted wings and flew, so long as they kept moving. He wasn't being cruel; he just didn't want to be attacked in the open by a vengeful Guthani warband or that bastard dragon. He had to get them to the monastery as quickly as he could; he wanted to be rid of his burden. He was tired of looking at faces full of sorrow and eyes full of hate. If Lorhine didn't get himself killed before journey's end, then Jamie would. Why couldn't they understand? It was just business. *So why do I feel so bad?*

They arrived at the monastery in the small hours of the morning. As soon as they were within hailing distance the gates swung open and a group of priests and priestesses rushed out, their pale robes glowing in the moonlight.

Trenham approached the woman who looked like she was in charge. "Lady, these people have been travelling for hours, they're tired and—"

The priestess waved him to silence. "Later. Let's get everyone inside where there's food and warm beds waiting—quickly now."

Trenham was suddenly on his guard, acutely aware that he was in enemy territory. "You knew we were coming?"

"Bad news travels swiftly my son," she said before shepherding the weary travellers within.

The brothers and sisters of the Order of Ashania quickly and efficiently tended to the wounded. Everyone else was ushered into the refectory where cot beds had been set out and pots of hot stew bubbled in the hearth. Trenham had to go in to explain the situation and make sure the Antian's were settled, but he ordered the Irregulars to wait outside the monastery. He didn't think it wise to mix with people they'd been trying to kill.

The company set up camp on the road. When he was done, Trenham headed to his tent with a bottle of brandy, Void-bent on getting drunk. Tomorrow Kiri would set off south with the company and his report, such as it was. If nothing else it would give the Council a laugh. *Fucking dragon.* How had Ali Stenna had managed to get a dragon? All that shit about honour, did she make a deal with a demon? Sell her spirit to Old Horny? He wished he'd asked her. "Too late now," he said aloud, the booze loosening his tongue.

Kiri was sitting just outside, smoking her pipe; she flipped back the tent flap, her head haloed in smoke. "Too late for what?"

"Nothing."

She drew on the pipe. "Tell me more about this nothin'."

"I was just thinking that it was too late to ask Ali Stenna where she got the fucking dragon." It felt odd, saying her name aloud.

Kiri gave a head toss of acknowledgement. She made to drop the tent flap, but didn't. Her face screwed up into a thoughtful frown. She took a deep drag on the pipe; scarlet bloomed in the clay bowl.

"Whassup?" he asked and offered her the bottle. She waved it away with the long stem of the pipe.

"I didn't want to tell you. 'Thought you might do some-thin' stupid."

"Nice to know you have faith in me, Lieutenant. What didn't you tell me?" he asked even though he really didn't want to know. The brandy was making him comfortably numb, and he didn't want to spoil it with bad news.

"They didn't kill Stenna. Remoya was scoutin' back, like you ordered. He saw 'em cut her down. She was still alive. Sorry, Boss."

"Why didn't you…? Nevermind. Kon Stenna's going to kill me."

"Don't go."

"I gave her my word."

"She won't know."

"I will. I might be a poor friend, but I'm no coward." He finished the bottle, closed his eyes and saw red.

Half a horse was slowly roasting in one of the hearths in the Great Hall. Hirths diced for spoils, while they waited for the meat to cook. Thorgulsen paced, nobody bothered him. Even Gathorl had made himself scarce. *Wise man that Gathorl.* He wanted to go back to camp, crawl into bed with Bethanglyn and rut, and then he remembered. *She's gone.* It felt like a stone in his gut, sinking deeper into him with every hour that she was missing. *Fucking woman.* She hadn't taken anything with her—no spare clothes or coin; nothing. She hadn't told anyone she was going either. He'd beaten seven shades of shit out of her servants, but they didn't know anything. The mad cunt had just taken to her heels in the middle of enemy territory.

He wasn't surprised she'd gone, not really. What sur-prised him was that she'd stayed so long.

Another scream died away, then nothing. He'd better go find out if the Priest had got anything out of the Steel-skin, before the slimy little prick killed her.

The hirths in the dungeon stumbled to their feet and made a show of being on guard when he came in. Thorgulsen told them to go get some food, give their ears a rest. Barziner was sitting at a table, neatly folding creases into his bloodied kerchief. He inclined his head to Thorgulsen. The Thane grunted, but his attention was drawn to the bloody body tied to the bars. If he didn't know it was the Steelskin, he wouldn't have recognised her.

"It's quite surprising what you can do with a fire iron, a fruit knife and an axe handle," Barziner quipped.

Thorgulsen shrugged and took a closer look at the Priest's handiwork. She was still breathing. "So what? I can mess someone up with a jagged rock. Breaking a body is easy, have you got her to talk?"

The Priest gave a sulky pout. "Almost, Thane Kasper, almost." He steepled his fingers. "I sense the Captain is on the verge of unburdening herself. It has not been easy working in these conditions, I—"

"Fuck's sake, Priest, we're running out of time." Thorgulsen was irritated as much by the man as the lack of results.

Barziner picked up his knife and marched over to the Steelskin. "I really wish we had more time together, Alyda." He flicked her matted hair from her swollen and bloody face with the tip of the blade. Her eyelids flickered. "I don't feel you've seen the best of me. It's because I hate to be rushed." He cut the ropes, she dropped. "Thane, if you would be so kind?"

Thorgulsen carried the Steelskin over to the table. The Priest sat down opposite them.

"If you could hold her, Thane Kasper, we're almost there now." He smiled.

Thorgulsen decided he really didn't like Barziner; there was something about the way he was smiling, the flush in his cheeks, and the brightness in his eyes. He was enjoying his work in entirely the wrong way.

Pain ripped through her leg, dragging her back to consciousness. She was kneeling beside a table, arm outstretched, held down by...was it that pig-fucker Thorgulsen? She wasn't sure; her vision, such as remained, was blurred.

She didn't have strength left to dread whatever new torment Barziner was about to inflict. Pain was the only measure of her existence: when it began, and when it stopped.

"If you could hold the Captain's hand down please, Thane Kasper. You are right handed, aren't you, Alyda?" Barziner wiped the knife on his kerchief. Thorgulsen pressed her right hand flat against the table, scars against scars.

"Now, Captain, you may not be able to ride again, but at the moment you can still wield a sword. I know how important that is to a warrior. If you tell me where the Queen is, I'll leave you your fingers. If not..." The Priest made a chopping motion with the knife.

"Don't be stubborn, woman," Thorgulsen growled in her ear. "You've proved you're tough; now prove you're smart."

Alyda blinked tears from the eye she could still open and shook her head. Barziner dug the tip of his knife into the table and rested the edge of the blade against her little finger. She tried to move her hand, but Thorgulsen held her fast.

"Please, Captain. I urge you to think about this carefully. You're still a young woman; is your life, everything you value—*everything you are*, behind you, or before you?"

Alyda struggled against Thorgulsen's grip, but even on a good day she'd be hard pressed to beat him in a contest of strength, and this was far from a good day. She could hardly think past the pain that wracked her body or beyond the fear of what lay ahead. But one word remained clear in her mind. It was a small word, but contained within it all of the defiance she had left. She drew a long, painful breath and said,

"No."

Thorgulsen held her. Barziner shook his head; like a parent who had failed to reason with a disobedient child. She looked in his eyes; saw nothing but her own bloody reflection. *Don't look down, don't look down, don't—*

He severed the tip of her finger.

The pain was excruciating, and far beyond the limits of her failing endurance. *Enough! Gods, enough!* She begged him to stop.

The Priest put the knife down. "Of course, my child. Now, where is the Queen?"

Between great wracking sobs, the Steelskin told Barziner that someone called Tain had taken the Queen north to meet up with Daris in Cathlan. The Priest was very patient during what he called, 'confession'. He gave her water and gently coaxed her back to consciousness whenever she passed out. When she began to repeat herself for the third time it was obvious that she'd told them everything. The Priest sat back and smiled at the Thane.

"Just one last thing," he said, taking a parchment and quill from the pocket of his robe, "and then you can rest, Alyda." He dipped the quill in the blood that had pooled around the severed digit. "Sign here, Alyda. Ah—let me help you." He wrapped her mutilated hand around the quill. Fresh pain ripped through her hand as he scratched her name on the vellum. "There. That will make the Eklesiasti a *very* happy man. He had nightmares about you, Captain. You quite vexed his Holiness. All better now though. Thane—the Captain looks tired. We should let her rest, don't you think?" Barziner tucked the parchment into his robe before going over to the trap door and hauling on the ring.

Thorgulsen carried the Steelskin over to the hole. He didn't mind the Priest's presumption—he'd got her to talk and dead was dead, no matter who ordered it. He peered into the darkness; he could just make out the rippling gleam of flowing water far below.

"You lose, Stenna," he said, and dropped her in the hole. There was a distant splash. The Priest slammed the trap door closed.

"Well there you have it. I must be going now, Thane. If you could provide an escort to Brindport as we agreed, I would be most grateful. The roads are quite hazardous at the moment." He put on his robe and patted the pocket with the parchment in.

"Of course. Safe journey, Priest."

"And you, my son. Good luck with the hunt!" The torturer skipped up the stairs, humming tunelessly.

Thorgulsen took a last look around the blood-splattered chamber, his gaze coming to rest on the trap door. He loathed the Steelskin, but that was a poor death for a warrior. He wondered if her spirit would find its way to her gods, or if it would lurk here, trapped forever in the place where she'd met her sorry end.

Hanser's cavalry charged off. They would hunt the Queen to Death's Halls if need be, their dead Thane's honour demanded no less. While his hirths feasted to their victory and sent lost comrades to the Land of shadows with fire and song, Thorgulsen watched the cavalry ride into the dawn. He didn't rate their chances of tracking down a

- 442 -

handful of people who could be anywhere between there and Cathlan. The battle had been won, at a price. The war…probably not. *Shit and blood, that's how it always ends.*

"Quite a talent, being able to torture and maim like Barziner," said Telvier, his expression and tone of voice a study in ambiguity.

Thorgulsen grunted. "Do you want to extend your contract?"

"Ah, well. I'd like to, but I already have work lined up… elsewhere. We shall be moving out on the 'morrow."

"You sure?"

"Quite sure. Thank you, Thane."

Thorgulsen eyed the Suvian, contemplated if it would be more trouble than it was worth to run him through and save his gold. While he was thinking about it, a hirth he didn't recognise barged into the tent. Blood streaked his beard; the man looked on the verge of passing out.

"My Lord, I have a message from Thane Redbear," he said and handed him a crumpled letter.

When Thorgulsen finished reading it he tossed it into the brazier. "It seems we're going to Cathlan."

"Prince Jerim has won?" Telvier asked.

"No, he's crow food, and Redbear's fighting for his life. I must go and either aid, or avenge my kinsman. You sure you don't want to come, Telvier?"

"Quite sure." He patted his stomach. "Too much glory for my humble tastes." The mercenary chuckled softly. "So, Stenna held out long enough after all? One has to appreciate tenacity, even in one's enemies. Don't you agree, Thane?"

Thorgulsen didn't answer. "Garuld!" he bellowed. The Talespinner stumbled into the tent. He looked half asleep.

"My Lord?"

"Rouse the camp, we march in an hour."

"What kind of a name is *Iris*?" Pytre asked her, a teasing smile on his full, kissable, lips. He was a handsome fellow, a little on the wild side, but that only added to his appeal. There was something about him, a touch of something dangerous and yet, terribly familiar. He handed Bear a slab of hardly-cooked venison. Just how she liked it.

"It's a family name, has been for generations, but my friends call me Bear."

He nodded approvingly. "That's much better. I'm going to scout ahead to the valley. You can come with me if you like? The others must be blindfolded, but there won't be any point for you."

Bear didn't have the faintest idea what he was talking about, but she found him utterly captivating, and a welcome distraction from Talin's hateful gloom. Damn his eyes, there was only so much she could take. It wasn't her fault that everything had gone to shit, but he was as angry with her as if she'd caused the war. She tore off a mouthful of meat and tossed the rest before jumping lightly to her feet. "Lead on, sir."

A knot of anger tightened Talin's stomach as he watched Bear follow the Hadami into the trees. He didn't care if he never saw her again. His heart was hardened to Bear Berwick for what she'd done.

Night was fast approaching and according to Tain, they were near their destination. His brother offered him a drink from a waterskin. Talin shook his head.

"You need to drink something, Tal," Olin pleaded, "please?"

His brother had cheered up considerably since they escaped the Arth. Talin didn't begrudge him the relief; he just couldn't share it. Not while Alyda was still in danger.

"Olin, please untie me. If you love me, let me go. I'm begging you."

Olin chewed his lip. "I can't, Tal. I promised moth—"

"Please, Oli! For Asha's sake, I'm your brother. I've always been there for you, now I'm asking you to do this one thing for me."

Talin could sense Oli's resolve starting to weaken. He tried to be patient while he waited for him to make up his mind. Oli stole a furtive look at the small group of fugitives. Talin did the same. Tain and his woman were talking with their mother, Bear had gone off with the male gypsy and the other Hadami was out scouting somewhere. Lady Beria was nursing her son and staring right at them. She put the child on a pile of freshly cut bracken, and much to Talin's dismay, came over.

She ignored him and turned to Oli. "I know what you're planning. You can't let him go, Highness. If you do he'll die. Do you want to kill your brother, Prince Olin?"

"Lady Beria, be silent, I command you!" Talin never spoke like that to anyone, but he had to get back to Ali and now was probably the only chance he'd have before it was too late. Beria looked at him with tear-washed eyes and snorted.

"Do you think I care? My life has been torn apart; all that's left is lying over there." She gestured to her son. "The rest is rotting in a pit at Gallen Arth. So you'll forgive me, but I'm beyond being cowed by princely commands. I'm not beyond stopping another mother's son from running to his death."

She turned back to Olin and took his hands in hers. "If you truly love your brother, you will make sure he stays bound tight and you will not let him out of your sight until this evil has passed. Do you understand, Olin? Only..." she paused, swallowed hard, "Only death waits for him at Gallen Arth. If you let him go, you'll be killing him as surely as if you stabbed him yourself."

The colour drained from Olin's face. He nodded gravely and turned to his brother. "I'm sorry, Tal. I can't."

After they'd rested, Suli led them deeper into the wood. Unlike the forest around Gallen Arth, the trees here were small and crooked. Their bent spines twisted together, their warty branches entangled. The ground between them was littered with tumbled stones, carved with faded patterns and robed in moss. When they reached the end of the trail, Suli ripped some makeshift blindfolds from the lining of her doublet.

Garian decided it wasn't treason to keep quiet about exactly where they were going. As far as the Queen, her sons and Lady Beria were concerned they were just going to a hidden valley. He'd lead them around the woods to disorientate them and then Suli would open the gateway to the valley and safety—in the Void. *The fucking Void! I must be mad.* His stomach rolled. Could he really take the Queen and heirs to a place he'd always believed to be the realm of evil? Could he afford not to?

When the others were blindfolded, he led them along a winding deer path before bringing them back to where they'd started. Suli had been carrying Lady Vorsten's baby, she passed the child to him before going over to a pair of stubby oaks off to the side of the path. They didn't look any different to any of the others.

The child gripped his chin and laughed. Garian watched Suli run her hands down the trunks of both trees. He could hear her whispering, but couldn't make out what she was saying. When she was done, she stepped aside and took the infant from him. Smiling, she gestured for him to walk between the trees. Garian drew his knife. Nothing had changed; there were no glowing runes or magical light, just two trees. That didn't stop his hackles rising. It was the Void. He took one last look at Suli and walked through.

The first thing that hit him was the smell. It was late autumn when he stepped between the trees; on the other side a warm breeze kissed his face, carrying with it the sweet scent of a flower filled meadow. Crouching low, he took in the view with a sweeping scan, then again, more slowly; just to make sure there wasn't anything with teeth or claws waiting to rip him apart. The two oaks he'd just walked between formed an arch leading into tangled undergrowth and darkness; they were also flanked by an impenetrable thicket that seemed to mark some kind of barrier but that was just a guess, his mind trying to make sense of what he'd been told and what he could see. For all he knew, none of it was real.

Overhead, the moon hung low and full. The argent sphere was reflected in a wide, glassy mere that lay a few yards from the portal. The pool was fringed with a cres- cent of graceful trees the likes of which he'd never seen, not even in books. They had clean, white trunks that shone like fresh snow. Elegant upswept boughs forked like antlers and darkened from pure white through shades of silver-grey to deep, gleaming black at the tips. The leaves were sickle shaped and silvery white. They sparkled in the moonlight as though rimed with frost.

Beyond the pool he could see a rolling meadow, dot- ted here and there with stands of the same luminous trees. *How big was this place?* It was beautiful. Hardly what he'd imagined the home of demons would look like. Within the snow trees by the pool, he saw dark shadows weaving between the trunks. He kept low, peered into the darkness trying to make out what they were. Suli appeared beside him. She was leading Prince Talin, still bound and blind- folded. He barred her way with his arm, and motioned for her to be quiet.

"There's something moving in the trees," he whispered.

"Don't worry; it's only 'Zia, Pytre, and Lady Berwick. They're staying out of the way so they don't scare the others."

"Why did they change?" Garian asked. "Why didn't they stay human?" He hated not knowing what was going on, and wasn't entirely comfortable with the idea of three shapeshifters lurking in the shadows. This place was making him twitchy.

"It's difficult for them in here. I'll explain later."

With that, she ushered the Prince to one side and went back through for the others. It was so strange, watching her walk between the trees, and then suddenly vanish. Garian removed the Prince's blindfold, but left his hands tied. They waited in icy silence for the others to come through.

When Lady Beria's blindfold was removed he quickly handed the child back to his mother. Lady Beria peeled back the blankets and gasped. Garian was immediately on his guard, but then he realised Lady Beria was laughing… at her faintly glowing son.

Garian got a closer look, sure that his eyes were playing tricks on him. They weren't. The child was glowing softly, but that wasn't all. His babyish features looked more refined, and his eyes had turned impossibly blue—like Suli's had. Other than the startling change in his appearance he seemed perfectly well, and giggled appreciatively at all the attention. He just didn't look quite human anymore.

Beria laughed. "Oh, Cass, I wish you could see this, my darling." Tears streamed down her cheeks and she hugged her son.

The nameless river that flowed beneath the Arth had narrowed over the centuries. Alyda slammed into the deep
bank of silt and sludge that had built up over scores of
years.

The shock of landing half in the icy water brought her
back to consciousness. She was lying up to her waist in
the water. Her ruined legs rocked gently in the sluggish
current. Instinct took over, and she began to claw her way
up the muddy bank, driven by the animal urge to survive.
Cold crept into her bones and numbed her flesh. She shivered violently until darkness claimed her.

She was falling into unending blackness. There was no
pain.

"I've been waiting for you," said a voice as ancient as the
bones of the earth, as powerful as a storm.

This is a dream. She ignored the voice; fell faster, the
pain of her ruined body a distant memory.

"Do you come to me now; through air, fire and water?"

She didn't want to talk, she just wanted to fall.

*"Speak—blood of my blood. You have threaded the path;
do you give yourself to me now in this sacred place?"*

She didn't know what it wanted, but a tiny part of her
thought she ought to. Whatever it was, she didn't want to
remember, she just wanted to fall, but she could feel it near
her, waiting. It wasn't going to leave her alone until she
gave an answer. She forced her eyes open. There was only
blackness, so complete, she wasn't sure she'd opened her
eyes at all.

"No, I damn well don't," she mumbled into the mud
before slipping back into unconsciousness.

The Anvil and three companies of infantry tore through
Gallen Forest. When the King had released them, Vanen
had done more than Vorbek could have asked to get them
back to Antia in time to relieve the Hammer and the Lanc-

ers. She'd even risked her ships by bringing them up river as far as Weyhithe. The black columns of smoke rising over the forest and the circling flocks of carrion told him their efforts had probably been in vain.

The poached road leading to the Arth was littered with debris, but there were no bodies, which was a good sign. Vorbek sent scouts off to follow the mass of tracks and find out who had gone where. He took the Anvil and the foot soldiers on to the Arth. The smell of death carried by the wind warned him of what lay beyond the trees. When they reached the edge of the clearing the Captain of the Anvil called a halt.

War had harrowed the battlefield, seeded the ground with ravaged corpses that lay mired in filth. It was a vile harvest, ripe for the crows to reap. Althus cast a hopeful glance to the blackened turrets to see if any standards still flew there. Today was not a day for miracles. With a heavy heart, he signalled for the company to ride within.

Inside the Arth the destruction was complete. Fires smouldered in the ruins, and the bailey was filled with rubble and bodies. The curtain wall was dressed in fire black and blood red, a cruel parody of the lost knights' colours,

"Arno!" Vorbek summoned his second. "I want this place searched for…for anything." Arno didn't answer. Vorbek swung round. "Arno! Did you hear me? I…"

Arno was looking at a child, standing by the barbican; he couldn't have been older than five or six.

"Perhaps today is a day for miracles after all," Vorbek muttered.

"In here!" the boy shouted and hared off down a flight of steps next to the gatehouse.

Althus cursed, leapt from his horse and charged after him.

The steps led down into a dank chamber, the embers of a fire still glowed in the hearth. Althus drew his sword. The floor and the walls were splattered with blood, cut sections of rope dangled from a grilled partition wall. It smelled of burnt flesh. Terrible things had been done here. Vorbek lit a torch from the dying fire. The child was standing beside an open trap door, he gestured urgently for Vorbek to come over.

"She's down there!" The child pointed into the blackness. "I lifted the lid and I tried to tie the rope so I could get her, but I couldn't do the tie, and the rope fell in."

Vorbek was a soft touch when it came to children. Gods only knew what horrors the little mite had seen. He reached out to the boy, but he danced away from Vorbek's hand—dangerously close to the edge of the hole.

Vorbek froze. "Easy now, little man," He lowered his hands. "It's alright. I won't hurt you."

"You have to get her," The boy demanded, a determined frown set on his dirty little face, his heels hanging over the edge of the hole. "Come see, come see!"

"Alright, lad, alright. Now don't you move; I'll take a look." Althus edged closer, very slowly. He peered down the hole; he couldn't see anything, but he could hear the sound of running water. He waved the torch in the darkness. When his eyes grew accustomed to the light, he thought he caught a glimpse of something pale, near a dark ribbon of flowing water.

"She's down there! Can you see the red knight? You have to hurry before the clouds come into her eyes." The child bounced excitedly beside Althus.

His heart skipped a beat. "What did you say, boy?"

The boy took a deep breath. "The Captain of the Hammer is down there."

"Sir, perhaps we should send someone else down first?" Arno ventured, "someone smaller—Keris maybe?"

Vorbek tossed his breastplate on the floor of the crowded dungeon. "Just hang onto the blasted rope, Lieutenant."

Vorbek stripped down to his shirt, breeches and boots, and strapped his sword across his back. Even without his armour it took three of the Anvil's biggest knights and two stout ropes to lower him into the hole. Distance was hard to judge in the near total darkness, but by his estimation the water was about twenty feet below the trap door. Vorbek's torch spluttered, hungry for air, but the flame steadied and his eyes became accustomed to the gloom. He was in an underground cavern, half filled with silt. He corrected himself as he went deeper and saw more. It wasn't a cavern; it was a chamber.

It must have been part of an earlier incarnation of the Arth. Crumbling stumps of columns jutted out of the mud and patches of ancient, painted plaster clung to the walls. When he reached the bottom he sank up to his calves in the cold slurry. He swung the torch towards where he'd spotted what might have been a body. Less than six feet away, he saw it, and his hopes were crushed. Whoever they were had their ruined back to him, and short hair. He was just about to shout up and tell them it wasn't Alyda when he caught a glimpse of a tattoo through the mud and blood. To a Tamalak, tattoos were as individual as a face. It *was* Alyda.

He thrust the torch into the mud, rushed over and scooped her out of the muck."Hang on Shorty," he whispered. She groaned. Shocked and elated, he shouted up, "She's alive!"

After the voice went away, she stopped falling and began to dream. In the dream she saw a stag running through a silver river beneath a lustrous moon. Someone spoke. Their voice was loud, commanding, but it wasn't the Stormbreaker.

It was Althus.

What's he doing in my dream? She opened her eyes and saw towers of smoke rising into the sky. Then the pain returned, and it was vengeful. She cried out. Someone fed her sweet wine. The pain went away again. She dreamed of a stag racing through a silver river beneath a lustrous moon...

They laid Ali by the fire in the Great Hall. Althus paced as he waited for the Company Surgeon to finish her examination. He could hardly bring himself to watch, Alyda looked more dead than alive. That the Queen had escaped was some consolation, but a lot of friends were lying in those grave pits. The surgeon covered Ali with a blanket and came over.

"Is there anything you can do, Jodi?" Althus asked her.

"Not here, Captain, and even were we elsewhere, I think she's beyond my skill, beyond the skill of most."

It wasn't in Althus to give up; being helpless put him in an ugly mood.

"The Order of Ashania has a monastery less than a day's ride from here," said Jodi. "They might be able to do something for her." She tugged her earlobe, something she did when she was worried.

"Spit it out," he prompted.

"I could give her more poppy juice..." she offered cautiously, "enough that she doesn't wake up."

He looked at Ali; clinging to life by the slenderest of threads. Perhaps that was the kindest thing they could do for her. He locked his hands behind his head. "Gods. I just don't know, Jo."

"I think it would be a kindness," said the surgeon.

Althus shook his head. "It's a kindness you give to a faithful hound, not a knight; not Alyda. I've never known her to back down from a fight; let her finish this battle on her own terms." Althus bellowed across the hall, "Arno! I want a ten knight escort to take Captain Stenna to the Ashania monastery. And form up the rest of the Company. We're going hunting."

It was raining when the cart trundled into the monastery courtyard. Jamie rushed out as soon as he saw the green and black of the knight's surcoats. Lieutenant Lorhine and Lieutenant Tristen followed him, all eager to find out the Anvil's news. Jamie was pleased to see Flea huddled under the sagging tarp covering the cart. He'd thought the child had been killed.

The boy beckoned him over. What he'd taken for a bundle of blankets, was a person. When he saw who it was he almost collapsed on the spot.

News of her survival got round quickly. Amid the ensuing chaos, Jamie kept everyone away except for the priests and priestesses who came to tend her. Lorhine eventually cleared everyone out of the infirmary who didn't have to be there, except Jamie. He refused to leave; afraid that death would take her if he let her out of his sight again. He wouldn't even leave when the brothers and sisters began tending to her awful wounds. He prowled the room much to their obvious—if unvoiced—annoyance. Later, when the poppy juice wore off, she woke up screaming in pain. He'd never heard her scream like that, it shocked him. It also made him angry, not with her; but with himself, with the world.

He gave her more poppy juice and held her until she fell asleep. People came and went like shadows; he sat by her side, willing her every shallow breath to be followed by another, and another…

"How long?" Kieran appeared at the door, a looming shadow against the torchlight, he didn't come in.

"They said it's a miracle she's lasted this long and…" He could barely force the words out. "…and that she won't last the night."

Kieran didn't say anything. Jamie went back to counting breaths. When he looked up again, the Lieutenant had gone.

He tried to pray, but there was nothing inside. He bowed his head anyway, and held the Captain's hand. The chain around his neck swung against his chest, reminding him it was there. His heart leapt; he tore it from his neck and closed shaking fingers around the Countess's gift.

He hadn't intended to fall asleep, and woke with a start. For a terrible moment he thought she'd gone, but then he saw her eyelids flicker. She was still wearing the pendent that he'd hung around her neck, proving he hadn't dreamed it. The simple wooden charm defied his every attempt to see anything magical about it, but he believed in it's power with all his heart; he had to, it was all there was.

Outside, the dawn chorus began to squawk raucous greetings to each other. He cursed the birds, and got up to close the shutters when it suddenly struck him. *It is morning, and the Captain is still alive.* Clumsy with sleep, he stumbled to the door and shouted for help. They would have to do something now. She'd held death at bay all night, he would damn well make sure they rallied—this time she would not stand alone.

"The knight insists on it, Mother. He's causing such a fuss! I didn't know what else to do." Lalin lowered her voice to a whisper. "I told him that you were very busy helping those who could be saved, but he was adamant that you come. I'm very sorry about this."

Jeneri listened to the novice gabble on. Lalin and the others had never seen casualties of war before. Shocked though they'd been, they'd done a wonderful job and had coped well with the influx; she was proud of them. Alas, Jeneri had seen it all before and it never got any easier to deal with. Lalin led her to the quiet corridor at the far end of the infirmary. It was where those deemed beyond help were taken to die in peace.

"It's alright, Lal. It would be a waste of the Goddess's gift if I only treated people who were going to live, don't you think? Although, it would make me look good." She gave Lalin a friendly wink.

"Well, yes, but I fear this warrior is beyond even your reach, Mother. She was as good as dead when they brought her in."

"There's nothing good about dead in my book. She's survived this long; perhaps it is Ashania's will that she lives. Ah, here we are." Jeneri knocked on the door and entered.

A red haired lad was sitting by the bedside. He looked up when she came in. His eyes were empty, his face bereft of emotion. Not cold, but utterly drained, everything was shutting down, even the muscles in his face. All of the survivors looked the same; they always did.

"I'm Jeneri. You must be Jamie, and this must be Alyda," she said, looking at the bruised and bandaged woman lying on the bed.

"They said she wouldn't last the night, but she has and I need you to…"

"It's alright, I'm here now."

The boy watched Jeneri closely, studied every flicker of expression that crossed her face, as she drew back the sheet and looked beneath the bandages. She made sure not to grimace.

She was born a healer, possessed of a Goddess-given gift, and if Ashania willed it, she could sometimes treat diseases and injuries that were beyond mortal skill. The girl's injuries were ugly, but not the worst she'd seen. The capacity to maim and torture was sadly not as rare as the ability to heal. The priestess took a deep breath and touched the girl's forehead.

She had to force herself not to recoil when she was assaulted by the fresh memories of violence trapped in her pain-ravaged flesh. She smiled at the boy and hoped he didn't notice that her hands were shaking. "She's hot, but not burning—that's good. There's no fever or sign of infection which is also, very good."

"But her injuries are bad?"

"They're crippling, to greater and lesser degrees. Goddess willing, I can lessen their severity." The lad looked crushed that she hadn't promised him the miracle he so desperately wanted, but she couldn't lie. She drew the blanket back over Alyda and paused. There was something else, something wholly unexpected. She ran her hands over the woman's body.

"Are you her lover?" she asked Jamie.

"Me? Gods! No. I'm her squire. I mean, I...no." He blushed as scarlet as his hair.

"I didn't mean to embarrass you. Do you know who is?" Jeneri asked.

"Aye, but it's not common knowledge. Why do you ask?"

Jeneri wondered if she should tell him. *Stick to healing Jen, and keep your own council.* "No reason. As for your Captain; some of her injuries may prove difficult to heal completely. She may not be as she was before."

"So you can you save her?"

The honest answer was that she didn't know, but he'd heard enough honesty for one day. "Goddess willing, Jamie."

Chapter Eighteen

"What have you done to me?" Bethanglyn tore aside the curtain of bronze hair to get a better look at her reflection in the grey puddle of what might have been water. Inhuman, scarlet eyes stared up at her. She rocked back on her heels, unnerved and excited by her appearance and the power she could feel coursing through her veins.

"I've replaced what you gave me, filled the hole I made in your essence with fabric of a richer weave."

"Sorcery then."

"Aye, sweetling—sorcery. I unlocked your pattern and re-wove it. Do you like it? I can change it if not."

He came up behind her pressed his naked body against hers and cupped a full pale breast in his rejuvenated hand. Her nipple hardened between his fingers, her barbed spine arched against him.

"I'm not sure. What am I now? Am I still human?"

"Does it matter? You wanted to learn, and I needed to be healed. You've fulfilled your half of the bargain, and I shall fulfil mine. Although you will find that I am a hard task master." He kissed her neck, trying to re-connect the act to the feeling of pleasure it had once given him. There was a distant stirring, not quite an erection, but closer than he'd come to one for several centuries. *All in good time.*

"So, what do you want to learn, sweetling? How to summon the Shadewalkers? Call lightning?"

"Everything." she leaned into him, hot against his cold flesh. "Teach me everything."

Feathery snow swept across the ward in a great white wave and drifted against the half built wall that enclosed the new inner bailey. It had grown at an incredible rate, but the harsh winter weather had forced work to stop for the present.

Hyram couldn't believe it would be Midwinter's Day in less than two weeks. Time passed so quickly these days. The two and a half months since the Arth had been razed had flown by in a frenzy of rebuilding and setting the kingdom back on its feet. There was still a long way to go, and much to do, but they had turned the corner. People could now look to the future in the certain knowledge that the worst was finally behind them.

Midwinter would not be an indulgent celebration this year, more a time of contemplation and remembrance. Many people had lost loved ones and were struggling with shortages and the other hardships gifted by war. Everything was set to improve once winter was behind them. Now that Herulth, the new Guthland Dragon King, had made peace with Daris, all that was left was to seal the alliance with a marriage. He wondered if he would see Merrin at Midwinter, but quickly brushed the thought aside. *Why would this year be any different to the last ten?*

He shivered and closed the shutters against the biting cold and drew the curtains. His new offices were more to his liking now that the walls were lined with bookshelves. Alas, they were quite bare. The bastards had burnt everything; his room, the tower, all gone. It would be years before the tower's more imposing replacement was finished, but already Thea's designs for a larger, and more importantly, *stronger* Arth were beginning to take shape.

Thea had bold plans for the new castle and the flinty determination to see them through. She had thrown herself into rebuilding the Arth and the city; to the extent that Hyram worried she was doing too much. He understood why. It was a distraction from the less than honourable, if totally necessary, plan she had caused him to set in motion.

He looked at the empty bookshelves and felt acutely the loss of years—centuries—of knowledge. It was nothing compared to the loss of human life…probably, but it saddened him greatly, those books were old friends.

There was a familiar knock at the door. He didn't bother to say, "Come in", the boy no longer waited to be invited.

Garian dropped his snow-dusted cloak on the floor and pulled a bundle of letters from his jerkin. He tossed them on the desk. As usual, he was scowling. Hyram snatched them up. Several were written in Prince Talin's hand and were addressed to the same person; *Captain Alyda Stenna.* The others were written by her, addressed to various people, the Prince among them. He noted that her handwriting was still little better than a child's scrawl.

Hyram swept the letters into the drawer, he'd read them later, when he wasn't under scrutiny. "What did our lay priest have to report? And he'd better not have been drunk this time."

Garian poured a glass of wine and went over to the fire. "No. He'd wisely taken heed of my previous warning and was sober when I arrived."

"Good. What did he have to say?"

His apprentice took a sip of wine and looked at him with an accusing stare. "That there wasn't much change. She's still bedridden, sick…isolated. He and the other little shit in your employ have intercepted every letter and every visitor since the First were ordered to Cathlan. Well done, My Lord." Garian raised his glass in mock salute.

"Don't you dare take that tone with me. This was necessary!" Hyram slammed his fist on the table, noting with some regret that his apprentice no longer flinched. Garian merely continued to sip his wine, and give him the lizard eye. The boy had already made it quite clear that he thought the Captain and the Prince were being treated poorly. Hyram took a deep breath, the pain in his chest a sharp reminder that he shouldn't lose his temper, not unless he wanted to spend another week confined to his bed. It also reminded him to drink the mixture of willow bark and water that had been sitting on his desk for over an hour. He swilled the milky liquid round the glass, and threw it down his throat, but still managed to taste the awful bitterness. The vile brew was almost worse than the pain.

"I'm only doing what's in the best interests of the kingdom," said Hyram, shuddering from the ghastly aftertaste of the medicine. "Thea was right to tell me. Their relationship had to be stopped. The treaty with Herulth will only hold if Talin marries one of his fucking daughters. Or do you want yearly visits from Guthani warbands?"

The boy glowered at him. "Have you tried explaining that to him?"

Ignorant pup. "No, no, no! What fool in love—even a prince, especially this one, would give up his heart's desire for the sake of a *mere* kingdom? Daris didn't, and look at the bloody trouble that's caused. No. I will not let it happen again."

"You would destroy anyone else who questioned the King's decisions."

"I am not just anyone. I am the King's Councillor!" He slapped his face into his hands. "Oh, why didn't she just die? It would have been so much easier for everyone—even her."

"Well she didn't. But you're right, her life is ruined. Even without you hammering nails into her coffin."

"So she is crippled?"

"Aye. Gustav said that Mother Jeneri's done all she can for her. He's heard that she'll probably be leaving the monastery within the month, weather permitting." Garian drained his glass. "I'm curious; what will you do then? When she's back at Trelanlith you won't be able to control what she reads and who she sees."

"Why would she go back there? What good is a knight who can't ride or hold a sword?" Hyram felt a stab in his withered conscience. *When did I become so callous?*

"She's still the Captain of the Hammer, and a hero or have you forgotten what happened at Gallen Arth? She has to resign her commission, but only after she's chosen her successor. That's how they do things."

Hyram steepled his fingers and considered the problem. He found it much harder to concentrate since his illness. His mind refused to focus like it used to; his best weapon had been blunted. Better to have lost an eye, a leg, two... "Damn it! Why can't she just disappear? Do you think she might have a relapse?" Hyram looked hopefully at his apprentice.

"No!" he gasped.

Oh, here we go. His apprentice was obviously outraged by the suggestion. *When did he become so moral? The boy who's rifled through guts before today.*

"Definitely not, and let me tell you this, my Lord; if she does have a 'relapse' as you put it, our working relationship will be over, and you and I will no longer be friends. Now before you start calculating how that will affect your schemes, let me help you out because I've already considered what you are about to. If you conclude that I need to have an 'accident' to keep me quiet, you will answer to my wife and her family, and you really don't want that, do you?"

Rigid jaw line, level gaze. The little shit means it. It was gone, he no longer feared him. The game had changed.

Hyram narrowed his eyes. "Are you threatening me, boy?" He was furious, *and* proud of his apprentice. The contempt was hard to take, but he couldn't pretend that he hadn't made him what he was.

"Just don't kill her, Sest's balls! I can't believe you're even thinking about it. Who are you trying to save the kingdom for if you kill the best of its people when they get in the way of your schemes? Why not take this to the ultimate conclusion? Why not drown all newborns! After all, some of them are bound to grow up to be traitors or get in your way. Slay them all! For the good of the kingdom, of course." The slender glass stem snapped in his fingers.

Hyram threw up his hands. "Alright, enough! It was just a thought. The relationship *must* die; I'll not be moved on that. The security of the kingdom comes above all else. This mess can never be allowed to happen again. Talin must marry a Guthlander."

Hyram sat back. He would have left it there but the sanctimonious sneer plastered across the boy's face was too provoking.

"Don't judge me, boy! Standing there, heart full of love's first flush, and a head full of idealistic nonsense. You think me unfair? Well let me tell you, the kingdom doesn't exist that was built on fairness. D'you think the Clan Lords were fair, or the Fey?" Hyram's temper roared back to life with a vengeance, it felt good. "Do not forget, Captain Tain; we *both* have blood on our hands."

"I couldn't if I tried." Garian wiped his bloody hand against his breeches. "Some blood won't wash off."

"What does he say?" Daris asked, adjusting the sling on his injured arm.

"He says, it's cold, but that the people are much less hostile now that food supplies have been restored. As a gesture of goodwill he's lifted the curfew. He also says he has a Sea Drake tooth for Oli, and that he hopes we have a happy Midwinter." Thea folded the letter without reading out the last part where Talin had written that Alyda was still too ill to write to him, or even receive visitors and that he missed her more each day.

"I know you miss him terribly," said Daris as he signed another of the documents Lord Hyram was feeding him from an alarmingly large pile cradled in his arms, "so do I—the wine cellar's never been so full."

Thea cast a furtive glance at the King's Councillor while her husband's head was down. He nodded his encouragement.

"I miss him very much. It's going to be strange not having him here for Midwinter and… I'm a little tired." She smiled at her husband. Hyram slid another document in front of him. Daris signed it without reading it and waited, quill poised, for the next.

"If this is your idea of "a few things to sign", I'd hate to see what your idea of "quite a lot" is. I'm supposed to be recuperating. Lorstadt will have your guts if he finds out how hard you're working me."

"'Tis your other hand that's injured, Majesty," Hyram replied. "The one you write with is perfectly able. But I know when to take a hint—subtle though you are. I'll come back later. Here, let me take those." Hyram scooped up the signed papers.

"Has the messenger gone back to Guthland yet?" Daris asked before Hyram reached the door.

"Yes, I believe the Iceheart's vessel sailed this morning."

"Good. I want the treaty ratified at the Spring Council. Herulth's daughter is a beauty, isn't she?" Daris picked up the miniature on his desk. It bore the likeness of a golden-haired girl, painted in exquisite detail on the polished oval of ivory.

"Yes, Majesty. *If the likeness is accurate.* I'm quite sure Talin will not balk when you show him that, but as I suggested; I'd leave it a month or so before you do. Give him time to get to grips with governorship before you tell him he is to be betrothed. One big step at a time and all that."

"Wise words, Councillor." Daris smiled.

Hyram bowed to the King, and gave Thea another reassuring nod. She looked away and slipped her son's letter into her sleeve. When Hyram had gone, Daris limped over and kissed her neck.

"What is it, my love? What's bothering you?"

She felt sick; there was no way she could tell him, not now. She had made so many terrible mistakes; one more would destroy her. The first had been asking Captain Stenna to lie to Talin. She was glad she hadn't obeyed, and deeply ashamed that she'd asked her. The second had been confiding in Hyram about their son and the Captain's relationship.

If only she'd let nature take its course, but she had been so desperate that they should avoid making the same mistakes she and Daris had made. Her arrogance appalled her. She had become just like the scheming courtiers who'd made her life so miserable when she'd come to court. By the time she'd realised what she was doing, it was too late. She couldn't undo what she had begun, not now. She was far too tangled in Hyram's webs, and had no choice but to continue with the deception or risk losing the love of her husband, and her son. She accepted her punishment, although it wasn't nearly as harsh as she deserved. Every day she woke up terrified that today would be the day Daris or Talin would find out what she had done and despise her for it. Anxiety had become her constant companion, and it was excruciating.

"Just hold me," she said and laid her head on Daris's shoulder for comfort—and so that he couldn't see the guilt in her eyes.

"When did you get him to sign this?" Garian was as impressed as he was disgusted by his master's cunning. Three days had passed since their last meeting. In that time, they'd separately concluded to pretend neither had said what they had said. Civil though they were, the ghost of their previous exchange still hung in the air.

"The day after we last spoke. I know you've only just got back, but I need you to return today and take that with you, and this." Hyram shoved a heavy pouch across the table. Gold glinted through the bulging thonging holding it closed.

"And how much is a guilty conscience going for these days?" Garian picked up the bag and weighed it in his hand. "Hmm, quite a lot it seems."

Hyram didn't answer, Garian didn't push. He put the pouch into the saddle bag, and slipped the documents inside his jerkin.

"No one must know," said Hyram, "not even your wife—and especially not the King."

Garian fastened his cloak, and threw the saddle-bags over his shoulder. "Surely the King already knows? Unless…You didn't forge his signature…did you?"

"What? Of course not. Ye gods! D'you think I'd commit the same crime as that turd Corvinius? No. The King signed it… He just doesn't *know* that he did."

Garian gave a curt nod. "I'd better get going before the weather turns." When he reached the door, he paused. "Happy Midwinter."

Surprised, Hyram looked up, the season's greeting on his lips. But Garian had already gone.

Slowly and carefully, Flea copied the letters on the chalkboard. Sitting by the fire, the boy was the picture of contentment.

Alyda tried to sit up again, but the strength in her good arm failed and she sagged back against the pile of pillows, drained by the effort. She would have cursed, but Flea had learnt far too many soldiers' oaths from her over the last few months, or was it years? Time had no meaning when every day was the same as the last.

She would be glad to be home, in her own rooms at Trelanlith, even if it would only be for a short time. The thought of choosing her replacement made her stomach churn. It would be Kieran, that wasn't her issue. What was hard, what was *impossible,* to reconcile was that she would no longer be Captain of the Hammer.

As happened often of late, her thoughts plunged her into a deep pit of despair. Tears pearled on her lashes. She scrubbed them away, and angrily dashed the small vase of winter greens off the bedside table. It smashed, spraying the whitewashed walls and red tiled floor with glass, water and greenery.

Flea looked up briefly, before returning to his chalkboard, completely unperturbed by Alyda's latest fit of temper. He was another unasked-for burden, as if she didn't have enough. She had no idea what she was going to do with him. She couldn't even look after herself, let alone a child. *Dear gods, a child.*

She wondered how Talin was—if he was well, if he ever thought of her. It had been such a long time since she'd seen or heard from anyone other than the sisters and brothers of the Order. She was glad that nobody had visited and seen her like this; she couldn't stand the thought of being pitied, but it hurt that no one had written.

The door opened, Sister Mirrin peeped inside and smiled nervously. "You have a visitor, Captain," the girl squeaked.

"Who is it?" She dared to hope it was Talin.

"A Master Garian Tain, Royal Cartographer, no less. Shall I show him in?"

Alyda hid her bitter disappointment with feigned indifference. "If you must."

"Oh, I thought…I'll come and clean up after he's gone. Shall I bring you something to eat? You need to eat something."

"Why? To keep my strength up?" Alyda laughed. "No food. I've told you, the very thought of it makes me ill."

"I'm sorry, Captain, maybe later." The sister ducked round the door.

"Flea," said Alyda. The boy looked up. "Go play somewhere."

Without comment or complaint, he tucked his chalkboard under his arm and wandered out. A short while later there was a knock at the door.

He was a master at hiding his feelings and knew he didn't look as shocked as he was when he saw her. Her hair was short and hanging loose about her face, which was thin to the point of gauntness. Her skin was sallow, except for a livid scar that ran across the right side of her face from her mouth to her ear. Her throat was bruised, and bore the tell-tale burn marks of a rope. Her right hand was bandaged, and her left leg was strapped in a splint from ankle to thigh.

With considerable effort Captain Stenna dragged herself into a sitting position. She'd paid a terrible price for her loyalty, which made it doubly hard for him to do what he'd been ordered, *for the good of the kingdom.*

"Yes, I look terrible," she said in a hoarse whisper. "Stop gawking and come in, Master Tain."

He hesitated. He wasn't sure he could do this. If Suli found out she'd never forgive him.

"Please come in, Garian. I couldn't bite you even if I wanted to."

Garian went in. "I've brought some letters, Captain. I've been ordered to wait until you've read them, if you don't mind." He handed her the document signed by the King.

With some difficulty she broke the seal. He watched her eyes scan across the flowing lines of script. These documents were always very elaborate, written by the most skilled scribes on the finest vellum. They took a long time to write, particularly those for high-ranking officers, so they were prepared in advance and a space left blank for the name of the recipient, to be filled in as required. The document was only binding when it had been signed by the King.

Garian could imagine how Hyram must have slipped it in with several others, half hidden under something else. He would have been chatting, making pleasant conversation to distract his Majesty from what he was signing. Hyram was a clever bastard, and completely heartless. No surprise that his own daughter hated him.

She must have been devastated, but the knight hid her feelings well. At least Hyram had been kind enough to make it an honourable discharge, but that was a small mercy.

"I knew I'd failed," she said quietly. "I shouldn't have surrendered the garrison, but I feel no guilt over saving those people. If anything, I should have found a way to do it sooner. That I broke does shame me. I didn't think it was in me to break. I told them everything, would have told them more if I'd known more." She shook her head. "So weak."

Garian didn't say anything, sure that if he opened his mouth, he'd blurt out the truth. He stood there and listened to her blame herself for something that he knew from personal experience, nobody could resist—no matter how strong they were.

"The King has been very generous; an honourable discharge is more than I deserve." She turned her face to the window.

"I have another letter, Captain, and this." He set the heavy pouch on the bed.

She ignored the pouch, but took the letter. Her hand was shaking, he pretended not to notice.

When she finished reading it, she tossed it on the bed. A hint of fire had returned to her eyes. "It's from Lord Hyram. Please thank him for me. At least now I know why no one's been. I don't blame them; they've every right to be angry. I let them down...all of them. Do you mind if I don't write a reply? I'm not very fast with my left hand, and you'll need to get going before the weather turns." She picked up the discharge letter again; perhaps to make sure that she'd read it correctly.

"I'd be happy to scribe for you."

She sighed. "Very well."

Garian asked one of the lay brothers to fetch some ink; he had his own quill and parchment. When the brother returned, Garian quietly whispered for Gustav to stay away from the door or he'd cut his balls off. Harsh, but the informant enjoyed his work too much for Garian's liking. After a drink of water, Stenna began.

"Lord Hyram, thank you for your kind words and sensible direction. Living with this is indeed going to be a heavy burden and yes, you're right; not only for me, but also for my family. You have considered matters that I have not, and I am grateful for your insight. Thank you, but I have my own means, and shall therefore decline your generous offer of assistance. With regards to leaving the country: you may assure my..." She paused, her jaw tightened. "You may assure the Royal Guards that I will not disgrace them further, and that I'll be leaving Antia as soon as I am able." She drew a long shuddering breath. "That's all. Goodbye, Master Tain."

Garian blotted the letter and slipped it into his satchel. After an awkward farewell he left. Disgusted by his cowardice he told himself what he'd done was for the good of the kingdom and if he said it enough, he might even start to believe it.

As he was leading his horse to the gate, Garian saw the boy they called Flea playing in the snowy courtyard. Gustav dismissed the child as a halfwit, but Garian very much doubted that was the case. Not many adults, let alone a child, could have kept their wits about them the way he had back at Gallen Arth.

Garian hitched his horse and took a small packet out of his belt pouch. He'd carried it around with him for weeks, too afraid to leave it anywhere, and unwilling to hand it over to Hyram. It was a Midwinter gift from Prince Talin to Captain Stenna. Like everything else it had been intercepted by Gustav and passed to Garian.

The package contained a pendant in the form of a golden hart. It was stunning piece, and bore the maker's mark of the most renowned jeweller in Antia. According to the note Talin had sent with it, the token was given with love—and an offer of marriage.

Dangerous as a snake though it was, Garian couldn't bring himself to hand it over to Hyram. His master would have disposed of it without a second thought. Not only that, he might also have deemed it necessary to ensure Stenna could never say yes, despite Garian's threats. If Hyram thought it was for the good of the kingdom, he'd risk death.

If there was one good deed he could perform, one small act of kindness he could do for someone who'd been treated so badly by those she'd served so well, there it was, gleaming in the palm of his hand. The small, anonymously-given gift could in no way offset the pain he'd helped cause, but it might at least bring her some small pleasure, wherever in the world she went. He had a quick look round to make sure they were alone and unobserved before approaching the boy.

"Good day, young sir. I wonder, d'you think you can do something for me, something very important?"

The child narrowed his eyes and drew his lips together in a thoughtful pout. Garian tried to encourage his cooperation with a friendly smile. It seemed to work; after what looked like serious consideration, the boy nodded decisively.

"Good lad. Now, what I want you to do is very important, and must be kept very secret…"

When Flea returned, he clambered on the bed to show Alyda a particularly interesting stone he'd found, and to give her the *very secret thing*.

"Where did you get this?" she asked, as he hung the pendant around her neck, small fingers cold as ice against her skin.

He shrugged, yawned, and curled up beside her. "'It's yours and a very secret thing," his said.

She watched his eyelids drift together, heard his breathing slow. Within minutes he was fast asleep. Alyda stared out of the window and watched the snow fall, the letter from the King clutched tightly in her hand.

Epilogue

Mist spat out the half-chewed rabbit bone and watched Lon's shadowy outline weave towards her through the gusting flurries of snow. She pushed herself off her haunches and changed back into her skin as he started the last, short climb up to the caves.

It was cold without fur, cold *with* fur these days; her blood was as thin as water. She quickly threw on her clothes and retreated inside the cave. It wasn't warm, but at least there was no snow, only the pool of stagnant green sludge that dominated the cavern. The thick fungus that covered the surface gave off a dull, green luminescence, but the walls shone brighter. Purple, pink, blue, gold, and yellow—a beautiful, mottled tapestry tattooed onto the walls by millions of tiny creatures, each no bigger than a pin head.

She turned from the pool when Lon ducked inside. He shook the snow off; his hair and beard were matted with ice. She waited impatiently while he dug himself out of layers of fur until he got down to his gleaming mail. She didn't need to ask if he had *it*. She could smell the Yorl, smell the blood and silver. He pulled off his gloves, took it out of his belt pouch, and handed it to her. It was in the shape of a spur, etched with vines and flowers; a thing of beauty—to some. She took it over to the pool.

Lon watched. She didn't ask how he'd got hold of it, and he wouldn't offer to tell her.

"That's what I like about him."

"What?" Lon asked.

When he spoke she realised she'd voiced a thought. Too much time spent talking to herself. *Too long up here, with only ghosts for company.*

"Nothing. Now hush or you'll make me do this wrong." She held the spur over the pool. Her wrist ached with the rheumatics, but this was how it had to be done—probably.

"*Asura'ta'ai. Lo't'an, Dwereneth,*" she said and felt the tension grow within the Yorl. Her palm tingled, grew hot, and then the spur melted. She jumped as the cold, silvery metal crawled between her fingers and slowly dripped onto the pool. It collected on the surface; a bright mirror of liquid reflecting the concern written across her age-carved face. It sat there a moment before sinking through the slime.

"Is it done?" Lon asked.

"Aye, I think…I've not done this before—not sure anyone has." She laughed.

"So what happens now?"

"What happens now? Fucked if I know. Ask the wind; ask the mountains. I'm going home. I've got some bread in the oven."

The End.

If you enjoyed reading
The Red Knight you
can leave a review
here:

HTTP://WWW.AMAZON.C
O.UK/THE-RED-KNIGHT-
K-DAVIES/DP/0957261519

Of course, if you
hated it, keep it to
yourself, K?

Kind regards,

KT Davies

Thank you for reading The Red Knight

To learn more about K.T. Davies
visit www.kdavies.net

And for more great books visit
www.anachronpress.com/books/

All Rights Reserved